50 £2.99

THE TOBACCO KEEPER

ALI BADER

Translated by Amira Nowaira

دار بلومزبري - مؤسسة قطر للنشر
BLOOMSBURY
QATAR FOUNDATION
PUBLISHING

مؤسسة قطر
Qatar Foundation

First published in English in 2011 by
Bloomsbury Qatar Foundation Publishing
Qatar Foundation
Villa 3, Education City
PO Box 5825
Doha, Qatar
www.bqfp.com.qa

First published in Arabic in 2008 as *Hareth al-Tabgh*
by Al-Moasasa al-Arabiya lil-Dirasat wal-Nashr

Copyright © Ali Bader, 2008
Translation © Amira Nowaira, 2011

The moral right of the author has been asserted

ISBN 9789992142622

Printed and bound by Clays Ltd, St Ives plc

Eat your chocolate, little girl;

Eat your chocolate!

Believe me, there are no metaphysics in the world beyond
chocolate;

Believe me, all the religions in the world do not teach more
than the sweetshop.

Eat, dirty girl, eat!

Tobacco Shop by Fernando Pessoa

Part One

I

Lives, maps and special documents

ON 3 APRIL 2006, less than one month after an armed group had kidnapped him near his home in Al-Mansour City, the body of the Iraqi composer Kamal Medhat was found near the Jumhuriya Bridge that crosses the River Tigris in Baghdad. Iraqi newspapers reported the fact of his death without going into detail. The real twist in the tale came when *US Today News* reported that Kamal Medhat was none other than Yousef Sami Saleh, of the Qujman family, who'd emigrated to Israel in 1950 during Operation Ezra and Nehemiah – that is, after the decision to strip the Jews of their Iraqi nationality and confiscate their property. He had married Farida Reuben, and their son Meir had been born in Iraq a year before he'd emigrated.

Yousef had found life in Tel Aviv unbearable and, in 1953, he'd escaped to Iran via Moscow, using a forged passport in the name of Haidar Salman. In Tehran, he'd married Tahira, daughter of a wealthy merchant named Ismail al-Tabtabaei, and she had given birth to their son Hussein. In 1958, he had returned with his family to Baghdad, where he'd remained until 1980 when, as an Iranian national, he was expelled to Tehran. His wife Tahira had died during the journey. His son Hussein had been held in prison for more than three years and upon his release he too had been deported to Tehran, where he had tried in vain to find his father.

Haidar Salman had lived as a refugee in Tehran for about a year. Then, at the end of 1981, he'd managed to escape to Damascus with a doctored Iraqi passport in the name of Kamal Medhat. Although he'd remained in Damascus for less than a year, he'd married a wealthy Iraqi woman by the name of Nadia al-Amary. Using his forged passport he'd returned to Iraq early in 1982. In Baghdad his wife had given birth to a son, Omar. It was also at this time, in the eighties, that Kamal Medhat had become the most famous composer in the Middle East.

That summarizes the American newspaper report that was published five days after the discovery of the dead body in Baghdad.

Two days after the publication of the report, *US Today News* contacted me and asked me to travel to Baghdad to write a thousand-word article on Kamal Medhat. The piece would not, however, appear under my name, but under the by-line of John Barr, one of the paper's senior correspondents. This is termed ghost-writing or shadowing, in which a reporter travels to a danger zone to write about a hot topic but whose report is attributed to one of the paper's big-shots. The local reporter gets a fee for his trouble and nothing else. The Press Cooperation Agency and AC Media & News also wanted a full-length biography of Kamal Medhat. They offered to cover all my travel expenses to the cities he'd lived in, provided that the book was based on documentary evidence and genuine interviews. They supplied me with a great many documents, newspapers and letters, and arranged for me to interview a number of his acquaintances in various places

4

around the world. They also organised my trips to the cities where he'd lived: in Baghdad I stayed for over a month at the Agency's bureau in the Green Zone. I then visited Tehran and tracked down the places he'd lived there. In Damscus I spent two months covering the final phase of his exile.

A portrait of Kamal Medhat

To make my work on this enigmatic character easier, and to form a portrait of Kamal Medhat, I drew together a number of threads.

He was a tall, very thin man with long hair and a light beard. He wore plastic-rimmed glasses and dressed elegantly. His love affairs were many and his emotions mysterious. His encyclopaedic interests included modern art, poetry, literature and politics. He had a deep belief in metaphysics but had indeterminate political views. His readings in philosophy were wide-ranging, if selective.

Kamal Medhat was also an outstanding violinist, winning several international awards. He could speak, and read, six languages: he picked up Hebrew and Arabic at home, studied English and French at school in Baghdad, learnt Russian while studying music at the Tchaikovsky Conservatory in Moscow, and Persian during his time in Tehran.

That would be a reasonable portrait of the man. During my work on his biography, a few surprises changed the whole course of the project. In his house I found a book of poetry containing a poem in a foreign language, which he had annotated. It is important to mention the poem here, before elaborating on its impact.

The truth is, when I visited Kamal Medhat's house in Al-Mansour City during my investigation into his murder, I came across two books. The first was the memoir of the French violinist Stéphane Grappelli. The other was in English; it had a red cover and was lying on a small teak table in his room. It was a collection of poems called *Tobacco Shop*, by the Portuguese poet Fernando Pessoa. In the margins, Kamal Medhat had written a lot of notes and comments in pencil. As I was leaving the house, I took the book with me. Having no clue as to the importance of the book or its significance in his life, I did not browse through it right away, but put it in a drawer until the following day. In the morning I started to read it, together with his comments and glosses. What I discovered stunned me. I realized that the book contained many of his secrets. I needed to study it and understand it, because it held important keys to unravelling the mysteries of his life.

In *Tobacco Shop*, Pessoa presents three different characters, involving three cases of assumed identity. Each one of the fictional characters represents a facet of Pessoa's own personality, who are all given separate names, ages and different lives. Each has different convictions, ideas and traits. With each personality, Pessoa develops a deeper and broader sense of identity, but ultimately we are left with the true ambiguity of identity. The first character is the keeper of flocks, Alberto Caeiro, while the second is that of the protected man, Ricardo Reis. The third is the tobacconist, Álvaro de Campos. Suddenly we find ourselves confronted by a game *à-trois* or a 3D Cubist image of a single face.

This is exactly what Kamal Medhat did. He, too, had three personalities, each with a distinct name, age, features, convictions and religion. Yousef Sami Saleh was an enlightened and liberal Jewish musician, born in Baghdad in 1926. When I looked him up in the *Encyclopaedia of Iraqi Music*, I discovered that he'd died in

6

Israel in 1955. (Curiously, Kamal Medhat himself had written the articles on both Yousef Sami Saleh and Haidar Salman in this encyclopaedia.) When he went to Tehran, he assumed the personality of Haidar Salman, a musician from a middle-class Shia family, born two years before his original persona. Haidar Salman had links with the communist movement throughout the sixties. According to the *Encyclopaedia of Iraqi Music*, he had died in Tehran in 1981. When he moved from Damascus to Baghdad, he had assumed the third persona, that of the well-known musician Kamal Medhat, born in 1933 to a distinguished family of Sunni merchants from Mosul. During the eighties he'd had personal ties with the regime in Baghdad and had become close to President Saddam Hussein. Kamal Medhat's entire life therefore proves without a shred of doubt that the notion of an essential 'identity' is false. His life demonstrates the possibility of exchanging identities through a series of narrative games. An identity turns into a story that one can inhabit and impersonate. In this way the artist laughs tongue-in-cheek at the deadly struggle of identities through a game of pseudonyms, fake personalities and false masks.

In the midst of the sectarian warfare underway in Baghdad prior to his death, Kamal Medhat's three sons visited him and revealed the collapse of 'identity'. Meir, the Jew from Iraq who'd emigrated from Israel to the United States, who'd joined the Marines and returned to Iraq as a US Army officer, was the product of his first persona. Hussein, who, after settling in Tehran, had tied himself to his Shia identity and joined the Shia political movement, was the offspring of the second father. Omar, a Sunni trying to bolster his identity in the face of the tragic ousting of the Sunnis from power in Iraq after 2003, was the outcome of the third persona. Each of them stood by a story that was constructed,

7

fabricated and furnished with narrative and imaginary elements. Each of them lived a life they believed to be true.

Kamal Medhat's life shows that identity is always closely allied to a narrative standpoint. A life is a story that is fabricated, formulated or narrated at a completely random moment, a localized historical instant when others turn into the 'other', into strangers, foreigners and even outcasts. The story of this artist shows that identity is a process of adaptation; no sooner has it located itself in one particular historical moment than it changes into a different moment. All these imaginary communities begin with a fabricated, invented narrative which denies that identities blend and overlap, but which at a certain point in time reveals such boundaries to be imaginary, constructed and fabricated, nothing but narrative concoctions. As a community loses its connection with its roots, it attempts to regain its lost horizons, which it may achieve only through storytelling and imagination.

A brief biography

The more I read of Pessoa's book of poetry, the deeper grew my understanding of the intriguing personality of Kamal Medhat. Before travelling to Baghdad, I'd already collected a great deal of detailed information about his life. And before starting to write his biography, I'd prepared maps of the Middle Eastern cities that he'd passed through on his journey. So I devised a brief biography:

3 November 1926: Yousef Sami Saleh was born into the middle-class Jewish-Iraqi Qujman family. In the year of his birth the Iraqi–British treaty was signed, as an

amendment to the 1922 treaty, and was ratified by the Iraqi parliament on 18 January. The same year also saw the births of the most important modern Iraqi poet, Badr Shaker al-Sayyab, and the leading modern Iraqi novelist, Fouad al-Tikerly. Yousef Sami Saleh had lived on Al-Rashid Street in the Al-Torah quarter. One of Baghdad's oldest quarters, this neighbourhood had been home to many Jewish families before the middle of the last century.

1927:   Oil, the liquid destined to play the lead role in shaping the country's history and future, gushed from the first well in Iraq.

1932:   As the first independent Arab state, Iraq became the fifty-seventh member of the League of Nations. The end of the British Mandate was officially declared.

1933:   Yousef Sami Saleh learned to play the violin under an Armenian musician, a graduate of Moscow's Tchaikovsky Conservatory. Also in that year, the first Iraqi Communist manifesto was published, written by Fahd, the historic leader of the Iraqi Communist Party.

1936:   Radio Baghdad broadcast its first programmes. Yousef Sami Saleh performed a piece by Mozart. That historic year also witnessed Lieutenant-General Bakr Sidqi's coup against the government of Yassin al-Hashemi. It was the first military coup in Iraq and the entire Arab world.

10 June 1941:   Yousef Sami Saleh met renowned Russian violinist Michel Boricenco, in whose presence he gave his first solo violin performance. In a small hall at Baghdad's English Club he performed Bach, Paganini and Ysaÿe. As a token of his admiration and appreciation,

Boricenco presented him with a violin and bow of the highest quality. In May, the Iraqi–British war broke out, accompanied by a nationalist revolt inspired by Nazism. Wholesale chaos enveloped the country. The Jewish community suffered assault, looting, robbery and murder. Massouda Dalal, Yousef Sami Saleh's aunt, was burnt alive before his very eyes and her property looted.

21 October 1946: The ninth government of Nuri al-Said was formed. That year also coincided with the Egyptian singer Umm Kulthoum's arrival in Baghdad in May, where she'd stayed at the Tigris Palace Hotel. She gave a few performances on the occasion of King Faisal II's birthday. That same year saw the opening of Studio Baghdad, which marked the effective beginning of the history of Iraqi cinema.

1948: The Portsmouth Treaty was signed between Iraqi Prime Minister Salih Jabr and British Foreign Secretary Bevin. Students declared a general strike and peaceful demonstrations for three days. They shouted slogans calling for the dissolution of parliament and the Cabinet. In response, the Deputy Prime Minister issued a statement that infuriated the demonstrators, and then ordered the police to open fire on them. Many students were killed and injured on the bridge. The following day, during the delivery of the bodies, police vehicles stormed the Royal Hospital Building at Bab al-Muazzam, opening fire and killing more students from the Faculty of Pharmacy.

The 1948 war began and the State of Israel was declared, the Arab *nakba*.

In that same year, Yousef Sami Saleh was awarded the King Faisal Prize for the violin. He embarked on a series of concerts at the English Club, attended by the most distinguished families of Baghdad. His fingers had mastered the violin, especially Bach's solo Sonata. In that same year, he married Farida Reuben.

1949: The founding members of the Iraqi Communist Party, Yousef Salman (Fahd), Hussein Mohammad al-Shebibi (Hazem) and Zaki Baseem (Sarim) were publicly executed in the streets of Baghdad. At the end of that year, Meir, Yousef Sami Saleh's only son by Farida Reuben, was born.

21 March 1950: The Afghan King Mohammad Zahir Shah arrived in Baghdad on his way to Europe.

Al-Rowwad, a grouping of a few plastic artists, was established in Baghdad. A law was passed depriving Jews of their Iraqi nationality. Yousef Sami Saleh left for Israel during Operation Ezra and Nehemiah, which allowed large numbers of Jewish families to emigrate. Their property and assets were confiscated.

1952: Yousef Sami Saleh moved to Kibbutz Kfar in Tel Aviv.

1953: He travelled to Moscow to attend a concert and to visit the Tchaikovsky Conservatory. There he met the well-known violinist Sergei Oistrakh, who helped him escape to Iran during the reign of Shah Reza Pahlavi. On the way, he stopped off in Prague where he met the famous violinist Karl Baruch and began a friendship that lasted until the latter's death. That same year, he began a new life in Tehran under the name of Haidar Salman and was embraced by the wealthy Iraqi family of Ismail al-Tabtabaei, whose daughter Tahira he married. He gave a series of concerts at the Tehran Opera House and became acquainted with the most renowned Iranian musicians.

1955:   The inaugural meeting of the Baghdad Pact countries was held on 21–22 November in Baghdad. It comprised Iraq, Iran, Turkey, Pakistan and the United Kingdom. On 25 November, Israeli newspapers reported Yousef Sami Saleh's death, based on a notice published by his former wife, Farida Reuben.

1956:   The Tripartite Aggression was launched against Egypt following the nationalization of the Suez Canal. Vocal demonstrations took place in Baghdad and in most Arab capitals.

3 September 1957:   Haidar Salman gave a solo performance of Henri Vieuxtemps' Op. 4 in D Minor, which he played before the aristocrats of Iran with absolute genius and exquisite musicianship.

14 July 1958:   A military coup d'état, led by Abdel Karim Qasim, was declared in Baghdad. The monarchy was overthrown and a republic proclaimed. Qasim became both Prime Minister and Defence Minister. The Rihab Palace witnessed the massacre of the whole royal family, including women and children.

Yousef Sami Saleh entered Iraq under the name of Haidar Salman, who had been born in Baghdad in 1924, who had studied music in Moscow and Tehran and whose family was made up of merchants from Al-Isterbadi market in Al-Kazemeya.

In the same year his son Hussein was born.

1959:   Haidar Salman became acquainted with the great

sculptor Jawad Salim and joined the cultural milieu, particularly the Baghdad Modern Art Society. During that same year, he gave several concerts in which he charmingly and masterfully performed Paganini and Bach.

During that period, rumours circulated that he was having an affair with the well known painter Nahida al-Said.

1960:   He started composing and departed for Moscow where he spent a year studying the arts of conducting and composition at the Tchaikovsky Conservatory.

5 August 1961:   He won an award bestowed by Elizabeth, the former Queen of Belgium, which he received at an event held by the queen to honour the winners.

8 February 1963:   A coup d'état initiated by the Baath and nationalist leadership overthrew the regime of Abdel Karim Qasim. Fierce popular resistance led by the communists continued for several days. Abdel Salam Arif became President of the Republic, while Abdel Karim Qasim, together with Fadhel Abbas al-Mehdawi and Taha al-Sheikh Ahmed, were executed. There followed mass killings of communists, including the leader of the Communist Party, Salam Adel, who died under torture.

At the end of February, Haidar Salman was smuggled into Tehran and from there to Moscow, where his wife Tahira was waiting for him. The painter Nahida al-Said was executed by hanging.

25 August 1964:   Haidar Salman began teaching violin at the Tchaikovsky Conservatory, where he became acquainted with leading Russian musicians. Rumours

13

circulated concerning an affair with the Russian pianist Ada Brunstein.

1965:   He took part in the Jacques Thibaud competition in Paris.

1966:   He participated in the Leventritt Competition held at the Carnegie Hall in New York.

5 June 1967:   Start of the Six Day War, which resulted in the occupation of the Sinai Peninsula in Egypt, the Golan Heights in Syria and the Palestinian West Bank. Haidar Salman stopped performing with the New York Symphony Orchestra in protest against this aggression and returned to Iraq, thereby ending his affair with Ada Brunstein.

17 July 1968:   A Baathist coup d'état in Baghdad installed Ahmed Hassan al-Bakr as President of the Republic and Saddam Hussein as his Deputy. The ousted President, Abdel Rahman Arif, was exiled to Turkey.

In May 1968 the communists declared an armed struggle and led the revolution of the marshlands in southern Iraq. The uprising failed, however, and the Head of the Central Leadership of the Iraqi Communist Party, Aziz al-Hajj, was detained. He gave a detailed confession that led to the arrest of all members of the Politburo. During that same year, the Baath Party executed large numbers of politicians on charges of conspiracy. A group of merchants was publicly executed in Baghdad's Tahrir Square on charges of espionage, amid the shouting and clamouring of the crowd.

1 February 1974:   Haidar Salman's son Meir emigrated from Israel to the United States. He became a naturalized American citizen and joined the Marines.

14

1979:   The year of the Iranian Revolution. On 1 February, Khomeini returned to Qom while the Shah left Iran for good. During that same year, Saddam Hussein led a secret coup and seized the reins of power after Ahmed Hassan al-Bakr had relinquished all his posts. This was followed by a Baathist massacre of all leaders that had no allegiance to Saddam Hussein.

4 September 1980:   The Iran–Iraq war began. Iraqi citizenship was withdrawn from all citizens with Iranian affiliations, who were deported to Iran after having their property confiscated, while many young men were killed. Haidar Salman was deported with his wife Tahira after his assets, his house and his property had all been confiscated. The Iraqi authorities deposited him and his wife by truck close to the Iranian border. His wife Tahira, who was in poor health, died at the border, while his son Hussein was detained in jail in Baghdad as part of the operation to detain all Iraqi young men of Iranian origin. Some of these men were killed while others were deported to Iran.

1981:   Haidar Salman was witness to the repercussions of the Iranian Revolution especially the conflict between the liberals and the radicals. Rumours circulated that he had an affair with Pari, the daughter of his host in Tehran, Mohammad Taqi. On 3 November, Haidar Salman travelled to Damascus on a forged passport in the name of Kamal Medhat. The name belonged to an Iraqi merchant who had died in a car crash in Tehran and who was the second husband of a wealthy Iraqi woman living in Damascus, called Nadia al-Amiry. Her first husband, who was Syrian, had been killed during the civil war between the Baathists and the Muslim Brotherhood.

1982:   He entered Baghdad under the identity of Kamal Medhat Mustafa, born in 1933 in Mosul to a merchant family that traded between Mosul and Aleppo.

5 March 1983:   His wife Nadia al-Amiry gave birth to their son, Omar. In that same year, Kamal Medhat joined the Iraqi National Symphony Orchestra, which turned him into a star. He became particularly famous after playing 'The Martyr' symphony with Walid Gholmieh. He developed into a well-known and well-liked artistic figure in political circles, particularly to former Iraqi President Saddam Hussein. Gossip had it that he had an affair with a cellist in the National Symphony Orchestra, Widad Ahmed, who was responsible for strengthening his ties with the regime at that time. He was also rumoured to have had an affair with a woman with a reputation, a failed pianist called Janet.

26 November 1986:   Kamal Medhat played a fantasia, including a beautifully performed cadenza, at the presidential palace in front of Saddam Hussein and a number of political figures.

8 August 1988:   The Iran–Iraq war ended. A year after this, his son Omar went to live with his maternal aunt in Egypt.

2 August 1990:   The Iraqi army invaded Kuwait and declared the establishment of a transitional government. On the eighth of the same month, Iraq issued a decree annexing Kuwait as its nineteenth province.

17 January 1991:   The second Gulf War began. The US-led coalition forces began to expel the Iraqi military from Kuwait. On 24 January, the land campaign began.

On 26 February, Saddam Hussein accepted UN Resolution 660 and withdrew from the city of Kuwait, which coalition forces then entered.

Nadia al-Amiry, who had been ill, died. There was talk of an affair between Kamal Medhat and a rural servant girl called Fawzeya.

1991–2003:   Kamal Medhat lived in Baghdad under the embargo imposed on the country. He witnessed poverty, disease, war and the decline of the arts. Although he withdrew completely from public life, he continued to compose.

20 March 2003:   The US launched the third Gulf War to remove Iraqi President Saddam Hussein from power. On 9 April, US forces entered Baghdad. In a dramatic scene, the statue of Saddam was toppled. Kamal Medhat's son Meir, now a major-general, arrived in Baghdad with the allied forces.

2004:   His son Hussein returned to Baghdad from Tehran, along with Shia political forces and joined the political system. His son Omar also returned to Baghdad from Cairo in opposition to the US occupation and to the whole political process in Iraq.

5 March 2006:   Kamal Medhat was kidnapped by an armed group in mysterious circumstances. On 3 April, his body was found near the Jumhuriya Bridge in Baghdad.

This is the brief biography that I prepared before leaving for Baghdad to write his story. I prepared it for one character, although

17

I could have created it for three. A complete report on his life was published under the name of John Barr, the well-known journalist at *US Today News*, which I had ghost-written. With the escalation of the conflict from 2004 onwards, it became impossible for foreign reporters to get into Baghdad. Newspapers, news agencies and TV and radio stations therefore decided to remove their crews to nearby Arab capitals, such as Amman, Damascus and Beirut. There, an Iraqi reporter would be commissioned to prepare reports that would not be published under his own name but under the name of one of the well-known reporters at the newspaper, news agency or TV station. This was intended to give readers the impression that the agency had a presence in Baghdad despite the dangers and hazards. The ghost writer, who undertook the whole assignment, simply got the money.

At this point we return once more to the game of assumed names and blurred identities. The person who changes his name is that of the tobacconist as he appears in Pessoa's poem. As for the ghost writer, his existence becomes dependent on that of another. There is, therefore, a basic difference between the ghost writer and the tobacconist, for while the latter assumes three or more personalities, the former lends his identity to another, in all likelihood a Westerner. Here we find what may be termed colonial textuality, which is a kind of absorption or extraction based on the total erasure of another being's existence and the creation of a vacuum. In order to explain how I constructed my report, I would like first to explain how I came to work as a ghost writer for those agencies.

II

Ghost-writing: an imaginary paradise or a journey into the unknown?

IN THE EARLY NINETIES, right after the ceasefire that ended the second Gulf War, I was demobbed from the army. I spent the whole summer unemployed, living with my family in our old house in Al-Karradah. I translated various poems from English and French that were never published. During that time I also tried and failed to write a long novel about my experience as a soldier and the dangers I'd faced during the war. In spite of the many drafts and manuscripts that I produced, they all seemed so worthless that I couldn't find it in myself to continue.

During that period, the orange trees in our garden were in bloom and the olive trees were laden with fruit. From time to time, I went to the Al-Hindiya Club where I swam in the clear water beneath the trellised roof. The blue water under the bright summer sun of Baghdad took my breath away. In those months following the war I didn't leave Baghdad at all. To make up for this, I used to visit a very rich friend of mine who was in the habit of throwing wild parties in his little house, with dozens of young women and men, and plenty of foreigners, all partying till the morning. I would go home at dawn, tottering drunkenly through the narrow alleys, and climb my stairs high on fun and summer.

I was unaware, at that time, of the huge numbers of people who were dying as a result of torture, poverty or politics. I was totally engrossed in myself, in my friend's parties, in the women I got to know, and in the priceless stories I wanted to write. By pure chance, however, I was introduced at one of those wild parties to a German activist of Iraqi descent called Katrina Hassoun. She was a reporter for the well-known German-language Swiss newspaper from Zurich, the *Neue Zürcher Zeitung*. She was also working as a researcher for human rights organizations and was a regular visitor to Baghdad in the nineties.

That evening at my friend's house, we stood together drinking white wine beneath a small green-glassed arched window. The music soared and the river breeze was fresh and soothing while Katrina spoke to me about the demands of her work in Baghdad, and particularly her dealings with the authorities. I wasn't really listening or showing much interest; I was just pretending to listen, for in those days I couldn't have cared less about such things. I didn't even pay attention to the news that was published or broadcast every day, although I was fully aware of the ever-deteriorating political situation in Baghdad. But the most significant turning point in this whole little episode occurred when Katrina Hassoun, whose Arabic wasn't very good, offered me a paid job as her interpreter. Seeing as I had no work at the time and my novel was at a standstill, I accepted her offer. My objective was, first and foremost, monetary.

At the house that she was renting on Al-Saadoun Street, I met groups of disabled veterans, former communists who'd been jailed and tortured, women who'd lost their husbands and mothers who'd lost their sons either in war or in prison. Their stories hardly made an impression on me. I listened to them as though they'd taken place in some faraway land. None of this was really my concern, for I was only the interpreter. I stood by the window, watching silently until the last visitor left.

One day, on my way back from work, I was arrested by the secret police. They asked me for the names of people who'd visited the activist and what they'd talked about. All of a sudden, I found myself implicated in affairs that I'd tried all my life to steer clear of. My understanding of the situation in my country was fairly poor at the time, for I was too busy drinking wine, smoking a variety of cigarettes and getting to know women of every sort to really bother about people's suffering. From that point onwards, however, I began to take a real interest in what was going on and wrote press reports for this activist under various pseudonyms. I chose foreign names, naturally, in order to be above suspicion.

It was from Katrina Hassoun that I heard for the first time about Fernando Pessoa's *Tobacco Shop*, the poem written by the third of Pessoa's characters. Katrina even suggested that I use 'the Tobacconist' as my pseudonym. As I was beginning to lose all my rights, both moral and financial, she then proposed that I work as a ghost writer, which meant I would write important stories on Iraq to be published under the name of a well-known journalist, while I would be paid handsomely.

For me the distinction between the tobacconist and the ghost writer is clear. Regarding the tobacconist, as Fernando Pessoa has said, two creatures co-exist in the soul of each one of us. The first is real, appearing in our visions and dreams, while the second is false, appearing in our external image, discourses, actions and writings. The ghost writer, in contrast, is a kind of negation, an abstraction. He represents a form of colonial discourse that is based on appropriation and rejection.

Months before she left Baghdad, Katrina Hassoun had introduced me to a correspondent for *US Today News*, a woman of Lebanese descent called Aida Shahin who became a close friend at the time. She commissioned me to write features that were off-beat, or at least unfamiliar and unusual, and I produced a great number of excellent stories for her. Among these, a piece on the English detective novelist Agatha Christie's time in Baghdad got noticed. She had visited and lived in the city in the forties and fifties. I tracked down the houses she'd rented and the guest-houses she'd stayed in with her husband, Max Mallowan, the famous archaeologist. I described the streets she'd written about in her novel *They Came to Baghdad*, the trains she'd ridden on her trips to Aleppo or Turkey and the places of entertainment in the Rusafa neighbourhood where she'd spent long summer evenings. This story encouraged the paper to give me further assignments, particularly about the foreign artists, writers and Orientalists who'd visited Baghdad and about the homes on the Tigris built by those Westerners during the nineteenth and twentieth centuries.

So I continued to work in secret for this newspaper, as well as for other foreign papers, until I got to know Françoise Lony, a well-known French journalist and correspondent who also directed documentary films. I made her acquaintance in Baghdad during the period of the sanctions, when Baghdad was making headlines and attracting reporters from all over the world. They were all drawn by sympathy for a nation that was suffering from the violence of the regime as well as from international sanctions.

I worked with Françoise on a number of documentaries while continuing to use an assumed name at her request. Our work included a film that we produced together on ancient Iraqi monuments. We were harassed in all sorts of ways by the authorities, in spite of the fact that my publicly acknowledged work with Françoise had absolutely nothing to do with politics. Our films were concerned with the antiquities of Babylon, ancient crafts of the Middle East or Babylonian musical instruments. During this period she always called me by my assumed name, and I almost forgot my real name, which I never used.

After a while, Françoise began to feel threatened in Baghdad and was in fear of her life and of mine. So she asked me to accompany her on a trip to Tripoli to shoot a film about Libyan monuments, entitled *Treasures of the Coast*. For six months we travelled together and worked continuously between Tobruk and Zawara. For two more years we shuttled between Damascus, Beirut and Casablanca. Those trips were as much for love as for work. I spent the best times of my life with Françoise Lony.

Françoise was a truly exceptional woman who radiated charm and sexiness. All the men of the media were greatly attracted to her. She was a natural in the art of seduction and was never reluctant to embark on a stormy love affair. Sexual pleasure, passion and the pursuit of society had far greater appeal for her than the romantic yearnings to which I was prone in those days.

Instead of concentrating on our work or the films we were producing in various locations, Françoise dragged me into a whole new world. We'd already made a substantial amount of cash from a hugely successful film called *Street Women*, about prostitution in the Middle East. It was shown at many big film festivals and aired on several European TV channels. It was then that she took me on a wild, stormy trip to Morocco. It was early summer and we went to the coastal resorts. I cannot explain the madness that overcame us. We felt that the Moroccan cities we were visiting had thrown open their gates to us, welcoming two carefree young people who longed to live in complete hedonistic abandon. Our next stop was Casablanca which, at that time, was on the verge of turning into an erotic myth: Sodom, as Françoise once described it in one of her reports, a home to vice and depravity. We were both on the brink of an abyss, as day after day we immersed ourselves completely in sensuality, pleasure and amusement. We haunted theatres, bars and swimming pools, and wallowed in sex, alcohol and evenings that lasted until the small hours.

As so often happens in collaborations founded on amorous relationships, my work with the French journalist came to an end when the love ended. We separated quickly. She returned to Paris; I no longer had any idea where to go. Travelling back to Baghdad was impossible, and I had no work or friends in Casablanca. Suddenly Aida Shahin came forcefully back into my life. Having learned that she was back in Beirut, I wrote a long letter to her address there, asking her to find me a job and a place to live. Her work was outstanding and she was still working as a reporter for *US Today News*.

Two weeks after arriving in Beirut, I moved into Aida Shahin's apartment on Al-Hamra Street. She was an exceptionally gifted photographer but a mediocre reporter. Her most prominent trait was her kindness, although this soon faded in the face of other, negative, qualities. She talked a lot, was always complaining, and had a penchant for criticizing and nitpicking. A rocky, on-off relationship developed between us. I should also mention one of the positive things she did for me, which was to get me more work at her newspaper. She also arranged a job for me at one of the Gulf TV companies, which gave me the opportunity to travel to many places around the world as a news analyst.

I went to Chad immediately after the failed coup in the nineties and to Rwanda following the civil war. I went to the Western Sahara, where the political situation was deteriorating. During that same period, I also witnessed the dramatic changes that were overtaking Eastern Europe, the radical transformations wrought by political revolutions and the total rejection of communism. From there I wrote about the war in Bosnia Herzegovina. I also wrote major pieces for *US Today News* on Iraqi communists in Africa, especially those who'd fled to Addis Ababa after the ascension of Mengistu in the eighties. They had escaped there from the hell of Saddam Hussein, and their aim was to spark revolution against Western interests in Africa. I found them frustrated and disappointed now that the illusion of revolution had entirely vanished from their lives. I travelled to report on Fascist jails in Portugal and Spain, comparing them with Middle Eastern jails. I was also witness to the major transformations in Afghanistan, especially following 9/11, and the international invasion of Kabul and the end of the Taliban era. In fact, I witnessed major changes taking place throughout the world: brutal civil wars, horrific atrocities of every description and cruel scenes of homelessness and deprivation. In Africa I saw things I could never have seen anywhere else: strange animals, birds with huge wings and crocodiles threatened with extinction. Awake all night, I also saw the blue minarets of Tehran piercing the sky and flocks of sharp-eyed birds flapping their wings on the domes of the mosques.

* * *

25

My relationship with Aida didn't last. She was too moody and demanding. Her moods also had an adverse effect on me. But this situation soon changed when she introduced me to an American reporter of Palestinian origin called Nancy Awdeh – I'm not sure whether this was an oversight on her part. We saw Nancy for the first time at a bar in Beirut. From that first meeting, Nancy and I were attracted to each other. The more deeply I got involved with Nancy Awdeh, the more complicated became my relationship with Aida Shahin. I tried desperately to explain to Aida that we should separate. It was even harder to tell her that I was going to live with Nancy. But in the end she realized that we couldn't possibly go on. When I moved into Nancy's apartment in Al-Ashrafeya, Aida gave me a beautiful memento: the blouse that she'd worn on the first occasion we'd met. This embarrassed me and made me sluggish.

Foreign reporters came to Beirut because it was a volcanic mass of contradictions, the place where all the conflicts of the Middle East were fought out. It was a permanent warzone where international and regional plans and strategies were executed. At the heart of an intricate web of contradictions and conflicts stood this coastal city, hovering over the dividing line between East and West but lying open to all. This was its distinguishing feature, and it was a permanent hotspot for foreign correspondents interested in the Middle East. They streamed to Beirut, preferring it to all other Middle Eastern cities. It offered so many attractions, including the huge number of bars, cafés and salons that made their lives comfortable.

It was also strange that reporters and journalists in Beirut were classified by the type of bar they frequented. The bars were categorized according to the political affiliations of their journalist patrons and given various satirical nicknames. There was the War Criminals' bar, the Terrorists' bar and the Lady Killers' bar. The bar I often went to with Nancy was no better named than any of these.

At that time, Nancy was working as a correspondent for a major American network. She had studied journalism in New York and worked as an extra at a radio station in Boston, so she had strong connections with the media there. She managed to get me a fair few assignments and commissioned me more than once herself. Although these jobs, for a variety of reasons, were not long term, they did help me a great deal with my living expenses and kept me in close contact with press circles. My relationship with Nancy reached its high point at this time. She was an irresistible paragon of femininity and desire. She had the figure of a model: tall, dark, slim and delicate. I was attracted to her soft features and shapely figure beneath her elegant outfits. Nancy had been married at twenty-three but had got a divorce from her husband, who was a well-known broadcaster at BDR New York.

Nonetheless, this love story didn't last long. We had many problems and rows and finally we decided to split up. I moved to Damascus to work with an Italian director on a documentary about Iraqis exiled in Syria. She went to New York. When I returned to Beirut two months later, she was back, having returned the previous month. Although she was in a relationship with José Paz, the famous Brazilian journalist who'd been working in Beirut for a long time, a vague connection remained between us via our work. Throughout this period, we continued to be close friends and met from time to time in Beirut and elsewhere. She tried hard to find me some work to help me earn a living. But I was still in a dismal state, having been unemployed for more than three months, with no real work either in journalism or television.

My situation began to worsen rapidly, for my savings from the Damascus documentary were gradually running out. Although at the time I believed that my move to Beirut would launch my career as an Arabic writer, my hopes were soon dashed. All my contacts had been with European and American journalists, which had made it easier to write for the press outside the Arab world, but I was an unknown in terms of the Arabic press. I had never had any contact with Arab journalists, writers or publishers, and they were the only conduit to a job. It was strange that work for me was always connected with a love affair or relationship of some kind. At that point in time, my affair with Nancy was virtually over, and since my journalistic work depended entirely on such relationships, I found myself isolated and lonely.

I knew that if I failed to form a relationship, I would probably remain unemployed. However, while seeking a relationship with a woman within Arabic media circles, I started to write the outline of a novel set in Baghdad. Being unable to finish it increased my sense of failure. I then met Nancy and her boyfriend at the Lady Killers' bar. We stood and talked for a long time. She was so genuinely distressed at my state that she invited me to Damascus to meet Jacqueline Mugharib, a Levantine woman well connected with the Arab and foreign press and media. I went back to Syria, and at Jacqueline Mugharib's I was introduced to an Iraqi director working for a TV channel. I started helping him with his work, which was by no means extensive, as he only produced brief news reports that he sold to various channels. On top of that, my collaboration with him was short-lived and fairly erratic, because it depended on a fast news turnover and last-minute assignments by the channels. I felt very unsettled. In order to finish my Arabic writing project, I decided to move to Amman, where I arrived feeling completely dejected. I rented a small, very cheap apartment, or studio, to be precise. I was completely cut off from everyone, moving only between the library and the studio. I started visiting the offices of the daily papers, where I got to know Salih, who was the culture editor for one of them. He asked me to write some literary articles, especially on foreign literature. I also translated chapters from modern novels and wrote some critical articles that he occasionally commissioned for the same paper. These were all pretty routine jobs that I took no great pleasure in.

Boring Amman afforded me plenty of time to read, watch movies and attend concerts, which helped me while away the time but filled me with little enthusiasm. So I didn't stay long, and soon moved to Damascus. Actually, I moved to Damascus at the invitation of a friend of mine who was working for a film company there. He commissioned me to script a film on behalf of an Iraqi cultural institution set up by Iraqi communists after the massacre they'd suffered in 1980. I stayed in Damascus for several months writing the script. After finishing the task and securing some funds, I decided to stay on. I rented a room in a very strange hotel in the Sarouja quarter of Damascus. It was a small and cheap hostel, with mostly foreign guests and an excellent library that contained books in every language. From my little room in this weird hotel, I started dispatching reports on cinema and theatre to a French newspaper that was interested in such events from around the world. All these jobs, however, were of short-lived interest and quickly faded away.

During those difficult days, Nancy called to tell me that she had found me a job as a copywriter for trailers and commercials at one of the Arab TV studios, without needing to leave Damascus. From the comfort of my hotel room I wrote amusing adverts, coming up with exciting and attention-grabbing catch-phrases for washing-up liquid, car tyres, rubber products and other stuff. This simple work in fact helped me move from the cheap hotel to a small apartment or studio in Bab Touma, near Jacqueline and Hanna Mugharib's house.

I remained like this until 2003. The occupation of Baghdad by the Marines and the toppling of Saddam's regime represented a real sea change in my life as a reporter. From that moment on, that Middle Eastern city became the focus for reporters, correspondents and documentary-makers from around the world; not just because of the war, but because of a real transformation in international politics that, on the one hand, reasserted imperialist discourse and, on the other, represented an opportunity for change throughout the Middle East. There were global, and media, expectations that Baghdad would be a turning point for the whole world. It was expected to become a modern city: politically, economically and socially. However, instead of becoming, as anticipated, a city safe for politicians and reporters, it turned into the most violent and dangerous place in the world. This created two contradictory perceptions of a city that was hovering on the brink of civil war. On the one hand, its media value rose to unprecedented heights, while on the other, it became dangerous and completely off limits to journalists. What were reporters supposed to do? They had to leave Baghdad for neighbouring capitals: Amman, Damascus and Beirut in particular were relatively close. Because these cities were safe, journalists could establish contacts there, acquire information and get reports and news about Baghdad. This was how my career as a ghost writer began, or 'black writer' as Nancy Awdeh used to say whenever she saw me. I'd see her sitting, with her sturdy build and full breasts, like a long-legged blaze of lust, and as soon as she saw me, she'd call out, 'Hi, black writer!'

It was thanks to Nancy that I got so many ghost-writing assignments as well as countless privileges. Through her, I became known to many newspapers and TV channels, and she introduced me to a large number of foreign and Arab news agencies, for whom I wrote reports and made documentaries about Iraq. I'll always be thankful to her for introducing me to so many famous international reporters and journalists. I'll never forget that it was she who introduced me to Robert Fisk, Pierre-Jean Luizard, Tariq Ali and others.

Nancy was everybody's best friend and she took her moral responsibilities towards her friends quite seriously. She was actually very different from anybody else I got to know at that time, for other correspondents seemed no more than brightly coloured bubbles. Most of them were proud, vain and worthless, while she was the total opposite. I became well known by the name that she had coined for me.

The fact is, no foreign reporter dared to enter Iraq during that period, so I was the one who wrote the news, reports and features for most of the major European newspapers. The names of their senior writers adorned their pages while they themselves sat in the bars and cafés of Amman, Damascus or Beirut, sipping cold beer and eating tasty *mezzas*. Their work was not unduly demanding. All they had to do was call and ask me to go to Baghdad, Basra, Al-Ramadi or Mosul to write their reports. In the meantime, they kept watch from a safe distance and, occasionally, directed reports to the destinations of their choosing. I moved from one hazardous area to another, time after time escaping death in order to write the reports and receive my cash.

In order to explain the dimensions of my new assignment on Kamal Medhat, I need first to describe my relationship with Jacqueline Mugharib, who played a great part in this.

Jacqueline Mugharib

Jacqueline Mugharib was a Syrian woman who lived on the upper floor of a small house in the Christian neighbourhood of Bab Touma in Damascus. The building was very old. On the ground floor at the front was a small bakery owned by a Lebanese Shiite man called Jaafar, who'd come to Damascus from south Lebanon some thirty years earlier. An elderly man, he employed five young Syrian bakers from Al-Saleheya City in addition to Iraqi immigrants who prepared the bread in the Najaf style. At the bakery, he also sold hot Lebanese-style pastries, whose aroma one could smell from far away. Next to the bakery was an olive-skinned Druze barber called Nabil. He had a very pretty red and green parrot with an extraordinarily long tail, which he said his uncle had brought him from the Caribbean.

The parrot perched on a long rope in the doorway, greeting passers-by in Spanish and Arabic. There was also a small, ancient-looking bar owned by a Christian from the Boutros family who lived in Wadi al-Nasara in Homs. This family had once been renowned for preparing and distilling *arak*, aniseed-flavoured liqueur. Posters of Hollywood actresses plastered the walls. This strange bar occupied a small part of the left side of the house. As for me, I lived just one street away from Jacqueline Mugharib's house, in a big guesthouse in the middle of which was a small fountain. We called it 'Katania House', which derived from the name of the woman who was in charge. Katiana was thirty years old, pretty, olive-skinned and rather plump, and wore the veil in the Syrian style. Her clothes were modest and for ten years she'd managed the house on behalf of its Syrian Christian owner who lived in New York. She called herself Katiana, a Christian name, to make the woman overseas believe that she was also Christian. The owner would contact her manager only by phone and receive the rents remotely through her lawyer. She was therefore under the impression that the manager of her hotel in Damascus was a Christian like herself.

I was in love with Bab Touma. My time there reminded me of some lost moments of my life in Baghdad because of the similarities between this neighbourhood and Al-Karradah in Baghdad, particularly the constant presence of foreigners, the bars and the round-the-clock noise. There was also a rowdy, typically Middle Eastern chaos that resulted from the presence, side by side, of mismatched businesses: ladies' hairdressers, cheap bars and modest restaurants. At a short distance from the house there were various shops and grocers: shops selling cakes and local sweets, Iranian and Arab bakers, shoemakers, tailors, small bookshops, a modern-looking church and a dentist's clinic. There was also the ever-changing flow of guests, particularly foreign students from the United States, France, Italy and even Asia. In this neighbour-hood lived Christian artisans, junior clerks of all denominations, carpenters, tailors and poor Jews. There were also Syrian painters who'd turned their homes into elegant museums, which every evening attracted the cream of expatriate Iraqi and Syrian society. In the midst of this international anarchy there were Iraqi artists:

painters, journalists, movie directors, novelists, photographers, dancers, musicians and actors, all living in old, semi-dilapidated houses in various parts of this cosmopolitan neighbourhood.

The house I lived in consisted of seven rooms, or eight, because the storeroom could be turned into a guestroom and one room was sometimes turned into two. These changes were purely logistical, undertaken during the tourist season with the arrival of Iraqi groups or for various other reasons. The permanent arrangement, however, was three rooms on the lower floor and three rooms on the upper, in addition to the courtyard facing the fountain at the centre of the house. There were always large couches for the benefit of anyone wishing to sleep out in the open and enjoy Damascus' refreshing summer breeze. There was also a tiny kitchen with simple cooking utensils. I would often bump into the other guests coming out of the shared bathrooms, especially in the morning.

The first room was occupied by two Iraqi film directors, Nazar and Adel. Next to them lived two sisters from Latakia who worked for a dress-making company in Damascus. They were extremely pretty and elegant. The lodgers called the first one 'the Romantic' because she always sat distractedly at the window or on the large couch in the courtyard in front of the fountain, reading a book. In contrast, her sister was called 'the Symbolist', following Adel's innovative appellation.

On the upper floor lived an eccentric Iraqi young man who was rumoured to have worked for Iraqi – that is, Saddam's, – intelligence. His first name was Helmi but we didn't know his second name, for he didn't speak much to the other lodgers. He would often stand in front of the outside mirror near the fountain in the centre of the courtyard, combing his hair for hours on end.

The first of the other two rooms was occupied by Shirley

Mendes, an American photographer and journalist, while the second was occupied by Karim, an Italian man of Syrian descent who worked for non-governmental organizations providing aid to Iraqi artists, particularly film-makers.

During this period I was a frequent visitor to the apartment of Jacqueline and her husband Hanna Mugharib. He was a Syrian physician who, though not at all rich, was very hospitable. He never refused his wife's wishes, for he was deeply in love with her. According to Nancy's gossip, however, he was also having an affair that his wife knew nothing about, with a young actress who'd once lived at Katania House. Still, he met all the demands of his Marxist intellectual wife without fail.

Like Nancy Awdeh, I became one of the regulars at Jacqueline Mugharib's salons and a fixture at her apartment on Thursdays. In fact I became one of her favourites. So, in addition to the regular Thursday evening sessions with a large number of foreign and Syrian intellectuals, I also met her almost every Sunday evening at a bar located at the intersection of Bab Touma and Bab Sharqi. At other times I would smoke the hookah with her and her husband on the pavement of the popular Dominoes café, near the police station in the main square of Bab Touma. At the end of our evening out, we would often go for supper at the pizzeria close by.

Jacqueline was an enlightened intellectual with mastery of both English and French and a law degree from the Sorbonne. Her views were totally communist. While in Paris, until her return to Damascus, she'd continued to work closely with French communists. For reasons unknown to me, she had no close ties with Syrian communists, but did sympathize a great deal with Iraqi communists, perhaps because, unlike other Arab communists, they had created armed militias to overthrow the regime. Jacqueline firmly believed in the culture of the coup and was convinced that change would never happen without armed struggle. This was how she came to look after a huge number of Iraqi communists, especially artists and journalists.

At her house I always met a bunch of correspondents. Some of them had been working in Baghdad and had fled, while others were based abroad but visited Damascus from time to time. Another group regularly seen at her house comprised film directors, painters, poets and political writers. But the most favoured group of all, one that was never absent from these meetings, consisted of guerrilla fighters or members of Al-Ansar, the communist forces that had taken refuge in the mountains of Kurdistan, where they fought against the Baathist and government forces with the aim of toppling the regime. The narrative of this period of history is certainly interesting.

The truth is Jacqueline didn't see me as a great journalist or literary star. But she, and her husband, believed that what I was doing was far greater than anything that those useless foreign journalists with little understanding of the region could ever achieve. Neither Jacqueline nor her husband had much confidence in the West or in Westerners, least of all in journalists in general and American journalists in particular. Their suspicions probably originated in the old communist ethic that they sustained for so long. Nevertheless, this never really affected them and they were not at all fanatical, especially Jacqueline, who was completely different from anyone I knew. She was never depressed, pessimistic or venomous, and was always kind and amiable. Moreover, she never got involved in the intrigues that some journalists engaged in.

In that modest apartment on the upper floor, where Jacqueline and her husband lived, you could always find a crowd of journalists, correspondents, actors and directors, Arab and foreign, of all races and creeds, including Americans. Both Jacqueline and her husband were friendly with everyone and offered them all possible assistance. The apartment, which I visited regularly, was so crowded that sometimes you couldn't find a place to sit. Within this amazing social melange, projects, reports and films would be negotiated. Foreign journalists lived almost exclusively in Beirut, Damascus or Amman, and sometimes in Iraqi Kurdistan. They might want to write news reports on kidnappings, sectarian conflicts, violence against women, anonymous murders, urban warfare or the US Army. So on their way to the Middle East, they might spend an evening or two at Jacqueline and Hanna Mugharib's apartment. It was there that I met journalists looking for a ghost writer. After concluding a deal, I'd be sent to carry out what was required for the report: taking photographs, conducting interviews, gauging public opinion and even meeting politicians. I was recompensed handsomely for my pains. For me, it didn't matter that the report would appear under the name of some other journalist, newspaper or news agency. Jacqueline, however, didn't like this one bit.

Nevertheless, it was Jacqueline who introduced me to them and it was thanks to her that I received many such assignments and became well known for doing a good job. The biggest news agencies and television networks would commission me to write features and short analytical pieces. They didn't want me to provide news stories or reports, as most correspondents did, which they had their own stringers for. They needed more than that, and started giving me serious assignments that greatly increased my

37

income. I dressed elegantly and drank beer at the most lavish restaurants. I also had numerous male and female friends. And from time to time, foreign newspapers and news agencies sent me on assignments to Baghdad.

Whenever my news reporting assignments dried up, Jacqueline would give me various jobs. These were mostly handling the affairs of Iraqi intellectuals who'd fled their country, finding them housing with friends, solving their other problems or, for those who so desired, smuggling them to Europe to become citizens and residents.

Jacqueline had vast experience in such matters. In the past, especially after Saddam's clampdown on leftist movements at the end of the seventies, she used to help fugitive communists, either by finding them refuge in Damascus or Beirut or, with the militants among them, by preparing for the revolution that would make Iraq the first communist country in the region. She helped many of them flee the hell of Baghdad, using two methods. Firstly, she would secure them regular jobs and salaries at Palestinian liberation organizations in Beirut. The Palestinian media in particular absorbed large numbers of them. Secondly, she would help some of them receive military training to go to northern Iraq, to hide out in the mountains and join the Al-Ansar communists' fight against the government forces.

Although Jacqueline had been jailed in Syria several times for her underground, conspiratorial activities, she never divulged even a single piece of information that might harm any of her Iraqi communist comrades or Al-Ansar fighters. During that period, the communists were at loggerheads with the Baathists, a conflict that had reached its peak during the Iran–Iraq war. As the communist movement became more militant, it was clear that its various wings were following the Syrian line in their struggle against Saddam. When Iraqi fugitives were unable to take immediate refuge in the mountains on account of the strict siege imposed by Saddam on Kurdistan, they would flee to Syria as a permanent transit point. They often carried a special card that enabled Jacqueline to identify them as communists. Only then would she be willing to offer them housing assistance. In the absence of a card, she would be suspicious that the newcomer was a spy planted by Saddam's secret service apparatus. She often spoke about contacts who later turned out to be spies.

After 2003 Jacqueline's programme underwent drastic changes. She turned from being the protector and supporter of communists to being the protector and supporter of journalists and writers, especially a year after the US invasion of Iraq, when they began to feel the brunt of the violence themselves. She disclosed to me some of her intricate plans involving Iraqis and asked me to help her carry them out. So I helped her by booking rooms in miserable hotels where we would cram journalists and photographers two or three to a room, according to the requirements of the situation. We once convinced a hotel receptionist to allow us to squeeze ten journalists into a single room. If the receptionist was Egyptian, our task would be much easier, because Egyptians were always sympathetic to the poor and needy and were constantly willing to facilitate humanitarian missions. We sometimes ran out of money or couldn't find places for them to stay, so Jacqueline would welcome them into her own apartment. Sometimes, when there were too many people staying in her apartment, she would go somewhere else with her husband, until lodgings were arranged for the newcomers.

The lifestyle at Katania House was so Western that you even forgot you were in the Middle East. There were young Iraqi and Western intellectuals, both men and women, living under the same roof. Music blared from the courtyard of the house: pop and rap, old and new, as well as classical music such as Wagner, Chopin and Verdi. In their rooms you'd find the latest publications in Arabic and other languages. There were new paintings signed by young artists and films whose directors and casts sat and laughed with you while lounging in bed. Almost every evening, everyone would bring a favourite drink and a dance party would begin to the music. Katania House was the destination of many young Iraqi intellectuals, the second generation of fugitives from the hell of Baghdad. While the first generation had fled Saddam's hell and the dictatorship that was now over, the second generation was fleeing terrorism, militias, occupation and religious censorship. Where the first generation had danced to the music of the Beatles, Cliff Richard, the Shadows and the Doors, and talked about armed revolution and the socialist state, the second generation danced to rap and hip hop, the songs of Fifty Cent, Eminem and Fergie, while debating democracy and human rights. There were also plans to emigrate to Europe, with Iraqis moving, wave after wave, to join their friends there. But they remained attached to those who stayed behind, especially in Damascus. So Jacqueline tried hard to make life easy for those who loved Western culture, music and a life of liberty.

Many Islamist journalists and intellectuals also arrived from Baghdad. Some of them rapidly became caught up in pop music, mixed society, strange clothing and accessories of every kind. Before long they would shave their beards and let their hair grow, dazzled by the freedom of life in the West and embracing Western values. Others did not. They stayed true to their principles but learned a new type of collective rejection of bourgeois ethics. But this was a peaceful tendency that inclined towards sensual gratification, a domesticated anarchy that loved nature and animals and rejected conventional morality.

Almost every day witnessed endless cultural discussions. You would find Arabic novels in people's bags. On their beds and on their bedside tables you'd find music by Léo Ferré or Georges Brassens. You would sometimes find them going to elegant movie houses to attend French or American film week. They were no different from rebellious youths throughout history. They stayed up late in bars and parks and read Tariq Ali's books against war and terrorism. They attended cultural events and, in the midst of crowds, danced to the music of well-known cult figures. Or they went to discos where their mere presence represented a rejection of traditional culture. You might also find them in theatres, captivated by the words of the Iraqi playwright Jawad al-Asadi or Salah al-Qasab, whose great plays challenged their minds and whose latest stage productions became engraved in their memories.

III

Journalists at the tobacconist's

ONE LIVELY SUMMER EVENING, I was at Jacqueline and her husband's apartment. It was noisy and animated. There were discussions of every type, loud laughter and the clinking of glasses. The place was so enchanting that it made me feel more preoccupied with others than with myself. Suddenly Jacqueline's voice rose above the din, telling me that Nancy was on the phone for me. I took the receiver and spoke as loudly as I could, while motioning at everyone to keep quiet. The noise was truly deafening, so I screamed into the receiver, 'Nancy, how are you?'

Her voice sounded calm as she said, 'I called Jacqueline to ask for you. I've got some work for you. Come quickly to Amman. I've got an important job. I have to see you.'

'Now?' I said in astonishment, while trying to silence the noise around me.

'Yes, now,' she said in her gentle voice.

'Can't it wait till the morning?' I asked.

'No, now.' Her voice was confident and enthusiastic. 'Now means right now.'

I went back to Katania House. It was as rowdy as ever and

the music was very loud. I knocked hard on the door, which was opened by a drunken girl. I went quickly upstairs and into my room. I took my photographs out of their frames and put them in my bag. I also took some of the books I always have with me, and a few films. I placed the camera in a leather bag and packed a few of my favourite possessions, insignificant objects that were worthless but which brought me good luck, or so I believed. These included a cup made of sandalwood, an empty ink bottle that smelt of cheap ink, and a very old silver ring with a stone that twinkled in the dark. I felt that at the end of a hard day's work, one needed the soothing warmth of concrete objects, even when they were silly and insignificant. Because I was heartened by its blue colour, I then bought a blue shawl and put it in the bag. I carried the laptop over my shoulder, hung the camera round my neck, put the small recorder in the side pocket of my trousers and rushed to the garage. At the border, I had to wait for hours and endure the cross-examination of the border guards in order to reach Amman where Nancy Awdeh was expecting me.

When I arrived in Amman, I took a cab and went straight to a lovely small hotel, the Select, a three-storey stone building with a glass door. Above the door was a sign where 'Select' was written in both Arabic and English. The hotel was located on Jabal al-Weibdeh. I dropped off my bags and went directly to a nearby bar, the Negresco. It was a small bar in a quiet, exclusive suburb, close to Amman's lively and noisy main square. This bar was a favourite spot for foreign journalists, correspondents and commentators. It was, in fact, the meeting point of foreign correspondents working for the international press, television, radio and news agencies. All of them had been stationed in Iraq during the outbreak of the war, before and after the early months of 2003. The bar was not distinctive, but with its wooden tables, paintings that reflected a taste for the primitive, its loud jazz, smell of alcohol and dim lights, it had a definite American character.

When I entered the bar, it was swarming with drunken, unruly journalists, and filled with the sounds of laughter, the chinking of glasses, shouting and discussions. The lights were dim and the place reeked of cigarette smoke and odd smells from the ashtrays that were full of butts and burnt matchsticks. Food and plates of *mezzas* littered the place, telling the story of what was going on. Waiters rushed from one side to another. There was nowhere to sit, but when I looked around, I saw Nancy sitting with a group of Arab correspondents who worked, I believed, for a foreign station. Next to her sat an Iraqi journalist called Faris Hassan, a man whom I totally detested. He was talking in a very loud voice and the sound of his laughter was deafening.

My very first impressions of this journalist had been negative and I never wished to have any dealings with him. He was a big mouth and always spoke as though he were an expert on Middle Eastern affairs. His reports on Iraq, which he sold to foreign newspapers, were mostly fabricated and exaggerated. We had no work connections and I couldn't bear the sight of him. The only time I'd talked to him in a friendly manner had been at Jacqueline Mugharib's apartment, where he'd gone in the company of Salina Quraishi, the Afghan journalist who wrote a famous report on the Taliban after the US invasion. At a later date, about two years previously, he'd said hello to me at the Box Café in downtown Amman.

*   *   *

Before Faris or Nancy could spot me, I made an exit by ducking behind the screen and heading out of the door. I stood in the street for a minute before deciding to go to the Piccadilly Restaurant. This was a small, English-style place located a short distance from the Negresco. It was also a minor meeting point for journalists and correspondents who couldn't find room at the Negresco. I pushed the door and went in. Two foreign correspondents I knew well were inside: a tall American journalist with blond hair, who worked for the *Christian Science Monitor*, and a German woman journalist, whom I believed to be of Syrian origin and who worked for Swiss television.

I sat with them as they spoke about the very same thing. They couldn't go to Baghdad because of the many risks involved, particularly after the spate of kidnappings and murders of foreign journalists since 2004. When the waiter began to remove the empty plates and glasses from the tables, they reordered. I had nothing to say, so I gazed instead at the evening outside, charmed by the mysterious view from the restaurant onto the wide street. As I sat there, I could see the light of the moon on the craggy hills that ran parallel to the great houses and buildings. The horizon was obscured by the fog while the lamps lit up the amazing tenderness of the night.

Nancy came suddenly into the restaurant. She was wearing a short denim skirt and a pink blouse, the top button of which was undone. She was accompanied by Faris Hassan, who was wearing the same clothes he'd been wearing last time: a light brown linen jacket and a pair of khaki trousers with lots of pockets. They came over and embraced me. After the waiter had managed to bring some chairs, they sat down at our table. Nancy sat next to me, while Faris Hassan sat opposite. She smiled at me with her

45

green eyes and her fair-skinned, rosy face. She pushed the hair away from her eyes and said abruptly, 'You have work, black writer!'

'So, what is it?' I asked. I also asked her in a whisper if that idiot, referring to Faris Hassan, was in the know.

'Listen,' she said, 'a major Iraqi composer has been killed in mysterious circumstances in Al-Mansour in Baghdad. We want a full report on his murder for *US Today News*. We also want a book for the Press Cooperation Agency.'

'Kamal Medhat?' I asked.

'You know him?'

'As a violinist he's very famous. As for his murder, I just read about it in the papers. Give me some information and tell me what you need exactly, and I'll do the report.'

'There's something else I need to tell you . . .' she said.

'What is it?'

'This idiot that you hate so much will be going with you.'

'Out of the question. I won't do it, no way!' I said.

'It won't be possible otherwise. I know what you've always thought of him, but . . .'

'Believe me, I can't work with that ass. Impossible!'

'But he was the one who turned up important information.'

'What kind of information could that numbskull have that nobody else knows about?'

'It's a long story. The three of us will meet tomorrow to discuss the whole thing.'

'You discuss it with him. Please leave me out of it.'

'Please listen to me and don't let your thick head get in the way!'

'Work with that donkey?' I said, while the donkey guffawed and talked to the American in his sickening English accent.

Nancy worked for a news analysis agency, or what is usually referred to as a press cooperation agency. On this occasion, she was looking for a short newspaper feature, to be followed by a book, about an intriguing personality. We started talking about various other things, without mentioning the important topic I'd come to Amman to discuss. Instead, she spoke to me in the way that other journalists did in those days, starting with a question to which she knew the answer, before getting to the crux of the matter:

'Have you ever worked in Sudan?'

'I've been there a couple of times,' I said.

Then she told me about her experience of spending a whole year in Darfur.

'Does the Middle East situation frighten you?' It was a question she might have posed to a politician. She went on to say that what terrified her was the fact that Middle Eastern countries were on the brink of disintegration and collapse or might splinter into pieces. But before she could finish what she was saying, a waiter came to take our order.

We drank some more while Nancy talked and Faris looked at me from time to time, without speaking. He took a packet of cigarettes from his pocket, nervously pulled one out and lit it with a match which he shook to put out the flame. Then he carelessly threw the matchstick away, not bothering whether it landed in the ashtray or not. He placed his glass of Scotch in front of him, took a quick sip and put it down again. When he spoke he would look you directly in the eye, and when he discussed something, he would not allow his interlocutor to finish a point. That had been my first impression of him. What was more important, however, was related to work: the way he wrote his reports.

I loathed his reports. He exaggerated so much in an attempt to draw attention to what he was saying. He hadn't the least sympathy for the people who were suffering from the devastating effects of war. He wrote in order to demonstrate his total mastery of his subject, however cruel. In fact, he wrote about people with utter disdain, caring little for people's feelings, especially his readers. He often lingered over rough, bloody, cruel and callous scenes. Whenever he talked about what was happening in Iraq, he would speak in a loud voice as he drank and laughed.

For example, he once mentioned an Iraqi soldier he'd found lying on the floor with his ribcage crushed. He described the intestines spilling out of the stomach like spaghetti between his fingers, with an eyeball lying a metre or so from the body. This was how he'd described an image of war, totally unconcerned about its impact on others. He never left a scene of carnage, be it an explosion in a market or the aftermath of a battle, without taking a photograph. He didn't mind photographing scattered, charred bodies, plastic shoes strewn all over the place, blood coagulating on the asphalt or human guts that resembled the shreds of food. He simply stood there and took the shot.

I knew little about his love life, although everyone knew he was having a relationship with a Brazilian girl called Paola, who worked for a local TV channel in Sao Paolo. She was a very tall mixed-race woman, with a strong, young body that was always in a state of arousal. I saw them together more than once, in Damascus, in Beirut, and in Amman. After 2003, I saw them together in Baghdad, where they'd created a furore at the hotel where we were staying because he didn't care where they made love. In spite of the state of unrest in Iraq during the war, the widespread insurgency, violence and murder, the formation of political parties and societies, and the overall chaos, he used to take her to the nearest bathroom to make love.

The first time I sat at a table with him was at Kataina House in Damascus, where he was drinking Scotch non-stop and lecturing a group of lodgers about his earliest sexual experience. It was when he'd been a soldier at the front. Although I hadn't heard the story from the beginning, I caught up with it in the middle. He said the woman had seemed submissive as she went down the stairs with him. He was using his torch to show her where to tread. After a few moments, he started running the torchlight over her body. The light on her dark thighs filled him with desire. When she'd raised her dress again on her way down the stairs, he'd touched her thigh with his hand. She'd sworn at him softly, with two words intended to arouse him. He was suddenly seized by an uncontrollable desire to possess her, and he pressed himself against her. Because there was space only for two people and his torch was pointing down, he reached out to touch her body. She let herself glide towards him, her hands on his shoulders. She didn't seem to be at all distressed; in fact, her smile had broadened invitingly. Rather than pulling back, she touched his neck and drew her face towards his. Swallowing his saliva, he devoured her with his gaze. She reached down with her hand and undid first the top button of his trousers, then the next. With his own hand he explored her body underneath her raised dress. It felt warm and soft, and quivered at the touch of his fingers. His breath became shorter as she leaned against the wall and pulled him towards her.

This was all I had to go on about the journalist that I was supposed to work with.

* * *

I took refuge in my room at the Select. It was small and clean and located on the upper floor of the hotel. It looked out onto a wide courtyard that had a huge, old pine tree in the middle. I sat by the window, staring at a beautiful church located two streets away. I opened my laptop and wrote a couple of paragraphs, inspired by my latest meeting with Nancy. But I was in total despair; I was afraid to miss this opportunity. It wasn't money that I was concerned with this time. I love this kind of work, but I was waiting for a better time to write a novel and also hoping it might prove both successful and financially rewarding. If it also got translated in the West, it might turn out to be a good source of income for me. But I still haven't managed to write it. The reason is mainly to do with my work as a journalist, but also because my connections and friendships with journalists and documentary film-makers were much stronger than those with writers. If truth be told, I hated the dead look on writers' faces and the lifelessness of poets. I couldn't stomach talking to literary figures, who sat in smoke-filled cafés, puffing on hookahs and speaking in hoarse voices about semiotics and structuralism. I couldn't stand their boring, incomprehensible babble.

I once said to Nancy, 'I hate writers ...'

'What?' she said in a slightly disapproving tone.

'I hate their ironed clothes and clean-shaven faces. I hate their lazy, boring lives. I've always preferred the lives of reporters who confront life head-on and go to dangerous places.'

I still remember this statement that I made to Nancy that day, although she couldn't work out why I felt like that. It might have been my love of travelling. I loved moving around and couldn't stay in one spot for long. I loved going from place to place, seeing the variety and vitality of life itself. I was as passionate about life as writers are about gloves, shoes, money and hatred. Writers' hatred smelt like tar. It was a smell exuded by the words of those whose souls had rusted away. They were prisoners in their stuffy rooms, in spite of the bustle of life on the streets, the delicious fragrance of a small flower on a table and the clean, ironed clothes they wore.

'But journalism also attracts some ghastly writers,' she said, 'and their numbers are on the increase. There are even more of them than authors. They fall into many types. There are the fake journalists who watch a massacre in cold blood and talk as though they're social reformers or sex therapists. There are others who write reports as though they're in possession of absolute and irrefutable truths. There are those who try to solve ethnic problems in a mathematical manner, and those who view democracy in the light of the agendas of sheikhs and clerics. And then there's a faction who might commit murder or go mad if a word of criticism is directed at them.'

Nancy's voice on the phone was like a divine intervention, injecting a dose of tenderness into my miserable night. It was dawn, around four or five in the morning. I'd been shaken abruptly out of my dreams by the sound of the phone. It rang many times before I opened my eyes and fumbled for the receiver. Her sharp and confident tone startled me: 'Don't hang up . . .'

Her voice had an imploring tinge. 'I need to have a word with you,' she said and then stopped.

'Nancy, I can't work with that person. I can't!'

'Listen. You can't go to Baghdad by yourself. It's too dangerous for you.'

'I've been there dozens of times.'

51

'But the situation now is much worse ...'

'I've been through all kinds of situations, Nancy. I know exactly what it's like.'

'Don't be so bloody smug.'

'And what can this person do that I can't?'

'My dear, he has an unbelievable capacity to deal with armed groups. He sometimes takes on the task of smuggling journalists in and out of Baghdad. He has shady connections, everyone knows that, but he knows how to deal with the militias. He's the one who leaks what they want the press to know. He sometimes passes militia recordings and information to the TV channels, like information about a foreigner who's had his throat cut. In return, he enjoys privileges. You'll be safer with him ...'

'Safer with a journalist who brings films of militias killing some reporter or hospital nurse? What do you mean?'

'Yes, unfortunately, my friend, that's what he does. But he's kind and useful. I won't let you go alone this time. The situation is much worse. You can't. This isn't just my opinion, but the agency's as well.'

I was happy that she really cared about me. The more insistent I was, the more I sensed her anxiety.

I hung up. But for the remaining hours I couldn't close my eyes. I stayed in this state of dismay and dejection until I saw the pale and hateful light of dawn in the Amman sky, coming through the curtains of the open window.

The following day, the three of us met at Fakhr el-Din restaurant. This was a swanky place located on Jabal Amman, designed like a huge palace with spacious gardens. The tables were situated in interconnecting rooms, and there was always a warm and intimate atmosphere. Faris sat on a black leather chair facing me. He was unexpectedly quiet, something I'd never witnessed before. He spoke gently and was extremely polite. He even raised his hands as if praying to the waiter to pour him some wine. His strange looks reminded me of a famous Hitchcock character, the detective in *Rear Window*.

At that particular moment, two explanations jarred in my head. On the one hand, Nancy might have been responsible for his state of calm. She might have convinced him to stop his silly babble. On the other hand, it was possible that my view of him had been wrong and based on a misconception. He might have been a very different man from the image he projected.

On that day, Faris seemed to me like a modern peasant responding to social challenges that he craved. He was not really a likable person, but he did display a kind of wild passion and an amazing love of food and drink. He was very tall, though not excessively. He wasn't the kind of man who was immediately appealing. He would express his views rather slowly. And in this meeting he revealed his *alter ego*, that of Assad Zaki.

'What! You're Asaad Zaki?' I asked him, as though trying to arrest the slippery Asaad.

'Yeah, I'm Asaad Zaki,' he said proudly.

'But Asaad lived in Brazil,' I objected.

As soon as he'd uttered the name Asaad Zaki, my conflicting and hostile emotions subsided. In fact, they disappeared almost entirely. Why was that?

Jacqueline Mugharib had told me about Asaad Zaki when I saw his photograph in *Kull al-Arab* magazine. He was a thin young man with a squirrel-like face and sunken eyes, an excellent, intelligent reporter who had good connections with Latin American journalists. He lived, if I wasn't mistaken, at Katania House, in the same room that was occupied later by the two sisters from Latakia. He stayed for a while in the house before leaving for Beirut, where he worked briefly as a journalist and then as a TV reporter. This was all I knew about him. Although I hadn't met him in person, I'd already heard dozens of his news reports. Those who'd worked with him spoke highly of his talent and exceptional abilities – he was a cameraman, editor, commentator and analyst all at the same time, a whole crew in one person. Moreover, he was greatly admired for his courage and daring.

But how had he created this new image and new life for himself?

He said he'd fabricated the image, and the life too, in order to avoid falling prey to Iraqi intelligence. I soon discovered that the name Faris Hassan was also an invention and a fabrication. So what was his real name? His father's name was Mahmoud Zaki. He'd worked for a long time as a lawyer. Being a highly cultured man, he'd been accused by the authorities of belonging to the Communist Party, a very serious charge at that time. He'd been arrested and imprisoned for more than a year as part of the notorious campaign against communist elements carried out by Saddam Hussein. During his time in detention, he'd been subjected to brutal torture. A short while after his release, he'd managed to escape with his family to Syria and from there to Warsaw.

Unable to find regular employment, he hadn't stayed long in Poland. He'd also sensed that the socialist regime was on the verge of collapse, due to devastating inflation, massive unemployment and defeatist attitudes. So in order to avoid sinking into the depths of despair like other immigrants, he'd decided to return to the Arab world. He'd soon settled in Beirut, where he'd worked first as a sales assistant in a small bookshop in Riad al-Sulh Square. Then he'd found a rather unusual job that had proved quite lucrative: he'd begun carving tombstones and other marble objects, such as memorials, that provided him with enough funds to emigrate to Brazil.

In Sao Paolo, the father had worked in trade and had been hugely successful, becoming one of the wealthiest Iraqis in the small Iraqi community that lived on the margins of the larger Lebanese and Syrian communities and mingled with them. It was in Sao Paolo that Asaad (whose real name was Emad Mahmoud Zaki) had studied journalism at Brazilian universities. He'd then worked for Brazilian television as a correspondent, moving between Beirut, Damascus, Amman and Casablanca.

So I found myself poised between two opposite personalities, one that I admired and the other that I loathed and couldn't stand. This brought me back to the characters of *Tobacco Shop*.

The situation was not easy for me to accept. But Nancy exerted great pressure to bring another personality out of Faris, different from the one I knew. On that day, Nancy was like a dramaturge, trying to extract from this great actor his best ever performance. She quizzed him about himself. She asked him about things she might have heard from him dozens of times before and perhaps even knew by heart. But she was determined to gather up all his pearls and put them on display before me.

She asked him about his work as a war correspondent in Afghanistan, particularly at the end of the Taliban era. He described to us in detail his visits to Mazar-i-Sharif and Kandahar, and the detention centres where many Arab fighters were held. Although I'd also been in Kandahar at the same time, we'd never actually met there. So I frequently found myself finishing off his statements and he mine, to the point that we spoke with one voice.

Faris spoke of many things. But to be fair, although I'd also lived in Kandahar, Kabul and Mazar-i-Sharif, I didn't know those places as well as he did. He had an extraordinary ability to remember the tiniest details, things that should be impossible to retain for long. He would talk about the drizzle on fighters' helmets or his visits to some Tajik camp buried beneath layers of snow. He knew the name of every single hill and didn't omit a description of the mules carrying jerry-cans of water up the mountain. Nor did he forget the camel caravans entering Kabul. When he talked about Mazar-i-Sharif, he gave a detailed description of the mausoleum where, according to the Afghans, Imam Ali is buried. He charmed us with his description of the white doves on the domes of the mausoleum and the sparkling letters carved on its walls and arches by the best masons of the region. He also spoke of the names of squares, the remains of statues, the traffic lights, the horse-drawn carriages and the types of camels and donkeys that were employed in transporting heavy loads. He told us how he'd ridden in a Jeep with armed Afghans and entered their camp.

He had access to many secrets there that were completely inaccessible to me. He had contacts with the prominent warlord General Majid Rozi as well as with General Atta Aswad. He was the man entrusted to carry a message from Atta Aswad to the Uzbek leader Abdel Rashid Dostom. Then he talked about the civil war, the warlords and the militarization of the country. He was always there, and seen everything, and he'd occasionally carried out tasks and missions beyond his duties as a journalist.

He sometimes oversimplified things, but at other times told us secrets we knew nothing about. His analyses had a tone that was neither journalistic nor scientific.

He spoke very simply but analyzed matters with remarkable accuracy. When he talked about himself, however, it was with a tediously self-congratulatory manner. Nancy must have told him my opinion of him, and he tried that day to present an image of himself that was different from the one we all had of him. It must have pleased Nancy to prove to me that what little I knew about him was nonsense and that he had other, unusual talents that I'd never suspected. At any rate, it was the first time I'd been able to put up with this pompous journalist among whose personalities I was lost, one of which I admired, and the other that I utterly detested.

But who was he?

He spoke that day about his memories and the reports he'd published in foreign newspapers. It was a funny coincidence that he'd also worked in advertising, writing commercials for Mexican rice, swimming pools and saunas in five-star hotels. He talked of services during the tourist season, of swimming pools and fishing tackle. He'd worked for a while making kids' cartoons. Perhaps this was the reason, he said, that he became so popular with children. This was before he started writing articles for a number of Arabic and foreign newspapers, and before moving on to work for well-known television channels. But all his writing was done under a pseudonym. I discovered that there was something else we had in common. Faris Hassan also wanted to write a novel. At least he regarded himself more as a writer than a journalist. This was a common feature of many journalists, who viewed writers as having a higher status than journalists.

'You probably hold the common view that a writer is superior to a journalist,' I said, without mentioning anything about myself. At least I didn't tell him that it was my own point of view as well. He didn't try to defend this claim but treated it as an indisputable fact, something to be taken for granted. He told me only that the main reason he'd gone into journalism was because he wanted to make a living from a job in some way connected with writing. He wanted to earn from his writing, regardless of genre. He also said that journalism gave him the 'editorial skills' that were so necessary for writing a major novel. It was the first time, I felt, that he'd spoken realistically, in a graphic, down-to-earth way. He talked with a great deal of sarcastic humour, which was reinforced by his despair. The conversation brought me closer to him, a person for whom I had earlier felt nothing but utter contempt.

The following day, we all had a business meeting at the Canvass restaurant on Jabal al-Weibdeh. This was a classy place that journalists avoided like the plague because of its exorbitant prices. Nancy called it 'the Guillotine' and its waiters the 'executioners'. We sat in the garden outside, drinking wine and eating grilled fish, while we discussed all aspects of the situation. At this point I should mention that our information on Kamal Medhat was very sparse. None of us knew much about the man. At the beginning, our discussion of him was sterile and hesitant, as if wading through a swamp. Nancy would talk and fall silent because of the yellow pollen falling from the blossoming trees, which clung to her eyebrows and lashes. She'd wipe her lashes with a paper tissue and look expectantly at us. Faris Hassan wiped his own face as though he'd just stepped out of a pool. With an unexpected jerk of his tall, lanky body Faris then said, 'Let's go straight to Baghdad.'

We moved on to the Negresco. We drank in the midst of the din, while reporters came and went and waiters ran to and fro carrying glasses, bottles and plates. There were cameras, papers, facts, numerous faces and beards, long hair and dim lights. There was also a strong smell of fermentation as well as shouting, conversations, loud noises and many languages. This was a place I really loved. Nancy sat by my side, her leg touching mine. I talked to her with my shoulder against hers stealing brief glances into her eyes. She felt my warm breath and my touch. She knew that I was choosing my words carefully with the express purpose of exciting her. She laughed loudly and wiped her brow.

We spoke, of course, about the murdered Iraqi musician. We also talked intermittently, in the midst of the clamour and the shouting, about the trip to Baghdad and the information that was available. Faris sat facing us. He took care of the orders and spoke to the waiters, a cigarette in his mouth and a glass between his fingers, loudly addressing some man or other, or a woman sitting nearby. He allowed me to get close to Nancy and talk of old times. Mostly we recalled things that had happened between us when we'd been together in Beirut. Then the restaurant began to grow quiet. Light-headed from drinking, the journalists in the bar started to head to their homes and hotels.

At Nancy's insistence we returned to the topic of Kamal Medhat.

The following day, Faris left for Baghdad in the hope of arranging a place for me at the agency site, in a building near the Associated Press inside the Green Zone. I stayed on in Amman, from where I set out to find information. I had to prepare a short biography of Kamal Medhat, as well as detailed maps of the capitals he'd lived in: Baghdad, Tehran and Damascus. I also had to find maps of those cities from the time of his residence and to assess the changes that had taken place.

I returned to my hotel at noon. The moment I stepped into the lobby, I saw Nancy sitting in the corner with her driver. She saw me come in and rushed over, saying that Faris was in Baghdad and that everything was ready for me. He'd be there to meet me at the airport. She gave me my plane ticket and a card with some important information. She also gave me a badge attached to some blue cord, to hang around my neck. This was my press card with the agency logo, stamp and licence. Nancy looked utterly exhausted, as though the volatility of the situation in the Middle East had left its mark on her face and hands. Although she was only thirty, the curls of her soft hair seemed ashen. She looked as though she were at a funeral. She was pale, worn-out and tense, and she was chain-smoking. Her appearance aroused strange and contradictory feelings in my heart. I reminded her that we were supposed to meet in the evening to spend some time together before I left, but she apologized, saying she had some urgent business to take care of in Damascus.

By dawn I'd flown to Baghdad.

IV

The imperial city and the emerald bars

'YOUR DESTINATION?' THE MAN at the entrance of Queen Alia airport in Amman asked me. He had a bushy moustache that hid his lips, and a blue beret pulled down over his forehead.

'Baghdad,' I said, putting my suitcase on the floor.

He shuddered a little, looked me straight in the eye and asked, 'What do you do?'

'I'm a journalist,' I said and showed him the card hanging from the blue cord on my chest.

He searched me carefully with his hands, tapping on my back and shoulders as well as between my legs. He ordered me to take off my shoes. So I removed my shoes, my khaki jacket, my glasses, my mobile phone and my belt. I placed all the items in addition to some coins in a grey plastic tray, which he passed through the machine. I was then allowed to go through the metal detector. There was a woman carrying an expensive leather bag walking next to a man dressed in a white suit and silk tie. He had a gold ring on his finger. There was also a foreigner with a cigar in his mouth and another person who was holding a string of prayer-beads and talking to a hefty policeman slouched in a leather seat.

I placed my small black leather bag, my Sony DCR-TRV461E camera and tripod on a small trolley, which I pushed in front of me. I headed quickly to a wooden counter inside the terminal. When I looked up, I noticed that the clock on the wall opposite showed two in the morning. The airport workers were sitting in their blue uniforms on wooden benches, yawning. Some were stretched out on the benches while others were fast asleep. When I reached the counter, I lifted my luggage onto the scales. A female airport employee gave me my boarding pass and pointed me to passport control. As I headed towards the white counter, I heard the last call for the British Airways flight to Cyprus. The call made one of the travellers jump up and hurry towards the counter.

I handed my passport to the airport employee, who flipped through it back and forth. A frown appeared on his dark face and there was a strange look in his eyes. He took a long time examining the passport and then asked me my destination. 'Baghdad,' I said, without adding a single word. I felt that he was taking his time and began to fidget. So he raised his head, glanced at me, rapidly stamped the passport and handed it back. Hugely relieved, I stashed it in the pocket of my jacket, picked up my little bag, put it over my shoulder and walked away. The terminal was filled with Marines heading for Baghdad.

I sat on a wooden bench watching them. Gathered in one spot, their loud voices were as piercing as an exchange of shots in a tennis rally. They wore camouflage uniforms and their heads were shaved. They were solid guys and carried their khaki rucksacks and kitbags on their backs. Some were stretched out on the floor, while others were sitting on benches. It was clear that they were booked on the same flight, bound for Baghdad.

At the wooden barrier, a few government employees were also preparing to board the plane with us. They were dressed in elegant suits and long ties, and carried Samsonite briefcases. The number of passengers increased as they were joined by bearded clerics wearing black turbans and holding long strings of prayer-beads between their fingers. Their veiled wives stood close by. On the benches sat families also preparing to go to Baghdad. They spoke fluent English without a trace of an accent. It was clear they were Iraqi families who'd settled in Europe and the United States and were now returning to Baghdad. Some of them were employed by the new government. The girls wore jeans and pretty T-shirts, and the boys had modern outfits and strange haircuts. They moved confidently and light-heartedly among the passengers, as though heading for a party. Their destination, after all, was the Green Zone, the location of the government and foreign embassies, and not the Red Zone, which was one of the most dangerous locations in the world.

Apart from the Marines, there were Asian workers: Filipinos, Malaysians and Pakistanis. They were employed at US military bases as cleaners, cooks, porters, dishwashers, ironers, salesmen and servants of all kinds. Other Asians were dressed in black suits and long narrow ties. It was clear they worked as personal bodyguards for businessmen, contractors or venture capitalists.

We all moved slowly through the hall towards the wooden barrier with the wide golden stripe. When we entered the departure lounge, the crowd grew larger and more diverse. Monks dressed in black cassocks sat on a distant bench. One of them had snowy white hair and wore a small, black cap. His head was turned towards a woman sitting near him as he listened to the voice of her playful child. There were Kurds in their baggy trousers and distinctive clothes. Near the barrier stood a tall woman leaning against the wall, looking very sexy in her tight trousers and light pink shirt that revealed the roundness of her breasts. She placed a camera tripod and a blue holdall full of various equipment beside her on the floor. She had the look of a reporter. Although I couldn't tell where I'd seen her before, it had been in more than one place.

In the farthest corner, a group of passengers was moving around, murmuring and gesticulating in a tense, nervous manner. Suddenly a group of American Blackwater guards passed through the small gate, carrying their luggage. This was the American private security company that specialized in providing security services to foreign embassies and US companies in Iraq. The way they looked stood out; you couldn't mistake them for anyone else. It wasn't only their uniforms that distinguished them – their bulging trousers and black shirts that revealed their chests – but also their burly, powerfully built figures. Their bare, muscular arms, their tanned skin, their broad, thrusting chests and their shaved heads gave them the look of actors taking part in a Hollywood action movie.

I suddenly noticed an old acquaintance of mine who worked for a local television channel. He was talking to the woman reporter in tight trousers whom I'd seen earlier and who was chewing gum in an overly sexy manner. He was bombarding her with rapid-fire statements, but when he saw me he waved and smiled. So I went over. As soon as I reached him, he introduced the woman, saying her name in a low voice, 'Nermine Haidar.' I didn't know where I'd heard the name before, but he told me that she directed documentary films. 'I might have seen a film of yours at some time,' I told her. It was unclear to me whether he knew her from before or had just made her acquaintance. But she seemed rather put off by him. Nevertheless, he dragged her by the hand to the duty-free shop and came back half an hour later, laden with bags of drinks, perfumes, belts, prayer-beads, jewellery, scarves and religious books. He told me he'd bought the items to make his work as a journalist in Baghdad easier.

We waited for around two hours. There was nobody that we could ask about the reason for the delay. The journalist, whose name I've forgotten, called several people in Baghdad, asking basic questions about his hotel or requesting help for his work there. When he spoke on his mobile, his voice was drowned by the voices of the other passengers. Then he hurried off to the cafeteria and returned with a tray full of cups of coffee. He gave me one and offered Nermine another. At the gate, we drank and chatted.

On the plane it was even more crowded because the seats were unallocated. Families and clerics were seated first. We put our little briefcases and bags in the overhead compartments. I took a seat next to the window. The nameless journalist pushed his way to the seat next to mine. In the aisle seat sat Nermine Haidar in her tight trousers and full blouse. She lifted her arms and with a rubber band tied back her hair, which was cascading down her shoulders. Then she took some papers out of her handbag and put them on her lap. Across the aisle from us sat three Marines who were returning from leave. It was clear from their looks and their language that they were of Mexican descent. Two soldiers from Fiji occupied the seats in the row in front of us. A plump woman soldier sat beside them. She was blonde and her hair was bunched with a khaki hairband. She'd left her khaki camouflage jacket open, revealing a khaki vest. In the seats near us sat young men from Iraqi families and three women soldiers. One of the women soldiers was very tall and blonde, with blue eyes and a small tattoo on her arm. A black officer stood beside her, talking. It was clear that his seat was elsewhere, but he was spending as much time as possible talking to her before the plane took off. Every time the air-hostesses hurried past to carry out the required procedures before takeoff, he would squeeze himself harder against the seat of the woman soldier.

When I'd finished drinking my cold beer, I dumped the can in a black bag beside me. The anonymous journalist turned and asked me if I wanted another one. I made a sign of agreement, so he reached into a large bag and brought out another can, which he opened and handed to me. The outside of the can was cold and covered with droplets of water.

'Where are you staying?' he asked me as he wiped his forehead with a handkerchief.

'Do you know Faris Hassan?' I asked.

'Yes,' he answered.

'He's coming to collect me from the airport,' I said to avoid any further questioning. I didn't ask him where he was going. He took the handkerchief out of his pocket, wiped his mouth and started drinking beer from the can in his hand. In the other hand he held a packet of Lays chilli-flavour crisps, which he was devouring eagerly. I drank my cold beer. Every now and again, he shook the packet of spicy crisps towards me. It was illustrated with a red chilli. I stuck my hand in the packet, took a few crisps, put them in my mouth and downed a sip of cold beer to soothe the burning sting.

I never answered the anonymous journalist's question nor disclosed to him the nature of my mission. I evaded his curiosity by pretending to be asleep until the pilot ordered us to fasten our seat belts for landing.

The descent was terrifying. The plane came down in a tight spiral, trying to keep immediately over the airport, because the militias would target slowly descending civilian airplanes with portable, shoulder-mounted, Russian-made Strela missiles. After the aircraft had landed and come to a complete halt, we all stood up. There was heavy spring rain. The Marines and Asians were the first to disembark and head for the terminal building. They were all complaining about the rain, except for the blonde woman soldier with the tattoo. A young man helped carry her heavy bag. He lifted it up for her to put on her shoulder. She thanked him without looking at his face and asked the others to make way for her. She then sprinted off.

As the crowd moved in front of me, I turned and took the newspapers that had been left in the seat pockets. I put them in my bag and stuck the empty beer can in a seat pocket in their place. I took my passport and mobile phone out of my small leather bag, which I then slung over my shoulder before leaving the aircraft.

All three of us stood in the queue: the anonymous journalist, Nermine the documentary director and me. The soldiers, Marines and Asian workers all went to the other side, except for the woman soldier with the tattoo. She'd been held up by the large bag she was carrying on her back. She finally caught up with them and left the place, accompanied by the black officer. Outside, the weather was terrible and we saw a flat green area, the portico of the building, and the wreckage of an aircraft still left behind from the days of the war. We all ran as quickly as possible towards the bus to take shelter from the rain.

Nermine was talking non-stop to a family with two young women. One of them was dark and wore very tight knee-length trousers. The other one was prettier, but rather plump, and wore a check skirt and blue blouse. She'd tied her hair with a ribbon as blue as the colour of her eyes. The mother was around fifty, very slim and elegant and with long hair that fell to her shoulders. She wore round glasses and carried a book in English. She told us that her husband was also a journalist working for a recently established paper in Baghdad. They'd been living in Stockholm for twenty years but had gone back to live in Baghdad after the fall of the Saddam regime. She talked about the hardships of life and compared the Baghdad of twenty years ago with the present day. I wasn't really interested in what she was saying, and didn't listen. Every now and again I'd check out the crowds of passengers of different ethnicities in the terminal. Then I'd gaze out of the window at the space outside. The clouds had partly cleared and the sun's rays fell warmly on the American soldier who stood holding his gun and looking in our direction. In the other direction, it was still raining non-stop. Our turn came at the passport control booth. The officer smiled at me and stamped the passport quickly without uttering a word.

We moved a few steps inside the hall and then stopped in front of the luggage conveyor, which was going slowly round. All eyes were fixed on it. Three tall, slim employees from the Fiji Islands appeared, accompanied by sniffer dogs trained to detect explosives. They moved around the bags with their dogs that sniffed one suitcase after the other. A soldier dressed in khaki then came out of the gate opposite. He walked towards us, buttoning his shirt up, examined our papers and passports, and then allowed us to move to another hall. The windows were very tall and revealed a large garden of fruit and willow trees, surrounded on all sides by a chain-link fence that was hard to get through. The only exit was through a gate guarded by a Marine checkpoint, beyond which stood a car from a convoy.

Faris was waiting for me in the hall as I emerged, pushing my luggage trolley. To my right walked Nermine and the anonymous journalist, also pushing their trolleys. As soon as Faris saw me, he waved and I waved back. When he came closer, he shook my hand. Then he shook hands coldly with the journalist, but shook Nermine's hands with great warmth. He stood with me for a while to allow Nermine and the journalist to leave with their trolleys. When they turned to me, I waved goodbye.

'Do you know him?' Faris asked, referring to the journalist.

'No, but he asked me about my business. So what's his story?'

'A suspicious character. No one knows his story.'

Faris was holding a cup of coffee that he'd bought from the airport cafeteria. He was wearing a pair of khaki trousers that I hadn't seen him in before. He looked as though he'd shrunk a little and lost some weight. He appeared different, perhaps a little paler than before. His bones seemed to protrude as a result of tiredness or premature ageing, and he didn't look well enough to be able to complete this assignment. His movements, however, were so swift and energetic that they seemed to be someone else's. He couldn't bear to stand still. While I went to exchange some dollars for Iraqi dinars at a bureau de change, he kept pacing round in circles. He polished off the hot coffee in three quick gulps, as though it were a magic potion, without saying a word. We stood in the queue again to exit through a narrow doorway. On the other side, the Marines were also standing in a queue, with their clean-shaven faces, their blond hair, their open shirts and their khaki kitbags. Dealing with them was a female official who didn't stop smiling, while we had a male official who frowned and pulled a long face. His hair was uncombed and he yawned incessantly, as if he'd just woken up.

As we left the airport, a grey Kia minibus was waiting for us. A fat driver was leaning on its bonnet, smoking. His head was shaved, his trousers were baggy and his shirt was buttoned to the top without a tie. His beard was unshaved. We placed our luggage quickly on the back seats. 'Do you have your laptop with you?' Faris shouted.

'Yes,' I said.

'Don't put it in the boot,' he said. 'And where's the camera?'

'With me too,' I said.

'Take it with you on the back seat.'

With a cigarette in his mouth, he carried his little bag on his back. From time to time he adjusted his glasses with his hand. He sat in front while I sat at the back. As the minibus gathered speed, we were met with tall concrete blocks and four- or five-metre-high barriers covered with an assortment of drawings: legendary heroes, trees and quails, luxury mansions and other colourful objects that were designed to disguise the lifeless concrete. Sparkling light flashed from electric lamps that hung here and there. As the daylight grew stronger, their light began to fade. There were cardboard paintings hanging down, posters that swayed gently in the breeze and political slogans of various types, attacking terrorism, advocating civil concord or calling for elections. There were pictures of politicians and clerics, of all sizes. Political posters and advertising predominated, some of them

70

imitating Iranian revolutionary and graphic styles. They were dominated by the bold, extremely bright colours so revered by the Shias, such as red, green and black. Many of the posters included writing as a complement to the image, in order to maximize the effect. This style of vulgar art or kitsch was prevalent during the Saddam era, produced mainly by amateur artists who filled the public squares with their own type of artistic expression. The recent posters, however, tried to redefine the cultural and social values of Iraq and express its new state of turmoil. They also represented a type of political protest, for they were designed to deface the walls that had been built earlier by the Saddam regime as emblems of its power and authority.

On the road, convoys of black cars passed by. Armed men in black suits and black glasses sometimes jumped out of their vehicles suddenly and urgently, pointing their guns at any approaching car. 'Blackwater,' Faris said and then fell silent.

The war had wiped the landmarks from Baghdad's streets. The Tigris was dry, the flowers were withered, the branches of the trees were scorched and the air was filled with dust. The gardens had lost their greenness and the buildings and houses stood randomly. Dust covered the pale green trees while rubbish accumulated on the pavements. There were potholes and ruts filled with stagnant water and high concrete walls shaded by blighted yellow palm leaves. The orange trees were dry and without fragrance. Only the smell of death was everywhere and its image haunted everything. The windowpanes were smashed to pieces by the boom of explosions, the walls alongside were cracked open and the streets were blackened by blasts.

*　　*　　*

As soon as our minibus reached a thick, high, concrete wall I knew we were about to enter the Green Zone. We stopped at an American checkpoint, which was considered the gateway to the most important area in the Middle East. The barriers were staggered so that the minibus had to zigzag between them. At the checkpoint stood a group of US soldiers in full combat gear, with their machine guns pointing at us. The driver followed the instructions given to him and moved forward slowly until the vehicle stopped near a wooden hut. Two very tall soldiers in Marine uniform looked out of the hut and ordered us to get out of the vehicle. As we stepped out, three 130 SM military helicopters flew out from a point beyond the concrete barrier. Their rotor blades beat like drums as they turned northwards and moved off into the distance like black insects. The sunlight was getting stronger. The muddy colour that dominated life and what was left of it in Baghdad began gradually to disappear and was replaced by a bright green. My watch showed midday. The temperature was close to thirty. The humid air was stirred by a refreshing breeze coming from the direction of the river that set the palm leaves and their shadows in motion. The American corporal came closer and started scrutinizing our faces and examining our passports, identity cards and papers. The driver was first, followed by Faris. The corporal finally placed his machine gun on his shoulder and took my passport. His face was not completely visible because of his steel helmet and the strap around his chin. As he stood there, four other soldiers behind him examined our faces.

'What's your profession?' he asked, looking intently at my face and then inspecting the photo in my passport.

'Journalist.'

'Your press card,' he said without looking up at me. So I handed it to him.

'How long have you been out of Iraq?'

'I was here a year ago ...'

He nodded his head, handed back my passport and press card and ordered one of the soldiers to lead the dog around the vehicle to check for explosives. Then we all passed through a metal detector.

There was more zigzagging between concrete barriers and barbed wire until we found ourselves on a wide road. It was paved and very clean, and shaded by thick green trees. Suddenly we were in the middle of a very modern city, a city more akin to the American Midwest than the Middle East. As we approached a small roundabout in the centre of the city, two black cars overtook our vehicle, sped through a huge steel gate and stopped in front of a stone-fronted building. Two formally dressed men got out of the first car. Their guards, dressed in black and wearing dark glasses, swooped out of the second car. The street was full of imposing buildings, expensive cars, security guards and surveillance cameras.

The minibus stopped in front of a modern building. We carried our luggage up to the second floor. I followed Faris into an elegant apartment consisting of three well-furnished rooms. There was also a spacious living room with Western furniture, curtains, a wooden desk, a large bookcase and a beautiful balcony.

'How much is the rent?' I asked Faris.

'A thousand dollars,' he said as he carried my luggage into the room assigned to me. It had a bed, a table, a wardrobe and a chair. I followed him into the room and looked it over. Then I went out and sat on the large leather sofa placed directly beneath the window. I looked around the living room as Faris entered the second room and came out holding a large wallet.

'Are you hungry?' he asked.

'Yes.'

'Let's go to a bar, then we can go to the Press Cooperation Agency and AC Media & News.'

Parson's Pub

'The Green Zone has changed a great deal,' I said as soon as we were out on the street. 'Are there any new pubs?'

'There are seven bars, a disco on Thursday nights, a sports bar, an English pub, a rooftop pub run by General Electric and a pub in a container run by Bechtel.'

'Which one do you like best?' I asked.

'Parson's Pub is quite nice and it's always open to Iraqis.'

'Only Iraqis?'

'No, there are other nationalities as well. But mostly reporters.'

We saw a beautiful pub on our way. When I asked about it, he told me it was the most luxurious of all, with bamboo furniture. 'Rumour has it,' he added, 'it's the pub that belongs to the CIA so it's known as Pub OGA.' He turned to me smiling, 'That's the codename for the CIA.'

'Is it really smart?' I asked, trying to find out whether he'd been there or not.

'Yes, I've been there once as a guest. It has a dance floor with a rotating disco ball and a games room.'

We passed a pizza place, two Chinese restaurants and a McDonald's. It wasn't long till we reached Parson's Pub. As we arrived, I saw a large tent pitched in a parking lot, which had clearly once been a petrol station. According to Faris, this was one of the most exciting places to relax in the Green Zone. It had a random assortment of Marines, politicians, interpreters and correspondents who came to cover press conferences. As we walked past the tent, we saw American women soldiers in camouflage gear smoking hookahs, their machine guns lying beside them. There were also contractors on the make, chuckling aloud while drinking their beer, and strategic-affairs experts in light desert boots, white shirts and khaki trousers. They drank beer and played *Risk*, the board game. Suddenly Nermine Haidar, who'd flown in with me earlier that day, emerged from among those seated. She came forward in her jeans and open blouse that revealed her round breasts. She shook hands with us.

'So, you're here!' she said.

I asked her about the journalist who'd been with her.

'Don't know how I got rid of him,' she said.

'Well, we're going to the bar to have a bite to eat and a beer, and later we're going the Press Cooperation Agency and AC Media & News. Would you like to join us?'

She paused for a moment. 'Fine, I'll join you later!' she said.

We went into the bar, which was in the shape of a hut and fairly dark inside. As soon as we'd entered the main door, a black South African guard approached us. His accent was hard to understand but he told us to write our names in the guest book. The bar was beautiful, like a neighbourhood bar in Los Angeles or Miami. There was a lounge full of tables and chairs, and a dartboard on the wall. An American employee was holding a glass of beer in one hand and throwing one dart after another. At the front was a wooden barrel with draught beer. The pub itself was huge and consisted of several rooms. There were a few black barmen standing behind the wooden bar, with all kinds of bottles of drinks behind them. On the right was a tiny back room, used as a store for whisky, vodka and wine that could be sold at almost twice their price outside the Green Zone.

Faris stood at the bar and ordered two beers, at two dollars each.

'Are you going to write your book on Kamal Medhat while you're here in Baghdad?' he asked.

'I'll write the Baghdad part here,' I said, wiping froth from my lips with a tissue, 'but I have to drop by the agency first to collect some important documents.'

'Is your role as a ghost writer?' he asked.

'No, not at all. The book will come out in my name this time,' I said. He nodded in agreement. 'You know, of course, that I've written many reports under other people's names,' I added, still wiping my mouth, 'but this time, I want the book to be mine.'

Then I began, I don't know how, to draw an analytical comparison between two images that obsessed my imagination at the time: the image of the tobacconist – or the tobacco keeper, as I called him – as presented in Pessoa's poem, and that of the ghost writer. I told Faris that each of us has two distinct personalities: one that we are born with, like the character of the keeper of flocks in *Tobacco Shop,* and one that we acquire, like that of the protected man. But few can distinguish the second from the first, whether regarding name, age or life history. What is even rarer is someone capable of creating the character of Campos, the tobacco keeper, who treated the other two personalities so condescendingly. He travelled and brought back the tobacco, guarded it, smoked it and lived his life stimulated by its clouds of smoke. That day, discussing the poem with Faris was like a hallucination, especially since he hadn't read it. 'Read it!' I said to him as I drank my beer and continued to rave. I told him that I believed the work of a ghost writer was totally different from that of the tobacco keeper. The latter was unique in being enriched by the other two personalities, while the ghost writer was always ground down by his role. The ghost writer represented total absence and existed on another unconnected plane, living an empty life in an absolute vacuum. No sooner soon had I become totally absorbed in explaining my theory, than Nermine came in. The bar was overcrowded, so I stood up and beckoned her over. She came towards us and sat beside Faris, facing me. She raised her hands to tie her hair back with an elastic band. This was the first time I'd looked closely at her face. She was pretty with delicate features, thick black hair and a very fine nose. Her thick lips made her very sensual.

'Would you like a drink?' I asked her.

'A beer,' she said smiling.

It was Faris who asked her about her current work. She told him she was working for the BBC, making a documentary about Baghdad. On that day we learned many secrets of the Green Zone from Nermine. She told us that there was more than one sort of pass that enabled Green Zone residents to move around. The pass was your key to the Green Zone. We had to get either the military press ID or the pass for the International Zone, which was the official name of the Green Zone. The first one was red and the second was pink. The pink one was clearly the better, and was naturally only carried by Americans and government officials.

Nermine drank as she talked about the guards of the Green Zone. 'They're the most dangerous in the whole world,' she said. 'They're authorized to kill, and you'd better keep a safe distance.'

She also explained the differences between the checkpoints. The ones closest to our residence were controlled by Gurkhas, the ferocious special security guards from Nepal. The ones further away were controlled by Irish guards.

'But in general, people here are pretty varied,' she said.

'How do the Iraqis live here?' I asked her, for I had, from time to time, visited the Green Zone but had never really got to know it. It was clear that Nermine Haidar had plenty of observations to make.

'There's always some misunderstanding,' she said. 'The translators, who are mostly graduates of English or American literature, think the American soldiers and officers will have some knowledge of literature and culture. But when they discover that those Americans are illiterate in every sense, it leads to friction. The Americans, for their part, believe everyone is ignorant or illiterate, and are then shocked to find that these people know more about their own culture than they do. While the Iraqis, who used to think Americans would know who Walt Whitman and John Steinbeck were, now realize they're only a bunch of ignoramuses whose knowledge is limited to porn mags and sports news. That's how the conflict starts.'

Speaking about Iraqi women she said, 'Iraqi women have misconceptions about Americans, based on Hollywood movies. They start out thinking an American will be liberal and cultured and will therefore respect women. But he sees her only as a whore. The Americans treat the Iraqi women who work here just like whores.'

Nermine also talked about a very pretty Iraqi woman journalist, who had gone to interview some American soldiers and never come back. She believed that the journalist had been kidnapped, raped and killed, and that all traces of the crime had been completely erased.

Many translators came in and out of the bar. I knew them well, of course, and they represented a phenomenon worthy of study. They were mostly young people, recent university graduates. After the total collapse of the state in 2003 they couldn't find employment. All they could do was work as interpreters in the Green Zone, a hazardous line of work where their lives were constantly under threat. They were everywhere: on the streets, with foreign troops and at checkpoints. Those translators, influenced by Western literature, were mostly well dressed, very civilized and highly Europeanized. They were far more sophisticated than the American soldiers and officers who treated them with such contempt.

What was truly astonishing, at least from my perspective, was that they all had Western names: Michael, John, Robert or Sam. They were never called by their Arab names. When I asked Nermine about this, she said the Americans had trouble pronouncing Arab names such as Abdel Rahman, Majeed, Rebhi and Fakhri. So they used those fake names instead, which were easy and accessible and created no psychological barriers. Iraqi names in general suggested a kind of tacit enmity, while Western names, on the other hand, allowed Iraqi translators to forget the realities of their situation and live the illusion that they were truly American. This led them to act arrogantly, as though they'd appropriated the white masks of the Americans for themselves. This was what French philosopher Frantz Fanon meant by black skin and white masks. According to him, colonialism, in effect, oppresses and crushes people, hollowing them out and filling the void with a fragmented image of their original personality. In other words, the character of the keeper of flocks in *Tobacco Shop* is replaced by the character of the protected man, with a new name that is always American. It's a dreamed-of character but one that cannot be fulfilled due to the oppressive, humiliating presence of the Americans. It is a character that is not 'protected'. The first character, the keeper of flocks, is spurned and discarded like rubbish. As with colonialism, a bitter conflict arises between Alberto Caeiro and Ricardo Reis, which renders the presence of de Campos, the tobacco keeper, almost impossible.

V

Boris, Samir and Farida Reuben's letters

THE OFFICE OF THE Press Cooperation Agency and AC Media & News was located in a quiet area full of small stone buildings and thick trees that gave it the feel of an old aristocratic neighbourhood. At the bend of Street No. 7 stood the building that housed the agency and other press organizations.

The entrance led us to a winding staircase that connected three floors. We reached a small white door on which was elegantly written 'AC Media & News'. It was an international press agency that maintained a neutral stance regarding the events in Iraq. It was also engaged in helping Iraqis overcome the effects of occupation, and tried to ease sectarian tensions and contribute to the development of an independent Iraqi identity. At its helm was a man known as Little Boris, a veteran reporter of Russian origins. He was a hefty guy with a bald head who looked like Khrushchev. The man in charge of Iraqi affairs was Samir Mohammad, a German journalist of Iraqi descent who spoke no Arabic at all.

Samir was a fascinating personality. I'd seen his photograph for the first time on the cover of an American or French magazine; I

81

don't remember which. I was surprised because he didn't look like any of the Iraqis I knew either inside or outside Iraq. With his healthy, ruddy complexion, his pale golden hair and his green eyes, it was difficult to associate him with the Middle East in any way. When I'd visited him for the first time in his office the previous winter, he'd been very friendly. We'd sat for over an hour, drinking tea and talking about various things. The meeting had been very genial and there'd been a low flame in the fireplace nearby. The chairs had had white satin coverings over their arms, and the table had been covered with black leather. Samir had sat directly opposite me. Beside him had sat a very beautiful woman who was quite plainly dressed. What she'd said was slightly strange and she'd spoken very quietly. I understood that she was a translator and had started translating an Iraqi novel into English.

During our short meeting this translator had asked me a few questions about translations of Iraqi literature into French. Although we hadn't talked for long, my first meeting with Samir being very brief, it had all been quite friendly. I'd come to see him at his request, as I'd written a long report on the problems facing the fishermen in the Gulf of Basra after 2003. This report was later turned into a piece for a French TV channel. I later forgot almost all about it, because the issues of fishermen, shoemakers and street vendors seemed trivial in comparison with kidnappings, assassinations, oil-smuggling operations and the militias' control over the port of Basra. Nevertheless, I'd received a message asking me for a meeting. During the meeting, Samir had wanted to commission me to write a report on the situation of Iraqi women in Basra. This had been triggered by the murders and kidnappings they were subjected to practically every day.

He'd given me many documents dealing with the numerous kidnapping gangs and the groups that specialized in killing women. There were photographs of graffiti that warned, and threatened to kill, women who did not adopt Islamic dress or the veil.

This was the second time I'd met Samir in his office. He recognized me immediately and said we'd met twice before. I was quite surprised because I remembered only the one occasion, those few months earlier in his office.

As he shook hands with me, he murmured a few compliments that didn't mean anything to me. He led us through the door to the agency. He walked quickly in front, while Faris Hassan and I trailed behind. Before inviting us to sit in his office, we stopped briefly at Faris's office. It was only then that I learned that Faris had his own office at the agency, which meant that he was officially an employee.

Samir immediately addressed the issue at hand. He was very practical and not given to small talk. One of his obvious traits was never looking directly at you or into your eyes. He spoke with his eyes directed elsewhere and his hands moving quickly. He jumped around the office from one spot to another, which made us struggle to keep up with him. He led us first to a small room near the kitchen from which a Sri Lankan worker emerged carrying glasses of tea. From there he went straight to his own office and invited us in.

He took some books off the shelf and placed them on the long table that was littered with papers, newspapers, magazines, teacups and pens as well as a laptop and other miscellaneous objects. He spoke while shuffling envelopes and packages around as if looking for something, and talking all the while.

I felt greatly relieved on entering his office. For some unknown reason, I was happy. The sun's rays were streaming through the open window and the beautiful sunny atmosphere contrasted sharply with my first visit back in the winter. The blinds had been drawn at that time and the outer window, in the shape of a concertina, had been closed. The room had been cold and damp in spite of the fireplace with its flickering blue flame. Today, however, spring was in full bloom and the windows were wide open, allowing the sun's rays to filter gently into the room. The soft cool breeze blew gently and intermittently. From where we stood near the large table, the view was stunningly beautiful. There was a green open space dotted with red and yellow flowers, and rows of lush green trees whose huge trunks rose high into the air. As we stood in the office, we could see the winding street teeming with cars and pedestrians. Shops were open, indicating the vitality and vibrancy of the city. It was a very different impression from what we'd seen as we drove in from the airport.

Samir didn't invite us to sit down, as if wanting us to enjoy the lovely view of the green landscape and the river in the background. He continued searching for various things that were scattered on the shelves. I had no idea what he was looking for or what he wanted to show me. Since our meeting the previous winter I'd learned to listen to his non-stop talk. He was chatting in a very animated way, as he had the first time when he'd urged me to visit Basra to write the piece on the situation of women in the south. This time, however, he urged me to travel to Tehran and Damascus to complete the report. For my part, I was all ears. He explained fairly precisely the importance of this investigation for the current situation in Iraq. He commented in detail on the stages of Kamal Medhat's life, for he knew much more about him than I did, down to the smallest details, as though he'd decided that I should know everything in advance.

The brown envelope

I stood before him in complete silence and looked intently at his face without uttering a word. I had no immediate response to what he told me concerning this personality whom I found quite puzzling.

Samir suddenly turned around and took a brown envelope off the shelf. He held it in both hands and looked at me, saying that a certain newspaper would be very happy to publish extracts in its Sunday supplement from what I would write about this man. At this point, Boris entered the room and stood near Samir's desk without looking at me. He spoke to Samir about some agency matter. When he'd finished, he suddenly fell silent, then turned to me smiling. 'You're ready for this assignment, aren't you?' he said.

Boris's confident statement represented the launch of the job, which I thought would be neither easy nor simple, contrary to what Samir had said. The differences between the two men seemed fairly clear, at least to me. The old Russian journalist had a great deal of training and expertise. In fact, he was the oldest foreign reporter I'd ever known. He'd visited almost all the countries of the Middle East and had been present at all the political crises, the years of tension, the civil wars and military coups. He'd written a number of books on Iraq, Iran, Palestine and Egypt. He was fluent in Arabic, Turkish and Persian. I learned that he had worked initially as a Middle East political analyst at Novosti News Agency in the former Soviet Union. After the collapse of the Soviet Union, he'd moved to the United States and become one of the most active experts on Iraqi affairs in particular and the Middle East in general.

My gut feeling proved correct, especially after Samir placed the envelope in my hands.

'What's this?' I asked, totally bewildered.

The envelope was heavy and smelled of the past. It was held together with a yellow elastic band. I brushed it with the palm of my hand but there was no dust on it.

He told me that the envelope was vital for my work, because it contained all the letters that Kamal Medhat had sent to his wife Farida Reuben over many decades. Boris had acquired the letters from the wife herself. I was to unseal the envelope and use the contents for my piece about him.

I took the envelope and went with Faris into his office.

Faris opened the windows, revealing exactly the same wonderful view that I'd seen from Samir's window. I sat at Faris's desk which was overlaid with a film of dust. There were papers, newspapers, pictures, envelopes, an ink bottle, a laptop and several other objects. I put the envelope on the desk and opened it. I was stunned by what I saw.

Inside the envelope were numerous photographs and letters written by Kamal Medhat to his wife Farida. It was clear that Farida had sent them to Boris, who in turn had given them to Samir, who had then passed them on to me in the hope that they might throw some light on Kamal Medhat's character.

Faris, who was sitting near me, looked in my direction without asking about the envelope, the letters or the photographs. He made no comment, significant or otherwise. It was clear that he knew all about the envelope and its story from the start. He probably knew of the correspondence between Farida and Boris Naumkin, but showed no interest in the subject.

I spread out the photographs, letters and official documents on the desk in front of me and flipped through them quickly without stopping to read. As soon as I'd read a date or a couple of lines, I pushed it aside and picked up another. The handwriting seemed to show real pain. I realized that I had to go patiently and systematically through the whole lot, line by line, word by word. But I was too impatient. I wanted to devour everything at once and absorb it all from the first glance.

I got up and, to relieve the tension, began to pace to and fro in the room, leaving the letters and photographs spread out on the desk.

While I was doing this, Boris came in and handed me the letter that Mrs Farida Reuben had sent to the Agency's manager, to which she had attached more letters and photographs. I began to read it, totally oblivious to Faris, who was sitting at the table drinking tea.

A letter to the manager of the Press Cooperation Agency in Iraq

Mr Boris Naumkin

It was with great sorrow that I learned from one of your reports about the sad fate of the Iraqi musician Kamal Medhat. I wish to inform you that the dead man's real name is Yousef Sami Saleh, who was my husband. We emigrated to

87

Israel from Baghdad after the birth of our son Meir. But my husband could not bear living away from his country, Iraq. So he escaped to Iran, where he stayed on. He used to write to me frequently from there until he married a Shia Muslim woman, Tahira al-Tabtabaei, as you can see from the letters I'm sending you. He then entered Iraq under the name of Haidar Salman Ali. He obviously stayed in Iraq during this whole period, as is clear from his letters. Our correspondence never stopped. Because he could not send letters directly from Iraq to Israel, he would send them via musicians living in Moscow and Prague. He told me in detail about the conditions of his life in Iraq and how he was deported to Iran as an Iranian national in 1980. His wife Tahira died on the journey. In a letter dated August of that year, he told me that he had solved the problem by going to Syria and from there to Iraq. On a trip to Europe, he sent me a letter informing me that he was now living in Baghdad and was married to a woman called Nadia al-Amiry, who had given him a son, Omar. He told me the details of how he'd got to know her and married her. He also asked me about his son Meir. I had told him earlier that Meir, like him, could not stand living in Israel, that he had emigrated to the United States and had joined the US Navy.

Because he travelled so often to Europe, he was always assiduous in sending me letters and pictures, especially because he wanted to keep in touch with his son. I learned a great deal from his letters about his life, about his fame and his attitude to art, particularly during the Saddam Hussein era.

When I read the news in the papers about the murder of Kamal Medhat and when I compared the photograph and the message that Meir had sent me, I knew that it was Yousef that had been killed.

That, then, was how Yousef departed this life. Though hard to believe, I almost expected it to happen at any moment. I always feared he might be arrested and executed for espionage or some other charge.

What I really want to know is how he died, who was behind his murder and why he was killed in the first place. I also know that until this day he is lying in a hospital morgue, unburied. In the other documents, I've provided a lot of information that may help you to write the report about him. I believe this report will not only be useful to me. If that were the case, I wouldn't bother to write to you or ask you to investigate. But I think it's important for all those who loved him, or even those who hated him enough to murder him.

With my best wishes.
Professor Farida Reuben
Department of Arabic Studies
Jerusalem University

P.S. I have added footnotes to each letter to explain certain points or ideas. I also enclose some photographs, along with his diaries, and have added marginal notes on several other things not included in the letters. There were also political issues that I felt needed explanation: to give the full picture, I had to clarify what he had not mentioned in the letters. On a separate sheet I have listed the names of some people who I think may have additional information on him, information that I don't personally have. I have also listed the addresses that I believe are important for tracing his life story.

So ended Farida's letter.

Before retiring to bed, I sat on the balcony listening to the silence of the Green Zone. I looked at the wide streets, the lavish palaces and the reception halls built in the style of the Palace of Versailles and surrounded on every side by impregnable walls. As I looked out, slowly smoking my cigarette, I could make out the glaring lights of the surrounding buildings while all of Baghdad slept in darkness. From my position on the balcony, I saw a journalist reading a book and, through their windows, a politician talking on the phone and another person writing reports.

Some of the buildings were illuminated, while others were sunk in total darkness. In the dark I could make out something that looked like a tank. I also saw some men sitting in a tent playing *Risk*, smoking hookahs and drinking beer.

That evening I started to write about Kamal Medhat. I was motivated by my visit to Kamal Medhat's house at Al-Mansour, where I'd discovered Pessoa's poem, to divide the biography into three sections: the keeper of flocks, the protected man and the tobacco keeper.

Part Two

VI

The keeper of flocks
From the life of Yousef Sami Saleh
(1926–55)

'I believe in the world like I believe in a marigold,
Because I see it. But I don't think about it.
I have no philosophy, only feelings.
... There's metaphysics enough in not thinking about anything.'

from *Tobacco Shop*
The Keeper of Flocks, Alberto Caeiro

The life of the musician, kitsch politics and foreign enemies

'ISN'T THERE MORE TO life than finding oneself a complete stranger among other complete strangers?'

This was what Yousef wrote in one of the most beautiful post-cards he sent to his wife Farida from Tehran towards the end of April 1956, when he was in total despair. The postcard showed the harsh landscape of the huge Elburz Mountains. This short line was like a stifled scream in the midst of an infinite emptiness.

The line reminds us forcefully of Alberto Caeiro's words when he says: 'The windows of my room, a room that belongs to an unknown person among the millions of unknown people in the world. And even if he were known, what could possibly be known about him?' I remembered this passage as I listened to Kakeh ('Mister') Hameh. With his nasal voice, thick lips and huge nose, he spoke with the enthusiasm of a priest about a long period of travelling and wandering, and of one city after another. He spoke vigorously, his eyes sparkling, his face unshaved, the ends of his white moustache shaking.

I ought to provide some information about this man. He was a Kurdish communist, and was conspicuously short and stocky. The oversized suit that he wore for our meeting, although fairly elegant, made him look almost comical. His hair was milky white and dishevelled and his large eyes darted about. It was clear that he rarely shaved.

Many people had a high opinion of him despite his incessant babble and tactless remarks. His passion for talking led him to dominate conversations. His Kurdish accent gave his Arabic a cetain beauty and eloquence. With his flamboyant style, his undu-lating voice, his intonation and local accent, he was often very amusing in telling Yousef Sami Saleh's story. His narrative made the character of this brilliant but childlike musician fascinating. Kakeh Hameh kept me listening for hours, like a leech stuck to a plant.

Kakeh Hameh was Kamal Medhat's friend, who had known all three of his personalities. He turned out to be one of the strangest characters I'd ever come across; strange in almost every respect. Because he knew a great deal about Yousef Sami Saleh and had been his companion for a long time, I sat with him until late at night. What had driven me to contact him was one of the comments Farida had written in the margin of a letter dated August 1956, that is, during Yousef's residence in Tehran. It was this letter that made me start looking for Kakeh Hameh in the first place. I thought it would be appropriate for me to meet him before travelling to Tehran.

I had no idea why Kakeh was so happy as he told the story of Yousef Sami Saleh. He was profoundly content, like an insect warming itself in the sun. As he spoke, he waved his short arms left and right. Behind him was a photograph showing him in an elegant outfit, while beside him stood a beautiful woman wearing a colourful Kurdish dress. From time to time, as I listened to him evoking the past, I looked at the picture behind him. His conversation had the smell of old cupboards and drawers, of cold wooden chairs. I noted down in my small notebook various names, cities and major airports in the north and south of the country.

Kakeh Hameh was being very friendly. It gave him great satisfaction to recount the remarkable chain of events. He seemed to be following the same sequence as the letters in Boris's envelope, which I'd arranged in date order. It was as if he'd sat me down on a stool in front of a peep box and was showing me scenes from a life that had gone forever. I tried hard to note down all the details without missing anything. There were new names, dates, cities, transformations and endless travels. It was a real journey for me, a journey that turned names into destinies and transformed our world into an incredible fantasy.

Was he talking about Alberto Caeiro, the keeper of flocks, the first of the characters that Pessoa had assumed for himself in *Tobacco Shop*? For Yousef Sami Saleh was as innocent as Caeiro; he contemplated things with his eyes and not with his mind. Wasn't Caeiro just the same? Furthermore, Yousef didn't come up with any great ideas when he gazed at the objects around him. His view of things was profound but neutral. He captured things with his feelings but never questioned anything. This great musician, like the poet Pessoa, accepted the world quietly and serenely, accepted it for what it was, far from any metaphysical complexity. His life had no hidden agenda, he was a wide-eyed child among the infinite formations of nature. There was little doubt that Yousef Saleh's character stood in stark contrast to his two subsequent personae: Haidar Salman and Kamal Medhat. While the second character was connected with symbolic forms (like Ricardo Reis in *Tobacco Shop*) and the third was attached to the sensual (like Álvaro de Campos), the character of Yousef Saleh believed in nothing. Such was the first persona of the musician, the one that carried the name of Yousef Sami Saleh and whose death certificate was signed in 1955, the year Haidar Salman's persona was born. It was strange that the character of Alberto Caeiro, who was born in Lisbon in 1889 and died of tuberculosis in 1915 after publishing his collection of poems *The Keeper of Flocks,* should have his biography written by Álvaro de Campos, the third assumed personality of Pessoa. When I later investigated the life of the Iraqi composer Yousef Sami Saleh, I discovered that his biography had been written by none other than Kamal Medhat.

So what was this character like?

Yousef was born in the Al-Torah quarter of Baghdad on 3 November 1926. His father, Sami bin Saleh, who came from the Qujman family, worked as an assistant at the Juri pharmacy in Al-Karradah. His mother was Huri bint Rahamin Dalal. Her father had been fairly wealthy in his early years, when he worked at the Spice Market and later at the Grocers' Market in Baghdad. But in the aftermath of World War I, he'd fallen on hard times. His slightly tattered childhood photograph portrayed him as a small boy with delicate features and black hair falling on his forehead. He wore shorts and a large white shirt over his skinny body.

Yousef's grandfather, Saleh, sold sesame paste at a shop on the left-hand side of Al-Rashid Street near Al-Murjaneya School. In that area, known as Al-Shurja market, were several oilseed presses owned by Jews. He then worked for a time pruning palm trees at the Mamou date grove. In the interwar period, he started brokering the date trade between merchants from Basra and Baghdad. Saleh's brother, Rabbi Shmuel Qujman, was the author of *Judaism and Life*, which was printed at the Shuhait Press and which later appeared in Hebrew in the thirties. Yousef never forgot his grandfather's house. In fact, for many years, he continued to remember the warmth of his grandfather's hand, which he'd held so tightly for fear of losing him in the crowd as they walked along Al-Rashid Street. He remembered the pungent smell of mothballs from the cupboard in which his grandfather hung his suits and the black caps that Baghdadis traditionally wore. His grandmother's carefully painted face and her sad, black clothes instilled fear in his heart. In her high-ceilinged room, she would maintain her silence. Her debilitating illness imposed a silence on the whole family. In his letters to Farida, Yousef never forgot her wrinkled, white face. In a letter dated 1954 he wrote that he would go into her room in the company of his mother. While his mother cleaned the room with a feather duster, his grandmother would keep her eyes shut as if she were dead.

Despite their poverty, his was an educated Baghdadi family, which had been hit by the post-World War II slump. All the members of the family used to read books, newspapers and magazines. Their small house was full of manuscripts and huge tomes. In one of his letters, Yousef said that books were everywhere: between drawers, on walls, beneath the stone banisters and even in the large rooms with their decorated ceilings. This was a source of humour and laughter among the Jewish families that had made their fortunes from business after the establishment of the Iraqi state in the twenties and thirties. However, this family grew ever poorer and had to sell the house. Nothing remained of their old wealth except Kashani rugs and Persian cutlery.

Throughout her life, his mother, Huri bint Rahamin Dalal, was plagued by a vague but deep anxiety. At the turn of the twentieth century she had studied at the school for girls run by Madame Danon. As a seamstress in the workshop at the Laura Khedouri Club she had acquired a reputation for embroidering pillows using gold and silver thread. In the thirties King Faisal I had paid tribute to her when he visited the club. Her family was proud of the fact that long ago the famous Turkish traveller Olia Djalabi had once stayed at their house on a visit to Baghdad. Not only had he enjoyed their hospitality for a long period, but he had also eaten from their *tebit* meal, which Jews customarily made on the Sabbath.

In a letter dating from his first trip to Iran in the fifties, Yousef gave a vivid portrait of his mother. She was like a frail chrysalis, always seeking solitude, for she had lost any joy in her work. Her naive smile, her quiet, pleading movements and her general weakness made her a complex mixture of the superficial and the tragic. On the large sofa in the small living room that was filled with colourful rugs she would sit quietly and peacefully, holding her needles and embroidering a satin pillow. The colourful woollen yarns rolled beneath her feet where little Yousef sat, overwhelmed by her silence and grief. He would try out some tunes on his violin, especially after taking lessons with Aram Garabian, the famous Armenian violinist in Baghdad. And as soon as the melody rang out in the living room of that little house, his mother would listen, as calmly and as silently as a statue.

The single photograph of Yousef's mother, which was included by Farida in the envelope handed to me by Boris Naumkin at the agency, showed the woman's personality clearly.

She was of average beauty, with fine features and very thin. Her beautiful eyes were covered by a film of translucent sorrow. She was in her thirties and wore small, round glasses. She was modestly dressed and stood beside her husband, Sami. He was a thin, tall man who towered above her in his old-fashioned check suit. His white shirt was ironed and his tie was as narrow as a piece of string. He had a long nose and a high forehead.

On the back of the photograph was written: 'Sami Saleh and wife, 1942. Photograph by Hajj Amri Salim at Ibrahim Twaiq's home.'

This photograph, as well as the letters written by Yousef to Farida and the testimony of Yousef's friends such as Kakeh Hameh, gave me a vivid picture of what Yousef would become in the future. I was able to refer not only to this important picture, which I kept with me for such a long time that I knew its details by heart; there were also the other pictures that interested me before I started on my journey. If I were to mention just one of them, it would be the only photograph I know of that depicts a group of Baghdad communists in the forties. It was a very rare photo with tattered edges and dated 3 August 1946 on the back. It showed Victor Menasha Yousef sipping a cup of coffee, Saida Sassoon looking cheerful, Zanoun Ayoub in short sleeves revealing his famous muscles and Sami Saleh, Yousef's father, standing tall and very thin, and staring with deep eyes into the unknown. They were all gathered in the living room of Victor Menasha's house and in the background one could see the arches of the house and its internal columns. There were also two pinewood columns by the wall.

The photograph showed very clearly the father in his youth. As a young man, Sami looked very much like his son was to become. His posture and self-confidence revealed his firmness and his ability to gather his strength before forging ahead. The picture also communicated to me his profound faith and how much he'd struggled to free his soul of all the harmful weeds that had threatened to choke it. His was a heart that tilled and sowed the void, in total ignorance of its destiny. Yousef referred to this in one of the important letters he'd written from Tehran, where he'd talked with great enthusiasm about his father, describing him as a role model who had held fast to his belief in human justice. Yousef even stated clearly that throughout his life he'd never met a man as principled as his father. So what was the father like?

Yousef was woken by his father's quiet, hoarse voice. He rubbed his eyes with his hands, blinked a few times to clear his vision, and saw his father standing by the window, his hair a little dishevelled, his collar turned upwards and his gaze unwavering. After a short silence, Yousef's father put on his hat, picked up his cane and went quietly out of the door. Yousef felt certain that everybody knew who Sami Saleh was: teachers in their old pressed clothes, rubbish collectors, painters, builders, waiters in cafés, prostitutes, drummers at the local café, the mayor, the policeman and the greengrocers.

Almost every afternoon, according to everyone we met, Sami Saleh would head home from his work at the Juri pharmacy and start his long walk through the streets of the Al-Torah quarter, around Hanoun Market or through Mamou grove. He would walk beneath the colonnades of Al-Rashid Street, a tall man with a dark face and a pointed chin. He had clear, penetrating, dark eyes that he'd probably inherited from his grandfather, the great rabbi, who'd left his mark on the whole family, who were still living in the old quarters of Baghdad.

Sami Saleh was lost in thought as he walked in front of the clothes shops. He passed quietly in front of the spice merchants in Al-Shurja market and in front of the shops that sold round boxes of sweets. He was constantly assailed by mysterious doubts. He would sniff the smell of the soil in the gardens, or pick up a piece of plaster and crush it between his fingers. He would always walk with his head held high, contemplating passers-by from above, his narrow eyes examining them as though they were little worms in a bright yellow field. He walked alone in his long, black coat, his large shoes, his wide creased hat and his glasses that were missing a lens.

The people in his neighbourhood called him 'Comrade' because of his great attachment to the communist movement and his support for the left. His leftist sympathies were not restricted to Iraqis, but included all people of the world. This internationalist Jew felt himself united with workers everywhere, whether labourers with hands as rough as crocodile skin or porters working in the blazing sun. He was detained and jailed more than once, but never abandoned his convictions. He was saturated with politics like a sponge with water. When walking along the pavement with his thin bamboo cane he never met anyone without talking to him about political issues. At first he would look at his interlocutor with his cloudy, dreamy eyes and would then address him. He saw in every item of news a political angle. He interpreted every bit of news in the light of the state's economic policies, parliamentary affairs, the constitution, or the difference between socialism and capitalism. His jacket pockets were always bulging with newspapers and magazines. Sami firmly believed that he was entrusted with one duty only, that of enlightening people about their rights.

So there was Sami Saleh, alert but silent and dreaming, lost in his habitual daily walk. In the spring he would inhale the pollen dust and sneeze; in summer, he would caress the wood carvings on doors and the plants as though saying goodbye to them; in winter, he would carry his dripping umbrella and head to Salman café in Ras al-Aqd. His feet would be wet and his body shivering with the cold; he would sneeze and wipe his nose with his hand because he had no handkerchief. Once, he saw a huge black dog standing in the rain, looking at him with sad eyes, its body soaked. He dragged it home behind him through the side streets, the wet, trembling, black dog walking dejectedly behind him. The residents of Al-Torah neighbourhood knew that Sami bin Saleh and his family kept no dogs. The children stood on the rooftops or on the muddy ground in front of the shops, houses and cafés, and screamed out, 'Comrade Sami, what's that dog doing running after you?'

'He's better and braver than you,' he replied scornfully. 'I told him about his miserable life, and he's decided to join the revolutionary movement.'

When he arrived home, Huri came out of the yard wearing her apron and her round glasses. Her hair was unkempt, and her sallow face looked tired and sickly. When she saw him, she stopped in her tracks, her eyes as wide as they would go and her hands held high as though transfixed. In one hand she held a large wooden spoon that she used for cooking okra.

She screamed in his face. 'Good God, Sami. What's that you're bringing home? Haven't I got enough with your children?'

'Huri, did you want me to leave it to die in the rain?'

That was how his father lived. After his father's death, Yousef never removed his coat from its hanger. He kept his hats, books, umbrellas, raincoats and boots until the day he emigrated in 1950.

(There were many anecdotes about his father. In his letters, Yousef penned a lovely portrait of his childhood in spite of the poverty of the family. This was particularly true of the letters he wrote from Tehran between August 1954 and July 1955. The 1956 letters, in contrast, spoke of his artistic life and how he'd joined the Iranian National Symphony Orchestra.)

The musician was in every way like his mother. Since childhood, he'd been captivated by her: her long fingers, her slender figure and her lovely bosom that showed above the low neckline of her dress. He was enchanted by a vision of her in her bedroom, for he saw in her a woman who never lost her femininity to motherhood.

This was how he saw her:

A large mirror with a teak frame hung prominently on the wall of the room. She was standing in front of it and gazing at her figure before taking him out to a concert. He sensed her beauty and femininity and marvelled at her lovely clothes. Although his family was not rich, his mother had the demeanour of a great aristocratic lady. She sewed her beautiful clothes on a Singer sewing machine in her room. Ibrahim Naji Shameel, the wealthy co-owner of the Juri pharmacy who had once been in love with her, would provide the tickets for the concerts to which she took her son in all humility and modesty.

Yousef entered the concert hall: his body was diminutive, his legs looking so thin in his blue shorts and his white shirt far too large for him. His eyes had a dream-like quality and his face was peaceful and beautiful. Throughout the time they sat there, he remained silent and solemn. He was more overawed than joyful. This was what his mother noticed. Classical music for him was akin to worship or prayer. He passed the time in silence, his eyes fixedly following the melodies as they intertwined. From the moment the music started he paid no attention to what went on around him. He was hopelessly romantic, for he held on to art as the final thread that attached him to life. It was clear that he would continue his musical education at the Iraqi music conservatory, which at that time was directed by Julien Hertz. Yousef would later help to create the Baghdad Philharmonic Society together with Boutros Hanna, Sandu Albu, Jameel Said and André Thoerè, with whom he continued to work until his emigration to Israel. The greatest and most important turning point in Yousef Sami Saleh's life was the scholarship he received at the age of fifteen from a wealthy Baghdadi, to travel to Moscow. There he had the chance to listen to orchestral pieces and chamber music at the Bolshoi auditoriums. He also listened to Rachmaninov and visited the Russian Composers' Society, the Academy of Music and the Opera House in the city of Bryansk. This visit made a great impression on him; indeed, it influenced his entire life. It was the first time that he'd seen such a large number of musicians and concertgoers. They dazzled him with their looks and their handsome outfits. He admired them so much that he wanted to follow in their footsteps and become one of them. So he bought a coat with large pockets, some elegant round glassses with gold frames, a pair of leather shoes and a crimson bow tie. He was so fascinated with the musicians that he met and their long beards that he wished one day to grow his beard long, too.

Yousef wasn't particularly handsome. He had high cheekbones, a large mouth, a slightly small nose and an expressive, sad face. His laugh was muted and he didn't speak much. On his return home, he felt he had grown up and become a man, even though he was barely fifteen. At that time he was overwhelmed by the most profound feeling of love, which struck him like an earthquake, demolishing his defences and leaving him in ruins. This was his love for his cousin Gladys, which woke him up every morning at dawn to the cockadoodledo coming from Moshe's house, the tailor in Tekeya market, or the chirping of the swallows in the eucalyptus trees. So, from dawn until sunrise, he would lie in his bedroom, awake and alert, thinking. As soon as an idea took hold in his mind, he would pick up his violin and express the thought in musical notes. Yousef realized without any shred of doubt that it was love that made him play with such intensity of feeling. It made him play with true passion and drew melodies from the depths of his heart. He knew that he was in the grip of a true and violent passion. He knew he was descending at full speed to the lowest depths. But he felt that nobody around him cared for his music. His beloved Gladys did not care either. Nor did any other girl that he had undressed in his mind or dreamt of in bed until he gasped in ecstasy.

105

But was his love in vain?

Not at all. For without love, he would not have played with such intensity, with such feeling, with every fibre of his being. He struggled hard to become a great musician. He willingly gave up all the choices and pleasures that life offered him, for he wanted only to be a musician. In Moscow, he stood for the first time in his life in front of the greatest conductor in the world: a thin man with a long beard and a face as red as wine, who wore a black suit and a crimson bowtie. He advised Yousef to find artistic inspiration from his own people and nowhere else.

The conductor stood there with his thick coat and wine-red face. 'Where are you from?' he asked.

'From Iraq,' answered Yousef, his palms sweating.

'Good,' he said, 'try to find a scene from your country and your people to turn into music.'

The conductor gave him this piece of advice without really knowing where Iraq was located on the map. After his return from Moscow, Yousef consoled himself with the thought that he would compose a piece of music inspired by local sights: the loud calls of the radish-seller, whose voice filled the lane; the coachman who drove his carriage through the streets, tooting his horn; the sight of Hamadi, the peddler, who walked with his stubborn, scabby mule tied to a colourfully decorated cart, carrying turnips from Sayed Hassan's farm; the music of a Kurdish beggarwoman singing in a melodious voice, imploring people to give her crusts of dry bread that she could sell in bulk to the bran-sellers. Or he might find inspiration in his love for his cousin Gladys, in the pleasure of eating kebab with Persian-made silver cutlery at home, or in the sight of his beloved Gladys sitting on the sofa and reading the Holy Book.

That day, when he got up from his seat, he felt that he had hit on an idea. The Russian conductor's advice might well be applied to Gladys's image, the indescribable joy he felt on accompanying his mother on her visits to his aunt Massouda Dalal in Al-Karradah and eating kebab, while his sisters Daisy, Rachel and Saida stayed at home. At his aunt's house, he would hear the grownups discussing grave and important matters for the very first time. It was there that he first heard names that never entirely disappeared from his life: Hitler, Mussolini, Nazism, the Axis, the Allies, the Boy Scouts and the Youth Brigades.

His cousin Gladys sat beside him and together they read the Holy Book. With her beautiful hands she lifted a jug that stood on the table, allowing him to see her smooth, white armpits. Their lovely fragrance made him feel intoxicated and entranced. He looked at her face that was encircled by a halo of henna-coloured hair, at the breathtaking beauty that never left his mind, even in his dreams. He looked at this girl who was prettier and more graceful than any other girl in the community, as well as being the most unassailable, even though she liked him and was friendly enough to him. Her full lips parted in a pleasing smile as she placed her hand on his shoulder.

She had once taken him and sat him on the red-brick wall of the house, where they'd been surrounded by a vast expanse of green grass. Then she had led him by the hand to a spot beneath a palm tree. They had stood and looked up at the thick bunches of dates beneath the branches that swayed in the breeze. As he watched the hens pecking and picking the grains from beneath the palms and around the red-brick wall he was blissfully happy. Gladys was wearing her gossamer white dress. Her arms were bare and her neck was like a swan's. That evening she had let him enter the house where she had hung the *tebit* lamp in celebration of the Jewish New Year. On the table, she had placed a chicken stuffed with spices, chickpeas and meat.

107

Yousef was surprised when Gladys put down the Holy Book and picked up her favourite book, the French *Syllabaire* that she had studied at the Alliance School. She ran off, singing a beautiful song with a sweet voice and a lively rhythm as she picked up the fallen dates. Listening to the French lyrics flowing so smoothly from her lips, Yousef felt assaulted by the ruthless, incomprehensible foreign words that hurt his ears like the cries of huge birds of prey. It was at that time that Yousef discovered the wild roses that bloomed in a little mud pond near the brick wall and the flowers that blossomed in the spring in the lovely, small garden. When the family were away visiting any of the synagogues nearby, such as Abu Saleh, Massouda Shemtov or Sami Twaiq, Gladys would sit beside him, reading to him from the *Syllabaire*, while together they looked at the old tree, its bark covered with lichen.

Yousef realized that he was the only male that his cousin paid attention to. One day she took him into a little room in the yard and lay with him on a rusty iron bed. The bed had been abandoned in a room on the upper floor, but her mother had brought it down in the hope that Bahiza, the daughter of the Muslim farmers who owned a pen and two cows near the grove, might come to work for them and sleep in it.

Gladys dragged shy Yousef by the hand, undressed him and made him lie down on the bed. She started to fondle him. When she asked him to suck her nipples, he obeyed. With his quivering lips, he began to suck the ardent, rosy nipples. He looked with expectation at the passion in her sparkling eyes. He heard the huskiness of her voice and saw the redness of her cheeks. The scent of her clean, white clothes was irresistible. There on the bed he could smell her arousal, as she breathed in the masculine charm that was impossible for an adolescent girl to resist. She drew him to her with with one arm and extended the other beneath her knickers until delirium overcame her whole body and she began to tremble as she hugged and kissed him. When she gasped, he was terrified that she might be in pain or dying.

This was the first time Yousef had experienced moments of intimacy, and been alone with a woman. It was not an easy experience at all. It was the first time he had actually seen a woman's breasts, white as coffee cups. It was the first time his lips had touched a real, rosy nipple after years and years of imagining it. He feared it might dissolve between his lips. For days afterwards, he had a devastating headache and his whole being was in a state of turmoil. His body throbbed and his mind wandered. He felt a similar kind of throbbing when his first long Mozart piece was aired on the radio. The presenter described him as the most gifted violinist in the country, the first to excel in classical music. This last description remained with him as an inspiration. It might even have erased the memory of his trembling, throbbing body, his headache and his obsession with the young Gladys. But how?

It was not, in fact, easy for Yousef to forget those moments, which distracted him for days on end. When he met Gladys days after the event, he was taken aback that she behaved so normally. He tried to avoid her gaze whenever her eyes happened to meet his. In contrast, she paid little attention to the whole thing and behaved quite naturally, as though nothing had ever happened between them. For his part, he kept repeating the radio presenter's words in his head in order to erase the memory of this experience and to relieve the pangs of conscience that began to torture him. He hoped that the presenter's words might wipe the scene from his mind. It was a strange scene that attracted and repelled him at the same time. Not a day passed without him dreaming about it or losing sleep because of it. It deprived him of the beauty of solitude and of clear thinking and meditation. The reason was that as a romantic he believed that sex was far more sublime than this image of animal passion. Sex was like music, with its variations, crescendos and mystic sublimation. It was not smells, secretions, gasps, or shameful moaning. It was a kind of soaring upwards, not bodies lying prostrate or lips shouting, 'Suck! Suck!' Gladys's angelic face at home was the exact opposite of her image during those intimate moments: her dishevelled hair, red eyes, sweaty face, trembling lips and hoarse, moaning voice.

So every time he remembered the erotic gasps and moans, he repeated to himself the words of the radio presenter, although he was not sure if the man even knew the meaning of classical music. The man's words seemed to him to contrast with the Russian conductor's advice to him to return to his native roots for inspiration.

Yousef had been urged to find inspiration in the morning splendour of Al-Rashid Street, the city squares with their insane congestion and the noise produced by the black leather carriages with their golden lamps. It meant that he had to find inspiration in large shops, in goldsmiths' and in the many cafés, on the pavement of the station where the vendors of chickpeas and grilled meat gathered, among the squatting workers and soldiers and the vendors selling single cigarettes. His music had to be drawn from cinema entrances and brothel doorways, from the sight of prostitutes strutting coquettishly in scandalous dresses beneath their black abayas, lifting their hems and walking slowly, noisily chewing gum. He had to find inspiration in Baghdad's twilight, when thieves, drug addicts and gamblers would gather discreetly in cafés by the river, in mortal fear of khaki-dressed mounted policemen, who wore wide leather belts and hats that looked like knights' helmets, and who carried black truncheons studded with nails.

Was this what the Russian conductor meant? If it wasn't, what had he meant by the statement that Yousef should find inspiration among his own people? He continued for days to raise his hands like an axeman and scream in the mirror: What did this Russian conductor with his wine-red face mean by this statement, when he had never been to this country nor seen its people? And what did the Muslim presenter with his dark complexion and Jewish looks mean by the word 'classical'?

Did it mean that he should represent Baghdad, through musical notes, as a raucous city filled with the noise of workers, craftsmen, rubbish collectors, porters and police?

Or should he distance himself and offer abstractions unconnected with this world or any other?

Yousef never experienced any difficulty in finding inspiration for his music in the simple lives of the people, among his siblings or the image of his little brother, who had died of meningitis at the age of two. He was inspired by the wooden buses on Al-Rashid Street, the sight of dirty Jews in neighbourhoods such as Al-Torah, Abu Dudu and Abu Seifein. He was inspired by people's talk about the war and about the English artillery that had bombarded Baghdad, by recollections of evening walks by the Tigris, by ruins, by ghosts, by his early years when he was discovering the world, by times of awe and of ineradicable pain. But was that what the Russian musician had meant, who had never seen Iraq nor even knew where it was, when he'd said that a musician should be inspired by his people?

How should he interpret this, when all he wanted was to write sketches, exercises, études and more?

Two images suggested themselves to his mind. The first, conjured up by the Russian conductor, was of music being popular and local, while the second, suggested by the local radio presenter, was of music as a classical art form. The second concept was akin to Alberto Caeiro's idea in *Tobacco Shop*, which saw music as expressing nothing and everything at the same time, patterns not ideas, sounds emanating from the essence of existence and not from existence itself. In expressing essence, it had no palpable forms. He had to create music that would force existence to lie prostrate on a table, where he would contemplate it with no fixed ideas; to create a body that did not fade because music does not fade; to create ethereal, eternal feelings, because it is only feelings that cannot disappear; to create music that was like a leap into the unknown, music that was elevated and spiritual. This was the type of music that the radio presenter referred to without understanding what he was saying.

But more importantly . . .

How could he continue to live in this stifling community? How could he develop and grow in a society that encased him like a hard shell, like a thick, impenetrable skin? First there was the thick layer of family. Then there were the barriers created by the Jewish community in Baghdad during the thirties. Finally there was the fortress built by the Muslim community around the Jewish community.

But without him realising its importance at the time, something momentous happened that was to change his life, transforming the course of his existence once and for all. This was his family's move, in 1945, out of the self-contained Al-Torah neighbourhood to Al-Rashid Street in Hassan Pasha district.

This was, in fact, the real turning point in his life, and in his personality, defining the nature of his existence in the years to come. But how did it happen?

Yousef moved from the small ghetto to the wide world outside, leaving the anxieties of the closed Jewish neighbourhood behind him. He broke through its thick skin and reached for the sun. It wasn't easy for him at the beginning, for it was an existential test in the full sense of the word, a test he would remember all his life. He would often try to imagine, with fear in his heart, what it would have been like if he had stayed his whole life in the claustrophobic atmosphere of a ghetto.

Moving out of the neighbourhood represented a significant leap in Yousef's life. On the one hand, he left the ghetto as a fully formed human being. On the other hand, he left his childhood behind him and was on the threshold of manhood. He no longer wore shorts, as he had done in the old house in the Jewish neighbourhood. He no longer ate the pieces of sugar that his mother brought out of the family cupboard. This was an extremely significant development in his life. For although the Jewish neighbourhood had given him a sense of security, as he mentioned in one of his letters to Farida, it had also instilled the fear of the outside world in his heart. Living in a heterogeneous community was a new test for him. The new environment removed his fear of the outside world and the terror he'd felt living within the confines of the Jewish neighbourhood. In his new home, Yousef learned many things that prepared him to stand on his own two feet. First, he could no longer bear to stay at home for long periods, because it was a sign of being a child. Second, he had to walk proudly and steadily to avoid being regarded as a cowardly Jew; now that he was a broad-chested young man, he walked slowly and proudly. Third, he no longer accompanied his father with his thick cane on his walks on Al-Rashid Street. Gradually he began to feel that he was part of the neighbourhood. He felt that he had taken root in this community and that he was not just a passing visitor. He would invite his Muslim friends to his home, and his mother would rush happily to the kitchen to make coffee in the silver-plated cups that she would take out of the ancient cupboard. Yousef saw with his own eyes how his mother sparkled and her face lit up as she heard him chattering loudly about their Muslim women neighbours.

His new residence also placed him in the middle of the action. It allowed him to see the world, to be among those who witnessed the bands that played on Al-Rashid Street to mark the establishment of the kingdom that year. He saw the military brass bands as they marched up and down the streets. In one of his letters to Farida, dated 1956, he mentioned another band made up of twelve musicians who used to liven up small dance parties at the English Club carnivals and the Laura Khedouri Club. It was the first year that national contests for *dabka* dancing were organized in the royal gardens. These carnivals were hugely successful despite the threats by clerics to ban them. Muslim alleys competed against each other in traditional wrestling while Christian alleys competed in the manufacture of *arak* and the organization of bellydancing parties. That year, there were at least three Jewish dancers, as well as two Muslims and one Armenian. For the first time in his life Yousef wooed a Kurdish girl, who lived on Al-Rashid Street. To the surprise of the whole neighbourhood the girl, called Dina, responded to his advances. Yousef, who had never performed live before, conquered his shyness and played the violin in front of an audience. For some reason, there was a shift in inter-communal relations that year. A Muslim officer got engaged to and married a Jewish woman who worked at the Khedouri Sassoon schools. A Christian man married a Jewish woman, while a well-known Jewish man fell in love with his Muslim maid and contemplated suicide when his family rejected his idea of marriage.

It was a kind of emotional unrest that struck the neighbourhood of Al-Rashid Street in the forties, a widespread turmoil that took some people very much by surprise.

But what became of Gladys? Where was she now? And what had happened to his love for her? She was his first love and perhaps his last. In spite of all the relationships he had in those years, he never forgot her. It wasn't that he just couldn't forget her; it was in Gladys' nature to be unforgettable.

Gladys had clearly left an indelible mark on his life, especially after she married a physician called Fawzi. Her escapades and scandals were not only the concern of her family, but were also the talk of the whole of Baghdad. Every evening during the daily ritual of tea and biscuits that brought the family together and lasted until very late at night, Yousef would listen attentively to the details of her adventures. He was intrigued by the stories but could not forget his love and admiration for her. Although they all resented her, criticised her, condemned her conduct, and hated and insulted her, Yousef was captivated by her wild life, which swung between extreme luxury and numerous infidelities. Gladys had married a handsome, wealthy physician of her own free will. She lived her life between her opulent home and her trips to Europe, torn between her new love – her husband's Muslim driver – a husband who loved her, and a third lover who pursued her like a shadow.

115

It was well known that her surgeon husband, Dr Fawzi, had been equally notorious for his own womanizing. But he, after his marriage to Gladys, had become a respectable family man. Rumour had it that it was he who had saved her life when she'd had a car accident while out driving one day, during the heaviest rainfall in Baghdad's history. Gladys was his beautiful, indifferent patient. He had fallen in love with her at first sight and spared no effort to convince her to marry him. But she was not faithful to him, and in no time at all, rumours began to circulate about her. Everybody knew that she'd fallen for his Muslim driver.

In a long letter, Yousef described how he'd listen greedily to the stories about this unfaithful woman, full of admiration. He loved to hear news of her. At that time she was pregnant, but she cared neither for her husband nor her baby. With real anxiety Yousef realized that love brought incredible pleasure and knowledge, and might also rescue people from loneliness and loss; but it could sometimes be painful, as with Gladys and her husband.

In the same year as Gladys' scandals, he met the famous Russian violinist, Michel Boricenco, in front of whom he gave his first solo violin performance. In a small auditorium at the English Club in Baghdad he played Bach, Paganini and Ysaÿe. As a tribute to his virtuosity, Boricenco presented him with a fine violin and bow. That May, the Iraqi-British war broke out, accompanied by a national uprising inspired by Nazism. There was wholesale anarchy throughout the country. The Jewish community were victims of assaults, looting and murder. Massouda Dalal – Yousef Sami Saleh's aunt and Gladys' mother – was burnt alive before his very eyes and her property looted.

Letters

In writing Yousef Sami Saleh's biography, or at least in documenting him by means of his era, his life, his thoughts and his youth, which were all similar or to a great extent comparable to the character of the keeper of flocks in the poetry collection *Tobacco Shop*, I have referred to the two phases of his life in Baghdad as outlined in his letters to Farida Reuben. The first extended from his childhood in Baghdad up to the Farhoud Incident in May 1941, which followed the rise of the Nazi organizations in Iraq and which saw the death of hundreds of Jewish victims in Baghdad. The second covered his life from the time they moved into their new home in the Hassan Pasha neighbourhood until his emigration to Israel in 1950. The Farhoud Incident, following the May 1941 revolution, occurred at the same time that everybody was busy talking about Gladys's adventures. The burning of Massouda Dalal, Gladys' mother, during the incident had a devastating effect on Yousef's life and destroyed Gladys completely.

The incident changed the life of everyone in Baghdad. It can be described as a real turning point in the history of this society, being the first attack of its kind against its own citizens, and opening the door to civil conflict. Although historians have devoted little attention to it and have done nothing to address our collective amnesia, we can safely say that all the subsequent civil strife in Baghdad may be traced back to what happened on that fateful day in 1941.

★   ★   ★

Was this incident like any other in Yousef Sami Saleh's life? Can it be considered as just one of those things that happen to people, whether or not they are violinists, whether they're like the hero of *Tobacco Shop*, and whether or not they're Jewish? But this was no ordinary incident. It instilled terror and humiliation in Yousef's heart and marked the end of the family's evening rituals, when Yousef had listened to the stories of Gladys while eating cakes and drinking tea. The beautiful stories of love and infidelity that had so captivated the family were now replaced by the news of Hitler's victories and the voice of the Iraqi Younis Bahri, whose 'Hail to the Arabs', broadcast on the Nazi radio from the Italian city of Bari, incited the people against the Jews. Instead of the accounts of Gladys' amorous pursuits, Yousef heard Younis Bahri's voice speaking enthusiastically about the victories of the Axis on all fronts and predicting an all-out defeat for the Allies at El-Alamein in North Africa. In those early days, Yousef had no interest in this kind of news, the news of things happening elsewhere in a very remote place. He was far more interested in what Gladys was doing with her three lovers: the husband, the driver and the third man who followed her like a shadow. What he wanted most of all was simply to recreate her in his wet dreams. He was more eager to imagine her desires, moans and lustings than to hear about Hitler's offensive, or any other, for that matter. That is, until the zero hour, the moment when the massacre happened before his very eyes. It was an incident that induced horrific images in his dreams instead of Gladys' naked body. He began to see figures that seemed to come out of a Breughel or Bosch painting, with huge noses, deformed bodies, frightening smiles and cloven feet.

How did he witness the Farhoud Incident?

When Yousef woke up that morning, he tried out a tune or two on his violin as usual. He then placed the violin on the table and went to wash his face. With his hands still slightly wet, he dressed his lean, dark body in white shorts and a large shirt. He flattened his hair with his hands, gazing into the mirror with thoughtful eyes and a bleak face. Suddenly he heard a high-pitched scream. He turned towards the window, but there were only the carriages going down the street, the sunbeams coming through the glass and the sounds of nightingales echoing in the house. Then there was another scream from next door. He emerged from his reveries and went to open the window.

At that precise moment, Yousef saw the fire starting in the house opposite, his aunt Massouda's other home. She had left her larger house in the Muslim neighbourhood of Al-Karradah because she believed that the Al-Torah area, being a closed ghetto, was much safer than a mixed neighbourhood. Al-Torah was an old area that was completely off-limits to non-Jews. She had no idea that this area would be now be swarming with strange, angry faces or that their houses would be looted by young men wearing caps and belts, whose bare and muscular arms held palm branches, wooden canes and iron rods that they waved in the faces of the terrified Jews.

From where he stood, Yousef watched the scene unfold in front of his eyes without forming any thoughts about it. He gazed as coldly at the scene as Alberto Caeiro, the keeper of flocks in *Tobacco Shop*, would have done. Standing by the open window, Yousef stared and watched cart drivers and coachmen with whips indicating their willingness to deliver the loot to the homes of the thieves. From his position, Yousef watched the crowds running in

119

the pale and hazy light and heard the hoarse screams of Jews suffocating and dying, but still he formed no clear ideas, just like Alberto Caeiro in *Tobacco Shop*.

He saw men brandishing swords and knives as they ran after Sabreya, the daughter of Daoud Effendi. She ran with her hair flying loose, pursued by a group of assailants who managed to catch her by the hair before she could enter her house. He watched them as they punched her on the ground, watched them as they stripped her of her clothing, as she screamed. He watched them place their feet on her head and stamp on it with full force. He watched two handsome men remove her bracelets and saw the angry mob break down the doors and enter the houses of the terrified, trembling Jews huddled together in the corners. The looters fled, carrying the furniture on their backs. He saw them emerge with linen and quilts, having thrown the occupants of the beds onto the ground. He saw them enter kitchens and remove all the cooking utensils, even the pots on the stove. They snatched the ladle from the hand of the gaping, terror-stricken Jewish woman. They went into rooms and took everything they could lay their hands on: bundles of clothes, carpets, rugs, children's clothes and even books.

'What will you do with those books? Can you read English?'

'We'll sell them at the market. There is nothing from Jewish homes that cannot be sold.'

Coldly and dispassionately, Yousef observed the scene of death that was all around.

What he would never be able to forget, however, was the burning of Rabbi Shmuel's books and the burning of his aunt.

He was looking at the books curling in the fire, shifting and hissing. At first there was a popping sound, then he heard

120

the stirring of the embers. The flames rose higher and higher, consuming clothes and wooden objects. He saw the covers of the books twist and twirl like rolls of cloth. When the fire began to die out, he saw his aunt on the ground, on her bare knees. Her skin was burning, peeling and blackening. Her facial muscles were contracted and her bones cracked, while the flames consumed her hair. The crackling sounds of his aunt's body burning stifled his screams, which emerged only as quavering, incomprehensible sounds. The flames flickered around her body before reducing it to charred dust that lay scattered on the ground.

He collapsed, unconscious.

When he opened his eyes, he felt as though it had all been a dream. His aunt lay a couple of metres away from him, her skin charred and her skull fractured. Her body had shrunk in size so much that it had become no heavier than her beautiful long black hair.

Did Yousef consider the move to the Hassan Pasha neighbourhood a significant change in his life? Certainly. Did it represent a departure from the terror that had dominated his life for so long? Certainly. But after drinking five glasses of wine in a row, he wiped his mouth with his handkerchief and told his friends that his feeble former life had gone for good. He was no longer dominated by fear as he had been in the past. Instead, his life and his character had been totally transformed. What had at root caused this change was going swimming with his friends in the river. At first he'd been hesitant, timid, holding back. From a safe distance, he'd watched the waves as they broke against the shore. Then he went alone to conquer the water, braving the waves with his chest. He felt the lapping of the gentle water against his body, as he moved his arms and swam towards the bridge. At that moment, Yousef felt an invisible force overtake him, body and soul, a kind of tyrannical joy that engulfed him until he began to laugh and breathe freely.

That year he also visited Al-Adhamiyah during the Prophet's birthday celebrations. He took part in the great festivities in front of the mosque. He drank juice and ate with his friends from the food that was spread out on long tables, enjoying the chaotic mixture of eating and talking as their hands reached for the stuffed roasted sheep. That year he also wrote a long poem in Arabic, glorifying the Iraqi army during the 1948 war against Israel. He described the valour of the Iraqi soldiers and how they were only defeated by betrayal. Then he delivered a long monologue in rhyming couplets in praise of the Arab Nation.

(In one of his letters to Farida, Yousef had pointed out how swimming in the river had erased the humiliating fear that had always dominated his life in Al-Torah. He felt then as though an earthquake had pushed him into action, forcing him to jump and leap in. Fear had vanished completely from his heart because he had been strong enough to overcome it.)

But did his fear really and truly disappear? Did it vanish for good with the splash of the water? Could the water wash away the terror that had made him tremble for days on end at the sight of the slogans and swastikas written on the city walls? Those slogans, cheering the victories of the Axis, had been on the lips of the young and old alike. Did his fear disappear when he read statements venerating Hitler and proclaiming 'Hitler, the protector of the Arabs'? Did he lose his fear of the sons of high-ranking army officers who wore uniforms with wide sashes and decorated their shoulders with the emblems of their ranks? Was he no longer afraid of the 'Boy Scouts' or the 'Youth Brigade' who paraded in their uniforms and searched Jews for wireless equipment and mirrors on the allegation of sending signals to British aircraft, and who, while searching the alleged culprits, would scream out, 'Exterminate the germs!'

In fact, fear never entirely left Yousef's heart, for as soon as he found himself facing any of them, his eyes would fill with tears and he couldn't utter a word. He wished he could hide away in a deep, empty well. He would try hard to collect his courage but could only stutter, his power of speech gone. When he went out walking, he would look the other way, avoiding all eye contact.

But we have to admit, however, that little by little, after moving to his new house, Yousef assuaged his fears. He gradually got rid of his fear of Muslims. He found himself more and more in the wider world, part of life itself, and not trapped in a musty fear behind walls. He no longer shut himself up at home with a book, as he used to, but was now captivated by the lights reflected in the waters of the Tigris. He revelled in the humidity of summer by the bank of the river. He paraded in a white outfit, throwing pebbles into the water as he walked along the bank, beside the cafés and bars, feeling completely weightless. He now felt that he truly existed in this life, in Abu Dudu, the Hanoun market, Al-Adhamiyah and even in Al-Karradah itself. In Al-Hindiya, the most exotic of Baghdad's neighbourhoods, which he had never gone near in the past, he felt liberated. He began to visit the countryside and other areas that Jews never ventured into.

In a letter to Farida, he wrote the following telling lines: 'To live in a Jewish area, like Al-Torah for example, was to live like a Jew among Jews, to live afraid and uncertain. But there was a much wider circle out there. That's why I wished to break into that new circle and destroy the old shackles that kept me chained. I could do this only by living among people, like everyone else.'

This meant that Yousef had now adopted the lifestyle of other Muslim and Christian young men and had became one of them. He had managed to conquer his fears for good. He acquired a new look that I saw in one of the photographs that I found inside Boris's envelope: a handsome, clean-shaven young man of twenty, wearing a black cap and a very elegant white suit. With his broad chest, beaming smile and formidable build, he looked perfectly happy. He had placed his large hands on the shoulders of friends who were standing to his right and left, laughing. Behind them was a new, white Chevrolet.

During those years, Yousef was in the habit of going out in the evening with friends to the bars in Abi Nawwas on the Tigris and to the nightclubs that had just opened in the square or in Bab al-Agha. He would stay out almost all night with his Muslim friends. There were times when his mother had to bail him out of the police station at dawn, for he was often involved in bar brawls or in exchanges of blows with broken bottles over some prostitute. With downcast eyes, he would walk home with his mother, noticing the wrinkles in her face and the hard look in her eyes, as though she were trying to conceal the feelings of tenderness and compassion she felt for him. In the evening when he left the house once again, she was seized by a renewed bout of severe depression.

His love story with the dancer Munira attracted much attention at that time. He described in one of his letters how two dancers had come to the Hilal nightclub in the square near Bab al-Muazzam. It was the same club where Umm Kulthoum had sung in 1933. Munira was a little shorter than her older sister Jamila, but much prettier. Originally from Aleppo, the two young women had inflamed young men's desires with their beauty, particularly Munira with her blonde hair and sexy clothes. When she rode with her sister in the black carriage from their lovely house in Hafiz al-Qaddi to the Hilal nightclub in Bab al-Muaz-zam, all the shopkeepers would leave their shops. They wanted to have a look at the two beautiful Aleppan dancers sitting under the hood of the black carriage, with its gold lamp at the front and its tall coachman standing with his slim whip, as they moved slowly along Al-Rashid Street.

When Yousef attended one of Munira's performances, he sat in a trance in front of the wooden stage, watching as she gyrated sexily and moved her facial features in time with the music. She bent her body and vibrated her waist more daringly than any other nightclub girl at that time. Munira seemed like a blazing fire at the mercy of the wind. She danced with a quick rhythm and unparalleled gracefulness. Her tall, graceful body shook from head to toe as she danced in front of the audience, smiling, singing softly, her arms raised, her knees exposed, lewdly shaking her waist and shoulders.

(Yousef didn't explain in his letters how he had got to know her, but he did mention in five of them that she was a real influence on his life and art. Furthermore, after my subsequent trip with Faris Hassan to Baghdad and our many meetings with some of Yousef's contemporaries, they all confirmed the truth of this relationship. They'd seen them together three times: once at a Friday matinee at the Roxy cinema, the second at a

New Year's party at the English Club and the third time during a Muslim Eid in the late forties, eating ice-cream on Abi Nawwas Street. That was before the expulsion of the Jews, the withdrawal of their Iraqi nationality and the confiscation of their liquid and fixed assets. Everybody affirmed that they had acted like lovers.)

A lot of people saw Munira walking by his side, looking gorgeous with her knowing black eyes and her luscious full-lipped mouth. In one of his letters, he pointed out that what he loved most about her was her Syrian dialect, which was so different from that of Baghdadi women, not only in its intonation and rhythm but also in its expressions, words and proverbs. He was not only charmed by her flirtatiousness, but was also utterly captivated by the Aleppan vocabulary that he didn't understand.

I tried long and hard to investigate the secret of this relationship and what became of it in 1950, the year of the expulsion. His illness at that time might have had something to do with the end of the relationship, when he was sent to recuperate at one of his aunts who lived on a farm in the suburb of Al-Karkh.

In that unusual place Yousef had got used to seeing grey skies and high buildings. He was charmed by the pure colour and fragrance of the flowers. The West Baghdad Railway Station, with its rails stretching across the fields, seemed a fantasy. He also travelled to Basra, boarding the train with his luggage at the tiny station that was surrounded by tall trees and that gleamed with a rosy hue in the sunlight.

The memory of those days formed an image of paradise. Al-Karkh was spacious and beautiful. Its wide streets were lined with trees and surrounded by green woods. In the spring the muddy roads of winter became sunny and picturesque. Yousef felt that the place represented the birth of a new world, one that was lush, beautiful and wide open. It was here that Yousef was introduced to Farida, who was later to became his wife. One day he picked up his violin and went to visit her family's house, which was next door to his aunt's. He played some pieces for them. At that time Farida was studying music at the Laura Khedouri School, and when he played a bar in a completely wrong key, she pointed out his mistake. For him this was as unexpected as it was shocking.

She smiled and indicated to him to stop.

So he stopped and looked at her silently for a few moments. 'Would you play that again?' she asked him.

So he repeated it. And in doing so, his fingers repeated the error.

'That's not right!' she told him.

'What?' he asked her in astonishment.

Yousef naturally did not acknowledge his mistake, for his passion for music was more an act of worship than a profession. He was preparing himself to become a composer, and he knew that composing did not require virtuosity. But his imperfection devastated him nonetheless.

He broke down in tears in front of her. But she soothed and reassured him, telling him that his musical talent lay in his ability to express himself through music and that he had his own individual language and style.

Those were Farida's words, she who later became his muse. They were married before he left for Israel.

* * *

In the late forties rumours circulated that there was a certain group of young Muslims, Christians and Jews who led a life of dissipation and were frequently seen in the Al-Midan Square, which fifty years earlier had been an old haunt of dancers. Even at that time, it was considered one of the oldest and most artistic districts in the Middle East. Dancers and prostitutes who had been trained in the past by the English survived there as curious relics after the end of occupation. Here in this neighbourhood Yousef found an assortment of women. There were those who wore vests, loose gowns, neck scarves or tight trousers. There were also fat women with large earrings and hair tied back in plaits, who squeezed themselves into tight dresses. When Yousef returned to Baghdad in the eighties and visited the area once again, the neighbourhood had changed so much that he asked himself whether women with such different dialects and looks still lived in sacred Babylon. Diversity was the source of the square's vitality. As the destination of people from all corners of Iraq, it teemed with different dialects, traditions and lives. It was, in truth, an entire country in itself.

In the late forties, Yousef used to go on almost a daily basis to high-end clubs in the company of his friend Mohammad al-Habib, the son of a rich Muslim trader in Al-Shurja market. Together they rode horses on a day trip to Al-Mansour and its great farms. They went on rides with some other local young men, in Mohammad's convertible Chevrolet. People said that Mohammad al-Habib would take his friends, including Yousef, on evening rides along the Corniche. On Thursdays, he'd invite them for a sumptuous banquet. And on summer evenings they would dine at exclusive restaurants and clubs where they usually stayed till dawn. After driving around Baghdad, Mohammad al-Habib would gave each and every one of them a lift home.

In fact, Yousef's remarkable presence, his distinctive way of talking, his cultivation, his musical knowledge and his elegance were the source of his Muslim friends' admiration. Yousef felt that a massive force had driven him to live in those times, to be inside the arena and not outside. When he turned twenty-one, his friends held a birthday party for him at an upscale restaurant. The newspapers wrote at the time: 'Seven Jewish, Muslim and Christian young men threw a large party at the English Club on Al-Rashid Street. After finishing their meal and drinking their glasses of Scotch, they started smashing plates and throwing food at each other. They then ran off.'

The other transformation that Yousef mentioned in his letters to Farida was his relationship with Mr Rashid.

Mr Rashid lived in Bab al-Agha on Al-Rashid Street. He was elderly and would laugh non-stop, never leaving his grocery shop. He moved among boxes of Persian sweets and bottles of cooking oil imported from Iran. He would sit with one leg stretched out into the passage and the other tucked beneath rolls of fabric. One of the photographs in Boris's envelope showed him wearing a grey jacket over a formal, white shirt. He had white teeth and a thick moustache. His eyes were the colour of Aleppan pistachios: a combination of green and brown, slightly lighter than his dark complexion.

Mr Rashid was the first Muslim for almost forty years to open a grocery shop in a Jewish neighbourhood of Baghdad. He had two lovely daughters: the divorced Lamiaa and the younger Noureya. For a small allowance, Yousef worked as an assistant in Mr Rashid's shop one summer.

One day Mrs Rashid was standing on the latticed balcony of her house. She asked him to wait until she called her adolescent daughter to see him. In those days, carnal desires had begun to take hold of him. It was the first time that he saw Lamiaa, Mr Rashid's blonde daughter. She was wearing a white nightgown that revealed her white legs and her small, rounded breasts. He once went to the cinema with Mr Rashid's son, Fouad, and saw a passionate kiss on the screen for the first time in his life.

Seeing Mr Rashid and his daughters confused Yousef and made life with his father much more difficult. This was because he would often compare Mr Rashid's relationship to his daughters with his own father's attitude and bookishness.

After getting to know Mr Rashid and his daughters, Yousef felt the chilling coldness of his father's house. The warmth and light-heartedness of Mr Rashid's home made him reject his father's high bookshelves, his house and perhaps his whole family. The library, and all that it contained of the thoughts of men and laws of life, with all its Jewish and non-Jewish philosophers, was worthless in comparison with the warm, spontaneous feelings of Noureya and Lamiaa. Furthermore, Yousef hated dogs. The dog that had entered his own home as a representative of the canine proletariat had a totally negative impact on him and had deprived him of all feelings of intimacy and warmth.

Yousef gradually began to feel revolted, bored and saddened by everything at home, including the lifeless family gatherings for tea, the windows permanently closed with heavy curtains, the wooden door, the dead quietness, the kitchen and its Persian cutlery, and the yellow library lamp. Every time he went home Yousef felt lonely and desolate. After dropping heavily into a chair, he would be overcome with a sense of dejection. A dark, heavy colour would descend onto the banisters, the empty rooms and the chill beds, on the walls lined with books and on the ancient furniture. He felt dismally lonely as he went into his room, hearing his father snoring in bed. He would switch on the light quietly and open his music sheets. But he couldn't play or write. He would sit and think. Facts, ideas, discussions and his father's sallow, depressed face, all made his life at home terribly hard.

His father spent all his time in his library, especially after his retirement. If he talked at all, it was about the socialism that could make everyone happy. Mr Rashid, however, was very different, for he never talked about the future, only about the present. He lived in the moment in its excitement and its essence. This was exactly what Yousef demanded of music. He wanted tunes that responded to the present moment. Whenever he saw Mr Rashid laughing or observed him making almost non-stop jokes, he thought of his own, very different, father, the man with the sallow face buried among huge books that he'd inherited from his own father. Like a lone dog, he would sit in the dim light of a single lamp, while Mr Rashid was sitting in his bamboo chair in front of his grocery shop, under the sun, laughing heartily and aloud with people all around him.

(We stopped, Faris and I, in front of Yousef Sami Saleh's house in Al-Torah, the famous Jewish quarter of Baghdad. The house stood near a windmill, which was now in ruins. All the maps going back to the fifties had shown it as a mill, although it looked like a derelict building. The house where Yousef had lived was still standing, but was now occupied by an elderly man, his sons and three daughters. From here Yousef had perhaps walked to Mr Rashid's grocery shop, which was also still in existence. Other houses in the neighbourhood were still intact: the houses of the Shaools, the Sassoons and the Rahoos, as well as other well-known houses.)

*   *   *

During those years, Yousef pursued his musical education with great passion, and practised his violin with obvious dedication. He stayed from morning till night at the music school where Muslim, Armenian and Jewish instructors taught. He also gave various classical recitals at the English Club in Baghdad. To sharpen his imagination, he read modern Arabic poetry, enjoying its innovations of form and diction. He read symbolist poetry and was fascinated by its imagery, language and modern form. He believed in the importance of the forties' wave of poets, who distanced themselves from classical Arabic forms. He wrote in his notebook that he felt alienated from traditional martial poetry, which lacked imagination, and was attracted to the modern spirit, which gave full rein to reflection. The Baghdad of Yousef's time was going through colossal changes. It was inundated by a flood of new ideas, trends, conflicts, schools of thought and cultures. He was the enthusiastic artist leading the boisterous life of a twenty-year-old young man. He got to know many artists and writers, such as Al-Sayyab, Al-Bayyati and Al-Tikreli, and would meet them at the Brazilian coffee shop. He also knew the rebellious, vagabond poet Hussein Murdan. Like the poets, he tried experimenting with musical forms of expression, especially after witnessing the bitter conflicts that arose out of political pressures or other social forces.

Yousef was witness at that time to the bitter conflict between new and outdated ideas, between an emergent spirit and another that was fixed and immovable. And although he was caught up in the chaos and populism of modernism, he had perceived the rebellious nature of the young wave and its connection with what was lived and felt, away from the hallucinations and anarchic mysteries of abstraction. He tried experimenting in music too, by composing pieces inspired by the poetry of Badr al-Sayyab,

Al-Bayyati and Nazek al-Malaeka. He attempted to transform the humdrum into melody, to add a mythical aspect to still life through music. He wanted to transform the intimate experiences of young people in Baghdad into immortal legends, finding inspiration among women's fishnet stockings and brassieres flung on beds, in love-letters and telephones, and in kisses, whether snatched or planned.

Yousef wished to create for himself an image that was similar to that of Hussein Murdan, who was a madman, a lost soul, a cursed renegade and a clown, all rolled into one. He wanted to follow in his footsteps and become the outlawed outsider par excellence. In the midst of the conflict between modernists and traditionalists, the intellectual disputes of Baghdad never ceased. They even reached the coffee houses, where the advocates of free verse and the proponents of classical poetry exchanged blows with chairs. But behind the artistic rivalry was an implicit ideological struggle. Communists and their supporters were on the side of modernity, while the nationalists and their supporters were in favour of traditional poetry and attitudes. Although he felt within his own soul a deep rebellious tendency, he was also affected by the political situation of the Jews in Baghdad, which was becoming a real cause for concern.

Faced with escalating, anti-Jewish Nazi and Fascist tendencies, the Jews reacted by adopting extremely traditional, religious and Zionist views. They tried to counter extremism by adopting their own extremist attitudes. This was represented by the increasing popularity of Zionism and the establishment of the Tenoua organization. In one of Yousef's letters to Farida dated March 1966 [*Note: The letter was addressed to the Czech musician Karl Baruch in Prague, but written to Farida*], he described his meeting with the

133

head of the Zionist secret society in Tehran, Benek Wilson Bennett, a British citizen of Russian descent. He was in control of the Jewish Agency in Tehran and, during that period, moved frequently between Ankara, Beirut, Damascus and Cairo. In 1948 he came to Iraq dressed as a Christian clergyman, ostensibly representing the Kashanian Company for carpets in Iran and Iraq. His assistant in Iran was the director of Orion Express, which had its headquarters in Tehran and a branch in Iraq. Bennett had facilitated the entry of a well-known Iraqi trader called Yehuda Meir Menasha into Iraq on an Iranian passport bearing the name of Ismail Mahdi Salhoun. Yousef had the following conversation with Bennett:

'You're an important musician and we'll help you travel to Israel.'

'Do you want me to be a refugee, to be in exile when I have a home and a country?'

'This isn't your country. One day they'll tell you to get out of here. Your country is over there. Today it's me telling you this, but they will tell it to you later.'

Feigned innocence was Yousef's latest strategy to protect himself. It was the last means he had of preserving his existence. He spent a miserable night before meeting Bennett at the library. Bennett sat beside him, smiling and being nice to him. Yousef, for his part, was immovable and held his silence for a long time. What Bennett didn't know was that Yousef was trying in vain to find a new type of reasoning, or a new orientation that was neither Zionist nor nationalist. Gazing at Yousef, Bennett saw drops of sweat frozen on Yousef's puzzled face. The cheerful hospitality with which he had first greeted Bennett couldn't hide his concern. But what, thought Bennett, were the ambitions of this obscure musician? Each evening he would obstinately place his music sheet on the stand and soar far away. His audience was made up of middle-class Christian, Jewish and Muslim families, mostly communists and intellectuals, who were transported in their own way while scores of seats remained empty. Those were Bennett's reflections, while Yousef had very different thoughts: What could he possibly do in Israel, a land he had never lived in or known?

A heavy silence descended over the place, punctuated by Bennett's sighs and Yousef's breathing. Bennett hadn't read the news item in the *Baghdad Times* lying on the table beside him, which reported that Yousef Sami Saleh had just been awarded the King Faisal Prize for the violin. It also announced a series of concerts to be given at the English Club in Baghdad in the presence of the most prominent families of the city. What would this young man, who had such superb mastery over the violin, especially Bach's sonata for solo violin, do in Israel?

That same day, Yousef went to the English Club to perform a new piece of his own composition. As soon as he had placed the violin on his shoulder and begun tuning it, he heard one of the Youth Brigade insulting him from among the audience, shouting out 'Jew'.

Yousef didn't look up at all. He who had received the highest accolades in the kingdom neither lifted his head nor looked in the direction of the insult, but continued stroking his bow over the strings of his violin. Although he didn't look up, he could hear the hubbub in the auditorium. He realized that some of the families among the audience had kicked the man out of the hall. This member of the Youth Brigade or Nazi Scouts had sneaked in to ruin the whole concert. After he'd been thrown out, the audience were ready to listen to the new composition. But Yousef stopped playing. His expression changed so much that he became almost unrecognizable. He fumbled in his pockets, brought out a handkerchief and adjusted his bow tie. He then stood up, examined his violin, sat down again, fixed his trousers and adjusted the music sheets on the stand. But instead of playing, he broke into burning tears.

Yousef realized that things had changed forever. Everywhere was turmoil. Angry young men were roaming the streets dressed in various uniforms, their heads shaved at the sides. He realized that new and violent ideas were circulating in society. There were anti-Jewish statements and graffiti on the walls calling for their deaths. It was a complete reversal. Stories that had never been told before were now out in the open. Massouda Sassoon told him that a bomb had gone off at Massouda Shemtov synagogue. Suleiman Chalabi told him that he'd heard from his uncle Yossi about a bomb that had exploded at the Beit Lawi Car Company. One morning, when he'd just woken up and was lying in bed, he tuned in to the news on the radio. His muscles froze as he heard the news of an explosion at the Stanley Shashou Trading Company.

At the same time, Zionist sympathies grew stronger among the Jews. They began to stockpile arms, study Hebrew and promote Zionist propaganda in the Tenoua organizations. But Yousef resisted that trend. He wrote in one of his letters to Farida, 'Before I could find answers or even ask questions, I'd rejected everything. My rejection was spontaneous and unsupported by any logical reasoning. It was just a profound, mute certainty coming from my heart.' This was what he wrote in an undated letter to his wife. Discussions became more heated and ideas clashed, while his enthusiasm for music grew. He wondered whether music was capable of bringing people together from different backgrounds and cultures. He believed that music could become a unifying force for all sects, religions and ethnicities, so each evening he played at the English Club where Muslims, Jews and Christians listened to his music in absolute silence and admiration, with pleasure and with passion. He tried to combine Western music, which he loved, with Iraqi music. He developed his style and ideas, and sometimes wrote articles on music for the newspapers. He believed that music was capable of making human minds more daring and more elevated.

This was how Yousef stood in front of the audience and began, as though in a trance, to produce tunes from his violin. He believed deep in his heart that his music had a magical effect on people, uniting them as human beings in an appreciation of beauty. He heard teachers presenting scientific or pseudo-scientific theories and researches. He read newspapers and was familiar with the public mood. He understood the meaning of sectarianism and realized that a whole movement existed that opposed his presence there. It was very difficult for him to resist or even to prevent himself from being destroyed. He knew without a shred of doubt that dialogue would soon be impossible and that all resistance would be useless. Nevertheless, he withdrew into his inner world, dedicating himself wholeheartedly to music. He wrote dozens of musical scores and filled his notebooks; he analyzed and studied music. He confronted the overwhelming propaganda machine of society with his own personal convictions.

It was in 1950 that Yousef stood in front of the audience at the English Club in Baghdad performing with the London Philharmonic Orchestra. Hundreds of people sat in silent anticipation.

As the tall, slim musician stood holding his violin, the hall became pitch dark except for the spotlight on him. On that day he wore a black tuxedo and patent leather shoes. He raised his violin and after a moment of complete silence he placed the bow on the strings and began to play. He felt himself soaring high as the music flowed from his hands, and his heart almost stopped with joy.

It was a day of historic importance for him, in the company of a hundred and twenty musicians. In the pitch dark of the hall he was close to losing consciousness. Ten violins sang out together. A high note from one of the violins almost snatched away his soul. The sounds of the music rose higher, punctuated by the light rumba rhythm of the tympani and double bass. In a duet with the piano, his emotions reached their peak. Yousef's soul burned, ethereal and volatile. He felt that he was infusing magic into the hearts of those who longed for love and human harmony. After just an hour, the lights flooded the hall once again and the sounds of cheers and clapping arose. Everyone applauded – lovely girls, society women, men and boys – while he merely bowed, overwhelmed by a sense of holy reverence in the endless recesses of his soul.

Yousef in those days was haunted by a single obsession, an obsession that said: 'Do not put me in a tight corner, do not place me in a little box. When you treat me like a Jew, you suffocate me.'

His gaunt face, his cold sweat and his great anxiety acquired a different meaning in the game of politics that forced people to wear masks. As a Jew, Yousef was required to play the role of a Jew and wear the Jewish mask, in the same way that Muslims and Christians had to play their respective roles and wear their respective masks. Masks made it easy for individuals to live in society. Rejecting the mask made the artist an alien forever, even though music, art and beauty refused to narrow the individual into a role.

Yousef was a stranger to everything around him. Everybody urged him to conform to his role. But he wished only to conform to music, for music had no religion. Beauty called for submission to an abstraction, a concept or a god, but not to a military uniform. Yousef refused to wear a specific uniform or to have a specific label stuck to him. He wanted to be neither one type nor another. He wanted to become whatever circumstances required him to be. He wanted to be one individual or another, to be 'here' or 'there', at the same time.

'How can I possibly take part in this human farce?' he asked himself. He had the overwhelming feeling that he didn't belong to this world at all. But he had to wear a mask, because the mask made it possible for him to regain his self-confidence. It calmed his fears, expelled his demons and quelled the violent cries in the depths of his heart, the depths that told of hell. That was Alberto Caeiro's feeling in Pessoa's *Tobacco Shop*, or what Pessoa himself had actually felt. Yousef found infinite joy in playing music. Every evening he ran as fast as he could to the music hall. He wanted to be on stage and to stay there, not only because he loved music, but also because his identity would vanish with the first step that he took on stage. His sense of elation, however, would dissolve and disappear in the morning, under the pressures of everyday life and the stamp of identities. On stage, he didn't occupy a particular slot, nor did he conform to a particular classification. But in the morning he found himself squeezed against his will into some pigeonhole.

139

Everything inside him wanted to attain the sublime, the transcendent. He longed to dissolve and vanish into the ethereal. The weight of his identity was too heavy for him to bear. It pushed him towards the past, to vanish into forgetfulness. He wanted to get rid of his identity by fading away, by escaping or hiding. If it wasn't possible to do that, he had to hide behind another character, a new name and a whole new life.

Had Yousef been thinking of changing his identity at that time? Of acquiring a new name and personality? Or of becoming a member of the *Tobacco Shop* club? This was what the events of his life would reveal.

Yousef's life was steeped in the identity conflicts of the Middle East. The present, he felt, was dominated by the spectre of war and civil strife. He thought that identities spelled the end of the world. He felt suffocated and almost dead, for the country was like a ship sinking slowly while his fears spiralled. The world around him was receding and collapsing. The country was plagued by successive defeats and being torn to pieces. It was being preyed upon by all-consuming ideologies and dominated by chaos and the total absence of rationality and ethics. His own existence was under constant threat.

Instead of feeling that he was at the centre of things, Yousef was overwhelmed by a deep apprehension. A massive force was pushing him towards a dark abyss. There was degeneration, regression and a sense of defeat and collapse. Eids became depressing and the festive spirit was almost gone. Society was no longer a beautiful presence but an intricate and frightening labyrinth. Everything had become much narrower in scope. As soon as he'd passed through one barrier, his head would bump into another. It was a new but terrifying world that smelled of blood. It rushed steadily forward, but only towards the precipice.

He was still alive, but without a present or a future. He seemed to be going through a succession of vertical falls into a black, bottomless pit or into nothingness. Since 1941, Yousef had felt that the abyss would swallow up the whole of society. Death would be everywhere, and all his acquaintances would have to emigrate or die. But emigrate where? Emigration was a vague longing, a leap into the unknown. Would emigration tear down the walls? Would it banish the persistent scenes that gave him nightmares? Would it eliminate the Jewish fear of society that had persisted throughout history? Would it end the feeling of alienation and the impulse to go back to the womb? Would it demolish the wall separating the self from others or the 'here' from 'there'? What would lie beyond these borders? Chaos, nothingness or paradise?

Travelling to Israel was never his objective. Although travelling in itself was fairly easy, leaving Iraq seemed to him to be entering a completely alien universe. He knew that visas were being granted to Jews, but would then be retracted and cancelled. Applications would be repeated time and time again, perhaps twenty times. Yet finally, Yousef had to get rid of his music sheets, his violin and his memories. The Jews had to leave for Israel because they'd been stripped of their Iraqi nationality. They would be deported with nothing more than the clothes they were wearing. So they put on their most expensive clothes and left for Israel. Inspection procedures at the time were terrifying and took forever.

Eventually he came to a conclusion of sorts. He opened his mouth and in a weak, inaudible voice said, 'I'll go to Israel.'

His wife Farida asked him to repeat this statement several times. She stopped reading her book and said in a apprehensive voice, 'Are you sure? How strange!' Then she fell silent.

At that moment, Yousef had little to say. The decision was simple and straightforward: All Jews had to leave their homes, furniture, and possessions and travel with nothing but their clothes. So the Jews bought the most expensive outfits, trousers, shirts, suits and shoes. Yousef, whose passion for music didn't allow him to leave his violin behind, smashed it into pieces.

He told Farida what he'd done. He'd left for the theatre and come back without the violin. When she opened the door for him, with Meir on her arm, she looked at him briefly and felt that in front of her stood a different person. She stared at him with new eyes, while he responded with a tearful, sorrowful look. She controlled her feelings but he could not. His trembling lips expressed the inexpressible. It was a silent dialogue, a kind of brief ritual in which each of them rediscovered the other.

The inspector of emigrants stood by the metal fence. Behind him were two policemen dressed in khaki uniforms with broad leather belts and heavy boots. Huge pistols hung heavily on their right sides.

Yousef stood in the long line with Farida carrying Meir, each with a 'final exit' permit and a photograph. The line was made up of Jews wearing their finest clothes. Unable to carry any valuables, they had sold their gold, their furniture, their elegant houses and cars, and had bought hats, tuxedos and starched shirts. The women were wearing elegant skirts and expensive suits. Yousef looked at the line and burst out laughing; it looked more like a queue for a party than for emigration. What a ridiculous sight! They moved slowly forward in front of the inspection officers. The officers

142

took the clothes out of the suitcases and ordered the Jews to take off their shoes, shirts and jackets. When the man standing in line in front of Yousef took off his clothes, the policemen burst out laughing, for the man was wearing four shirts and three pairs of trousers, one on top of the other.

'He has to remove his shoes! We need to check he's not wearing another pair underneath,' the customs officer shouted.

Neither Yousef nor Farida were wearing anything new or expensive. They went in their ordinary clothes and bought nothing new for Meir. They gave away all their furniture and books to friends. Like two philosophers, they stood with a small suitcase containing essential clothes and items. Neither of them felt any sense of weariness. They felt numbed as they stood in line, watching the other people. As though in a dream, they couldn't believe what was happening. They gazed with cold detachment as their steel suitcases were inspected, their few clothes spread out, their documents and certificates torn to pieces, their soap bars crushed over the clothes and their shoes inspected to make sure that no gold was being smuggled in.

In two important letters that I received in Baghdad, Farida detailed the history of Yousef's immigration to Israel and the years he'd spent there. It's also important to say a few things about Farida.

(Farida Reuben was a woman of average beauty. She was very slim and had large dark eyes. After graduating from Laura Khedouri School in Baghdad, she joined the Women's College to study Arabic literature. Because she felt that her college education was rather removed from practical life, she embarked on the task of educating herself, especially as she was proficient in English and French, in addition to Hebrew and Arabic. Hoping to become a full-time writer one day, she enrolled at university as soon as she

143

arrived in Israel. She majored in Arabic literature and continued her studies until she obtained her doctorate. She then started teaching at Jerusalem University.)

Farida related that as soon as the plane landed in Israel, all the passengers shouted, '*Shalom Haber!*'. But the Ashkenazim didn't respond, they just sprayed them with DDT to prevent them from carrying their Iraqi germs into the Promised Land. They were then transported in cattle trucks to the quarantine camp in Shaar Ha-Aliya, the 'Immigrant Gateway'. They stood in line for vaccination and in food queues for half a boiled egg and five olives each. Two days later, Yousef, Farida and Meir were taken to another camp, with two other families, in a large vehicle designed for transporting cattle. At the camp, Yousef had to learn to stand in line for water, for the toilet and for bread. He had to learn to buy meat, eggs and butter using coupons and to work as a builder.

Yousef sat, moving his fingers in the air as though playing music.

In Israel, time had come to a complete standstill. Life was monotonous and unchanging. Yousef watched the passing of the seasons, one after the other. He recalled the old days in Baghdad and relived them in the present. He felt that he was living outside time. His little diary was full of the tedious rhythm of immigrant life: the pale faces, the dismal routine of soldiers and the total absence of joy, wonder and beauty. He searched for an answer but found none, although what he was looking for was to be found in a mysterious and simple enough explanation. It was to be found in a simple metaphysical image that was like an invisible bridge between him and the unknown. He realized that truth was granted to no one and that the Promised Land had been promised long ago. Although he felt hesitant and giddy, and was full of sorrow and conflict, the whole world seemed to urge him to leave.

His decision to return to Iraq was final and categorical. He had no doubts. [*Farida wrote in detail about his idea in an explanatory note appended to one of the letters sent to her from Tehran, dated January 1952. He also offered the same explanation in his diary.*]

At the beginning, Yousef joined Rakah, the Israeli Communist Party. That same year, he met Emile Habibi, who was rather plump with black hair combed back and a moustache that gently outlined his upper lip. Yousef spent lovely evenings with the communist intellectual Emile, who later became a writer. They had heated discussions about the changes that were happening to Arabic literature. All the evidence proves that it was Emile who arranged Yousef's escape to Moscow once Yousef had told him of his desire to return to Iraq. One day Emile came running, his face sweating, and wearing a striped navy blue jacket and a white shirt. He stood in front of Yousef smiling, an elegant silk scarf tied around his neck. (Yousef Saleh used to call him the elegant communist.) Emile gave him a piece of paper written in Russian, an invitation to give a concert in Moscow. Yousef felt extremely happy. Not only would he travel to Moscow, but he would also be returning to music and giving a recital in front of an audience.

The following day, Yousef stood with his arms dangling at his sides in front of comrade Klausner. The curtains were drawn in the modest office located in an area far from the city centre. Without looking at him directly, Klausner said, 'You're travelling to Moscow for this big concert and coming back, right?'

Yousef answered him coldly, 'Yes.'

In her letter, Farida said, 'He didn't sleep a wink from the moment he got the plane ticket. He stayed up late, distressed at the prospect of leaving me and his son Meir. But he was also happy that he'd got a ticket to Moscow, and on to Tehran. According to his plan, Baghdad would be the next leg of his trip. He said that we could join him later.'

Yousef believed that the Iraqi Jews would return to Baghdad, or at least most of them. He believed that the government would retract its decision to strip them of their nationality and would return their property. It would be natural for them then to return because Israel was nothing but a wasteland compared to the sophistication of Baghdad. Why should all those traders, craftsmen, employees, army officers and doctors work as casual labourers in a tiny, underdeveloped country?

All the documents in our possession confirm that Yousef arrived in Moscow in the evening. But it's not clear how he spent his first week there, for he didn't write anything about his feelings during the concert or afterwards. The only person he met in Moscow at that time was Kakeh Hameh, who told me about it when I met him later. But Hameh didn't attend the concert and knew nothing about it. The only thing he told me was that a comrade had asked him to contact another communist who wanted to go to Tehran. That was how he'd arranged for him to get a fake passport in the name of Haidar Ali, which would allow him later to enter Iraq. That was the only task assigned to Kakeh Hameh. But Yousef later wrote about this task in more detail. In a separate letter that he sent to Farida from Moscow, dated one week after his arrival, he told her that he'd succeeded in contacting some Iraqi communists and had told them of his wish to return to Baghdad. He also told her about his meeting with Kakeh Hameh and many other things, including attending concerts given by Mark Goezler, the thin, silver-haired German musician. Yousef created a venerable image of him in his imagination, which lived on in his memory for some time. In the same letter, he described to her how he had walked in the freezing cold of Moscow, filled with ecstasy as he took a route that crossed fields and passed buildings wrapped in mist. He'd walked with his hands in his coat pockets, condensation rising from his nose and mouth and vanishing in the air. Nothing disturbed the stillness except the screams of seagulls diving in the air and the sounds of sledges as they slid hastily away. When he'd entered the large concert hall, all the seats and stalls had been completely empty. He'd remained there until the hall began to fill up. When the conductor began and the music started, his eyes welled up with tears. By the end of the concert, he was totally oblivious of everything around him. He later walked along the wet roads, passing pedestrians, cars, cows, dogs and sledges, and overwhelmed by a profound feeling of ecstasy.

When Yousef returned to his apartment in a small suburb of Moscow, there were piles of snow on the pavement. He felt the cold breeze hit him in the face as he turned the key in the lock. He was utterly exhausted. Taking off his heavy coat, he threw it on the sofa and sat on the black leather chair, stretched his legs onto the table opposite. In no time at all he fell into a long nap from which he was woken by the ringing of the telephone. He looked at his watch and discovered it was very late. Kakeh Hameh's voice came over the line, inviting him to meet up again at the Novoslobodskaya train station, which was near the house.

Yousef got dressed in a hurry and went to the great station. He heard the harsh, grating sounds of the brakes as the trains ground to a halt. The passengers got off. Kakeh Hameh was waiting for him at the telephone booth, with a Russian musician called Sergey Oistrakh, who was wearing a black hat and was standing with his wife, a tall, blonde woman. Oistrakh spoke only Russian, so Kakeh Hameh translated. To the ringing of the station bell, the four of them walked through the crowds and arrived at a wooden house nearby. It had an iron gate and was surrounded by linden trees. Kakeh Hameh talked to Yousef for a long time and gave him a lot of information about getting to Tehran. He then gave him a fake passport in the name of Haidar Salman, musician. He told him to stay for a while in Tehran and then move to Baghdad.

Two hours later, they headed for the Sheremetyevo airport on the outskirts of Moscow. In the evening Yousef boarded a plane bound for Prague. A Czech musician called Karl Baruch collected him from the airport and took him to a place outside Prague. In an isolated wooden house in a vast forest near the city of Mladá Boleslav, they sat together and chatted about music for a long time. Yousef thoroughly enjoyed talking to him, for Karl Baruch was a young man in his twenties, like him. He had blond hair and blue eyes. He wore a white coat and carried a leather briefcase. He gave Yousef a beautiful violin as a present, which he hugged in an expression of his gratitude. Yousef didn't sleep all night long. Every time he opened his eyes and caught sight of the violin, he smiled and tried once more to sleep.

In the morning, Yousef went straight to the Iranian embassy in Prague. As soon as he had obtained an entry visa to the country, he booked a flight on a Norwegian plane bound for the Iranian capital, Tehran.

Did the composer feel that he had left the personality of Yousef Sami Saleh on the seat behind him and acquired a new one? In one of his letters he mentioned that it was on that day that he heard from Karl Baruch about *Tobacco Shop*. Did he realize that his new persona would be that of the protected man?

VII

The protected man in the tobacconist's
From the life of Haidar Salman
(1924-81)

'Don't plan your destiny, for you have no future. Between a glass you drain and a glass you fill, who knows whether your destiny lies in the middle of the abyss!'

'Odes de Ricardo Reis', *Tobacco Shop*

An immigrant, an obscure composer and ideological gangs

The second character in Fernando Pessoa's poetry collection *Tobacco Shop* is the poet Ricardo Reis, who is protected by the first character, Alberto Caeiro. He has a date of birth and lifestyle very different from the other two. This protected character believes in the Greek gods even though he lives as a Christian in Europe. He feels that his spiritual life is fixed and constant, and that real happiness is impossible to achieve. He also believes in fate and destiny, and in the existence of an overarching power which, despite everything, ignores his freedom.

All these ideas lead the character of the protected man towards a kind of Epicurean existence and compel him to avoid pain at any cost. In spite of his wisdom, the protected man tries as best he can to avoid emotional endings. He tries to look at life from a certain distance and accept his fate with equanimity, looking philosophically at identities and casting doubt on everything and everyone, including himself.

This character has close affinities with the second persona assumed by the composer, that of Haidar Salman. After his escape from Israel to Moscow, he immigrated to Tehran with the help of the Russian musician Sergei Oistrakh and the Iraqi communist Kakeh Hameh, who lived in Moscow. The fake passport he carried gave him more than just a new name. It gave him a new history and a date of birth that preceded that of the first character by two years. In other words, he was now born in Al-Kazemeya in Baghdad in 1924, just as the character of the protected man in *Tobacco Shop* was born nine months before the first character. And he was a Shia.

When Yousef Sami Saleh sat with Kakeh Hameh in Moscow, the latter gave him a great deal of information that would help him become familiar with his new personality as Haidar Salman. The son of a merchant at Al-Isterbadi market in Al-Kazemeya, Salman had angered his family by studying music in Moscow instead of medicine. That was the reason he was unable to return to Baghdad at that time. He wanted to travel to Iran to visit an Iraqi merchant called Ismail al-Tabtabaei. The latter was a real not fictitious person, a wealthy merchant who traded between Tehran and Baghdad and was known for his great sympathy for the left. The history of this second persona was clearly very different from that of the first. Yousef Sami Saleh was naturally required to impersonate and embody this new persona, which was fairly similar to that of Ricardo Reis in *Tobacco Shop*. Reis was a protected young man from a wealthy, influential family, the son of a very rich merchant, as well as a musician and a rebel. Both Ricardo Reis and Haidar Salman were spontaneous, self-indulgent high-achievers. They enjoyed wealth and the simple pleasures of life, and tried to avoid emotional endings.

All the evidence confirms that Haidar Salman arrived in Tehran early in the winter of 1953, that is, a few months after the overthrow of the Mossadegh government. In this Eastern city the composer embarked on a totally new phase of life and with a very different personal history. He arrived at Tehran's Mehrabad Airport with a small, black suitcase containing a few items of clothing. These were, with the exception of a black scarf and a pair of leather gloves that he'd bought at a small shop in Moscow, the same items that he'd carried with him from Iraq. All he had in his pockets were a few tomans that had been given to him by Kakeh Hameh, his passport and his gloves. He carried the violin that the Czech musician Karl Baruch had given him as a gift. [*Karl Baruch later became the best-known violinist in Czechoslovakia, and received numerous prizes and accolades. He fled to the United States in 1975 and died in New York in 1983.*] Kakeh Hameh had given him the address of Ismail al-Tabtabaei [*a well known Iraqi merchant who was a friend of the Communist Party and had spent many years between Tehran and Baghdad*]. Hameh also gave him a book to teach himself Persian in seven days. As he presented him the book, he cautioned: 'Don't believe the seven-day thing, though!'

* * *

At dawn on 13 December 1953 the plane landed at Mehrabad Airport. When Haidar Salman disembarked, he felt the cold, sharp air strike his face. Snow had been falling and the airport was brilliant white. He walked unsteadily towards the passport control officer. When he stood before him his smile was full of fear. He handed over his Iraqi passport.

The Iranian officer, a captain by rank, asked him to sit on a wooden bench near the passport booth. Without looking at the passport, he placed it to one side and began to stamp the passports of the other passengers, one after the other, until Haidar was the only person left. The young officer then picked up Haidar's passport and flipped through its pages carefully and attentively while talking to several people on the phone. Haidar was extremely anxious and confused, unable to overcome his anxiety and doubts that the passport officer might discover the passport was fake, in which case his whole life would be in serious danger. Haidar sat on the wooden bench reflecting on his fate, realizing that both his return and his love of music were totally incomprehensible to others. He belonged to a different world from the real one and had a vocation that was alien to his environment. To alleviate the worries and sorrows that had taken hold of him, he started gazing around the airport hall and up at the ceiling. He waited for the official procedures to end, not knowing what to expect either now or later. He looked anxiously through the window and saw some high trees, the sky overcast with clouds and an empty carriage pulled by a pair of horses. When he looked up at the airport ceiling, he saw the Nazi swastika decorating its centre. He later wrote to Farida about this: 'The airport and the central railway station in Tehran were built in the thirties by Nazi Germany, when there were close relations between Hitler and Reza Shah,

Iran's former ruler. The ceiling was constructed in such a way as to make it impossible for the swastika to be removed without the whole thing collapsing.'

In the morning, having surrendered himself to sleep on the bench, hugging his suitcase, umbrella and hat, he felt a hand patting him on the shoulder. The Iranian officer handed him his passport and allowed him to leave the airport for Tehran. Overwhelmed with unspeakable joy, he felt that he'd been born anew. He had a new personality that had erased the old one and its history. He went straight to a third-rate hotel where he decided to stay for some time until he found the address of the Iraqi merchant, Ismail al-Tabtabaei, the one who traded between Iraq and Iran.

The Tehran of those days left a powerful and lasting impression on his imagination. It charmed him with its undulating hills, its solemn, silent forests, its light-filled, rounded peaks and the statue of the poet Al-Firdawsi, who affirmed the potential integration of heaven and earth. During the reign of the Shah, Tehran was a modern city, with impressive avenues and hotels, luxurious palaces and dense forests. Its grey buildings, constructed in the nineteenth century, showed the influence of English architecture on Nasser al-Din Shah, who began to copy Western architectural techniques and designs. This was Haidar's first vision of this fascinating, oriental city. In his room, which was made of teak wood and lay on the upper floor of the hotel, he wrote a long letter to his wife, Farida. The hotel was a beautiful old building surrounded and shaded by poplar trees. One wintry afternoon he went down to the hotel lounge and found the owner squatting on her knees, dusting the furniture with a feather duster and arranging the books elegantly on the wooden shelf. A book with a grey cover suddenly fell off the shelf onto the ground. Haidar picked it up, rearranged his scarf and began browsing through it. It was the *Rubaiyat* of the Persian poet Omar al-Khayyam, translated into five languages, including into Arabic by Ahmed al-Safi al-Najafi. Haidar had previously become acquainted with this poet at the Brazilian coffee shop in Baghdad. So he asked the owner to permit him to borrow the book to read it at leisure in his room. He read the book throughout the night as if to protect his silence and solitude from the falling snow. At dawn, before falling asleep, he wrote a long letter to Farida in which he described Tehran's bazaars and outstanding museums, including the National Museum of Iran, the National Jewellery Museum and the Gulistan Palace. This fortress, built in the Safavid era, had been turned into a late-nineteenth-century Western-style palace by Nasser al-Din Shah, one of the important rulers of the Qajar era. The letter, which included some verses of al-Khayyam, was the very first to carry the signature: Haidar Salman, Hotel Sarjashma, Tehran, 1953.

This means that from his early days in Tehran, Haidar Salman began to discover this huge imperial city, visiting not only the deprived, congested areas to the south, but also the northern aristocratic neighbourhoods. Each morning, he went hurriedly out of Hotel Sarjashma. With his hands in his coat pockets, his hat on his head and his scarf over his face, he began to explore Tehran's wide streets. He was captivated by the high, snow-capped Elburz Mountains, the long rows of huge, ancient trees and the winding side alleys that seemed to overflow with the secrets of craftsmen and small traders. He sometimes took his violin and sat in a large city square. On sunny winter days the fountain in the middle of the square seemed to whisper as though it were chirping. So he would play a piece or two on his violin and in the evening would return to the hotel, his ears filled with the sounds of lovers' whispers mixed with the water that trickled down the mountains and flowed in streams through the streets of the city.

It is certain that Haidar Salman called more than once at Ismail al-Tabtabaei's address. But he didn't find him, because the latter was in Baghdad on account of his daughter's illness. After a few days, when Haidar's funds began to run out, he contacted Kakeh Hameh in Moscow. He told Hameh that Ismail al-Tabtabaei was not in Tehran and that he was running out of cash. Hameh sent him some money to tide him over until the left-leaning Iraqi merchant returned from Baghdad. During that period, Haidar Salman started to frequent the Khanzad restaurant, which lay at the crossroads of Fakhrabad and Qizard Streets, a few steps away from the main square in Tehran. This was because an Iraqi, Hekmat Aziz, worked at the restaurant. So Haidar Salman often went in the evening and sat by the back door of the restaurant, waiting for Hekmat Aziz to appear with a kebab sandwich wrapped in newspaper, which he would devour at a park nearby.

On the basis of the information that I have, I don't actually know how Haidar Salman came to know his new friend Hekmat Aziz. Farida sent me a letter in which she thought that Kakeh Hameh was the one who introduced them. But when I questioned Kakeh Hameh about this and told him of Farida's view, he denied the suggestion, telling me that he only became acquainted with Hekmat Aziz after the 1958 Revolution, when he saw him in Baghdad. Haidar Salman, however, wrote in one of his letters to Farida from Tehran that Hekmat Aziz had gone to Tehran to study architecture at the university. He had then found a menial job in the kitchen of the Khanzad restaurant. This was when he'd started to cooperate with the Tudeh Party and other revolutionary and leftist forces that opposed the Shah's regime. During the fifties, Iraqis lived the fever of revolution. Revolutionary parties swarmed with young men and women who dreamed of change and hoped to repeat the revolution of Lenin and his bearded men in their own country.

Haidar and Hekmat's friendship might have been strengthened by such café conspiracies, where they met with young Iraqis of the type that the right-wing newspapers nicknamed 'kids of the left' or 'revolutionary adolescents'. At Naderi café on Pahlavi Street, they met various groups: Iraqi students studying at Tehran University, some junior clerics from Qom who were influenced by Marxism and later became members of Ali Shariati's movement, and some migrant Iraqi workers in Iran. When Hekmat Aziz learned of Haidar Salman's financial difficulties, he offered him the surplus food that the restaurant would otherwise have thrown out.

According to Haidar Salman's account, Hekmat Aziz was a handsome, pitifully thin young man of twenty. He lived in an old, dilapidated apartment surrounded by rubbish in the Tobkhana district of south Tehran, an area of craftsmen, carpenters, shoe-makers, tailors and poor Jews. Hekmat Aziz was preparing diligently for the revolution, the great coup d'état that would establish the republic of joy in Baghdad. This idea so dominated the hearts and minds of young people in those days that they travelled far and wide in order to bring it about. But what exactly drummed this fiendish notion into Haidar Salman's head, an idea that was out of keeping with his first character? Was it the impact of the second character, one that was based on rebellion and dissent, the character of Ricardo Reis, which was assumed by the character of Haidar Salman? Was it the image of the protestor embodied in Shia Islam? Or was it something else?

Hekmat Aziz actually offered Haidar Salman what might have been the ideal way to enter Iraq once again, for no method was safer or more certain than the conspiratorial activities of the left. The method might have been a little fanciful and rather far-fetched, and it required some patience, but there it was all the same. Revolutionary leftists were being smuggled in and out of Iraq, either through Iraqi Kurdistan in the north or via the marshes in the south. The Jewish musician was never in fact as rash or reckless as Hekmat Aziz, who'd broken with the Communist Party and arrived in Tehran two years earlier. He'd received training in guerrilla warfare while Haidar Salman was a petty-bourgeois with no prior clandestine adventures. All he wanted was to return to Iraq, and for him returning to Iraq meant no more than going back to the place where he used to play music in front of the families of Baghdad.

On the final day of his first week in Tehran, Haidar Salman went to look for Ismail al-Tabtabaei's house, hoping that he might have returned from Baghdad. After asking several people on the street, he managed to locate the house in the aristocratic neighbourhood to the north of Pahlavi Street. He visited it one evening carrying his suitcase, violin, umbrella, hat and black gloves.

The house, hidden by thick trees, was totally isolated.

He stopped in front of the house and knocked on the brass knocker in the middle of the grand door. After a few moments a maid opened the door, wearing a red pinafore over her beautiful clothes. No sooner had he started speaking to her in English than

Ismail al-Tabtabaei came out in person to greet him. He was a handsome, tall, grey-haired, fifty-year-old man in an elegant outfit. He took Haidar straight to a small room upstairs. The room was decorated with strange old drawings and its furniture was faded with age. It was to be his room.

The mere fact of entering the house represented a huge turning point, not only in his whole life but also in his second personality as the protected man, although it was not protected by the first character as in Pessoa's *Tobacco Shop*. Haidar Salman became in fact the protégé of the great merchant. From the moment they first met, they both realized that their relationship would go way beyond the simple assistance offered by the trader to supporters of the left. Did not the protected man in *Tobacco Shop* also believe in the workings of fate and destiny?

The following morning, when Haidar Salman discovered that Ismail al-Tabtabaei had a sick daughter called Tahira, his conviction grew stronger that his presence in that house was an act of providence. The father spent most of his evenings sitting beside his daughter's bed.

During the early days of his stay, Haidar Salman spent most of his time in his room. He was always extremely shy, reluctant and uncomfortable with the aristocratic lifestyle. He was daunted by the oppressive stillness and opulence of his host's house. He therefore preferred to spend his evenings sitting alone in his room, dreaming of music. He confined his passion for music to his wild dreams, and in the morning would explore Tehran's sidestreets, crowded with workers, voices and passers-by. When he returned at noon, the sun would be high above the windows of the house and, after lunch, its golden beams would fill the dining room and hall where Haidar would sit for many hours with Ismail al-Tabta-baei and his daughter Tahira.

Everybody stayed in the sunny hall during the winter. Tahira sat with her pale, withered, beautiful face and her golden hair falling down over her shoulders, while Ismail stayed at her beck and call, his gaze unbroken. Haidar Salman looked down shyly and kept quiet. He seemed to be listening to the noises coming through the window, to the vague sounds of winter that kindled his imagination. It was a mysterious space filled with the scent of trees and melting snow. But a dreary atmosphere gradually infiltrated the room. One evening, when Haidar Salman came home late, exhausted from having walked the length of Reza Pahlavi Street, an idea suddenly hit him. He decided to dedicate an hour each day to playing music to the pale, sick girl who was lying in bed and to her poor father who always stayed by her side.

He had no idea how much his short pieces would raise the spirits of the young woman and make her so much more jovial and optimistic. The father became very attached to him, for the young man not only played the violin for the lovely girl, but took her on outings during the day, particularly after she began to feel much better. Instead of the painful headaches she used to suffer from, she had a sensation akin to an ecstatic dizziness, a feeling closer to passionate love than to illness. Tahira was exceptionally sensitive and highly impressionable. She received the young man into her father's house with a mixture of profound sadness and joy. When she stood in front of him, the muscles of her face twitched painfully and her eyes filled with tears, for she was burning with love. She came to realize that she was desperately attached to him and could never let him go. Although he reciprocated her thoughts and feelings and continued to treat her with a great deal of tenderness, he tried hard to avoid falling hopelessly in love with her.

[*In a letter to Farida, Haidar Salman expressed his wish to release Farida of her bond to him so that she might be free to remarry. Three days later, he sent her a long letter telling her about his new life with Tahira, who was, he said, his last chance to get back to Baghdad. Although he wasn't completely happy, he enjoyed his strolls along Tehran's wide boulevards and his visits to breathtaking parks where ancient cypress trees had provided shade and exuded fragrance since the times of the Qajars. He also admired the magnificent mansions with their large grounds and coloured windows. In another letter, he told Farida about his visits to the most important sights of Tehran, such as the Caravanserai market with its passages and low rows of domes. With Tahira he also visited the peaks of the snow-capped Kallus Mountain and the beautiful resort of Kelardasht and together they swam in hot springs at the coastal resort of Ramsar. They toured the monuments of ancient Masule, strolled through the markets along the Caspian Sea, and visited Persepolis and the inscription at Naqshe Rostam. Then they stood in front of Hafez's grave, its dome rising high as a symbol of the soul soaring up to heaven.*]

The intimacy between Haidar and Tahira was at its strongest during this period. They would spend whole mornings hanging out on Tehran's streets, either strolling on foot or cruising in Tahira's car. The time they spent together allowed Ismail al-Tabtabaei to turn his attention again to his business, instead of being the constant companion of his daughter. Haidar therefore became important not only for the daughter but also for the father's business. As far as Tahira and Haidar were concerned, their outings represented almost a sacred ritual. They would start their walks from north of Reza Pahlavi Street, with its congested traffic, cars and motorcycles. They would then move on to the middle section of the street where the statue of the sage, Al-Firdawsi, the writer of the epic Shahnameh, stood. They would walk in front of the great gate to Tehran University which was designed by the French architect Godard as an extension of the Dar al-Funun, itself established by the first Iranian reformer of the nineteenth century, Mirza Taqi Khan Amir Kabir, in an attempt to import Western science into Iran. They would also go to the Talar-e Rudaki theatre, which was built in the shape of a tulip and named after the Persian poet Abu Abdullah Jafar Rudaki of the fourth century of the Hijra calendar.

It was at this theatre that Haidar Salman gave a concert a year after his marriage to Tahira, thanks to the good offices of the influential merchant Ismail al-Tabtabaei. Haidar gave a solo performance of Henri Vieuxtemps' Opus 4 in D Minor, which he played with absolute brilliance, precise phrasing, soaring melody and unparalleled genius, earning him the admiration of Tehran's upper echelons and the approbation of the aristocratic families who attended the concert.

Haidar Salman wrote several letters to Farida at this time, telling her of his adventures and his exploration of that beautiful city. Tahira was his constant companion on these trips. His letters overflowed with a marked fascination with mosque architecture, sparkling blue domes and gilded minarets. He was captivated by silver and wooden decorative patterns and mirror-encrusted ceilings, which were also found in wealthy homes. But the question that perplexed me was whether Haidar Salman became a true Muslim in his heart. Or was he just a Ricardo Reis, who believed in Greek gods despite living in Christian Europe? It was certain that Tahira was filled with instinctive religious faith and whole-hearted acceptance of Shia rituals. But was his own complete identification with the persona of Haidar Salman motivated by religion or by art? He later made countless comparisons between elevated art, on the one hand, and the visual and graphic vulgarity of politico-religious propaganda, based on total superficiality and crudity, on the other.

I don't know why, but from the time he arrived in Tehran he insisted on talking about a painting by Andy Warhol. This painting by the master of kitsch showed Shah Mohammad Reza Pahlavi sitting on the throne, the very throne that had been stolen by Nader Shah when he invaded India. Known as the 'Peacock Throne' and inlaid with thousands of jewels and precious stones, it was the seat of Iran's emperors in coronations and formal cere-monies. There the Shah sat, in Warhol's painting, wearing his Shah-of-Shah's suit and giving his distinctive look. The emperor sat on the plundered Peacock Throne itself, wearing the crown of former emperors and surrounded by their jewels and gold objects. But at that time I wasn't aware of all those things. It was clear that he made frequent comparisons involving art. This tendency may be traced to his first persona when he first visited Moscow and stood in trepidation and apprehension in front of the Russian conductor, waiting to hear the advice of the bearded man whose face was as red as wine, urging him to find in his people the inspi-ration he sought for his art. It may also be traced back to the statement made by the local Muslim broadcaster with his dark, Jewish-looking face, who complimented him on embracing clas-sical art. But the most significant change no doubt happened later in the sphere of politics, with the increased use of kitsch as a tool of political propaganda both in Tehran and Baghdad.

The key question that preoccupied me at that time was when had Haidar married Tahira Ismail al-Tabtabaei, for he never mentioned the date in his letters. There was a letter from a later date, however, which he sent while on one of his trips to Europe, and where he told Farida that he'd married Tahira and had had a son Hussein from her. This question puzzled me until Faris and I went to Tehran.

Faris Hassan and I landed at Tehran Airport on 3 May 2006. The Elburz Mountains were still snow-capped despite the warmth of spring. The airport was very busy. We left the terminal building at night, took a cab and went straight to the city centre. At that hour, it was virtually impossible to find a room at any cheap hotel or *khan*, so I asked the driver to go straight to Sarjashma. I had no idea why I told him that we were staying there. I imagined that the Sarjashma Hotel, where Haidar Salman had stayed in the fifties, was located in the Sarjashma neighbourhood, and had no idea that there was also a popular district in the southern and more deprived part of Tehran with the same name. When we got out of the cab, of course we didn't find the hotel we were looking for. Instead, we found a number of cheap hotels and small *khans* all along the main street. We started knocking on the doors of the hotels and *khans*, one after the other, but we received only rejections or apologies. Because our hair was dishevelled, our clothes creased and our faces sullen, our appearance didn't encourage anyone to offer us a room.

After much trouble we found an extremely shabby hotel, barely adequate as a stable or barn. Still, we slept in clean but uncomfortable beds. The room lacked furniture and the toilets and bathrooms were communal. The place was also extremely noisy. When the sunbeams began to penetrate the room, I woke Faris. After washing our faces and brushing our teeth, we picked up our bags, paid the bill and left.

We walked along the street opposite the old hotel. In the middle of the large square, a very tall and bearded policeman stood directing the cars, bicycles and motorcycles ridden by turbaned clerics. Around the square were shops selling spices, nuts and groceries, in addition to barbershops, traditional bone-setters, small restaurants and bookshops. Tehran in its glorious beauty represented the Eastern city par excellence. Women wore the chador, men strolled peacefully through bazaars, chickens pecked at the grain in the rubbish and cows looked in the grass for watermelon rinds. At the corner of Old Zorkhana Street, men as hefty as Sumo wrestlers appeared.

Haidar Salman's letters proved to be my guide to the city. My task was to find specific information concerning his residence in Tehran, both in the fifties, when he arrived from Moscow for the first time and in the eighties, when he was expelled back to the city as an Iranian subject. Despite this, I was as charmed by the city as he had been. Most amazing for me were the faces of people in that oriental, impoverished neighbourhood, for they seemed to be identical copies of the faces of the Iranian poor as depicted by Sadeq Hedayat in his fiction and the characters of Bozorg Alavi in his novel *Her Eyes*. Our curiosity led us to bookshops, where we found the works of Mahmoud Dowlatabadi, considered the Naguib Mahfouz of Persian literature, and of Forough Farokhzad, who was in many ways similar to Ghada al-Samman. We also came across the plays of Reza Burhani and the works of Saeed Sultanpour, who was executed by Khomeini and whose banned books were only released after the latter's death.

The streets of south Tehran were teeming that day. Faris suggested that we dine at Khanzad restaurant, where Hekmat Aziz had worked, and from there head north. The restaurant stood on Vali Al-Asr Street, which, in his letters from the fifties, Haidar Salman had called Pahlavi Street. The street was, as he had described it, extremely long. It stretched as far as the eye could see, from the south of Tehran to its north. Along the sides of the street were ancient Qajar trees with their huge trunks, as well as modern buildings, hotels, museums, cafés and restaurants. Women's attire ranged from the chador in the south to Western clothes in the north, where they paraded with their colourful headscarves, jeans and high boots, and dragged little puppies by gold chains around their necks. The restaurant occupied the wide pavement of a street that was flanked by ancient trees. Dewdrops trickled from the leaves onto the white stones, and grass sprouted from the cracks in the pavement.

As we sat at a table outside, we felt the cold breeze blowing. At that moment, a blonde woman of about thirty walked past, wearing a loose scarf on her head and a pair of tight jeans. A police car suddenly stopped beside her. A bearded policeman and a policewoman in a chador got out. A heated discussion ensued among the three of them. The woman spoke loudly to the policeman. The policewoman came up to her and tried to drag her into the car, but the woman deflected her and screamed. Then, all of a sudden, she turned around and tried to run. The policewoman, however, took hold of her and, with the help of the policeman, dragged her by force into the car, slamming the door shut.

The north of Tehran was completely different. There were posh hotels, foreign restaurants and modern villas, which were hidden by walls and surrounded by large gardens that reflected

166

extraordinary wealth. Their inhabitants were Iranian technocrats, high-ranking state officials, wealthy merchants, businessmen, engineers, doctors, writers and publishers, who were constantly travelling to the United States and Europe. In this area the women didn't wear the chador at all, but went about in full makeup and elegant clothes.

We took rooms at the Siren Hotel. As soon as we'd dropped off our suitcases, we rushed out, took a cab and headed for the city centre. We wanted to visit the grand bazaar because a man there called Bahzad had been connected with Haidar Salman and his father-in-law. At the bazaar, we sat and stared at people's faces until the prayers at the mosque were over. White birds flew in the blue sky and perched on the domes of the great bazaar. The vaulted arcades were lively and vibrant with faces and cheap outfits. The faces of the men were bronzed and wrinkled while those of the women were beautiful as they chatted nonchalantly. Everywhere were religious posters bearing invocations such as 'Ya Fatima', 'Abul Fazl al-Abbas' or 'Ya Hussein'. These were placed on the façades of the shops that sold women's clothes, on the city's public and private transport system, on restaurants and, of course, on mosques and religious schools.

After meeting with many people who'd known Haidar, Tahira, or Ismail al-Tabtabaei, we were sure that he'd married Tahira in Tehran. But when did he go back to Baghdad? Everybody confirmed that it was after the July 1958 revolution, when Abdel Karim Qasim took power in Iraq. But the date of his return remains uncertain. That he was exultant at the Iraqi revolution, which overthrew the king, was clear from a letter he'd sent Farida from Moscow during his trip there with Tahira and Hussein.

Nonetheless, several people categorically affirmed to us during our visit to Baghdad in 2006 that he'd been living in Al-Karradah neighbourhood immediately following the revolution. He'd lived in a beautiful brick house surrounded by a small garden near Saint Raphael church and opposite the nuns' hospital that had been built in the sixties. It was a relatively old house, overlooking the Tigris from the back and Al-Karradah Street from the front. The street, which boasted numerous hotels, nightclubs, bars, book-shops, stores and markets, was fast becoming the most important commercial and cultural centre in Baghdad.

It is clear that during this period Haidar Salman went back to music with a passion. He actually became very famous, especially among the cultured elite, a class that established itself after the revolution. He gave concerts in venues that differed markedly from the halls where he'd performed in the past. His new audiences consisted mainly of middle-class communist families, a group that had supported the revolution and come to prominence during that era. This new class was also radically different from the aristocracy, which had been eradicated by the revolution. It wished to create its own cultural, political and social symbols and to present them as viable alternatives to the former aristocracy. As a result, an important association of artists, comprising sculptors, architects and musicians, was created in support of the revolution.

Accompanied by a large ensemble under the direction of Russian conductor Vladimir Glepov, Haidar Salman gave concerts not only in Baghdad but also in various world capitals, particularly Moscow and Prague. These two cities, which he absolutely loved, represented turning points in his life. It was there that he formed relationships with two musicians. One was Sergei Oistrakh who, together with Kakeh Hameh, accompanied him to the airport in Moscow. The other was Karl Baruch, the Czech composer who later escaped from Prague to New York. Both gave him enormous help in his difficulties, especially by facilitating his correspondence with Farida, for it was not possible for him at that time, or in fact at any other, to send a letter or even a piece of paper from Baghdad to Jerusalem. So he used to send his letters to these two foreign musicians, the Russian and the Czech, and they in turn would forward them to her address in Jerusalem.

A couple of important pieces of news were published in Baghdad's papers. The first, published in *Al-Jumhuriya* in 1960, stated that the composer Haidar Salman had travelled to Moscow for one year to study conducting and composing at the Moscow Conservatory. The second appeared in *Sawt al-Ahrar* in 1961, stating that the leftist composer Haidar Salman had won the Queen of Belgium's violin prize, and the Queen had handed out medals to the winners at a huge celebration.

This proves beyond doubt that Haidar Salman was living a totally new lifestyle during this period. His life was no longer as unsettled as it had been. Nor did he give himself up totally to dancing, partying or endless affairs with beautiful women as he had done in the past. His life had become highly focused and organized. He wrote a letter to Farida dated 1959 in which he mentioned that musical inspiration would often hit him suddenly while in the street, in his car or at the cinema. It would sometimes strike him during heated political discussions with friends and, when he went home, he would note down his ideas. In another more detailed letter, he once spoke of leaving the house one winter morning when it had been pouring with rain, and the silent, empty Nation Square was drenched. Baghdad was looking beautiful with the wet balustrades of its bridges and the sight of coats and umbrellas. When the Baghdad clock struck seven in the morning, he went back to his room, threw off his wet coat, sat by the fireplace and began to compose a piece of music. We naturally don't know the genre of the piece that he composed, particularly because, starting from this period, Haidar Salman underwent a radical political and cultural transformation. Without a doubt, he must have experienced a profound shock, and his general outlook must have been deeply affected. In another letter to Farida, he expressed the feeling that the world around him had changed. It was though he was on an intense inner journey. Pure colours had been replaced by opaque counterparts. A new state of spiritual revelation had overtaken his whole being.

This letter brought to mind the elements of revelation and visionary insight that characterized the second personality of *Tobacco Shop*. I was personally astonished to see his new persona come to life. His complete identification with that character seemed to me almost 'diabolical', for it showed that he had discovered himself almost totally and completely. Through constant training and continued creativity, he was no longer playing a part but had become the new persona.

We also need to discuss the major changes that were happening to him.

It is well known that after the revolution, Haidar Salman began to visit Hekmat Aziz's house on a regular basis. Hekmat was his revolutionary friend that he had got to know at the Khanzad restaurant in Tehran. He'd returned after the revolution and was living in a beautiful house shaded by tall trees in Al-Adhamiyah. Writers and musicians frequently visited him there. Jawad Salim, the famous sculptor, was often there together with his retinue, which in those days was made up of young artists of both genders, fans of his art, the poet Boland al-Haidari, Hussein Murdan, the dancer Afifa Eskandar, the artist Lorna Salim and several musicians including a few Russians who lived in Baghdad after the revolution and who taught music or painting at the musical academies or institutes of fine art. Some were Polish and had immigrated to Iraq during and after World War II. They would all meet at Hekmat Aziz's house, sit near a small fireplace and revel in its seductive warmth. In a state of great euphoria, they would grill chops on this beautiful fire, one at a time. Hekmat's wife, Widad, a Turkmen from the north of Iraq, would offer them glasses of cold beer which they would clink together merrily and noisily. They would eat and drink, totally absorbed in heated discussions and loud laughter. Those meetings generally ended with poetry readings, musical interludes or card games, of which Haidar became very fond.

But life didn't always follow this exciting rhythm. The first year of the revolution was happy to some extent because a decisive victory had been achieved. But the euphoria of victory masked huge atrocities. Haidar Salman might have turned a blind eye to many violent scenes that accompanied the revolution, such as the murder of the young king, the army's shooting of the princesses in the courtyard of Al-Rehab Palace and the lynching and murder of the prime minister. Were these violent scenes so different from the events of the Farhoud that befell the Jews in 1941 and left an indelible mark on the mind of the first character, the keeper of the flocks? Didn't the masses also perpetrate those atrocities?

I can now draw connections between two basic themes. The first is the ongoing influence of his meeting with the Russian conductor who, without really knowing where the country of the young man before him was, advised him to find inspiration in his people. The second is his research into folklore, which started with the numerous comparisons he made between low and high, or classical, art. This was what the Muslim presenter had pointed out, although Haidar Salman was not sure at that time whether the man understood its full meaning and implications or not. And, of course, there was his visit to the Iranian Museum and the letter he wrote about the Shah's portrait, painted by the Andy Warhol.

It's clear that Haidar Salman felt considerable hostility towards the mob, the masses and the populace in general. His aversion was perhaps born out of the public's inability to understand his music. He'd always felt something of a rift between him and the masses. But this hostility grew after the Farhoud, which proved to him that the masses were the prime enemy of everything beautiful. Those who opposed beauty, according to him, stood against all that was life. His attitude towards the masses suddenly changed from indifference to pure enmity, from acceptance to denunciation. How did this happen?

Since the revolution had its own artists, engineers and leaders, the officers also wanted to create a composer for the revolution. Haidar Salman was their first choice. He would be created and presented as a model made wholly in the revolution's laboratory. They made the proposal to him openly. They suggested turning him into the revolution's musician and composer. He thought that the proposal was ridiculous, although he didn't say so, and his refusal of their offer was clear and categorical. Classical music, he believed, couldn't move the masses and was therefore of little use to revolutions. Music that didn't appeal to the base instincts of the populace couldn't possibly work. Revelation and insight, which were part and parcel of the second persona, were far from revolutionary. Classical music was by its very nature indifferent to words, but revolutions depended on them and used them in patriotic songs. The revolutionaries asked him to compose an opera about the people breaking their chains and were willing to send him to the Soviet Union to compose the work. But he didn't like the idea, for he didn't care for the masses, or their history of outbursts, and feared them.

He remained silent for a long time following the departure of Jawad Selim in the company of the painter Nahida al-Said, whom he'd met at the house of his friend Hekmat Aziz. Then one of the people present raised his glass to toast the masses. So they all did, except for the revolution's composer, who refrained from raising his own glass.

Haidar wanted his music to emerge from his inner self and not from external ideas.

Although his ideas at that time were neither coherent nor fully clear, he wanted to mould them into something new. He wanted to compose pieces that people would view in the same way as a woman looking at the living being coming from her womb. He wanted to construct his thoughts in the same way a painter constructed a scene on a blank canvas. Art was taste, first and foremost, and then harmony and proportion. Revolution, in contrast, was the destruction of all harmony. He didn't wish to make a fortune with his music or see admiration in the eyes of ordinary people. He wanted his music to mould people and push them forward. But how?

The revolution naturally focused its entire attention on the masses.

The first year of the revolution represented a total break with the past. But the revolution later followed a different course, with an increased tendency to appeal to the masses. Haidar hated this populist tendency. He feared the masses and regarded them as a source of danger. He was overwhelmed with apprehension every time he saw their faces and bodies moving with a uniformity that obliterated individual distinctions. They moved with tremendous force to destroy everything. That was the cause of his fear of them. During that first year it was not an issue. Only in later years did he begin to sense it. The lines were still too faint to form a complete picture. But matters became clearer bit by bit. A whole new culture emerged, generating a new vocabulary that hadn't existed before. This was what he wrote to Farida: 'There are new slogans such as "Death to mercenaries" and "Death to imperialist collaborators". Everybody here speaks of death and calls for it. Can you imagine that the masses are cheering their leader, Qasim, asking him to "Execute, execute, don't say it's too late"? Post-revolution Baghdad has become a totally different place. The revolution has strengthened populist and vulgar tendencies and the mob's hold on the streets.'

On his return from Moscow, he looked out of the window as the plane banked over the airport. Baghdad seemed no more than an arid stretch of land through which the River Tigris meandered, its waters as muddy as milky tea. Thin green belts encircled the towns, which looked like barracks protected by barbed wire and reddish mud-brick walls. Once the aircraft had finally landed, he made his way across the worn and dusty airport carpet. The walls were plastered with violent slogans and tasteless, vapid pictures. He felt disgusted, offended by the march of ugliness and the hostility to beauty that always accompanies revolutions. It touched him to the quick that mob culture was growing rapidly, and that this would inevitably lead to an explosion of sorts. Pure force had the upper hand on Baghdad's streets. They were full of armed soldiers with yellowish khaki uniforms, trim beards, berets, machineguns and revolvers. Militiamen walked the streets while the masses carried posters demanding that the revolution or the leader be protected, and asking for the execution of secret agents. There were long marches, unbearable heat and endless lines of students, soldiers and workers who clapped rhythmically, shouting out slogans, their faces enraged and excited. There were men and women travelling on buses to greet the leader. The radio stridently urged them all to take to the streets because the revolution was under threat and conspiracies were being hatched all the time.

The revolution, on the other hand, did nothing at all for the people. Houses collapsed amid clouds of reddish-brown dust, while shops, which looked like cubes with their front face missing, were in a miserable condition. The roads were full of potholes and grime was everywhere. Anarchy dominated life in general.

He wrote to Farida: 'Baghdad has turned into a military tribunal handing out death sentences. The leader receives his well-wishers as well as the angry masses, for the revolution is always threatened by many powerful enemies. There have been twenty-three attempts on the leader's life. Military justice is still putting people to death and the number is steadily rising. Things will become more complicated in future if we legitimize the use of arms, for the bullets will never stop.'

Just as Haidar had discovered *Tobacco Shop* through Karl Baruch, it was through Sergei Oistrakh that he came upon the idea of kitsch.

Haidar Salman saw a congruence between kitsch art, which is

a vulgar form, and political kitsch, which portrayed Qasim, the leader, in gaudy colours. He was shown sitting with a stern expression, or with a smile on his face or wearing his military beret. Photographs showed him from different perspectives: in profile or portrait, full-length or three-quarters. The leader alone embodied post-revolutionary existence. Life was portrayed in terms of kitsch, with tasteless, fiery colours representing the revolution crushing its enemies.

After the revolution, the Folkloric Art Society was set up, ushering in a new artistic movement in Baghdad. It aimed at representing life in positive, upbeat terms, to represent the changes that hadn't happened because the enemies of the revolution did not want change. The reality of the streets exposed this as a lie. They were narrow, crowded and suffocating. Buses tooted incessantly amid the throngs of the tired and angry masses. Emaciated horses pulled their poor carts while lines of donkeys carried the tatty furniture of immigrants from the countryside to the city. Black-clad, barefoot women carried huge bundles on their heads, and porters tied ropes around their waists to indicate their willingness to carry any loads. Dirty, barefoot children were assailed by flies.

The letter that Haidar sent to Farida, dated 1 November 1962, was brief and clear. He couldn't specify exactly what he wanted, but he felt that he was in mortal danger. His wife Tahira was in Moscow for medical treatment. He wrote to Farida that Tahira was always pale, thin and in very poor health. His son Hussein went to Saint Joseph's School in Al-Alweya. He spoke incessantly about his wife's illness but never about their relationship. His real interests at the time, as his letters indicate, were music and politics.

He believed that the decline in artistic and aesthetic taste had left a huge mark on politics and vice versa.

Haidar Salman's family life wasn't in the best of shape, for his relationship with Tahira was vague and undefined. Many rumours linked him with the painter Nahida al-Said, who was introduced to him by Jawad Selim who was visiting Hekmat Aziz. Selim came to know Aziz in Tehran and would always visit him at his house in Al-Adhamiya.

Selim was the one who built the Freedom Memorial as an outcome of the revolution. The brilliant sculptor had created this memorial in the shape a Sumerian cylinder seal. But the man who wished to be the revolution's architect created its base and the frieze in the form of a populist poster. That was why Haidar Salman loathed the memorial so much. He often argued about it with Nahida. Nevertheless, he frequently mentioned Nahida al-Said and her ideas in his letters to Farida. What was it that attracted him to the painter's ideas so much?

He wrote to Farida that he'd recently made the acquaintance of a young woman painter. The young, pretty woman caused a drastic change in Haidar's outlook. At least he found in her vision and ideas some consolation for his music. Her paintings didn't tackle the populist, folkloric and patriotic themes that were so popular in those days. Rather, they were informed by universal concerns and represented absolute subjectivity and idealism. Such traits were abhorred then, because it was generally accepted that art shouldn't be separated from life. Art, according to this view, came close to political propaganda. It had the function of re-examining existing tradition in order to create new modes of expression. This was what Jawad Selim and his school did.

The US-educated young woman, Nahida al-Said, was only looking for intellectual, emotional and intuitive forms and not for any ideological meaning or content. This was what attracted Haidar to her and what he needed at that time, although he couldn't articulate it. He refused to express stereotypical images of people or realistic events through his music, although he believed that the grounded and spiritual aspect of music could elevate people and enhance their intuitive capacity. Music was able to unite and refine people, to urge them to work hard and respond to the instinctive beauty within their souls. He believed that it was for art to eradicate ugliness and introduce beauty to the world. It replaced the anarchy of clashing colours and discordant rhythms with harmonious melodies that embodied absolute beauty.

But who among the artists or any others was listening to him at the time? In fact, very few of his friends paid much attention to such ideas. There was heated debate in the newspapers and magazines as to whether art should exist for its own sake or for society's benefit. Despite the vulgarity and crudity of the arguments, everybody accused Haidar of falling prey to the influence of bourgeois aesthetics. This was a serious charge at that time. He felt truly lonely and alienated. Almost every day he would leave his house and walk Baghdad's streets with his hands in his pockets, wondering if there was anything uglier than the environment surrounding him or more repellent than the prevalent vogue of political and folkloric kitsch. Was there anything more sordid or distasteful? As soon as any discussions started, he would burst out in their faces. He believed that kitsch would produce greater violence in society. Lines, dots, surfaces and three-dimensional forms would disappear and be replaced by corpses left hanging in public. The people, who had been encouraged to be resentful, with strident colours, vulgar music and loud anthems, would become a hugely destructive force that might be impossible to reverse.

Haidar's friends in turn would flare up in his face as they defended the people's art and the crowds, except for Nahida. Her ideas were close to his and she often defended the views he expressed at the meetings held at Hekmat Aziz's house.

It was probably Nahida al-Said's defence of his views that attracted him to her. A new sensation was impelling him. As she approached him with her pure, fair complexion, her clear eyes and slim arms, he was in flames. Looking into her eyes or smelling her scent, he was overcome with both terror and infatuation. He felt completely numb in front of her. Were they involved in a relationship at that time?

All the evidence points to the fact that the composer spent most of his day at her apartment. He also spent most of his nights with her when his wife Tahira travelled to Moscow. The only surviving piece of evidence for this relationship is the painting that she produced of the composer. He is completely naked and holding his violin in his arms like a woman. The warm colours and technique of the painting represent the playing of music as a kind of sexual encounter. These were naturally Haidar Salman's views of music. In one of his letters to Farida, he described the half-naked Nahida painting in her studio while he lay on the couch drinking vodka.

Almost everyone knew of their affair. Haidar Salman even felt that his sick wife tolerated the relationship. This was what most of the people that we met confirmed, particularly those who knew the two of them at that time. But what we were looking for was

179

the reason behind Haidar's admiration for Nahida al-Said. Was he attracted to her anti-revolutionary ideas or the way she was influenced, like him, by bourgeois aesthetics? In fact, all events point to differences in their views regarding the revolution. All those whom we asked about Nahida al-Said and her life confirmed that to some extent she believed in the revolution. But her thoughts were vague and inconsistent (incidentally, Nahida al-Said was a committed communist). Haidar's own ideas were clear. In his view, revolution destroyed harmony. It was a violent blow that disturbed peace and serenity. No fruitful or consistent change could possibly happen in the midst of overriding chaos. He thought of revolution as the serum to cure us of a minor illness. Instead, it destroyed the harmony between our bodies and nature, leaving our bodies weak and exhausted. We should point out, however, that Haidar Salman never completely broke with the Communist Party, unlike Al-Sayyab, who abandoned the Party altogether and attacked it. The Party preferred at that time to keep Haidar within reach, even when his ideological stand was different from theirs. That was deemed much safer than engaging in a headlong confrontation with him, as happened with Badr Shaker al-Sayyab, who opened fire on the Party and published a series of articles entitled 'I was a communist'.

Did Haidar Salman intuitively understand certain things that others didn't? The events of the evening preceding the 1963 coup suggest that he did. All the guests who attended Hekmat Aziz's party at his house in Al-Adhamiya that night agreed that Haidar's behaviour was very strange. It was February and the cold had descended on the wet trees in the garden, while the warmth of the living room inside the house made the artists who were sitting in a circle around the fireplace woozy. None of those who were present knew anything about what the next day would bring. Haidar stood near the fireguard with a glass in his hand, while Nahida al-Said stood beside him, also drinking. When he came too close to her, a horrified scream flew out from Nahida's mouth as he flung the wine at her face and clothes.

There was a blazing row between Nahida and Haidar, which disturbed all the guests. In a little while, at the request of Hekmat and his wife Widad, they both went upstairs to resolve their problems quietly. Almost an hour later, a tearful Nahida ran down the stairs, but none of the guests were aware of her leaving until she slammed the front door behind her. When he rejoined his friends Haidar was totally drunk. Everybody was in high spirits that night. They roasted lamb cutlets on the fire, sang loudly and danced; at one table, there was a card game going on. Then Haidar screamed. It was hard for those present to understand the meaning of this scream until he told them that Baghdad stood on the edge of a precipice: a volcano of burning lava was erupting and the city was concealing a new weapon, ready for a new day and a new era.

So how did Haidar Salman know about the coup? Who told him that the following day would usher in a huge turning point in the history of the country and that there would be an unstoppable eruption? Did Haidar have any contacts with the insurgents? That was impossible. Everyone who knew him confirmed that his name was on the list of people to be liquidated by the coup.

Nevertheless, Haidar Salman awoke the next day to the clarion call of the coup. He had a hangover and a splitting headache. He was stunned to see the tanks of the nationalists and the Baathists on the streets. He trembled to see the populist trend in Baghdad at its most extreme. The winter sun was casting its slanting rays on the wall opposite, and a deathly hush had filled the house. Tahira was still in Moscow and Hussein was with his grandfather, Ismail al-Tabtabaei. At that moment, Haidar felt a vague anxiety. He had a strong sense of déjà vu as horrific images passed through his head. The country he was longing to return to reminded him once again of the events of 1941 when he was a child.

The phone rang. He ran to pick up the receiver. Hekmat's voice came over the line, warning him against staying in Baghdad, for the nationalists and the Baathists had issued statements vowing to crush all communists. Orders were given to the youngsters carrying machine guns and wearing National Guard armbands to kill and hang the communists. He hung up, his hand trembling. He couldn't get any detailed information from Hekmat because the whole country was under curfew. What he could hear was the sound of bullets going from house to house and street to street. Two images haunted his mind and would not be dispelled. He saw Nahida's face, tearful at his behaviour the previous night, and he saw her coming out of the bathroom, wrapped in a towel. As she changed her clothes, he looked at her beautiful body, totally entranced by its grace and firm roundness.

The phone in the corridor rang. He raced to it, his heart beating fast. It was Ismail al-Tabtabaei informing him that he had sent him a car to take him away from Baghdad for his own safety. His name was on the list of communists to be liquidated that was being distributed by the insurgents. He felt disturbed and shaken by all the terrifying images around him. He heard constant screams and shouts, and he could not stop trembling and moaning. It was almost ironic that the insurgents wanted him dead while a day earlier he'd been criticising the revolution. The whole thing had no connection with ideologies or ideas, but only with bloodlust and mob mentality. He wasn't wide of the mark, for as soon as he arrived at his father-in-law's house, he heard of the massacres and violence that was being carried out against the communists. On his way, he saw military personnel leading blindfolded, handcuffed young men in pyjamas. They were taking them on large trucks out to the desert where they would be executed and buried. After darkness fell, he found Ismail al-Tabtabaei standing in front of the door. 'Haidar,' he said, 'I know about your affair with that artist!' He spoke in a firm, unwavering voice as he looked downwards.

His father-in-law pointed to a black Chevrolet that was standing outside the house. A bald chauffeur wearing glasses stood beside the car. A second tall, dark man put Hussein in the back, while Haidar sat in the front. The car headed to Tehran in the darkness of the night.

Why did Ismail make this remark to Haidar at that particular moment? Ought he not to have mentioned it at another time and place? Why did he make it clear that he had known all about the affair with Nahida al-Said and had kept quiet about it? Although he could have easily left Haidar to his fate, he had reached out and saved him from the insurgents' bullets. Did that important merchant who had supported the left and was well-connected with government circles always behave in such a way or was this behaviour inconsistent? If Ismail was simple, decent and tolerant with his daughter, was he the same with other people?

In his childhood, Ismail al-Tabtabaei had tasted all kinds of cruelty and humiliation. His life history provides ample evidence of this. These inconsistencies were the result of a confused, and also inconsistent, upbringing. His father had been a poor Arab from the Al-Mukhayam neighbourhood of Karbala. He had worked as a market porter for Iranian merchants at Bab al-Murad. His mother was from a very wealthy Iranian family in Karbala market. That was Ismail's first scar. He felt humiliated and disgraced by his father. At the same time, he was excessively proud and boastful of his mother's elevated origins. He tried to compensate for this conflicting and confused background through his work. He worked hard and doggedly despite all the frustrations that led him to a few failed attempts at suicide. As a result, he immigrated to Iran to find work at the bazaar, but came back equally frustrated when no merchant at the Tehran bazaar in those days was willing to employ a poor Arab living on aubergines. It is clear that his sense of superiority towards others was the result of the ethnic marginalization he had suffered during his stay in Iran. In his dealings with women he became an example of selfishness, emotional tyranny and sadism. His torture of his wife Jehan, Tahira's mother, led to her death after she had given him his sickly daughter. He loved his daughter in a humiliating, confused way that made him lead a life full of guilt, regret and self-torture. Not because she was the only thing he loved in life, but because he constantly felt that he was the cause of her tragedy, particularly after the death of her mother.

Jehan, his first wife, had come from a well-known, wealthy family of traders who worked at Al-Isterbadi market in Al-Kazemeya. She had got to know him when he was working as an accountant for her uncle. From that time, he had shown a unique competence in his work. She had fallen in love with him and written him letters that overflowed with love. She defied her family's will by marrying him. Their relationship, however, soon deteriorated because of Ismail's complex and contradictory personality, for he was both loving and full of hate and spite. He was the helpful, generous man as well as the person who sometimes cut a worker's wages just to degrade and humiliate him. He was the civilized intellectual who was at the same time attracted to all kinds of filth. On the political level, he symbolised all contradictions. He was a wealthy merchant who vehemently supported socialism against the comparador class in the third world. In his capacity as a red millionaire, he had strong connections with important political personalities in the socialist states. But at the same time, he had equally strong connections with capitalists known for their contacts with Western intelligence agencies. The same contradiction was clear in his relationship with his wife, Jehan, whom he undoubtedly loved but who, at the same time, he abused and scolded through no fault of her own. He wanted her to be respected by people but at the same time he also wished to humiliate her. He was bent on taking revenge for the old and forgotten abuses he had suffered in the past.

Jehan was therefore always confused and tense in front of him, for she had no idea how to deal with him. But she later understood that the man was truly sick, and not just with her. He was a bundle of contradictions and fantasies. Jehan later learned that her respectable husband liked to sleep with prostitutes and had never felt that sex was in any way connected with love. Only prostitutes could arouse him. During this period, Ismail made the acquaintance of an Armenian prostitute in Al-Karkh called Beatrice. She found happiness in being his slave and in submitting to his whims and his desire to dominate. In turn, he found enhanced erotic pleasure in her submissiveness. The things he loved most about her were her stupidity, her sensuality and her lust for sex, drink and food. For him she represented pure carnal pleasure. Everybody knew that he used to beat her so hard that his hands would be bruised. The following day, Beatrice would walk on the street with the cuts and bruises he had inflicted on her. She became pregnant several times and each time he asked her with the utmost indifference to have an abortion.

Hurting Beatrice wasn't enough for Ismail. He also went to great lengths to wound his wife, Jehan, by letting her know of his relationship with the Armenian prostitute. He made fun of her and humiliated her in front of his guests. He even threatened to leave her for the whore. At night, though, he cried at her feet and implored her like a child to comfort him.

So much for Ismail, Haidar Salman's father-in-law, and his diverse affairs and contradictions. Were the people around him not right, then, to wonder where Haidar Salman had learned of the date of the coup? Could Ismail have been the source of the warning? Due to his wide contacts with merchants related to various international intelligence agencies, he must have known of the date of the coup. Or we could say that Haidar, with his marked analytical abilities, had simply predicted the event? He had always stated that if we gave legitimacy to arms, the bloodshed would not stop. Could we say also that the second character in *Tobacco Shop* had outstanding intuitive abilities?

Haidar Salman was once again in Tehran.

He couldn't stay long inside the stone house with its wooden façade and poplar trees. He couldn't stay in the beautiful house located in north Tehran, where he'd met Tahira for the first time a few years earlier. It was bitterly cold on that February day. Tehran was completely covered with snow and he felt moody and confused. What could he possibly do? At noon, Tahira called him.

Her faint, sickly voice entreated him to travel to Moscow. She seemed to be in the depths of desperation as her tone of voice, her tears and entreaties indicated. She was overwhelmed by despair because she hadn't received any reassuring letters from him. 'You didn't even call me when you arrived in Tehran,' she complained tearfully.

'Please forgive me. The events of the coup left me no time to call.'

No excuses could possibly convince her. She sobbed and sobbed, reproaching him for remaining in the country after the outbreak of anarchy. She begged him to join her in Moscow.

Moscow, he felt, would mean a real release from the state of depression into which he had sunk during the past few days. It would free him from the fear of death and torture, and would take him back to music, which brought so much joy and happiness to his heart. All he wanted to know at that moment was news of Nahida al-Said, who he was so anxious about. His hands and lips trembled with apprehension for her. But it was impossible for him to receive detailed news in Tehran. He spent two weeks filling in paperwork for his trip to Moscow, but because there were no direct flights from Tehran to Moscow on account of the Shah's close ties with the West, he had to go via Prague or Budapest. There was also the SAVAK's strict monitoring of the Iraqis living in Tehran, particularly those arriving after the coup. But finally he managed to evade them and left for Moscow, taking Hussein with him.

His wife trembled with joy as she stood wrapped in her fur coat. Her face was sallow and her body emaciated. As soon as she set eyes on her family, she cried out loud. The news from Baghdad had talked of bloodbaths.

Haidar took off his woollen coat and tossed it on the chair

opposite. He dialled Kakeh Hameh's number. The latter's voice sounded faint over the line, as though he were a prisoner. Kakeh Hameh told him that Nahida al-Said had been hanged at the hands of the insurgents. Hekmat Aziz and his wife had also been murdered on the escape route to Basra. Haidar's hand shook so much that he dropped the receiver. He cupped his hands to his face and broke into bitter tears.

He wrote the following passage to Farida: 'With the help of the Tudeh Party, dozens of people managed to slip across the border with Iran into Soviet territory. Some of those who tried to enter the Soviet Union via the Caspian Sea died from the storms that capsized their boats. It's worth noting that some Iranian opposition organizations, realizing the nature of the coup, offered to shelter the fugitives. These included the Melli Iran Party, which was nationalist and was part of the National Front led by the late nationalist leader Dr Mohammad Mosaddegh.'

From Moscow, Haidar wrote a long and significant letter to Farida. This was dated 23 March 1963, that is, more than a month after his escape from Iraq. He mentioned many details and referred to several important events. He believed that his views on the people, the rabble, on populism, mob mentality, revolution and the culture of coups had been proven correct by the latest coup and by the insurgents themselves. In other words, one coup engendered another, which in turn caused yet another, ad infinitum. Then he described in great detail the frightful events, including the image of the murdered leader lying on the floor of the broadcasting building, dressed in the same yellowish khaki suit and looking exactly the same as the day Haidar had seen him walking among the frenzied masses who crowded around his car to greet him.

'The faces were distorted by love and the mouths gaped open repulsively; the same faces that were disfigured by anger and indignation as they murdered, lynched and hanged in the name of the new revolution.'

One of the puzzling facts of Haidar Salman's life was that Tahira and Hussein returned to Baghdad while he stayed on in Moscow. Three months after his arrival, Tahira returned with her son to the house in Al-Karradah. According to Kakeh Hameh, it was her father, Ismail, who asked her to go back to Baghdad. In the meantime, Haidar Salman spent all his time developing his musical skills, composing the symphony he'd been dreaming of and giving concerts in Moscow and the other republics. He played in a small music institute near his apartment. He followed a strict regime of practice that extended from the early morning until the evening. By working like a slave, he tried to avoid thinking about anything. He felt utterly devastated by the colossal events that were taking place, especially the image of Nahida al-Said's hanging, which he couldn't banish from his mind.

One day, the fat, middle-aged, Russian director of the institute stopped him in the middle of the corridor. 'Wouldn't it be better Mr Haidar,' she said, 'if you practised the more technically challenging works of Schönberg?' To this he had no response, for he didn't care whose music he played. He played incessantly and unthinkingly, without paying much attention to the composer. True, he developed his skills and prepared for a number of concerts in Moscow and elsewhere. But he was a fugitive from the events around him, which he could neither comprehend nor decipher. Work was a form of escape from the images that haunted him. One day, he left early to go home. He walked slowly out of the building, buffeted by the wind. A large puddle left from the previous night's heavy rain stood in his way. He skipped over it to avoid stepping in, without looking at the faces of the men and women coming from the building. He saw only their muddy boots, shabby trousers and wet coats. Before reaching the door to his apartment, he stopped in his tracks and lifted his head. The first phrase of the composition he wished to create leapt into his mind. Henceforth, he realized that he was looking for an untraditional form and was trying to avoid using old forms such as the sonata. He was looking to recombine the raw material of melody to inspire listeners and transport them to broader horizons. He was looking for an orchestral texture that was colourful and a harmonic language that was unique, employing counterpoint as an essential base in the harmonic structure, far from traditional forms.

On 25 August 1964, he began laying out the plan for his first composition. He'd already found a job at the Tchaikovsky Conservatory in Moscow, and was working from morning till noon. Instead of going home directly after work, he would go to the top of the hill, where lush, shady trees grew beside the walls of an ancient fort surrounded by large gardens. He lay down on the thick grass beneath the branches of poplar trees, enjoying the peaceful atmosphere and the cool breeze. He meditated and gazed at the beautiful houses that were ranged in neat rows. It was from this spot that he began to compose his own musical pieces. He was inspired to write a concerto that would start with an improvised melody (a cadenza) and would use the full orchestra, especially the string section. He jumped to his feet and went down the hill, as the first tunes took shape in his head. He walked quickly as he listened to the distant melodies. Immediately, while still on the street, he began to write down the notes. But when he arrived back home, he felt too exhausted to continue. After taking a short nap, he woke up and began to work on the technical aspect of the concerto. He sat at the table thinking. He thought first of violin techniques but then realized that the strings could support the percussion instruments. So he began with the latter.

He told himself that the cadenza could replace the exposition of traditional works. It could be used to introduce new elements that would be delicate and tender. It could be created out of the harmony that distinguished Arab music. He felt elated as he discovered this world. He felt able to uncover the capabilities of the violin, this powerful instrument that was so close to the human voice, while preserving at the same time the character of Arab music.

He couldn't banish the idea of linking contemporary art with traditional forms, perhaps because the idea of preserving and using the heritage was so strong in Iraqi art. He had become firmly convinced of this view years earlier, after a conversation with the sculptor Jawad Selim.

As they sat at a wooden table in the Waqwaq café that was established by Boland al-Haidari and Hussein Murdan in Al-Adhamiya, he heard Franz Liszt's Concerto No. 1, which he loved so much. They each had a cup of coffee as they sat opposite each other. Jawad Selim, with his handsome face, sharp eyes and thick, black beard, told him in a low voice, 'You can't possibly introduce anything new without getting inspiration from the past.'

Jawad Selim seemed like a traveller of old, sailing across the oceans of the Sumerian and Assyrian heritage in order to produce novel ideas. Al-Sayyab was experimenting with the two-thousand-year-old metres of Arabic poetry in order to make them compatible with the rhythms of modern life. So Haidar Salman diligently searched Arab and Islamic traditions. He wanted Arabic music to seep into Western classical music as stealthily and quietly as sand.

'Stealthily and imperceptibly,' he said to himself.

Was he looking for a moment of absence in his music?

There was no doubt about it. He wanted Arab culture to be present in Western or classical music. As he composed his pieces, he felt his fingers grow hot with the spiritual warmth of the desert. When he was in Europe, he felt that musical notes soared high like butterflies fluttering in the depths of the desert. He wanted melodies that would awaken the phantom of fertility in the blazing heat of noon. He wanted to produce music that was like the birth of creation and the trembling of life's genesis.

Haidar tried to make music achieve the extraordinary feat of submitting the soul to artistic experience. He did not believe in heroism, only in art, for art was the search for goodness. Was moral virtue really capable of solving society's problems? Was there a radical difference between morality and art?

He believed that art was virtue itself. He had no idea that this view would later collapse in Baghdad, under the destructive pressure of the people. He had innumerable questions, because he wanted his artistry to lead to the good of humanity. He looked for epicurean pleasure in music, like the second character in *Tobacco Shop*. He felt that he was creating something important, that creativity was for him a mystical act, a deep conviction that the work he was creating had a spiritual dimension.

Could he possibly deny the presence of a spiritual force in the work of art? Not at all. Haidar felt that he was embarking on the creation of something palpable, something that drew its power from the music of the universe. At the beginning, he felt drawn to abstractions that were, nonetheless, strongly present and palpable. This was faith, no doubt. It was a belief that reconciled the different religions inside him: Judaism, which he had absorbed as a child, Christianity, which had seeped into his soul through classical music, and Islam, which became part and parcel of his inner self after his marriage to Tahira. God was One, although He appeared in various texts.

Haidar rejected Ada's materialist interpretations of music. As they sat on the balcony of her house in spring, watching the trees change colour, he told her that he was trying to reconcile the various strands and tonalities of the three religions. He saw the presence of sand everywhere, the changes of colour and of natural phenomena. This was immortality itself. A piece of music represented partial immortality while music in total represented complete eternity.

He spent his evenings at the house of the Russian pianist, Ada Brunstein, located on a narrow street behind the Bolshoi Theatre. She had a large room on the upper floor, where a sofa overlooked the street, flanked by small windows that were permanently open. On the opposite side was a large window that overlooked the dense garden. Ada sat cross-legged on a second sofa to the left. On the mantelpiece above the fire stood a nightlight and a vodka bottle. Ada was a petite, blonde woman with full lips and a short nose. She spoke softly and was very happy with him. A world-famous virtuoso pianist, Ada was also cultured and fluent in several European languages. She would receive Moscow's most important writers in her house, and it was through her that Haidar became acquainted with many of them.

As for how Haidar came to know Ada Brunstein, we only have

the account given by the Czech violinist Karl Baruch in his memoirs. He said that Haidar Salman had taken a cruise on the Baltic Sea. On the same boat was Sergei Oistrakh's son with his pregnant girlfriend. After the son had disembarked, it became known that the girlfriend had run away with the Iraqi composer, Haidar Salman. The girlfriend was the pianist Ada Brunstein.

So Ada Brunstein was Haidar Salman's new girlfriend. But did she have anything to do with his trip to Paris? That was something we could never ascertain. It was a detail missing from all his letters. Nor did Farida ever comment on it. But all events indicate that Haidar and Ada were closely attached at that time.

Why wasn't Haidar Salman a faithful husband? He never once wrote about this, as though it were natural to be married and also have mistresses. Throughout his life he experimented with these relationships and sought to avoid unhappy endings. This was predicted by the character of Ricardo Reis in Pessoa's collection *Tobacco Shop*.

But why didn't the disgraceful incident on the boat affect his relationship with Sergei Oistrakh? That was something we never discovered either, as the man died in 1990. We couldn't get through to any of his family members either.

Whatever the case, Haidar's relationship with the pianist was common knowledge. In 1965 he travelled with her to Paris, where he took part in the Jacques Thibaud competition. It was his first performance in front of a Western audience – most of his concerts in previous years had been in front of Russian audiences.

On a large stage in Paris, Haidar Salman stood in total darkness except for the spotlight above him. The large audience appeared to him only as ghosts. After breathing deeply, hc closed his eyes and rested his bow gently on the strings. As the music soared, he felt the sounds flowing savagely but serenely along with the streaming of his soul. It rose above the wilderness and connected intimately with the Creator, expressing His true relationship with all creatures. Haidar felt that music was to be found in savage isolation while the soul grew within and rose higher and higher. As soon as the music stopped, he heard the applause in the hall. The lights came on and he could see the audience offering a standing ovation. Among those who applauding was the director of the Carnegie Hall, who later invited him to travel to New York and take part in the Leventritt Competition.

He wrote to Farida from Paris:

'I don't really know, but this is my first encounter with the Western world. The East carries a great symbolic legacy that I sense as it moves across all time periods. I wished to play music in an Eastern manner. You may find this ridiculous and you may laugh at my statement, but I cannot ignore a dynamic culture whose dimensions of meaning and content reach deep into my soul. When I play music, it's as if I'm producing colours, clear lovely colours, for I understand the playing of music in terms of serenity and light. The moment I place my bow on the strings, I feel the colours emerge from the sounds.

'When the bright light of the sun is present, nothing can possibly be absent. I kept playing music in this cold, bleak environment until the audience could feel the brightness of sunny summer days in Baghdad. That was why the audience clapped and clapped.'

Did Haidar Salman visit Baghdad between 1963 and 1967? The evidence indicates that he lived most of those years in Moscow. The reason was his fear of the political regime in Baghdad. He might have visited his family from time to time. But he always used his work at the Tchaikovsky Conservatory and his composing as excuses to stay in Moscow. Tahira, accompanied by their son, Hussein, went to Moscow from time to time, either for medical treatment or to spend the summer with him. His affair with Ada, however, remained a mysterious matter, even to those closest to him. Nobody could confirm or deny it. But why did he return to Baghdad in 1967?

Was it because his work at the Tchaikovsky Conservatory came to an end? Was it because his affair with Ada had lost its spark? Or was it the 1967 War, which took place when he was playing in New York?

His visit to New York was a great opportunity for him. He played at one of the grandest halls of the great city, with its famous Statue of Liberty looking out over the ocean and the amazing Brooklyn Bridge. He stayed in the Hudson neighbourhood, the artists' quarter. Ada always accompanied him when he walked the streets. For the first time they felt free. It was New York. He gazed at the deep darkness of the night, which was broken only by the lights emanating from hotels and huge buildings. He was charmed by the city. With its skyscrapers, its wide, crowded streets, its suspension bridges and the ships that conquered its ocean, New York seemed the total opposite of Moscow. The artists' quarter where he lived was full of concert halls that were so different from those in Moscow. There were many other differences as well, but the real surprise came when the *New York Times*, commenting on his visit, wrote the following: 'This communist did not hide his deep admiration of America.'

Carnegie Hall captivated him, with its historic building shaped like a library. He watched people as they crossed the large court in their elegant clothes as though they were living in a different era, as though they had stepped out of the nineteenth century. The building had two round towers, a thick surrounding wall and Gothic stone windows. He stood there gazing meditatively at the court and the silent walls. From the window, his gaze fell on the icon of the Virgin Mary hanging on the wall, her forehead hidden in the darkness and her dreamy eyes lit by lamplight. The New York Philharmonic asked him to join them for a concert in this great hall. It was by pure coincidence that his concert was scheduled for 7 June 1967.

All the evidence suggests that Haidar Salman refused to play while the Israeli forces continued to invade Arab territories. He was so angry that he was shivering all over. His confused state didn't prevent him from contacting the director of the Hall to cancel the concert. Instead of going back to Moscow, he returned to Iraq while Ada returned to Moscow.

He spent the year after his return from New York in near total isolation, meeting no one. Instead of mixing with people, working in public places or meeting friends, he began to develop in his mind a new type of Sufi music. He hardly left his house on Al-Bolskhana Street in Al-Karradah in Baghdad. He would always sit near the large window, gazing at the verdant garden and watching the changing of the seasons. A kind of deep spiritual mood had taken hold of his soul. At that time, he was looking for a type of music that could not be heard and that he tried to grasp in the growth of trees and flowers. He was looking for a soft music that arose from these life forms that changed and transformed with the seasons. We can only understand his state in terms of a mystical mixture of Islam and Kabbalah. He felt that Mendelssohnian music was invading him little by little, making his soul expand and grow larger and larger. His playing made rapid progress

During this period, he sent Farida a long letter at the end of which he wrote: 'Through music I can discover places. I can see the colours of dimension and depth. Music liberates me from fear and takes me to the mysterious and obscure recesses of life. With music I get rid of the body's filth. But, Farida, what is the body but a return to primary elements and the intense desire for salvation ...'

He broke up with Ada Brunstein and spent a difficult year regretting what he'd done to his friend Sergei Oistrakh's son. He sent Oistrakh long letters expressing his regret for having made the gravest mistake of his life and asking for his forgiveness. In the midst of this emotional fever of regrets, he was swept off his feet by another affair with an Armenian cellist at the National Symphony Orchestra in Baghdad. In the middle of his involvement in this affair came the 1968 coup, which put an end to the second character, that of the protected man, and paved the way for the third character, that of the tobacco keeper. Only one year after his return to Baghdad from New York, he was witness to another military coup. He was forty-two at the time. He had some awful moments when Tahira woke him, her face pallid and sallow, telling him in a hoarse voice about the coup. Nobody knows whether or not Haidar Salman thought then of fleeing Baghdad as he had done in the earlier coup. He told Farida that the new coup brought back the spectre of death and the ritual of killing in a renewed form. Coups were always accompanied by a series of public executions on account of alleged conspiracies. It was all reminiscent of the savagery of the Middle Ages. There were anthems and victory songs, men in white shirts hanging by the neck, their bodies dangling in the air, while families sat at their feet feasting as if celebrating a national wedding. In one of his letters in 1969, he described to Farida how he'd watched a woman advance to the middle of the park, stop in front of the corpses dangling in the air and tie up her hair with an elastic band. She'd looked gleefully at the men hanging from the ropes. He'd observed her thick, crimson lips and her high cheekbones, and was stunned to see her erotic pleasure at the sight of such murder and death.

So what was his maxim at that time? It was 'Have a light head, and a lighter foot. Live your life with the person you love and enjoy the shit and the kitsch'. It accurately described his affair with the Armenian musician, which was mysterious in every sense of the word and which nobody knew anything about. Despite his life having taken a new turn at that time, events brought him back to earth whenever he climbed too high. His contacts with the world were largely pale and colourless. The images of his wife and son began to fade slowly while his interest in music grew. Was he still working on the great symphony that he had dreamed of composing since he'd stood as a fifteen-year old lad in front of the Russian conductor? Was he still thinking of the work he wished to compose after his escape to Moscow?

All those questions were drowned in the Iranian Revolution that changed the course of his life once and for all.

It would be appropriate for us to mention Tahira's uncle, who was intimately connected with this narrative. His name was Saleh and he was in the habit of visiting their house almost every week to see Tahira. He had a dark complexion and deep, dark eyes. He wore glasses with black plastic frames and his beard was sparse. He buttoned his shirt at the collar but never wore a tie. His hair was also unique, for he left a black lock of hair falling over his forehead. His jacket was always too broad. He was a Muslim intellectual in the Shia tradition. He read books by theologians such as the Iranian thinker Ali Shariati and Mohammad Baqir al-Sadr.

Saleh wasn't a fanatic in any sense, but was fairly broad-minded. He had a girlfriend at university and didn't care whether Tahira wore the veil or not. But the real turning point in his life came when the Iranian Revolution took place. He felt ecstatic that he was no longer the humble individual talking reasonably about the revolution to come. The revolution, he said, was the avalanche that would demolish everything, the earthquake that would shake the whole earth to its foundation. It promised salvation for the nation and declared the appearance of the Imam. It predicted the dawning of the Islamic age of the Caliphate, Saleh screamed at the top of his voice. The promise had finally been fulfilled. Haidar tried to talk rationally to Saleh. He had no argument with the revolution, but he was terrified by the popular mood and by the mass psychology, which was at its peak. Sickly Tahira did not see Haidar's anger those days as he read the papers or followed the news of the revolution on television. But he was angry. He was so angry that he trembled when he saw the crowds on the streets. On their faces he detected a loss of individuality that happened only in traumatic situations. Hundreds of people who were essentially different from each other suddenly became copies of each other, clones. Their wild gestures and absurd shouts were indistinguishable. He stared at the escalating frenzy of the masses. Although he understood the causes of popular anger and the state of political, social and economic turmoil in Iran, he hated mass hysteria. He hated the agitation that took hold of the people and guided their actions.

With his beard and plastic-rimmed glasses, Saleh reeled and swaggered through the house, and declared that the East had changed. Haidar Salman smiled at him and said in a low, scornful voice, 'But the people cannot create any real change. The people are dangerous, very dangerous, because they represent the disappearance of rational behaviour. The people are against critical thinking. In fact, their thoughts are completely different from mine. Their ideas and movements are driven by pure chance. They do not think, but only flare up and become wild. They combine the most contradictory tendencies and represent the dissolution of the particular into the universal. One word is enough to transform the people into a bull in a china shop.'

'No,' screamed Saleh, 'these people wish to abolish the tyranny of the individual and establish a communal society. They want to re-establish the Islamic Caliphate and the precepts of the prophets.'

Haidar was absolutely terrified, for he never had any faith in the people. Something in them inspired fear in his heart and made him tremble. He was scared of the mob and tried to keep as far away from them as possible. He had very little confidence in angry popular fervour. Perhaps the Farhoud was the reason, when he'd seen the same ecstasy in the eyes of the mob, the ecstasy of sacrificial offerings, which turned individuals into a herd in a state of exhilaration. The mob's anger would break out at the slightest provocation and was impossible to control. He feared all impassioned appeals to the emotions.

The passion of the mob spiralled higher without end, as was to happen later with Saddam. Extreme agitation seized people's minds and hearts and drove them to rush forward. When Saddam climbed the podium, the masses beneath ran like maniacs. The same thing was happening in Iran. Like Saddam, Khomeini depended on manipulating the masses with his personal charisma. The people, the public, the crowd went out in a state of agitation, shouting so hard they became senseless.

Poverty, deprivation and loss were responsible for creating charismatic leaders. Those leaders exercised their authority and hegemony in order to compensate for their own sense of inferiority and their absolute spiritual vacuum.

'Do you think that Khomeini has declared the revolution against the Shah?' asked Tahira.

The small sitting room looked out onto the garden. The windows were open and the sunbeams cast their golden rays inside the house while the birds sang outside. Tahira poured more tea into Haidar's cup as she sat in front of him with her oval face, still sparkling eyes and tender lips. She had a beautifully aristocratic expression.

He realized that the country was in a perpetual state of mass turmoil, especially after announcements in the press that Khomeini had left his exile in Neauphle-le-Château, twenty miles west of Paris. He read the papers almost every day and stayed from morning till evening in a state of constant apprehension. He walked along Al-Rashid Street, thinking of the demonstrations that marched out of Tabriz's mosques and which the security forces were unable to control. Haidar walked past the statute of Al-Rusafi as if unconscious. One image dominated his mind. It was the image of Bloody Friday, when four thousand people lay dead on the ground. His ears tried to pick up the news, for the Tabriz riots had just broken out, which led pro-Shah Iranian officials try to find a solution to the problem. Then the media embarked on a self-critical evaluation of government institutions and the activities of the ruling Rastakhiz Party, with the aim of appeasing the people whose anger extended to Tehran, Qom and Tabriz.

He went home with a heavy heart. He felt that the crazed scene was pressing on his mind. The Shah was sticking to his guns, refusing to acknowledge opposition, whether moderate or extreme. He even described the opposition groups as outlaws and murderers. His categorical refusal was the green light for the opposition to ignore their basic ideological differences and unite against him.

Haidar read in the morning papers that General Nasser Moghadam, the director of the SAVAK, had gone to see the Shah wearing all his medals on his chest and dressed in his pressed military uniform. But the Shah had looked at him haughtily and rejected his proposal for reform. Haidar had heard at a tea shop at Bab al-Moazzam that the great bazaar merchants, almost a quarter of a million shops, had decided to stop working. The sky was clear with just a few white clouds tinged with crimson streaks. Dust rose high into the sky and pollen filled the air. He felt a childish joy that made his heart dance. He stood at the corner of the street, listening to the news of demonstrations everywhere. A man in a black tie told another that demonstrations in Iran had spread to forty cities. When Haidar came closer to the man who was providing this information, he recoiled in fear. When Haidar went home, Tahira was sitting on the sofa, wearing a striped white shawl. Her dark eyes sparkled magnificently like two jewels outlined by kohl. Her complexion showed that even though she was much older, her body hadn't lost its physical lustre. Nor had her lovely eyes lost their sparkle. She offered him *sahoon*, the traditional Iranian sweets that Abadi wrote about in his novels. She offered him fresh water out of mosaic and alabaster vessels. Her Iranian maid slept in the shade as though she had materialized out of the books of Gobineau or Chardin a hundred years earlier. He took out the photo album. Tahira had invited him to discover the mysteries of Tehran and its art through a tour of its old museums. She was the one who lured him into horse-drawn carriages to put him in touch with society. For a change, she accompanied him on a visit to Tajrish Bazaar, whose passageways they walked for hours. Then she took him to the wonderful museums and to Marshad Jaafarpour. They climbed Mount Toshal, played backgammon near Al-Ghareeb cave and sat at the celebration of the birthday of Hazrat Fatima. They went to an open-air pool, where Tahira swam in her swim-suit, and then visited the Shahr Park, south of the city. Haidar Salman remembered the Tehran bazaar where Tahira had taken him for the first time. They sat on a bench in the shade of a large tree near the mosque. A Sufi wanderer passed in front of them. There were cypress and sycamore trees. He heard the sound of water falling from a tap. He heard a swallow singing on a huge tree, and beneath it there was a vendor selling a cold ginger drink in copper cups.

The sun was disappearing behind pink clouds and the evening star was hanging in the sky, while at Tehran Airport more than six million people stood to welcome Khomeini. Crowds surrounded the eighty-year-old man as he took a helicopter to resume his journey and flew over the heads of those who thronged to welcome him. The helicopter was like a black insect flying and hovering above the people's heads. In the morning, the state and the government dissolved before his personality.

On the following day, as Haidar sat in the leather armchair in the hall, he knew that what was happening in Iraq was loaded with significant historical implications. There was a prevalent satirical tone that was full of anger. Saddam's statements were indirect but pointed ultimately to war. Revolutionary Iran stood in confrontation with revolutionary Iraq. Border discussions and skirmishes were all trumped-up stories that portended doom ahead. The dogs of war were undoubtedly barking, for when war came, it knocked on each and every door.

One month after Saddam had assumed power and executed his old comrades, and one year after Khomeini had taken power in Tehran, Haidar and Tahira went out of their small house on Al-Karradah Street in their red-and-gold Cadillac to visit the Sofer restaurant in Al-Mansour.

Haidar Salman was keeping a piece of bad news from Tahira. Her uncle Saleh had been arrested and, only two days afterwards, executed.

Tahira was ill and nobody wanted to tell her the news.

Haidar and Tahira sat near the door and ate carp cooked in black pepper, with apple tart for dessert. Then they went back home.

'Do you think there'll be war with Iran?' Tahira asked.

'Of course, there's no doubt about it.'

He later wrote to Farida describing how he was deported with Tahira to Iran: 'None of us realized that a war would be waged against us the very next day.'

At the beginning, there was an escalation of warmongering in the papers, which in both countries turned into a vulgar kind of celebration, with idiotic, shabby rhetoric using superficial, lame and deceptive language. History was being falsified and people were dancing on the edge of a bloodbath. Slogans were being formulated in elevated, poetic language in order to glorify death and destruction.

Baghdad had more than its fair share of poets who excelled in the art of flattery, and Tehran had its artists who mastered the art of kitsch. Baghdad was full of slogans; Tehran was full of slogans and posters. Elegant poetry had gone and was replaced by shocking platitudes and vulgarities. Art and ideology had become one, and more and more the events of the past were being exploited, with each side trying to unearth a hidden and forgotten history. New genres appeared, other than biography, history and essays. In the beginning Saddam depended on folkloric poetry. The popular poet was the true voice of the philosophy of vulgarity and the anger of the people. In Tehran, the visual artist, the creator of posters, controlled the streets with their revolutionary slogans and images that made use of Persian rhetoric.

But where was music?

In Baghdad, music was greatly abused. It was put in the service of anthems that incited people to kill.

In Iran, where singing was banned, music was put to a different use. Classical music was promoted, but it was a type of music impressed with anger and outrage. In Baghdad, music contained a marked streak of ugliness that was created by tyranny. But it was an ugliness that was cleverly presented. Tehran, for its part, banned singing and made Shahin Farahar turn away from composing symphonies about Omar al-Khayyam and al-Firdawsi to composing religious rhapsodies.

Baghdad was settling its score with the past, as was Tehran. They stood in headlong confrontation with each other.

Haidar Salman naturally realized at the time that everything in Tehran and Baghdad contained a streak of kitsch. He tried to develop this idea further, thinking quickly and ecstatically. In the course of one night, he realized the presence of common fictions in these two enemy states. It was a strange experience that was very different from anything he could possibly imagine. The art promoted by dictatorial regimes took its power not only from the scandals it propagated, but, more importantly, from its vulgarity and depressing futility.

Both word and image were debased. Iran used images to create impact by presenting the thronging crowds raising their hands mechanically and shouting. The revolution depended on the image of the masses. Iraq, on the other hand, turned popular phrases into poetry and vulgarity into verse. The meanness of everyday existence changed into perplexing nightmares.

There was anarchy in both countries. Each confronted the other with an artificial system that was eloquent and ridiculous. Pure chaos merged with raucous anarchy and old romantic babble.

Vulgar art endorsed politicians and encouraged their violence. Cheap eloquence endowed murder, destruction and annihilation with a high aesthetic value. Vulgarity was elevated onto a moral plain, causing hatred to increase. Baghdad's songs and verses created irrational zeal, while in Tehran the images on the posters, placards and advertisements became rhetorical tools. In Baghdad, art embodied insolence, while in Tehran it represented faecal obsessions.

Each country went back to its heritage. Arab Baghdad went back to poetry and words, to the spellbinding rhetoric that the Arabs had mastered. It went back to the undiminished magical power of prose, but with an additional strain of chaos and obscurantism. It was like being lulled to sleep by words without meaning. Iran, on the other hand, went back to its love of imagery, to its drawings and miniature paintings. While the former was lost in its verbal muddle, the latter fell into the vulgarity of revolutionary artists who were far from professional.

In the Green Zone, I established friendly relations with some of the neighbours that I felt might be able to help in some way with my work. I got to know an Iraqi woman from a fairly aristocratic background called Aida al-Nadim, who'd been the wife of an Iraqi consul in Tehran. She was now divorced. She had blonde hair and a very solemn look, and lived in the apartment opposite to mine. We sometimes met on the landing, passed face to face on the stairs or saw each other at the entrance to the building. We exchanged greetings, mostly in the evenings. After a week had gone by, we began to shake hands and exchange news. Our friendship soon grew and she invited me into her apartment to listen to Iraqi music and to have coffee. She made me understand a great deal about life in Tehran before I travelled there. She had important information that wasn't to be found in books or tourist guides. She knew about men and women's lives, people's views on the situation in their country, the names of cheap hotels, the names of shops, the names of Iraqi families living in the city, as well as a host of other things. One day I asked her whether her husband still worked in Tehran.

'You mean my ex-husband?'

'Yes. Do you think I can benefit from his knowledge and experience? I want to go to Tehran to write a newspaper article.'

'My daughter lives there. I'll call her and tell her.'

'Great,' I said.

I was over the moon with happiness that day. It was important for me to find someone to help me deal with information and put it to use in that country, for naturally my stay wasn't going to be for long. I would have to do things quickly. Having someone familiar with life there and with expatriate Iraqi families was of the utmost importance. Nevertheless I kept noting down details connected with the subject. I also worked on the documents in my possession, spending whole nights writing. I would often work until five in the morning, go to bed and wake up at noon to find my bones aching all over. I used to placate my conscience by working so hard. When I got up, I'd go out for a pizza.

One day, Nermine Haidar, the documentary maker I'd met at Queen Alia airport, introduced me to a Turkish official from Istanbul, who worked for a humanitarian organization that helped Iraqis with local government administration. Nermine introduced me to him and his wife Jamina, who was Czech and worked as a primary-school teacher in Limassol. They were a wonderful, cultured couple, who spoke and wrote English. The day Nermine introduced me to them, they invited me for a glass of wine, which strengthened our friendship. They began to invite me almost every evening to their house where I sometimes stayed with them until the small hours. Occasionally I would take along some wine bought at a shop near Al-Khawarna bar. They'd get angry with me and say, 'We have an endless supply of wine. What's the pointing of bringing more!'

They had a wonderful library, and I was always borrowing books in English from them. They were real intellectuals and spent a great deal of money on new books. They felt it was almost a duty to keep up with what was being published in Britain and the States. They were eager to get the latest novels and political books on the Middle East and on Turkey in partic-ular. His wife would say to him, 'Did you know there's a new novel out by Tariq Ali?'

'Really?' he would ask with great interest.

'Yes,' she'd answer, 'I read about in the paper.'

'I'll order it today.'

Orhan, the husband, was almost forty. His beard gave him the look of a leftist, which he was, for he believed categorically that the communism that had collapsed in Russia would re-emerge in Turkey. He always wore elegant but loose outfits over his plump figure. He wandered through the house in a slipshod manner, carelessly leaving things lying around. He ate and drank excessively. He had the look of a revolutionary who'd just been engaged in a blazing row.

His wife Jamina, who was so hospitable she embarrassed me, was very attractive and elegant and, even at home, she dressed well. I can't remember a single time when she looked unhappy. She smiled constantly and told clever political jokes, especially about her husband.

When I talked to them about Kamal Medhat, they were fascinated by his life history and offered to make inquires as to whether or not he'd been to Turkey. They also helped me with Iranian contacts, putting me in touch with a friend of theirs, Khisro, an Iranian intellectual and historian who lived in Tehran. He helped me a great deal with Kamal Medhat's life and his relationship with Hassan Qazlaji and Farrah Nikdahar during his third trip to Iran. But how did Kamal Medhat reach Tehran this time?

Towards the end of 1980 and in the quietness of dawn before the cock crowed, there was the sound of urgent knocking at the outer gate, which made Haidar Salman jump out of bed. A car engine rumbled outside and there were the loud voices of men all talking at once as the violent knocking on the door continued. Half-awake, he heard heavy footsteps approaching, doors being opened and then being slammed shut. Out of terror, Tahira jumped up after him and followed him to the hall with her small, shivering, bare feet.

The roofed balcony of the hall was covered with vines. The garage lights were on, causing the shadows of men wearing khaki and green suits and with pistols holstered at their sides to fall on the walls. Haidar's memory was lit up by the frowning, angry faces, the thick, droopy black moustaches and the cruel, brutal eyes. A tall officer rushed forward in his dark safari suit and wide, thick leather belt and raised the gun in his hand. The door was open and the sound of footsteps continued on the stairs. The whole family had been woken in the middle of the night and were standing there, tense and fearful, their eyes burning. Haidar stood in the corridor in his unbuttoned pyjama shirt. Tahira was right behind him in her nightgown, her bare feet on the tiled floor. Hussein stood behind his mother trembling with horror and expectation. The perplexed father placed his hands in the pockets of his dressing gown while the scared mother stood behind her husband for protection, looking at the terrified child by her heels. In an unsteady voice Haidar asked them why they were there. The answer came clear and unwavering, 'You're Iranian subjects. You have to leave for Iran now.'

The trucks transported them for some time before arriving at a warehouse-like building. The doors were shut immediately, making the place pitch dark. A man with a powerful torch shone its light into their faces, one after the other. They were unloaded from the truck and ordered to walk in the dark. Following the torch they felt their way until they came to a tiny doorway cut into the metal wall of the warehouse. They had to bend to go through it and found themselves standing in front of a group of officers holding registers. There were guards with guns tucked beneath their loose outfits. From the inside, the building, with its concrete floors, patches of black oil and thin metal poles, seemed like Central Security.

A staircase led up to a senior officer who stood watching what was happening.

The rooms on the upper floor had dangling electric bulbs and tables on which typewriters were placed.

One of the officers started calling out the names of the detainees. Young men between the ages of fifteen and forty were taken aside, while the others were pushed through a narrow passage. Haidar shouted out, 'Hussein!' But the sound died on his lips. They were told to get into the covered military truck. Haidar climbed with difficulty into the back of the truck as the guards urged him and his sick wife with gestures and curt phrases to get a move on. The truck took off so suddenly that they all tumbled on top of each other in the dark.

Haidar and Tahira had no idea where Hussein had been taken. Together with many other families, they'd been thrown into huge cattle-trucks to be dumped at the Iranian border.

When they got out of the truck, they were led like cattle towards a deep valley. Haidar couldn't tell how many there were, but he saw huge crowds. There were women carrying screaming babies in their arms, some of whom were dying of cold or hunger. The numbers were large, but Haidar felt certain they would dwindle on the road that led from the Iraqi border to the Iranian city of Qasr-e Shirin. Some of the refugees who'd been beaten up by the security forces were walking heavily, their legs bruised and swollen. The faces of others were black and blue. The soldiers who searched them took any money that remained in their possession and which they'd hidden away in their clothes.

He held Tahira's hand, trying to encourage her. His eyes were full of tears but his hands were strong. He looked ahead and saw the deep valley lying beneath a blue sky that was overcast with scattered white clouds. After two hours of walking, Tahira felt very ill and had a horrible pain in her legs. So he supported her while she walked beside him, wearing a large scarf on her head as protection from the heat of the sun. She sometimes fell down on the ground out of sheer exhaustion. Her slippers were torn, her eyes red and her face withered and sallow. She felt as though she were in a trance. 'How can we leave Hussein behind and go?' she asked him.

He felt that she was dying, but he couldn't do anything for her. Totally desperate and on the edge of an abyss, he couldn't fully absorb what was going on. She spoke to him with a voice that seemed to come from the grave. Her closed lips stopped moving and her eyes froze. Other families walked side by side. Tahira said that she wanted to rest by a tree. So he supported her with his shoulder, made her sit down slowly and threw himself beside her. When he looked towards the distant horizon, he saw the crowds still advancing, with tears in their eyes. His mind was paralyzed, but he reflected on the use of the imagination for the purpose of torturing people. Human beings, he thought, were the only creatures on earth with the capacity to torture their fellow creatures and destroy themselves. Their excessive, preternatural imagination allowed them to envision torture. Thousands of men and women were removed forcibly from their homes and countries, and compelled to settle in strange lands. The irony was that most of these refugees could hardly locate Iran on the map.

'I want you to bury me here,' Tahira told him. 'I want to be buried in Iraq and not in Iran.'

'No,' he said. 'I'm taking you to Tehran.'

'Listen, I'm already dead. Bury me here.'

The expression on her face told him that she was really dying. After half an hour, she fell into a coma. Some of the refugees nearby said she was dead. Some men insisted on staying with him, while the families with children had to continue walking. After an hour, Tahira left this world and became as cold as ice. But her beautiful pale face remained unchanged while the strands of her soft, blonde hair fluttered in the wind.

One of the refugees that we met in Baghdad, Dr Mohammad Ali, reported that Haidar Salman hadn't shed a single tear in spite of the heaviness in his heart. With the help of some other men he had dug the earth with his bare hands to make a grave for her. It was hard because they had no shovels and no tools. But they succeeded, even though the hole was not deep. They covered her with a black gown and sprinkled dust on top. Everybody offered their condolences. He didn't say a word or open his mouth, only stared at the others, feeling that the calamity of death was infinite. The absurdity of the situation bordered on the nonsensical. He felt that words could not express anything, they could only multiply as in an absurd play. Everyone who offered their sympathy to him seemed to be playing a role in a play, with set speeches to give and ready gestures to make. People had become marionettes and reality had became fiction. In a parrot-like fashion they repeated the same phrases, the same conformist statements and the same ready-made ideas without fully understanding. He wished they would keep quiet and say nothing, for they had little to say or share with others. They had no inner existence and nothing but mechanical expressions for such occasions: 'May she rest in peace'.

He said nothing but felt that his silence unsettled them a little. They didn't know how to react. At that moment, he had no feelings and didn't know what to say. He hadn't just lost Tahira, but his entire existence, his personal world. He became a mere number, a person that might easily be replaced. He was like an empty shell, echoing uselessly. Tahira was gone and Iraq was behind him. Hussein's destiny was unknown. The environment in which they existed had collapsed. So he prepared himself to become someone else, to become the tobacco keeper.

They walked beneath the cold, winter sun. He suddenly heard the sound of running water and saw trees and farmers' houses. Men were walking up a grassy hill and the cows were on their way to the fields. Behind him on the left was a pile of wood ready for making charcoal and on the right was a vegetable nursery. There were a few clouds and a flock of birds on the horizon. Life went on, he thought, while Tahira was buried in the dust. Didn't everyone realize that they would be buried in the same way one day? Nature alone would remain: cruel, silent and constant. It was healing and sorrowful to look at nature, for it alone was eternal and had a monopoly on survival.

Iran emerged on the horizon. The border and the refugee camp appeared. Greenery invaded the earth. The serenity was breathtaking and the cold wind blew from a new land, a land that had to become his new home. Whose decision was it, then? The authorities decided. The director of the play decided. Life was a huge stage where form was often confused with content. Life as he knew it was made up of actors performing roles. Two days earlier, he had been the Iraqi composer Haidar Salman. Today things were different. The old play was over and he had to find himself a new performance. He was about to enter a new world, a new life.

The previous play had been tedious and its speeches lifeless. He had to find a new role that had no comical or satirical elements and no paradoxes, a role that was much clearer.

After the expulsion, he wrote the following to Farida: 'We must not forget ourselves entirely, even if we surrender to a role that we've invented, even when it is incompatible with our personalities, because we have chosen to play that role. But I see that others, instead of playing their roles, are played by them. I wish I could find myself another role and stop playing myself. We often imagine that we control the game, unaware that it actually controls us. We often imagine that we uphold values contrary to those we were raised to uphold. But in truth we are only surrendering to them.'

When he arrived at the refugee camp, he managed to procure for himself a tattered, dark coat with a worn collar and a shirt with soiled edges. His beard was long, his face was pallid and his hair was a mixture of black and white. He had become so thin that his cheekbones were protruding. He walked with confident steps towards the guards' tent. The Iranians looked different to him: their faces were surly. They carried machine guns and their beards were long. Photographs of political leaders and revolutionary posters were everywhere.

The camp leader spoke to him through the translator by his side.

'Mr Haidar, you have friends here in Iran. You know that according to Islamic Shariah we have banned songs and depraved music, but we've retained classical music. Would you be willing to co-operate with us? We would like you to compose music about the revolution, about the leaders of Islam. We'll give you everything you want, including Iranian nationality.'

'I won't lie to you and say yes. What I really want is to be released from this camp. I know Tehran well and I lived there a long time ago, but I can't live in a refugee camp.'

The man looked straight at Haidar. He was quite perplexed, but he felt it was useless to try arguing with this tall, thin man who had intelligent, confident eyes. He let out a sigh and said: 'It's lucky you're not a prisoner. You can move out whenever you want, on condition that you don't become involved in politics. When you need anything, we'll help you.'

Two days later, he received an Iranian ID card on which his name was written: 'Haidar Salman Merza, of Iraqi affiliation'. He laughed inside himself at this ridiculous comedy. They also gave him enough tomans to last a whole month. Less than two days after his arrival at the camp, he left and headed directly for Tehran, unlike most Iraqis, who went to Jalalabad.

All he thought about was how to get out of this labyrinth. By hook or by crook he had to find papers to allow him to leave Iran. With clarity of vision, he decided not to stay in the country, but to find a way out. He thought about all this as he walked along Wali al-Asr Street, which had been called Reza Pahlavi Street when he'd walked it for the first time. Ismail al-Tabtabaei's house was located at the end. It was one of the ironies of fate that he should come now, after the al-Tabtabaeis had completely gone. Ismail, in spite of his advanced years, was detained in a Baghdad prison, all his property and wealth confiscated and charged with collaborating with the Shia movement. His brother Saleh had been executed and his body dumped on the street. Tahira had died during the expulsion. But here he was, at a small café on the main street close to hotel Hazrat Fatima. He examined the waiter who was pouring the tea for him. The man's beard was long and he looked sullen and morose. Haidar sat, warming his hands with his tea and watching customers as they tossed coins onto the tray of the café owner. They exited onto Joseph Stalin Street, although the name of the street had been changed after the revolution to Sattar Khan, one of the leaders of the Iranian Constitutional Revolution. The new names of the streets meant that he got lost a few times. He also decided to brush up his Persian. Since leaving in the fifties and sixties, his command of the language had deteriorated. To practise his language, he decided to buy a Persian book by Ahmad Shamlou, a favourite poet, as well as a dictionary from a large bookshop on Revolution Avenue.

Tehran's winter was bitterly cold as he looked for somewhere to stay. He placed his hands in his pockets after wrapping the coat tightly around his body. Walking along the street, he saw two fat men in long coats tailing him. They had thick lips and stern eyes. He felt he was being watched by the Pasdar, the revolutionary guard. Nevertheless, he walked on quietly, observing the changes that had occurred in Iranian life, not only in the women's clothes and the style of life in general, but in political posters too. This was a new feature of life, a kind of collective imagery represented in murals. High walls offered the perfect space for artists to display their graphic skills. It seemed to Haidar Salman that there wasn't a single wall left without murals, posters or writing covering it. People were being mobilized through the use of ideological and political propaganda that depended on a minimal use of words to produce the maximum effect.

218

The Iran that he had known well had disappeared without a trace, replaced by a new Iran. The posters showed this clearly. Shia themes of traditional Pardeh-Khani narratives now completely dominated Iranian visual culture. Haidar Salman had seen those old images re-enacting the battle of Karbala since the fifties. Now they were everywhere in Tehran, even in the cafés. They represented epic themes in a primitive form, but were now used to embody the revolution. They combined the Pardeh graphics with new revolutionary propaganda. He later explained this to Farida as follows: 'What's happening in Iran seems to me to be a kind of Pardeh-Khani art, where a painter controls a large canvas of five feet by twelve. The painting depicts Karbala, a centuries-old battle in which Hussein, the Prophet Mohammad's grandson, was killed. The painter begins his dynamic project by taking a large sheet of canvas stuck to the wall or hung between two poles. What he does then is to bring people by force into the circle of pain. Everything here is designed to drive you to tears . . .'

Haidar Salman realized that this artistic genre was the product of politics but also left a huge impact on it. This art proliferated on coins, stamps and school textbooks, although there was a brief honeymoon between religious groups, on the one hand, and progressive and institutional forces, on the other. Soon enough, Islamic ideologies launched a campaign to reclaim and appropriate the revolution. They organized an army of primitivist and religious artists to mobilize people and defeat their rivals and opponents through visual art.

Only Hotel Azadi remained from the old Tehran. When Haidar walked down Evine Street, he stopped at the hotel. A concierge stood in front of the door in his elegant outfit. Haidar had stayed at this hotel with Tahira during their honeymoon. They'd taken a large suite with windows looking out over the mountains from one side. On the other side, the windows looked over the city. The suite had a small sitting room with a table in the corner. In the evening, they dined in the panoramic restaurant on the upper floor with a view of the whole city.

What would Haidar Salman do now? I managed to locate everyone that Orhan suggested, especially Dr Khisro. Haidar had known Dr Khisro for a while and would sit with him at Naderi café in Wali al-Asr Street. Everybody confirmed, too, that he'd been involved in a relationship with a girl called Pari. They also suggested that he'd escaped to Syria, either directly or through Turkey, with the help of Farrah Nikdahar and Hassan Qazlaji. So who were all these people and how did he get to know them?

First, who was Pari? What kind of relationship did he have with her? And how did he make her acquaintance?

The Pari story actually goes back a long time and cannot be told here. But we can trace the relationship as far as her father Mohammad Taqi, who worked as an accountant for Ismail al-Tabtabaei in Tehran. Haidar Salman had made his acquaintance before Ismail liquidated all his assets in Tehran. At any rate, Haidar, who no longer had any acquaintances in Tehran, felt that Mohammad Taqi was the only person he could turn to. The revolution had produced drastic changes in lifestyle and in the class system, which had driven most of his father-in-law's acquaintances to emigrate to Europe. He realized that only the poor stayed behind, whatever the changes, revolutions and coups.

Mohammad Taqi lived in the Hazrat Hussein neighbourhood, the area closest to Hussein Square. On the afternoon of Haidar's arrival in Tehran, he felt hungry and miserably cold, so he took the bus from Revolution Avenue and told the driver that he wanted to get off at the point closest to Hazrat Hussein. After about a quarter of an hour, the driver, with his thick moustache and hat, signalled for him to get off. Haidar found himself in front of a number of small shops with high metal shutters. In between was a narrow, paved street that led to a poor neighbourhood. He stopped briefly and took a cigarette out of his pocket, lit it and blew smoke into the air. He walked beside thick wooded gardens that lay in front of a group of houses. He saw a casually veiled young woman in her twenties wearing jeans and standing at the door of a small, two-storey house with a beautiful ceramic façade. He stopped and asked her about Mohammad Taqi's house. She looked up at him with startled large dark eyes, and told him that this was her house and that Mohammad Taqi was her father.

The young woman spoke a little Arabic and his own Persian was adequate for basic communication. The girl asked him to follow her. With quiet nervousness he obeyed, passing by the screen that stood at the entrance of all Iranian houses to prevent evil spirits from entering. They followed a winding path across the small flower garden to a sunlit living room that was filled with the pale rays of the winter sun. The room was very warm, so he took off his coat and handed it to her. He sat on the sofa facing the girl with the large, dark eyes and fair-skinned, moon-like face. He waited for Mohammad Taqi to come home from his downtown shop on Gragh Barq Street in Tobkhana Square, also named Artillery Square, which became Khomeini Square after the revolution.

Pari disappeared briefly and came back with a cup of tea. He took the cup in both hands and began to drink. His clothes were very shabby, his beard long, his hair was falling onto his forehead and streaked with grey. The girl eyed him tenderly, thinking that his shabby clothes, pale face, exhausted, thoughtful eyes and melodious voice made him appear more handsome. She was as overwhelmed by his presence as she would have been by a prophet.

Almost an hour later, Mohammad Taqi came home. He was a tall man with a slight stoop. His old clothes were ironed and his hair was completely grey. Before Haidar Salman could shake his hand, Mohammad Taqi embraced him. He'd known Haidar since the latter had met Tahira. Mohammad Taqi was one of the people whom Ismail al-Tabtabaei depended on in his work in Tehran and who had looked after Tahira when she was a little girl.

Everyone we met confirmed that Haidar Salman had lived in Mohammad Taqi's house in the Hazrat Hussein neighbourhood and gone with him to work every morning in Gragh Barq, where he'd watch the passers-by and customers that came to the shop. At Mohammad Taqi's house, he'd started relearning Persian with the help of his daughter, Pari. Did Haidar and Pari's relationship become formal? Nobody really knew much about the nature of their relationship. Other people were perhaps less curious than we were. Haidar Salman, however, wrote about it in some detail.

Pari was twenty and had been divorced for two years from her husband. She had no children of her own and since her divorce had worked at a women's hairdresser's on Wali al-Asr Street. She used to spend the morning at the shop. On her return in the afternoon, she'd fling her handbag on the sofa and, in full view of her parents and sister, head straight upstairs to Haidar's room. She would sit close beside him on the sofa, indifferent to everyone else. She was wildly, though quietly, happy to be with him and never tried to conceal her feelings. Her face radiated sweetness and docility as she sat in front of him and sang in Farsi. He listened to her with great joy. While she sat embroidering a linen sheet for him, he would watch every thrust of her needle. He would sometimes stand silently and look out of the window at the stars encircled by halos of trembling white light. As he stood there, his body was infused with a sweet, quiet power. He sensed Pari's ripe, youthful body, and was aware of every part of it. He desired her legs, her waist, her arms, her neck and her full bosom, which pressed against the window as they stood together watching the trees in the garden.

In a letter to Farida, he said: 'Pari's body tells me that the world is infinitely large. Every time I stand in front of her, I see the huge mountains behind her and the stars sparkling in the pitch darkness of the night. I feel an infinite power residing within this living flesh. What exactly do I want from her? Why am I so fearful, so hesitant? I don't really know what to do.'

During this period, he began taking delightful strolls around Tehran with Pari to the very same places he'd visited with Tahira thirty years earlier. As they wandered through Revolution Avenue or Azadi, he noted the great transformations of post-revolutionary Tehran. The poor south was dominated by religion and the chador, while the north was full of grand houses and large stores playing all kinds of songs and music. In the north, women went about unveiled and discussions were free. Pari would carry a scarf in her bag, which she put on when in the south and took off when in the north. But with the coming of winter the weather was changing fast. Haidar Salman smelt the cold humidity of the earth when he stood with Pari on Azadi Square. He knew that the war with Iraq had taken a new turn. Mobilization and the boosting of morale went on relentlessly. Clerics gave sermons from pulpits with machine guns slung over their shoulders. He felt that a huge explosion was bound to happen. It was as certain as death. In his mind's eye he could see angry crowds sweeping over the squares. Once again the incensed, raging masses would go on the onslaught. The revolution, he thought, had turned the people into mobs. Distinctions of class had disappeared and easily manipulated groups had emerged onto the scene. The mob would march and burn and destroy with a blind, random force that knew no bounds.

The streets were damp, the trees bare and the houses miserable behind their rusty fences. At the back of the three-storey stores, beyond the stone-arched entrances and through a swirl of fog, were little yards with small recesses, old pigeon towers and tables fixed to the ground beneath ageing linden trees.

Haidar felt that things in Tehran couldn't go on like this, for there were huge campaigns against the liberals. A secret war was being waged against music, the cinema and unveiled women. He witnessed the burning of cinemas and the banning of free discussion. One day, he was standing with Pari on Wali al-Asr Street, looking at the buildings shrouded in fog. He didn't want to go to a café, but found his attention caught by a sudden mythical apparition: a girl wearing a blue shirt, leather jacket and jeans was selling newspapers. Around her stood a group of young men and women. They started to engage in a free discussion or what was called an 'Azadi debate'. Haidar turned to Pari and told her that such scenes would not continue for long. Groups of bearded peasants from the countryside were carrying truncheons and breaking up leftist demonstrations. They would use stones to disperse any group of young people. He wrote to Farida: 'With the support of the authorities, the militias have begun hounding women on Tehran's streets, especially in the north. It's a maddening,

224

infuriating sight. The bearded scum of society are pursuing girls and women with the claim that their veil is "incorrect". These riffraff shove the women, attack them with abusive words and bundle them into cars.'

As I told Faris Hassan in Tehran, I firmly believe that at that time Haidar Salman was beginning seriously to plan his escape from Tehran and once again head to Baghdad, either via Syria or Turkey. This was confirmed by Dr Khisro too. Haidar's decision came from observing the huge changes that were taking place in Iranian society and the political programme of the revolution. He thought seriously of forging papers in order to get to Baghdad. But the questions that now pose themselves are: Who was Hassan Qazlaji? Who was Farrah Nikdahar? And how did they help him escape to Syria and from there to Baghdad?

I met Dr Khisro at the Naderi café, the same place where Iraqi leftists had met to plan their revolution and which Haidar Salman and Hekmat Aziz frequented. Dr Khisro told me that after his return from Bulgaria, Hassan Qazlaji had seen Haidar Salman by chance in this café. By then, Qazlaji had become an elderly, grey-haired man with glasses. He recognized Haidar Salman immediately, and screamed out loud, 'You're the famous musician Haidar Salman!' He embraced Haidar and asked, 'What's happened to you? Look at your beard and your shabby clothes! What are you doing here, Maestro?'

Hassan Qazlaji was a Kurdish man who took part in the political struggle against the despotic rule of Reza Khan. After the downfall of Reza Khan in the early forties, following the invasion of Iran by British, Soviet and US forces, he established with a group of young revolutionaries the Komeleh Party, an anti-Fascist,

Kurdish nationalist group. The party was later joined by Qazi Mohammad, the leader of the Republic of Mahabad, which was declared in 1945 but collapsed in 1946. Qazlaji was one of the founders and leaders of the party. After the fall of the Republic of Mahabad, however, Qazlaji fled to Iraq, where he published the *Regay* newspaper. He remained in hiding in Iraq, doing various jobs at restaurants, cafés and tobacco farms. He worked in the business of dying shoes and as a photographer in Sulaymaniyah in order to keep body and soul together. He was then arrested in Iraq and sent to jail, from which he was freed only after the 1958 Qasim revolution. He stayed for a while in Baghdad, and was introduced to Haidar at the house of his friend Hekmat Aziz. He then immigrated to Bulgaria, and after the success of the Iranian revolution in 1979, returned to Iran to take charge of the Kurdish edition of *Mardom*, the mouthpiece of the Tudeh Party of Iran.

Haidar Salman stopped in front of him and said: 'Would you help me?'

'Of course, Maestro!'

'I'd like to escape to Syria!'

'Consider it done,' he told him.

Haidar Salman waited for the signal from Hassan Qazlaji. Pari knew nothing of the matter, nor did Mohammad Taqi or anybody else. Qazlaji insisted that the matter remain a closely guarded secret. Otherwise, the Pasdar (the revolutionary guard) would surely kill Haidar Salman. To vary his daily routine, Haidar stopped going to Naderi café and started a new itinerary. Every morning he would walk from Azadi Square to Khurasan Square, and then take the bus to the bazaar, where Mohammad Taqi and his friend Mirza Tabrizi sat at a small café.

Mohammad Taqi sat reading the morning papers and drinking his tea, while Haidar Salman sat facing him reading a biography in Persian, translated from the Russian, of the composer Tchaikovsky. Next to Mohammad Taqi was his friend Mirza Tabrizi, a merchant from Tabriz who'd been a farmer living off the pistachio trade, but who, after the revolution, had become a great merchant. Tabrizi naturally supported the clerics. Every time the two friends met, a heated political discussion took place. Mohammad Taqi adjusted his collar as he spoke; he wore thick glasses and his grey hair gave him a dignified look; when he coughed, his dry voice was sharp and raucous.

Haidar realized then that the liberals constituted a huge force in Iran. They were supported by President Abulhassan Banisadr and his intellectual ally, Engineer Mehdi Bazargan, the leader of the Nehzat-e Azadi movement, as well as his team at the Shura Council in coalition with the members of the nationalist Melli Front. He saw that they were supported by the largest organized popular and political opposition force on the streets. This was no less than the Iranian Mujahideen Khalq Organization, under the leadership of Massoud Rajavi. It was also supported by the Democratic Party of Iranian Kurdistan and the Fida-e Khalq Organization as well as other leftist organizations such as Al-Kifah, Al-Kadehin and Komeleh.

'Do you think the clerics can snatch the revolution from the thinkers and intellectuals?' asked Mohammed Taqi.

Haidar felt the weight of history in Iran as he felt it in Iraq. He suddenly found himself caught up in the fray, in the conflict between the clerics who wanted an Islamic republic and the Islamic liberals who wanted a democratic Islamic republic. He sensed this conflict in the old leftist Mohammad Taqi. From the moment he entered his house, he was extremely agitated. He would unbutton his shirt which he wore without a tie and throw the papers onto the sofa, shouting, 'This isn't an honest fight for power between the clerics and liberals, it's an attempt by the clerics to dominate. At the beginning, they wanted to secure a few seats but now they want them all. Establishing a religious state means that they alone will be in charge.'

Haidar realized that the clerics wanted to tighten their control and authority, which was why the assassinations and imprisonments had begun. The clerics were staunchly supported by the peasants who'd come to the cities, by the faithful and their children, by the illiterate and the ignorant. Haidar Salman watched the political events unfold in Iran. At the café he'd find Mohammad Taqi trembling because the government had shut down the opposition papers. He explained the situation with great agitation, his eyes red and his lips trembling. In front of him sat his friend, Tabrizi, who was also furious.

Haidar Salman stopped going out with Pari. He would walk the streets aimlessly. He let his beard grow long and buttoned his shirt at the top in the manner of the Islamists. He continued to watch the demonstrations, conflicts and civil unrest until the Mujahideen Khalq Organization declared an armed struggle, which made it impossible for him to go out. So he would watch the streets from the window of his room. On 20 June at four o'clock in the afternoon the Mujahideen Khalq took to the streets to begin the armed revolution. They attacked some government buildings in Tehran and other cities. The Revolutionary Guards, Hezbollah and the Revolutionary Committees stood against them, and before darkness fell they had succeeded in defeating and dispersing them in Tehran and other cities.

He wrote to Farida: 'There are fires everywhere. Buildings, cars, offices, theatres, headquarters and houses are on fire. Fights, assassinations and executions are taking place. In Iranian Kurdistan, where the Democratic Party of Iranian Kurdistan controls large areas, there have been firefights with the authorities. The party has allied itself with Banisadr and has begun expanding its sphere of influence.'

One day, he was surprised to be contacted by Farrah Nikdahar, one of the young people connected with Fida-e Khalq, an organization specializing mainly in assassinations. Farrah wanted to meet him at Naderi Café on Wali al-Asr Street. He was extremely civil and courteous. He was also clean-shaven, with long dark hair. His eyes looked remarkably serene.

A book in Persian and a few newspapers lay on the table.

'We know you well. You're the leftist composer, Haidar Salman. I've been sent by Reza Shaltoki.'

Shaltoki was a leftist officer who'd spent more than twenty-five years in the Shah's prisons and had been tortured mercilessly by the SAVAK.

'What exactly do you want from me?'

He smiled. 'On the contrary, we ask you what you want from us. Hassan Qazlaji has been murdered by the Revolutionary Guards. You'd asked him for something, and we'll do it instead.'

'I want to get out of here.'

'Where do you want to go? We can guarantee your exit from Tehran to the country of your choice.'

'Syria. Damascus. The closest place to Baghdad. I need to try to get to Iraq.'

The following day, Haidar told his host Mohammad Taqi that he wished to move to another house. Mohammad Taqi felt that

229

Haidar Salman might be worried about living under the roof of a man known by the Revolutionary Guards to support the liberals. 'This is your home,' he told him. 'Any time you wish to come, you'll be most welcome.'

When Pari came home that evening, she learned from her mother that Salman was planning to leave the house.

During the night, she went up to his room. He was so totally engrossed in his writing that he didn't notice her come in. She caught him in the act of writing with invisible ink. He sat near the bed, with his suitcase packed and placed in the corner. He took off his scarf and gave it to her. With tearful eyes, she took off her own shawl and fell into his arms, kissing him and crying. She showered his lips with kisses and melted in his embrace.

She stood up slowly, her hair falling luxuriantly on both sides of her face. She took off her jacket, her dark eyes sparkling and her breath heaving. She took off her shirt and trousers. She took his shirt and threw it aside while he took off his trousers himself. She wrapped herself around him, her belly white and her hips warm. She then began to move her belly towards him. In a final bending motion that seemed like dancing, she took off her knickers and threw them on the sofa. Her arms reached out to embrace him, her elbows bent, her torso motionless, her pelvis shaking. Her body produced a faint noise as it rubbed against his. He ran his hands over her firm body, bronze buttocks and smooth pubic area. She spoke some words in Persian that he didn't understand. Their eyes met with an increasing intensity until they fell onto the bed, drenched in sweat.

On the following day, he found a small apartment on the second floor of a two-storey building near Revolution Square. He obtained a ration card from the mosque. The woollen collar of his dark coat was speckled with dandruff. In his left hand he carried a suitcase tied with rope. His shirt cuffs were not clean and he was utterly exhausted. The small room he'd rented echoed with the sound of emptiness. He sat in a corner that had no windows. An unmade bed, a tattered rug, a small paraffin cooker, a pot and a frying pan, as well as his suitcase, were the only objects in the room. After untying the rope he took a sheet and a blanket out of the suitcase and spread them beneath the dusty window. Without a pillow or a quilt he settled down to sleep. The room seemed like a cave. The ceiling lamp reflected off the cold floor. He had nothing with him except his suitcase and a book on contemporary art that he'd bought at a bookshop on Wali al-Asr Street. He felt that his life was without meaning or value. He curled up facing a bare wall that was splattered with paint.

In a couple of days, he was contacted. The organization had got him the passport of a man who'd died in a car accident a few days earlier. It was in the name of Kamal Medhat Hassan, an Iraqi merchant married to a woman from Mosul called Nadia al-Amiry. She had married him a year earlier and was now living in Damascus. She had been the widow of a Syrian called Mohammad Aqla from Hama, who'd been killed in the confrontations between the Islamists and the state. That was all he knew about his new identity.

A journalist came by and dropped the passport in the tank of one of the toilets at the Royal Park Hotel in the north of the Iranian capital. Haidar picked it up a short while later, to avoid it being discovered.

As soon as he read his new name and saw his photograph and date and place of birth in the passport, he felt that the persona of

Haidar Salman had vanished without a trace. Suddenly he felt so alienated from it that it seemed to have been imposed on him. He had a far greater sense of identification with the new character of Kamal Medhat.

VIII

Tobacco keeper
From Kamal Medhat's life
(1933-2006)

'Oh! I know him. He is the tobacco keeper, devoid of metaphysics.

The tobacco keeper goes back to his shop driven by a divine
instinct.'

From Álvaro de Campos *Tobacco Shop*

Spartan wars and the end of romanticism and love

He entered Damascus with the new name of Kamal Medhat and
a new passport with a new date and place of birth. This was his
third character, the personality that corresponded to Álvaro de
Campos from the poem *Tobacco Shop*. It was the sensual character
of the tobacco keeper, the man obsessed with gratifying the senses
of taste and touch, the person wishing to live in a stupor off the
two previous characters and soar in a world of smoke, pleasure and
sex. In every corner of his soul there was an altar to a different

233

god. But would the shadows of the previous two characters vanish for good? Never.

The strength of the new character lay in the fact that although it stood in contrast to the earlier characters, it depended on them and often overlapped. This was the source of Kamal Medhat's strength. Although he lived in a state of isolation and nihilism, his personality was more solid than the other two. Pessoa created a clear biography for this character. Álvaro de Campos was born on 15 October 1890 in Portuguese Tavera. After studying marine engineering in Glasgow, he travelled to the East to find pleasure, relaxation and laziness. He justified the trip on the grounds of his relentless search for opium to take back home. For the East, opium represented consolation for its honour. Like Álvaro, Kamal Medhat had a well-defined biography. Born in Mosul in 1933, he became a well-known merchant who frequently travelled to Iran and back. He was a man who indulged in enjoyment and pleasure. It would not be surprising, then, if the authorities in Damascus suspected him of bringing a quantity of opium with him from Iran.

This is what we'll discover from the answer to the following question. On what day did Kamal Medhat arrive in Damascus and how?

The latest date for his arrival in Damascus was early November 1981. But how did he travel? There are actually two contradictory stories. The first alleges that he escaped to Turkey (though Orhan didn't confirm this view) and went to Damascus through Mardin. The second story claims that he flew from Tehran to Damascus on Syrian Air. The airfare was paid with a sum of money offered to him by Mohammad Taqi's daughter, Pari. He arrived at Damascus airport in early November, although we couldn't verify this piece

234

of information because he never mentioned it in his letters. What is certain, however, is that he was arrested on his arrival at Damascus. He referred to this clearly in one of his letters to Farida: 'When I arrived in Damascus, I was detained by the authorities for four days. I was held in a room that was no bigger than five square metres, together with more than twenty others: smugglers, common criminals and Syrian politicians. They all stank and their hair was infested with lice.'

In prison, he was taken blindfolded through a dark corridor. Two gigantic wardens on either side lifted him by his armpits and dragged him along. Suddenly they stopped, removed the blindfold and allowed him to walk along the corridor with his eyes dazzled and half-closed. There was only a small window looking out onto a yard that was empty but for a single tree.

Kamal Medhat had no idea why he was being detained. But when they seated him on a wooden chair in a small room lit by a dust-covered bulb, with cigarette butts littering the floor, the officer asked him: 'Be brief. You have opium.'

'No, I swear to God. I'm a small merchant and I have no use for such things.'

'We have information that you're bringing opium with you from Iran.'

'That's never been my job.'

At the beginning, the investigator didn't believe him, although he didn't force him to confess or torture him. After two or three days of interrogation, he was released. That was the end of his detention. Some of the people we met in Damascus, however, believed that Kamal Medhat did enter Syria with a package of opium that he'd brought with him from Tehran and that he sold it at one of the cafés in Al-Bahsa. The money that he spent in

Damascus, they argued, came from selling that package. The question we asked was whether Kamal Medhat himself smoked opium. Nobody, in fact, confirmed this, except one of the political exiles that we met in Damascus, Saadoun Mohammad. He was the one who introduced him to Jacqueline Mugharib. He told me that he once went with Kamal to a secret café in Damascus where he smoked hashish in hookahs specially prepared for the purpose. We can neither confirm nor deny whether he entered Damascus carrying a package of opium. But it is worth noting that he thought music produced a kind of trance similar to the effect of opium. Furthermore, he composed a piece of music, the 'Opium' Concerto, which was permeated with Iranian culture. All this made me wonder where and when he consumed opium for the first time. I'm sure that he got it from Iran because opium was widely available there. His first use of opium must have been during his stay in Tehran rather than anywhere else. But when, exactly? Was it in the fifties, when he lived with Ismail al-Tabtabaei at Pahlavi Street? Or in Enqelab in 1963? But that wasn't a long enough period for him to experiment with opium. Or was it when he stayed at the house of Mohammad Taqi and his daughter Pari?

Concerning Kamal Medhat's life in Damascus, all the documents confirm that he arrived at noon with his new passport and new personality. He tried to find some space for his new hedonistic, pleasure-seeking character within a politically explosive landscape. His arrival corresponded with the most violent confrontations between the regime and the Muslim Brotherhood. This was a period rife with ethnic, sectarian, racial and ideological hatred. The region was at the height of uncertainty and indecision. It seemed to have muddy feet and a savage, cruel face. So how would this self-indulgent, indolent character fit into this context?

The cab that Kamal Medhat took crossed the Victoria Bridge with its freshly lacquered handrails. He sat looking out of the window at the people as the cab drove through the streets of Damascus. When he heard the news of a booby-trapped car that had been blown up near the Cabinet building in Seven Seas Square he felt he was inside a simmering cauldron. Any suspicious person on the streets was arrested without much ado. In this environment was it possible, as the double of the tobacco keeper in *Tobacco Shop*, to find an outlet for his passionate, pleasure-seeking nature? How would he treat his sense of self-importance, his unsettled view of himself and the image he wished to create for his own identity?

'What's your name?' he asked the driver.

'Ammar. If you want some fun, I have a beautiful young girl,' the driver said. He was a dark man with thinning hair, sharp eyes, a thick moustache and a broad, athletic chest. Kamal Medhat wasn't surprised at the driver's offer to pimp for him, for drivers almost everywhere in the world did exactly the same. But he didn't feel completely at ease with this driver. He was unsettled by the man's acne and his high cheekbones. He disliked him and found his conversation tiresome, but he wished to use him to find somewhere to stay.

'I want somewhere cheap,' he told him in a low voice, wiping his forehead.

'Fine, I'll take you to Umm Tony's house. She has cheap rooms,' said the driver.

He looked out of the window at the streets of Damascus, which he was seeing for the first time. It was his first experience with his new identity, name and personal history. He realized that part of his personal history would be created here, while the other part would be tied to the past. This was the first time he felt that he'd usurped the identity and history of someone else, a person called Kamal Medhat. He knew nothing about his history and realized the risk he was taking in coming here to Syria. All he knew about Kamal Medhat was that he'd gone to Tehran from Damascus. He also knew his wife's name and bits and pieces of her personal history. He later wrote to Farida: 'Sitting there in the back seat of the car, I knew nothing about my new character. Was I being sought by the authorities here for political reasons? Had I been charged with any offence? I knew that I'd been married for a year to a woman from Mosul who was the widow of a Hama Islamist. When I was questioned, I came to know that the regime was preoccupied by the conflict with the Islamists and had no time for me. That was a relief. But I knew little about the traits of my new character.'

The boarding house was located in the Al-Bahsa area. It stood in a semi-dark, urine-soaked alley that the residents called Hamdan Alley. The boarding house was a dilapidated building owned by a forty-year old Christian woman called Umm Tony. She opened the door and led him to an upstairs room. It was an attic room with a bed covered by shabby sheets and two worn-out, ancient-looking, but newly washed, blankets. A low iron cupboard and a kerosene primus for making tea were also in the room. The bathroom was shared by all the lodgers.

Umm Tony told him that the monthly rent was 500 liras, which he had to pay in advance. He agreed immediately, opened his wallet and gave her the required amount. She took the money and stuffed it down her ample cleavage. After she and the driver had left, Kamal Medhat shut the door and threw himself on the bed in exhaustion. When he later lifted his head and saw the peeling paint on the damp walls, he replayed the events of the past few days in his mind. He recalled Pari's changed face, her posture as she sat in front of him, her legs, her arms and her heaving breasts. He was in the grip of a welter of dreams and hallucinations. He felt like a disembodied soul, as transparent and clear as water. But in his throat was a stickiness that suffocated him. His body was limp, as though he were under sedation. His head was awash with memories, details, desires and rosy-cheeked women with long hair. Then he fell into a long sleep from which he awoke in the evening.

He felt hungry when he woke up, so he went out to look for something to eat. On the stairs, he met Umm Tony's daughter, a pencil-thin, teenage girl with long, slender legs called Aida. In the courtyard, he saw her other daughter, also a teenager with boyish buttocks and round breasts, called Dalia. Umm Tony lived on the lower floor with her two daughters and her son Tony, who was a schizophrenic. The other four rooms were rented by two Iraqis, an Algerian and a Syrian. This was what the Iraqi living next door told him when he met him on his way out to the courtyard.

The man's name was Saadoun. He was good-looking and elegant and, in his loud voice, spoke a dialect that was a mixture of Iraqi and Syrian dialects. He stood in the yard flattering Umm Tony's daughters, who were having a good laugh at his silly jokes in front of their mother. On the rug near the fireplace two cats were purring. He turned to Kamal and said, 'I'll come with you. I know a restaurant nearby.' And they went out together.

Kamal looked at the street as though he were in a trance, while Saadoun was cheerful and in high spirits. Saadoun, who was an architect, was highly cultured and exceptionally elegant. He had the superior air of an aristocrat. He was a fugitive communist who'd escaped from Baghdad two years earlier, after Saddam's crackdown on communists in the late seventies. He earned his living publishing well-written articles in newspapers for which he was paid badly. He ate at a cheap restaurant for students near Seven Seas Square.

They went into the restaurant. Kamal saw the mixture of colours in the onion slices and the green of the rocket and the parsley. He saw the rusty colour of plates piled with liver, the crimson of shrimp heads and their white undersides. Cold beer was also served. He drank two bottles, ate a plateful of liver and felt somewhat full and happy.

Saadoun asked him about his work. He told him he was a violinist.

'I know a nightclub in need of musicians. You might find work there,' Saadoun told him.

Kamal didn't know how to respond. Work at a nightclub when he hadn't accepted the Iranian musician Shahin's offer in Tehran to play with the largest orchestra in the Middle East?

He felt the pain of an old wound being rubbed. His rectangular face was pale and sallow. Was it really *his* face? Then the colours disappeared once again. He got up and went to the toilet. He crossed the crowded restaurant and the light-filled floor and climbed the stone staircase. The toilet door was at the end of the corridor. He slid slowly into the darkness and, for one moment, silence seemed to have descended on him. There was absolutely no movement. He felt only the accelerating beat of his heart. Then he threw up in the sink. He washed his face and went back.

The following day, Saadoun took him to the Al-Rawda café. It was a large café with a big, planted terrace and numerous tables. Mint tea was served, along with hookahs with aromatic tobacco. It was the meeting place of Iraqi refugees, especially journalists and writers who'd fled Iraq in the seventies. With so many people, faces and questions, the noise was unbearable. Everyone he met there bombarded him with questions ranging from the political to the personal. Saadoun told him he had to get used to such questions, because Iraqis mistrusted one another and suspected each other of being Secret Service agents sent by Iraqi intelligence to penetrate the opposition. The place was rife with anger and filled with highly strung faces, constant questions and suspicions. Their mistrust appeared not only on their lips but in their eyes as well. He couldn't stay in that place for long, where he felt suffocated and tense. Above all else, he was troubled by everyone's curiosity.

The same day, Saadoun took him to Al-Tahouna nightclub near the Russian consulate. They sat beneath a blue lamp and the music was truly mediocre. The semi-naked dancers danced in a lewd fashion. Facing the nightclub was a garden where cats slept beneath benches. Some of the people sitting there were stoned on hashish, staring vacantly in a cheap daydream. Others sat with their backs against the wall, gazing at the horizon. After drinking several beers, he thought hard about how he might stay in this country. Saadoun asked him how he felt about working as a violinist.

'I want to go back to Baghdad.'

241

'Go back?' he asked him.

'Yes, I want to go back there. I have no life here.'

'What's your real story?'

'No story! I was in Iran and I don't want the Iraqi authorities to know I was in Iran.'

Kamal Medhat learned a few important things from Saadoun. First, he found out that Umm Tony, who hailed from Wadi al-Nasara in Homs, was in the business of forging passports, or at least in the business of handling them. Her husband, Abu Tony, was most probably the chief forger, or perhaps the contractor in charge of handling identities and passports. It was by pure chance that Umm Tony sold passports to some individuals who were later discovered to belong to the Muslim Brotherhood and who were being hunted by the authorities. Although they managed to flee the country, one of them by the name of Khaled al-Shami got arrested. He was the one who secured the contacts between Islamist leaders and some army officers that were planning a coup. Umm Tony was arrested and received a prison sentence of seven years at Tadmor Prison. Her husband managed to get away with it and flee the country. After she'd spent one year in prison, the authorities had released her with the proviso that she worked with them as an informant.

'Can she help me?' asked Kamal.

'Don't even try, she's an informant. But we can use her later.'

Afterwards, a girl of twenty called Noosa appeared. She was dressed indecently. Her back was completely bare and her transparent dress revealed her breasts and her red knickers. Her eyes were very large and intensely dark. She wore heavy makeup and puffed smoke in their faces, which came out mixed with the smell of cheap whisky. She sat at their table and ordered a Scotch on their bill. She was either drunk or high and laughed out loud. After she'd got up to continue her performance, Saadoun told him that she was the wife of the driver, Emad, who'd given him the lift to Umm Tony's guesthouse.

Although Kamal needed money to continue his stay in Damascus, he didn't have the slightest desire to work at that joint. He felt so repelled by the idea that thinking about it made him queasy and brought tears to his eyes. When he went back to the guesthouse, he lay in bed and thought hard. How could he stay in the country if he didn't have a job? He felt that he could use part of his musical talent, though not at that type of nightclub. So he decided to look for a place where he could work as a musician. The next day, in the morning, he left the guesthouse to look for work. But he had no idea that a secret war was going on in Damascus.

He walked along Baghdad Street, which stretched from Seven Seas Square to Al-Sadat Square. Then he went to Murshed Khater Street in the Al-Azbakeya neighbourhood, which extended from Al-Qasaa area to Al-Sabaa. It was around half-past eleven when he suddenly heard the sound of shooting on Murshed Khater Street. A minute later, there was a huge explosion. He saw everything around him fly up into the air. The screams of women and the sound of cars blowing up were deafening. There was complete chaos everywhere. A coach on the Duma–Damascus line stood parallel to the blown-up car. A charred part of a human back landed on the street. Kamal also saw burnt and crushed limbs on the pavement. All the pedestrians on the street had been seriously injured. Faces had been mangled by flying glass and the windows of the houses on the street had splintered over the residents.

The perpetrator of the operation ran in the direction of the traffic lights some fifty metres away. He was followed by a policeman dressed in khaki and carrying a heavy revolver. As soon as the perpetrator entered a sidestreet connecting Murshed Khater to Baghdad Street, the policeman shot him and he fell, drenched in blood. Kamal Medhat came closer and looked at his face. The man writhed and his head fell on the pavement. He was dead. Kamal Medhat passed by the body, his legs shaking.

Did Kamal Medhat have any options? None whatsoever. Damascus was tense and had no need for his talent. So he decided to look for Nadia al-Amiry, or at least get as much information about her as possible. He knew that she lived in Bab Touma, this much was was documented on the card given to him by the man who'd secured his passport in Tehran.

One day, he woke up in his room on Hamdan Street in Al-Bahsa, went out of the boarding house in a hurry without anyone seeing him and walked along several criss-crossing streets leading to Bab Touma. When he arrived at the place, he fell in love with it straight away. The old neighbourhood was the site of many historical events. The white statue in the middle of the square facing the police station seemed to him like the garrison of the city. It was like a minaret that shot up to heaven. When he walked further on, he was amazed to see the walls of the old church with their iron drainpipes that jutted out to the edge of the pavement and its round stone towers that rose high. The neighbourhood was full of winding streets that seemed dormant and forgotten. Along both sides of the streets were old houses, thick trees and hundred-year-old bars. There were squares immersed in mist and lofty drawing rooms with unlit chandeliers.

The dome of the church attracted his attention most of all. He walked on a little, gazing at the houses, and then took a few steps up to a shop. He asked the assistant about Nadia al-Amiry's house. The man's moustache was crooked and his paunch protruding. He pointed to a tall, one-storey house, whose black, iron gate stood open. Two large windows looked out onto the street. When he went through the gate, he saw a fountain and a small, well-tended garden filled with leafy buckthorn trees with intertwining branches and thick trunks. A beautiful woman sat on a chair, her face pretty and round, her eyes large.

Feeling confused, he turned away and went back to the market. A butcher's shop with Kashani tiles stood near the house. The walls of the shop had been scrubbed with shampoo, and the slaughtered animals dangled from hooks, their bellies open.

He took the first bus that he found in the square and returned to the boarding house. When he went in, he saw Umm Tony's plump body as she smiled at him. He said hello and she told him that someone was waiting for him in his room. Opening the door to his room, he found Noosa sprawled in bed and looking quite different from the drunken girl he'd seen before at the nightclub. Her round face now openly exhibited her lustfulness. Her thighs were full and her hair was black. She walked barefoot around his room, her two small feet looking very beautiful. She went to the table and poured herself a glass of water. She took an aspirin out of her bag, put it in her mouth and downed it with the water.

The conversation between them was brief.

When he asked her why she'd come, she didn't answer. At the beginning, he thought she was part of a conspiracy against him. But he soon dismissed that idea. He was intrigued by the way a

245

woman became attracted to a man. He knew that she fancied him, without any particular reason. He also fancied her himself. In a few moments, he took off his shirt and trousers and took her in his arms. She soon melted between them.

Noosa in fact stayed in his bed until the evening. She talked to him about herself and told him that she'd married Emad three years earlier and had a child that she rarely saw. She'd spent five years in prison for circulating counterfeit notes and prostitution. Her first sexual experience had been at the age of fifteen, with a man she had loved. But after sleeping with her, he'd vanished. Afterwards, she'd begun to frequent the shop of an elderly man, who offered her everything for free in return for sleeping with her in a small room behind the shop. Although the room was originally intended as a storeroom, it had a bed. Her poor, large family forced her to marry Emad. When he proposed to her, he wasn't a driver but did a little bit of everything: smuggling, robbery, dealing in counterfeit notes and more. Two months after their marriage, he came to her one evening and told her that he was no longer able to pay the rent or the costs of the child. He also told her that he'd found suitable work for her. Important guests were going to visit them a few days later and she had to look after them. And so she started to work as a currency trafficker in the morning and a prostitute at night. She was arrested and sentenced to five years in prison. There, she became acquainted with Umm Tony, who gave her a job when she came out.

Kamal Medhat spent those days in Damascus hearing the sounds of explosions and watching people rushing around everywhere.

Security guards and foot patrols filled the streets, especially after the Russian advisors' building was blown up by a booby-trapped car. The explosions continued for days and the security patrols frequently clashed with the extremists. In the midst of the chaos, Kamal Medhat managed to contact Nadia al-Amiry. But how did he manage that? How did he tell her about the reality of his situation and convince her that he might be the substitute for her dead husband? What if she thought that *he* had killed her husband in order to replace him? He never mentioned any of that in his letters or his diary, which he sent to Farida after his departure for Baghdad.

All the evidence suggests that Jacqueline Mugharib had introduced Kamal to Nadia. Jacqueline. arranged a meeting for Kamal and Nadia at a family cocktail party given especially for young people. At the time, they couldn't have been introduced in any other way. Although the party was given for Jacqueline's young relatives, among the guests were Kamal Medhat and Nadia al-Amiry.

Kamal couldn't resist Nadia al-Amiry's voice. Before meeting her, he wouldn't have believed that he would become so enraptured by her.

He mentioned in a letter to Farida the effect that their first meeting at that cocktail party had had on him. Walking towards the buffet, Nadia al-Amiry stopped in her tracks when she heard someone calling out to Kamal Medhat. She went up to him and asked, 'Iraqi?'

'Yes.'

He heard her lovely voice for the first time when they were standing at the corner of a long corridor, near the foot of the inner staircase. He was captivated from the first instant. Her angelic face and beautiful voice charmed him. She, too, was infatuated by him from the first moment. The first syllable that he uttered elicited an expression of satisfaction on her face. They seemed to be on the same wavelength from the start, for both their hearts were filled with unspeakable sorrow. They'd both lived through difficult times. Kamal Medhat, she felt, was a bright man, whose intelligence was carved into his face. But she detected in him an underlying bewilderment as well as a silent, intense passion. It was his charming smile, however, that quickly won her over. For his part, he felt that this seemingly ageless woman had indescribable charm. With her well-groomed hair and beautiful scent, she was extraordinarily elegant. He also noticed that she was as flattering to him as a young servant. Although she possessed great wealth, she was also the victim of circumstances.

Despite all appearances to the contrary, and the fact that this was his last chance to be rescued, it was not he who tried to get close to her at that strange cocktail party; it was her. Actually, both of them looked out of place in the party, for most of the guests were very young. With his grey beard, shoulder-length hair and black coat, he seemed like an oddity. Similarly, with her short figure and the plumpness of her forty years, she looked odd among the slender young women at the party. She had tied her greying hair back with a piece of black tulle fabric and wore a long, black coat that made her look even shorter than she really was.

Every day after that they went for a walk together and ate the fried mezze they saw on display in restaurant windows. They would start in Al-Hamideya market, walk parallel to the dry Barada River and end up by the Umayyad Mosque. They walked like two lovers along the cobbled street beside the brick wall of the high mosque. They were passionately in love. Nadia al-Amiry began to feel enhanced pleasure watching the flocks of birds turning and swooping for grains. She was in love for the first time in her life. With every step that she took on Damascus' narrow streets, she heard the restless beatings of her heart that yearned for him. Almost every day, after lunch they went to drink mint tea at a tree-shaded café.

They became a familiar sight during this period. With his long black coat, his attractive, slender figure, his handsome, dark face and his long, greying hair, Kamal Medhat sat at a café on a tree-lined street close to the Umayyad Mosque. Nearby was a wide courtyard, a stone staircase, a two-storey house and a pool in the centre of a garden. Nadia al-Amiry's face was lit up by a bright light.

Their relationship became common knowledge. It's surprising that he didn't treat her as his wife from the beginning. It's clear that he led her to believe that his connection with her husband, who had died in a car accident in Iran and been buried there, was no more than a coincidence of names. Everybody, including Jacqueline Mugharib, was convinced that Nadia al-Amiry had no idea that her husband had died in a car accident until Kamal Medhat, the musician, had told her. It's also clear that after the man's death his papers had been stolen and he'd been buried without the Iranian authorities having access to information about him. Both the revolutionary and the opposition movements were willing in those days to buy documents at any price to help them smuggle their members out of the country. Equally clear is the fact that he never mentioned the secret directly to her. But no one knew what she thought of her fugitive or missing husband. That remained one of her closely guarded secrets. To clear up some of the mystery, we need to mention that Nadia al-Amiry's first husband, the merchant from Hama, had not been a particularly pious man, but he had been close to religious circles. He'd bought her a house in Al-Mansour City, a wealthy neighbourhood of Baghdad, after she'd given birth to a boy and a girl who now lived in Hama. One of her Syrian husband's friends was a certain Kamal Medhat, who was a good, honest man but was in love with his friend's wife. Her husband had became implicated in a coup hatched by Islamists in collaboration with army officers, and had been executed. Kamal Medhat had then married her. Their marriage was short-lived, he'd left for Tehran, where he'd been killed in an accident. She had left Hama and gone to live in Bab Touma. With her new husband away and with no information about him, she'd been utterly desolate. She'd wanted to return to Iraq, which wasn't easy because relations between the two countries were so strained. What Kamal Medhat now wanted was her help to return to Iraq, while all she wanted was his company. That was how they decided to return to Iraq and live in the house in Al-Mansour that had been left to her by her first husband.

Before discussing their return, we must describe the final scene between Kamal Medhat and Nadia al-Amiry in Damascus. Kamal Medhat had managed to change this woman completely, to convince her to demand her pleasures more forcefully than she had ever done in the past. Was he not, after all, the tobacco keeper, the guardian of ecstasy and pleasure? They were spotted together on New Year's Eve.

His head sank onto her shoulder out of pleasure. She wanted to breathe in his scent. He pressed her to him and she closed her eyes, almost collapsing from joy. She was gripped by powerful trembling as she stood in total darkness during the blackout in celebration of the New Year. A number of other men and women also took advantage of the darkness. The sound of music rose high from a corner and he thought he was about to be driven to orgasm. As she continued to lick the lobe of his ear, he was on the point of exclaiming, of falling down. But something saved him. Those sitting around thought he was simply drunk.

When the lights were switched back on, everybody was hopelessly drunk. Kamal was very hot because of the heating and the drink, but the breeze coming through the window cooled him down and relieved his erection. He lay on the sofa and heard the rhythms of the music like muffled blows. When she put her hand down his trousers, he came immediately. His face convulsed as he threw his head back.

Kamal Medhat reached Baghdad late at night; it was pouring with rain and pitch dark except for the flashes of lightning that lit up the city rapidly and briefly. Torrential rain continued to pour down from the sky. Nadia al-Amiry's house in Al-Mansour had a brick façade and all its windows, which were made of pine wood, reached up to the ceiling.

'What do you think?' she asked him as the car moved towards the entrance across the paved driveway. 'This is your home!' She turned to him sighing, and reached for his thigh.

It was still raining when the car stopped. Nadia opened her umbrella and stood in front of the car door. As he got out of the car, she held the umbrella over his head to protect him from the rain. He walked towards the white stone wall that separated the house from the garden. He walked until the water seeped into his shoes. He removed the umbrella from above his head and let the rain fall on his hair and face. His beard and hair were soaking wet. He looked at Nadia, raised his hands into the air, spun around in circles and roared with laughter. It wasn't a frivolous or sarcastic laugh, but a laugh straight from the heart.

In the morning, he opened his eyes slowly and felt his face. He looked to his right and found Nadia sleeping next to him. Still drowsy with sleep, he smelt a delightful fragrance emanating from her.

He got out of bed. Looking around the bedroom, he realized it was awful and a complete mess. On the floral wallpaper were family photographs and a painting of white horses. Magazines were scattered on the table and there was clutter everywhere. The decoration was primitive and artificial.

That morning, Kamal Medhat looked at the garden. A pomegranate tree was covered with a delicate film of water, which made it gleam and shimmer. From the closed window of the room, winter glowed in the morning light and the green garden was wet with the rain. Everything sparkled and shone. He felt that he was where he had always wanted to be. Trembling with exultation, he felt his heart pound as he stood behind the window. He was once again a child looking at a tree spreading its shade over a plot of roses and at the rooster swinging its long, red tail in the air. His homecoming was pure bliss.

So what was the cause of his elation?

Years later, he wrote to Farida: 'Simple-minded patriotism has never been one of my traits. In fact, I loathed patriotic feelings because they were the source of all fanaticism and hatred. But I felt like a rain bird coming back through the rain. I had to return on a cold, rainy day filled with thunder and lightning. When I think of this, I feel my heart fluttering and thumping like a great squirrel.'

He left the house in the evening and took the bus to Al-Saadoun Street. As he passed in front of the door of the Semiramis Cinema, he stopped briefly to read the declarations of war pasted beside posters of semi-naked actresses basking in the summer sun on a European beach. At that time, he became a regular visitor to a bar at the corner of the street. He went there almost every week, sitting alone and speaking to no one. He would watch the clusters of coloured lights coming from the music shops. He saw women standing in the rain at cinema box-offices. He smelt hamburgers coming from a nearby shop and the wet stones of Baghdad's streets on a rainy evening. He'd be happy walking in his heavy coat, black gloves and grey scarf. He entered a music shop and bought a medium-quality violin. At that particular moment, he realized how much he loved this part of Al-Saadoun Street in winter. So he stopped some distance from the Al-Nasr Square buses, took a cigarette out of the packet and lit it in the cold, damp air. He blew out the smoke and looked straight ahead at the street. He walked on until he reached the tunnel leading to the eastern gate. There he discovered a very different city. He was appalled by the posters for the war effort. Deep in his heart, he felt that the longer the war continued the more barbaric and deadly it would become.

Baghdad, unlike Damascus and Tehran, was a cosmopolitan city. There were foreigners almost everywhere and women went about the streets dressed in modern clothes until the small hours. There was a bar on almost every corner of Al-Saadoun Street; even *shawerma* restaurants served draught beer with sandwiches. The cinemas showed the latest movies, and the walls displayed posters for concerts like any modern metropolis. Plays and operas from around the world were performed at the most prestigious theatres in the Middle East. But Kamal Medhat sensed that behind the modern, civilized veneer of the city lurked flagrant examples of decay and death. He sensed that the soul of the old city was fretting and moaning because its powerful imagination was being bridled and suppressed by the political rhetoric of tyranny.

When he got home, he found Nadia sitting embroidering a dress for the baby she was expecting. He placed the stand near the large window overlooking the garden and began to play. That day, he wanted to regain his skill and recover his technique through various exercises on the violin. He soon found himself responding emotionally to the instrument, swaying as he used to do in the past. His heart thumped with pure joy as though he were under the influence of opium.

The Opium Concerto was the piece he'd composed on his return from Tehran in the late fifties. It was his most beautiful creation, but it had been confiscated together with his books and documents after his expulsion to Tehran. What if it was resurrected once again? He tried to recall the basic melody and introduce new variations. This was what he told Farida in one of his letters. But it's clear that he went back to his old habit of watching trees and flowers as a way of feeling the music of the universe.

Kamal Medhat played the music as he looked at the garden. He saw the trees with their huge trunks and their long branches towering tall and magnificent. The lush green colour emphasized the will to life, while wars emphasized the wills of their individual perpetrators. Wars were the conflict of different wills, embodying destruction and death. That night Kamal could not sleep. His soul was ablaze with the violin and he felt happy and fulfilled. He wanted to take a long walk in the rain, so he went out in his raincoat and strolled along Baghdad's wet streets. He sat on a bench in Al–Zawraa Park, his back turned to the cars and the buildings. He sat under the pouring rain the whole night, until his shoes became soaking wet. When the sun came up, he wandered a little in the park till he reached Al-Mansour Street, where he stopped in front of a man selling tea. The man had a large white moustache whose ends were yellowish from smoking. Kamal ordered a cup of cardamom tea and began to take one sip after another.

After a break from music of nearly three years he went gradually back to practising and playing.

Through practice his fingers, which had become rigid and stiff, began to grow supple, light and flexible. What was he going to do now? He was back in Baghdad, but what was he going to do? During this period his wife Nadia gave birth to a son, Omar. But like most artists, Kamal felt that children were of no great importance to him. The questions of art and work continued to plague him, until he was introduced to a Russian pianist, Maria Ivanova, who played in the large hall of the Sheraton Hotel. He began to accompany her on the violin at this place that was more of a café than a concert hall. The customers talked, drank and laughed as Kamal Medhat stood tall in his black suit and long hair, playing music and accompanied by the twenty-year old Ivanova, who wore a long dress with a slit that reached up to the thigh.

Kamal stood in front of Maria Ivanova as she bent over the piano and played. He stood tall, with his dark face and light, greying beard inclining as he slid his bow over the strings. He was much happier with the music than he was at being in a hall full of chattering people.

One day, a couple were sitting in the corner, listening to the music of this astonishing violinist who swayed with his violin like an accomplished dancer. This tall man with the greying beard and hair was no ordinary musician, for he never kept still while he played. He plucked the strings with tremendous force, moving his bow and turning this way and that. He leaned forward and produced exquisite, plaintive sounds amidst the noise of people drinking and laughing. The Russian pianist worked hard to keep up with this skilful violinist who swayed from side to side and produced such beautiful and technically accomplished music.

The young couple got up and came towards him.

'Who are you?' the young man asked in surprise.

A trembling Kamal Medhat stood stock still. His heart fluttered like a little squirrel within his chest. He felt that somebody had discovered his identity and wanted to arrest him. He realized his mistake in expressing himself through music, for his skilfulness might betray him. His talent, if discovered, would lead people to ask who he was. But it was music that tempted him to display his skills in front of Maria Ivanova.

'Kamal Medhat,' he said in a low voice.

The young man extended his hand to shake his. 'I'm Amjad Mustafa, a violinist,' he said, 'and this is my wife Widad, a cellist at the Symphony Orchestra.'

'Lovely to meet you,' he said, out of breath.

'I've never seen such ability or such technical competence. Where did you learn your music?'

'In Russia,' he said reluctantly.

'I studied in Budapest, at the Franz Liszt Conservatory.' He stressed the word Liszt, then added, 'May I give you my phone number? I would love to see you.'

Kamal Medhat placed the scrap of paper in the pocket of his black jacket, adjusted his red bow tie and went back to Maria Ivanova, who was enchanted by the way that he swayed and danced while playing the violin. He wasn't, in fact, playing music at all. He was dancing and making love to the instrument. He held it gently as though it were a woman, swayed with it as though he were kissing her, rising with her as she responded to him. He would probe deep inside her and mount higher and higher with her until he reached the zenith.

During the interval, Kamal Medhat went with Maria Ivanova to her room upstairs for an hour's rest before returning to the hall. He stood in front of the low table, opened a bottle of vodka and poured himself a glass. Then he poured another for her in the cut-crystal glass. He turned to her and asked, 'Would you like a drink?'

With her black hair falling over her shoulders and her soft features, Maria Ivanova stood, beautifully tall, before him. She took off her dress and let it drop to her feet. She stood completely naked in front of him, with her small, firm breasts, her smooth, round, white belly, her long, soft legs and her sparse pubic hair. Choosing erotic words intended to arouse him, she told him in Russian, 'I want you to play me ...'

'What?'

'I've never felt as jealous of a woman as I have of your violin today. You were making love to it, and I want you to do the same to me.'

Maria Ivanova's room was like a brothel. There were rugs on the floor and animal furs spread on her bed. The hot air made the atmosphere intimate and lustful. She discarded her dress and lay naked on top of the fur covers. She made animal-like noises as Kamal Medhat felt her body and passionately sucked her rosy nipples. She took his other hand and led it over the contours of her body.

He wrote to Farida: 'I'm keenly aware of my carnality. Like an animal, I'm hungry for every sensation, every sexual technique. I kissed her passionately, I bit her lips and groped her legs. I did everything.'

During this period, Kamal Medhat felt that Baghdad's winter had a sad, grey colour when the rain poured down on the buildings. He was overcome with sadness and reverential awe when he practised a piece by Schönberg every day in the living room. His furry, white cat opened and closed its large loving eyes as it sat on a chair observing him. The green grass of the garden outside the window was wet. During those days in particular he didn't know why he was reminded so much of Tahira's death. He was obsessed with the idea that she had wanted to die. The death wish was a real fact that couldn't be ignored, for it came from within the human soul and not from without. A person willed death and invited it from its eternal space. And death responded and came. The mystical feelings that dominated Kamal's mind at that time were linked with the mysterious death wish within him. He didn't fear death, but considered it a kind of flight into the unknown. Tahira might have succeeded in destroying the walls that encircled her. Death might perhaps free him, too, from the persistent images and nightmarish visions that had haunted his dreams and tortured him ever since the Farhoud. Death might destroy the wall that stood between him and his self, the wall that blinkered the narrow perception of his soul. It was as if he was being sucked in by the whole world, by noises, gentle arms, soft colours, escalating joy and an unbelievable force that pulled him upwards.

It's clear that it was Amjad Mustafa and his wife Widad who took Kamal Medhat out of his solitude and introduced him to Baghdad society. Widad, in particular, had family connections with the Iraqi political regime. She pushed him to find his rightful place as an artist of genius. For his part, he felt that his life had changed almost overnight. He became more attentive to his clothing and started to wear black suits, Italian gabardine coats and expensive glasses. He spent most of his time outside his home and enjoyed the company of musician friends for the first time. He was invited to the most important concerts in the world and accompanied the most famous orchestras that visited Baghdad. In addition to playing the violin, he began to compose pieces based on the ideas he had developed during his time in Tehran and Damascus. He played the violin in an intricate, highly skilled manner, and his ideas were fresh and plentiful. Those ideas helped him to develop spiritually. They were his first attempts at breaking down barriers, for some of his past compositions had been overly dignified. In brief, he managed to break through the solidified crust and allow the burning lava inside to erupt. But those works, after he'd put them aside and then gone back to them, became utterly nauseating to him.

He wrote to Farida: 'I use the word "nausea" in the physical sense of the word. Don't think that I'm exaggerating or using the word simplistically or foolishly. The truth of the matter is that I compose my pieces at amazing speed, by defeating the inner resistance which might stop me. I was like someone moving the radio tuner quickly. But when the notes were ready, I would leave them for a day or two.

259

And on returning to them, I'd be overcome with horrible nausea. Only aspirin could relieve me of the nausea and the headache.'

He had an intuitive feeling that his achievement was trivial and worthless. He procrastinated, waiting for the great idea to take shape in his mind. He never tried to capture it in its early stages of formation.

Amjad Mustafa brought him into the National Symphony Orchestra, which had been formed in Baghdad in the fifties and which performed at the Al-Rabat Hall on Al-Maghreb Street. For decades, the hall had been the venue of concerts almost every Thursday, with a huge audience always in attendance. Kamal Medhat became the first soloist in the orchestra and the most famous and best-known musician, even among ordinary people.

Kamal Medhat was immensely grateful to Amjad Mustafa, who helped him a great deal to achieve this position. Although Amjad was a much younger man than Kamal, his wide contacts within artistic and official circles made him seem much older than his years. He thus gave Kamal immeasurable help in his work in spite of the fact that everybody spoke of Widad and not Amjad as the prime mover. It was actually Widad who pushed Amjad to be the smokescreen while she was the one who performed the valuable services that put Kamal on the map.

Faris Hassan collected important information about Amjad Mustafa, who was born in a house with a view of the river in Al-Adhamiyah near the royal cemetery. His father was a mechanical engineer in the army. Amjad wasn't even five years old when his family moved to the privileged Al-Haretheya area in Baghdad, towards Al-Karkh. He lived in Baghdad until the age of twelve, and then travelled with his family to Britain, where his father had been appointed military attaché at the Iraqi Embassy in London.

His memories of London were of lush, green trees, of splendid, cool parks and of large squares where ponies pranced and trotted. He retained his passion for ponies all his life. Amjad never experienced the harshness of life, although he lived through a very difficult historical period, because he was born and lived at an important turning point in the history of the country. His father was a committed Baathist. After a rapid rise up the ladder of the Baath regime, he soon enough fell victim to the politics of terror and was executed while in his mid-forties. At that point Amjad and his mother returned from London, bearing the stigma suffered by families in similar situations. Two years later, Amjad travelled to Budapest to study music at the Franz Liszt Conservatory.

After his return to Baghdad, he got to know Widad Ahmed, who was studying cello at the Academy of Fine Arts. They met after his return from Budapest, when he gave a lecture about Bach at the Academy. She was the daughter of a senior official at the presidential palace who'd died in mysterious circumstances. Widad secured Amjad a good position in Baghdad, for she belonged to a family of important government officials and had authority, influence and wealth. Her brothers were top-ranking government officials, a category that included ambassadors, ministers and councillors. Thanks to her status, she succeeded in easing the political pressures on Amjad on account of the stigma that was attached to him. Amjad, moreover, took full advantage of his wife's influence and frequently travelled with her to Brussels, New York and Paris. In Paris, he strolled with her in the alleys and parks, and visited the cafés. Then he decided to stay on for a year to study at a Paris conservatory, where he became acquainted with a famous violinist called Eric Luc and with whom he became close friends.

*　*　*

In winter, there were always soirées at the house of Widad and Amjad Mustafa, in the roomy, light pink lounge. Huge chandeliers hung from the ceiling and the piano stood in the corner. Drinks were ranged on a shelf, as if in a bar. Friends and their wives all met up, especially on Thursdays, to drink wine and have supper.

Amjad Mustafa's friendship was of paramount importance to Kamal Medhat. After meeting him, he didn't stay at home much. He spent a great deal of his time practising the violin at the Al-Rabat Hall on Al-Maghreb Street; he also gave more and more concerts. He visited Amjad, in whose house he was introduced to artists, writers, intellectuals and painters. Among them were the oud player Munir Bashir, the famous Armenian pianist Beatrice Ohanessian, the sculptor Mohammad Ghani Hekmat, and Khaled Al-Rahhal. Everybody confirmed that Kamal Medhat, who had emerged on the scene out of the blue in 1983, spent most of his evenings talking to the musicians, painters and poets who gathered in Amjad and Widad's house, where the large window of the lounge looked out over a wooded garden and where birds could be heard chirping and could be seen hopping about. Nothing disturbed the peace and joy of those ambitious artists or hampered their artistic creativity, except the sound of bombs. Iran's artillery shelled Basra and the cities of the south. Everybody realized that Saddam was slowly giving up his *Blitzkrieg* tactics. In fact, the war's toll was heavy and costly, and people despaired of seeing its end. Every evening Baghdad TV showed a programme about the war. This presented images of dead Iranians torn to pieces by fighter planes, their guts strewn over the ground, their heads severed and their smashed faces covered with dust. The programme didn't relay footage of the battles between the two armics, but only the maimed bodies and scattered limbs of the enemy. The camera moved along rows of laid-out bodies and panned over piles of corpses, zooming in on a burnt face, a severed hand or a half-buried body. Such scenes were the focus of conversations about the war among Amjad's artist friends.

The group held different, conflicting views. Kamal Medhat was greatly dismayed by the war, although he didn't give clear expression to his views. He was surprised by Amjad Mustafa's ideas and convictions, for he was the only one among the artists to use a racial justification for the war. He would say, as he drank a glass of Scotch on the rocks, 'The war broke out because of Persian malice towards the Arabs, because Arabs are superior. They'll never give up waging war against Iraq.'

Amjad Mustafa gave a racial and ethnic justification, in contrast with the religious justification that Kamal Medhat often heard from Iranians in Tehran. Iranians believed that the war had started because of the Christians among the Baath leadership. These Christians, according to Iranian views, were bent on destroying Muslim unity. Kamal began gradually to understand his friend's ideas and beliefs, ideas that were common among a particular class of intellectuals and artists. Discussion between them became heated. Kamal didn't believe in the totalitarian ideas imposed by the state on people, while Amjad's arguments grew more vehement every time there was a discussion of the war. He stood in the corner, describing the enemy's dead in the most violent terms. He felt that killing was sometimes justified and necessary, because it involved the survival of the fittest. Kamal, on the other hand, sat quietly in the same corner, near the mantelpiece on which stood some wooden and silver decorative objects. He held a glass of Scotch and quietly stroked his long, greying beard, which enhanced his looks so well. Facing him stood Amjad with his large shaved head and his black drooping moustache. He represented the nationalist image of masculinity that was prevalent in Baghdad at the time. Standing in the corner, he held his glass and attacked Kamal, who didn't believe in the manifest destiny of nations.

Amjad believed that the Arab nation had an immortal message, which was the spiritual development of the world. The statement made Kamal burst into laughter. Kamal found it mind-boggling that this talented artist could be a convinced Baathist and an extremist Iraqi, who read Nietzsche and Fichte's *Addresses to the German Nation*, and admired Chamberlain, especially his book *The Foundations of the Nineteenth Century*. Amjad also read the literature of the Baath Party, which was influenced by Gustave Le Bon's ideas that race and nation were identical. Amjad, in fact, believed that Arabs were surrounded by inferior races who were created for barbarity and savagery. At best, these races were the recipients of civilization and not its makers. These inferior races felt nothing but hatred and envy for the Arabs. He threw a book entitled *Iranian Wars Against Iraq*, at Kamal an old publication with torn covers and yellowed paper. It was a primitive edition published for the first time in the nineteenth century.

'Read Suleiman Faïq's book and you'll find all the information you need there.'

His fundamental idea was the necessity of returning to history, an idea that nauseated and suffocated Kamal Medhat. Was it possible that anyone could hold such views? Thinking of human history in terms of perpetual conflict would negate all other forms of relations. Kamal Medhat started to read the papers every day in order to follow up on the historical school of thought that Saddam Hussein himself endorsed. This school aimed to prove that the three-thousand-year history of the region was evidence of the unceasing hostility of the Persians, Kurds and Turks towards Arabs. Kamal Medhat believed that this view saw history as controlled by the human will. It was an idea that was intent on highlighting one type of relationship at the expense of all others, negating commercial, cultural and other connections. Was warfare the only connection that existed between Persians and Arabs? The historical school wanted to ignore the conflicts among Semitic peoples and emphasize only the Persian malice against Arabs. This was the view that the regime and its ideologues wished to impose on art. It made Kamal wince in disgust and revulsion.

Then Amjad got up, took a book from his library and read aloud a text by the Assyrian King Sennacherib: 'I slaughtered them like sheep and cut their throats with a single strike ... And on the battlefield, the entrails and heads of soldiers were covered with dust and the flanks of my horses sank deep in streams of blood.'

Amjad trembled as he read the passage. A patriotic tremor shook his whole being. The passage filled him with ecstasy at the scenes of killing, destruction and devastation produced by war. It was his joy to achieve overwhelming victory over the enemy.

On that day, Kamal felt that cruel, sadistic minds were turning Baghdad into a Spartan society, a city built on the ethics of warfare. The citizen was basically a soldier. He was violent, pompous, impulsive and coarse. Military uniforms were the object of pride, something to boast about among young people, and military jargon was widespread among people. Cruelty became the hallmark of that militarized, Spartan society. Military uniform was the wedding suit for officers and soldiers getting married. Kamal frequently saw a soldier in battle gear standing beside his bride in her white wedding dress, while the music played in the background.

The execution of deserters from the front also became a familiar sight.

Simple peasant soldiers, who were barely twenty, were driven violently in front of the assembled crowds and placed on top of tall, white columns in public squares. In a short while, other soldiers arrived wearing black masks. They aimed their rifles at them and shot at their heads and chests in an orderly fashion. It was a sacred ceremony of slaughter, where bright red blood streamed from chests and cheeks in full view of the roaring crowds.

All these displays concealed the bitter anger everywhere and the hidden cruelty that came to the surface from time to time. Kamal felt that the population was clearly suffering from schizophrenia, a split between the false claims of grandeur, superiority and uniqueness, on the one hand, and the dismal realities produced by a despotic regime that crushed, marginalized and humiliated every single individual, on the other. He felt that he was living in a rebellious, introverted nation, one that was characterized by fanaticism and other negative qualities, which it had acquired in such abnormal conditions.

At the end of 1983, Maestro Walid Gholmieh would lead the National Symphony Orchestra in playing his Martyr Symphony. Among the musicians were Kamal, Amjad and Widad. More than anyone else, Kamal was aware of the noble and pure spirit of the martyr within him. But for him, this martyr was every martyr to war everywhere. Once, at the end of a practice session, the three of them, Kamal, Widad and Amjad, went to a restaurant near

Al-Maghreb Street. As soon as they settled at a table, Amjad Mustafa began his talk about martyrdom, pointing out that the Iraqi dead were martyrs while the Iranian dead were no more than harmful insects. Amjad's talk reminded Kamal Medhat of his time in Iran, when the Iranians believed that the Iraqi dead would go straight to hell, while Iranians would be rewarded with heaven. Amjad Mustafa, however, added a philosophical twist by pointing out that the Iraqi martyr had achieved harmony between life and death. Kamal Medhat felt then that discussions with Amjad were utterly fruitless. So he stopped talking and contented himself with drinking his beer. From time to time, he joked and laughed with Widad. Amjad, in contrast, became very tense as he elaborated on his views. Banging the table with his hand, he told them that the Iraqi martyr had became one with the tragedy of Iraq itself, for the country was in an isolation imposed on it by Arabs. So the Iraqi martyr was a kind of tragic hero whose sacrifice was an expression of the national character.

Kamal Medhat wasn't capable of making fun of these ideas because he was scared. But he realized clearly that the nationalist ideology in Baghdad gave the oppressed people a sense of false grandeur and led them to believe that Iraq stood alone and isolated. Of all its neighbours, it was the only country without a coast. It was also the least dependent on commerce, travel and collaboration. Martyrdom therefore was a necessity. The symphony composed by Walid Gholmieh would, therefore, be played by the Iraqi orchestra and broadcast everywhere on the last day of December. Cars and people would stop in their tracks and car horns would blow continuously. Church bells would ring and mosques would praise God as the Martyr Symphony was played.

Were Iraqis the only martyrs? This was undoubtedly a revolting question for Kamal. After all, what was the difference between being martyred and being killed? But it was Amjad Mustafa's opinions that forced the question on him. Amjad used specific epithets in his description of Iranian soldiers: they were mercenaries and harmful insects that deserved to die. The discourse was no different from that of the Iranians, who described the Iraqi dead as apostates. On both sides, there were sadistic, political speeches that concentrated on crushed bodies, broken necks and severed heads. In both Iraq and Iran there was a kind of pathological morbidity that revelled in people's destruction. Kamal realized that discussions and debates about these matters were utterly futile.

There was another factor in all this: Widad was more attracted to Kamal Medhat's views than she was to her husband's. She pushed Kamal Medhat into a brand new area, for she not only introduced him to the National Symphony Orchestra in Baghdad, where he soon became the lead soloist, but she also introduced him to the political elite. Using her wide connections and her wealthy family's contacts in high places, she put him in touch with influential politicians, who encouraged a limited kind of social and cultural modernity in literature and art. They used modernity as a double-edged sword: on the one hand to mobilize people, and on the other as a movement to counter the medieval political power in Iran.

Widad greatly admired Kamal Medhat. A great intellectual and a peerless musician, this affectionate man in his fifties was a mass of feelings and sensations. Soft-spoken, handsome and impressively tall, with delicate features and attractive, dandyish gestures, he may have inspired more than admiration. She took special care of him and was particularly interested in his welfare. For his part, he was aware of her feelings and had no wish to stop her. This became known to everyone, even his wife, Nadia al-Amiry, who became suspicious when she saw Widad's excessive concern. But who was it that introduced Kamal Medhat to Saddam Hussein at that time? All the evidence suggests that he was invited to the presidential palace through Widad Ahmed's highly connected brothers. It was also through Widad's good offices that he performed several times in front of Saddam Hussein.

Groups of intellectuals were transported in large coaches to the great presidential palace, which wasn't easy to reach. With their tinted glass windows, the coaches passed through thick wooded gardens and stopped in front of a towering palace. There were flowerbeds, small artificial ponds, swimming pools and bright green grass. At the various entrances there were armoured vehicles and tanks. In the watchtower were special guards dressed in their uniforms and helmets, holding machine guns. At the entrance to the grand hall there were the latest models of cars, with guards armed to the teeth.

They entered the palace and waited for a very long time until the president appeared. Once he'd arrived, Saddam was received with cheers. He was in his khaki military uniform made of high-quality broadcloth and wore no beret. He advanced cautiously, smiling and waving with his right hand to the people standing around. The artists clapped rhythmically and chanted slogans. The waiters in white jackets served glasses of juice from large trays. Saddam gave a long speech on art and its political function. Kamal Medhat, who wasn't listening to the speech, was awoken from his reveries by the sound of the clapping. At last, everybody stood up and the president shook the hands of each and every guest. Kamal

Medhat saw the president at close quarters when he approached, accompanied by his secretary, Abd Hamoud, who noted down everything that happened in a little notebook.

It was the first time that Kamal had seen Saddam in person, after having seen his photographs everywhere on the streets. He felt that Saddam exercised his power through those photographs, which deputized in his absence. The photographs filled the spaces and absences with images of Saddam smoking, eating watermelon, mending his daughter's dress, hunting gazelles or eating grilled meat. He was photographed parading in a military uniform, wearing an American cowboy outfit or dressed as an Arab and riding a horse. Now here was Saddam standing in front of him, placing his hand on Kamal Medhat's shoulder and bursting out laughing, revealing his white teeth and gold crowns. He ordered his secretary to arrange a special meeting with him.

After the reception, Kamal was called by a man with marked peasant features and a thick Bedouin dialect. The man's hair fell onto his forehead and his moustache covered his mouth. His head was twice the size of a normal head and he had the profile of a bird of prey. His large, dark eyes looked like two smudges beneath his eyelashes. He spoke slowly, but his hard, stern gaze provoked fear even when he smiled.

The man was sitting in a strange-looking office. Near the door were large rolled-up maps and in the corner stood a stuffed fox, all covered with dust. The place looked more like a shop than an office, for the shelves reached the ceiling and were filled with mysterious boxes. There were also boxes containing foreign books and three cupboards that were filled with archives, records and files. On the wall were paintings by well-known Iraqi artists such as Jawad Selim, Faïq Hassan and Atta Sabri. There were also original statues and cheap copies as well as an elephant's tusk and African masks.

'The president wishes to throw a private party. Give me your phone number and we'll contact you.' This was what he'd told him, in a tone between an order and a request. Within a month, Kamal Medhat was playing in front of the president.

Kamal wore his black tuxedo with tails. He stood tall and thin; his face was dark and his eyes sparkled as he held his bow and violin in the spotlight. After a moment of silence, he began, creating out of the melodies a constellation of stars in the air. To his right was Widad holding the tip of her cello. She sat in her chair with the instrument stretched beside her body, like an eternal beloved. Kamal Medhat's gaze was fixed on the tip of the conductor's baton and on his eyes. With Kamal Medhat were forty musicians, playing the Opium Concerto. The president sat at the front, surrounded by a cluster of guards.

When the music stopped, Kamal Medhat was jolted back to consciousness by the applause of the president and the sideways smile that appeared from beneath his moustache. He heard the clapping of the ministers ranged in a row and saw the stern looks of the guards. The conductor bowed his head, then stood erect and pointed to the soloist, Kamal Medhat. A beautiful, tall blonde girl carrying a bouquet of flowers advanced and offered it to the conductor. He took the bouquet with a smile and offered it to Kamal Medhat, who moved it to one side and bowed again. He wondered if these politicians and guards appreciated the music and felt its strong rhythm. Did they know that they'd once confiscated and torn up this piece of music? Did they understand its meaning or its dimensions? What was this performance? And what lay behind the thick silence of existence? Chaos?

271

Nothingness? Or the sap of life, free energy released to engulf everything?

What were these presidential rituals? Did they symbolise something else? Such were Kamal's thought on that day. He wondered where they came from. From religion, for example? Did they symbolize anything else? Did they hide other things? He often reflected on his doubts and uncertainties, for he didn't know the truth. He wondered whether presidential ceremonies were as absorbing as music was to him. Years later, he wrote to Farida saying: 'Throughout my life I've never been immersed in anything except music. There has always been an ego that watched me and made fun of everything I did. Don't those great politicians possess a similar ego that watches them and makes fun of their acting and role-playing?'

Kamal realized that the truth was never granted as a gift. Every time he was required to take a single step towards the point of no return, he hesitated and was afflicted by vertigo and a horrifying sense of disappointment. During this period, rumours circulated of a love affair between him and Widad, Amjad's wife. But what was the truth of this rumour? Widad was a woman of only average beauty, but she was extremely gentle and delicate. Her dark eyes were full of reflections and insatiable hunger. They were lustful and frank. Her lips were savage and highly sensitive, while her looks were sparkling, contemplative and intense. Her unruly hair flew wildly in the air. Men admired her delicate complexion and her fair-skinned forehead. But why would she fancy Kamal, who was so much older than her?

Widad, in fact, saw in Kamal's personality a kind of madness, a crazy rebellion. He had an aura of savagery that she adored. She saw in him a man without inhibitions, a man with a sensitive, elevated soul. He was like a refined animal. But an animal with an ailment, albeit an intangible, obscure ailment. Widad wanted him at any price. She wanted to possess him even though she knew he was not available, for he never gave himself to anyone but himself. She watched his every move, his every gesture. She tried with all her might to claim him. She might desire him but she could never lay hold of him. His phantom haunted her everywhere: in the glass that she drank from, in the music that she played, in the fragments of broken marble and in the wood that fed the fire. When he played one of Bach's famous pieces in the hall, she felt totally numb. His music was harmonious and highly polished. His performance of the long first movement of Bach's opus was superb. He crowned the performance with a cadenza that was brilliant and exceptionally fluid, like a spring gushing out of the dryness of desert dunes. Kamal Medhat added lustre and richness to the arid desert. He burnt his fingers with a flame that glowed from the ashes of ovens.

Only with music could he grasp the balance of nature and return to the moment of creation.

When Kamal advanced smiling towards Widad, she started to stammer. It made him laugh out loud to see her confusion. He felt no pity or sympathy towards her. She, in contrast, pined for him. Every time she sat in front of him, she felt the pain of longing. She saw him falling prey to weariness without being able to offer him a helping hand.

Infatuated, she watched him as he moved around the living room of her house. She adored everything he touched, from the glass to the ashtray. He, on the other hand, never settled in one spot, moving quickly between the bookcase and the fireplace.

When he sat down, he sat quietly as though it were a dictate of fate. His clothes had a special charm, for he always wore loosely around his neck, like a bohemian, a scarf as red as bull's blood, gabardine trousers and a black coat that gave him the look of a monk. When leaving the house, he would kiss her on the cheek. The brush of his beard against her cheek excited her; for her this innocent kiss was erotically charged. One day, she decided to seduce him.

I don't know when this actually happened, but it may have been some time before the second Gulf War, while Amjad was out of the country. One evening, Widad left the Al-Rabat Hall after giving a concert there in the company of Kamal. When she took hold of his hand, he shivered at the touch. She drove him to her house and tried to seduce him there. But Kamal was scared. She held his hand between her palms and sensed his agitation. He didn't know what to do. But she enjoyed the state of turmoil he was in, for he was like a little sparrow fluttering and trembling in her hands. In a few minutes, his reluctance disappeared and his anxiety vanished. He felt elated to be loved and wanted.

After moments of silence, he leaned towards her and began kissing her with great passion.

Did Amjad Mustafa love Widad for her money? Widad was the pampered favourite of many men, including her late father, the senior presidential official, and her uncle, an Iraqi ambassador to Europe. This uncle was a middle-aged man with a fine nose and good posture thanks to diet, physical exercise and frequent massages. His tanned complexion came from sunbathing. She was also the favourite of her three brothers, who were all close to

274

political circles in Baghdad. Before Amjad, Widad had been married to an army officer who'd been killed in the first months of the war. She married Amjad a year after the death of her first husband. But her only taste of true love was when she was studying music at the Academy of Fine Arts, with a man twenty years her senior. He was a womanizer who had sex with her in his apartment near the Academy.

Her story with Amjad was both simple and spontaneous. She met him while he was giving a lecture on Bach, and a relationship started. Through her, Amjad established contacts with Baghdad's high society, which opened its arms to him in spite of his limited financial means. Some people even asked him to introduce them to Saddam Hussein himself. He'd become a famous musician at the National Symphony Orchestra. He harboured a passionate love for Widad, and although his attempts to court her and ask for her hand in marriage were initially unsuccessful, his persistence and resolve finally made her relent.

Such were Amjad's feelings towards her. But where did Kamal place her within the tapestry of his own life? He was the old, impetuous hedonist, the saintly sinner and the opium keeper. He was Álvaro de Campos, who forced together the traits of all his various personalities. He turned music into a dynamic instrument that could fine-tune his mood and his principles. Wasn't music, after all, the substitute for real opium? Where did he place Widad, then? Where did the tobacco keeper, who owned a whole warehouse full and not just a shop, place Widad? He was the adventurer who faced the entire universe using all the strategies at his disposal, who carried within his soul the essence of cities as diverse as Tehran, Baghdad and Damascus. He was a legend who, with his manic depression, turned music into a replacement for opium, and sex into a substitute for tobacco. If he failed to create a utopian identity, he overcame his shortcomings through women and music. All he wanted was a woman's body and a tobacco shop.

During this period, he became acquainted with an unusual Assyrian Christian woman from Basra called Janet. She was a novice pianist who, after the war, turned to prostitution. She worked at a brothel for young prostitutes in Al-Elweya neighbourhood. She then became a fixture in musical circles. Kamal Medhat got to know her after a concert he gave at the Al-Rabat Hall, where the National Symphony Orchestra played almost every Thursday. It might have been Widad who introduced him to Janet, who was her colleague at the Academy. Janet began to invite Kamal to go out with her. Widad had no idea that Kamal Medhat would like or desire Janet, for she was very thin, malnourished and hysterical. In addition to other undesirable qualities, she was also an alcoholic.

One day, Janet invited the playboy musician with his impressive height and his good looks to her apartment. Having got drunk, she broke the furniture and smashed the windows. She went out of the front door and began to scream so hard that people gathered around. So Kamal Medhat carried her, by force to begin with, back to her apartment. She kept screaming and struggling for a whole hour, after which he took her to hospital. The incident brought their affair out into the open, and aroused Widad's jealousy immensely.

Widad felt murderously jealous of Janet.

'How could that wretch, that cockroach, take Kamal?'

In a moment of weakness, Widad approached Nadia al-Amiry and told her of Kamal Medhat's affair with Janet. Nadia was upset and extremely sad at the news. Although she suffered many sleepless nights as a result of the affair, she didn't talk to Kamal directly about it. Instead, she called Janet to her house, took out her chequebook and asked: 'How much, to leave Kamal?'

Kamal Medhat felt that Nadia al-Amiry's love for him was excessive and extreme. It was a sick and unnatural kind of love, tainted by the enjoyment of pain, something akin to the delight of saints in suffering. She knew that he was unfaithful to her. But his marital infidelities became for her a kind of sacred rite of purification. He was like a spoilt child, so his infidelities were always forgiven.

Janet, on the other hand, was obsessed with sex. She started her life as a lesbian, but was converted at the hands of a male lover who then abandoned her. She then fell into the arms of Kamal Medhat. One day, Widad slapped him in the face and told him that she was the one who'd introduced Janet to him. She wasn't his pimp, she screamed at him.

For Kamal Medhat, Janet embodied all human contradictions. She was like one of the sacred prostitutes of the Al-Torah whom he'd desired so much while reading the Holy Book in the company of Gladys. She reminded him of all the sacred harlots whose erotic sighs he'd heard coming out of the yellowed pages of the Al-Torah. She was an angel and a vampire at one and the same time. A politician had fallen in love with pale, anaemic Janet just because she was damaged. He couldn't put her out of his mind, and sent a warning to Kamal Medhat, who had stolen her mind and stopped her thinking of him.

Janet was a true legend. In spite of her ugliness, she managed to attract a huge number of men with her lewd and whoring attitude. One day, after Kamal had left his house, he was astounded to see the car of Janet's lover intercepting his vehicle on the bridge. A sixty-year-old man got out. He had grey hair that was dyed pitch-black, making his head look like fleece. He took a picture out of his pocket. 'Do you know this person?' he panted, his eyes sparkling.

Kamal Medhat was silent for a moment and nodded. He realized that the man was hopelessly in love with Janet, for he held the picture with all the tenderness that a mother would show towards her child, even though she knew how ugly it was.

Janet was obsessed with sex. She did many evil things in her life, but men loved her because she opened her legs like an animal and allowed them to do as they pleased, which respectable women never did.

Kamal Medhat wrote to Farida: 'At times of war, animal instincts are always on the rise. Sex becomes the antonym of death, and not of love. Nobody really thinks about this, but there are forms of sex that reach the height of perversity and irrationality: lesbianism, infidelity, sado-masochism and all types of tenderness and cruelty rolled together. Such is war. It means the sheer insanity of extremists, fools and hysterics. It means people suffering from hallucinations, paranoia, waking dreams and bouts of depression, despair and crying. It is a hunger for blood and a thirst for filth.'

During a hunting trip to Diyala, Janet insisted on coming, along with Widad, Amjad, Kamal and Nadia al-Amiry. As Janet was standing among the palm trees, she was shot in the chest and fell dead, drenched in blood. An hour later, the police arrested a farmer with a gun in the vicinity. Everybody believed that her politician lover had arranged for one of his guards to kill her.

* * *

During this period, Kamal Medhat acquired a reputation for loose and dissolute living that paid no attention to custom or form. He regarded Nadia only as a ceremonial wife and had numerous mistresses. He became a walking, talking sex legend, loved by women for his looks, his music, his complex personality and his fretfulness.

He wrote to Farida: 'Nadia forgives me everything I do. My lapses are naturally quite bad in some respects but they are also fairly simple. I can't say that I haven't hurt her, but my relationships with women make me love life more. It's not something I can get away from. I often think of her and I'm overwhelmed with dread. One word could be the end of me.'

Did he fear her? Was he scared that she might betray him to the authorities? She, after all, was the only one who knew the truth about him. And then, what was the story of his nightmares? Kamal Medhat would often wake up screaming. Two or three times a week he was seized by nightmares. They came randomly: at midnight, at one in the morning or sometimes at five in the morning.

He tossed and turned in bed, then gave a loud scream. It was a sharp, high-pitched noise like the croaking of a man dying a violent death or one committing suicide by jumping off a building. It was the scream of a man hit by a speeding car. The whole house shook with the sound of his screams. Nadia would wake up and sit by his side. Every muscle of his body pulsed and his heartbeat thumped like a drum. He trembled all over and his voice rose high. His hands were cupped on his face. After the screaming had suddenly subsided, he opened his eyes and looked at Nadia with his eyes flashing. He then fell into a mysterious silence and lay back quietly on his pillow. She held onto him to make sure that he was still breathing and that his heart was pulsing with life.

He once wrote in one of his letters to Farida: 'How long can a man continue to be afraid? How old should a man be before he eliminates his fears? Here I am at fifty, and until now I'm as scared as I was at ten, or even twenty. How old should I be to be able to sleep without nightmares, tears or fear?'

If this was Kamal Medhat, what was Nadia al-Amiry like?

Nadia al-Amiry was a sick woman who lived a contradiction. On the one hand, there were those who admired and revered her on account of her beauty (or on account of their personal weaknesses), and on the other hand, there were others who did not fall under her spell and felt nothing but contempt for her.

Nadia al-Amiry was a deranged, pretentious woman, who bequeathed her arrogance to her son Omar. Nevertheless, she flattered Kamal as if she were a servant and would never embarrass him. She dedicated her life to raising her son, while Kamal was engrossed in his friendships, affairs and his love of art, while neglecting everything else. But Janet's murder transformed the lives of the two families entirely.

It's clear that Widad and Amjad reached a point where they could no longer go on together. Nobody knew whether Kamal was responsible for the rift, but everybody confirmed that Amjad's relationship with Kamal was not affected. This implies that the breakup happened for other reasons, related to the nature of Widad and Amjad's relationship. Widad got divorced from Amjad and after a while emigrated to the United States. One day, Widad got in touch with Nadia al-Amiry, who was spending the summer with her son Omar in Beirut, as usual, and suggested they meet in Beirut. It was the summer of 1990. She received Widad's letter a week before her departure. Widad actually went to see Nadia at the Hilton Hotel on Al-Hamra Street. Nadia was sitting in the lobby when a woman came up and said hello. Nadia didn't recognize her, because Widad had become very fat. She'd cut her hair so short that her scalp showed through and her eyes were lacklustre and empty. She confessed that she'd been unfaithful to her husband and committed adultery. But she didn't deny that her love for Kamal was overpowering and destructive.

When Nadia returned to Baghdad, she was bitterly angry with Kamal. Her anger grew when she saw the huge transformation in Amjad Mustafa. He'd become flabby and was doing the rounds from one nightclub to another, staying up late and drinking too much.

During that time, Baghdad was commemorating its victory over Iran and the celebrations continued for a whole week. Kamal Medhat stood in front of Saddam Hussein for the second time on Victory Day, before the Arch of Triumph that had been erected by Saddam for the anniversary. Near the Arch the helmets of the defeated Iranian soldiers were piled up. Saddam was extremely happy and his eyes gleamed with the joy of victory. It was the first time that Kamal could scrutinize Saddam's face. His eyes were jaundiced and twinkling, and his dark face had a yellow hue. Everything about him suggested order. When he smiled it was from the left corner of his mouth. The lips parted, revealing a section of his teeth, while his eyes remained fixed on the person in front of him. The place was deathly silent. But Kamal wasn't afraid of him, even though he knew that this was a man who would stop at nothing. He was a force moving forward and capable of demolishing anything that stood in its way. He wasn't a mythical creature, but he was strong and had powerful instincts. A number of artists, playwrights, writers, architects and physicians were among those who were offering their congratulations. At the beginning, Kamal counted down from ten to zero, in order to conceal his confusion. He advanced towards Saddam. Forgetting himself, he bowed his head while shaking hands, as he often did at a musical performance.

'Good to see you,' he said to Kamal, 'we want you at a private party, to play music for us at the presidential palace in celebration of Victory Day.'

'With pleasure, Sir,' he said, smiling.

He later explained to Farida the exchange between him and the president, making the following remark: 'I looked at the president, who was flushed with the victory he'd achieved. His eyes sparkled and his face was cheerful. He must have been extremely happy because he'd crushed his adversary, while Khomeini, who'd been defeated, had to swallow poison. I ask myself what happiness means. Those politicians always follow their instinctive feelings. They enjoy the pleasures of life to the utmost and take ruthless revenge for the slightest offence. Their anger is bitter and their demolition of their enemies is brutal. As far as I'm concerned, I feel nothing. Music gives me a kind of comfortable oblivion that drives away all the fear and anxiety I have felt throughout my life.

'You may ask me about the person who caused Tahira's death and the disappearance of my son, Hussein, the person responsible for destroying my whole life. Do I have a sense of malice towards him? Do I want revenge? Never. I have no such feelings. All my feelings can be summed up by the Iraqi song that you loved so much: "If I cannot take revenge myself, God can."'

*　　*　　*

Kamal Medhat pushed the violin under his chin and held it with a supple arm. He looked at the bright sun and the swimming pool in the presidential palace. He was tempted to remove his clothes and take a dip in the water.

The president laughed with his guests, while Kamal felt some pain in his fingers as he pressed on the strings. The spirit of music was gone from the instrument and it seemed to produce an unfeeling moan. Mozart was no doubt turning in his grave because the musician didn't feel the music but was obliged to continue producing the notes nonetheless. Nobody paid any attention to Kamal. All he had to do was to play louder. He thought of Mozart, who played music for the king in the morning and in the afternoon sat at the servants' table and played for them at the orders of the chef, the king of the kitchen.

When Kamal Medhat performed in front of an audience, he soared with the sounds until he became totally oblivious to everything around him. His body, however, remained firmly on the ground like a dead shell. At the end of his performance, he felt that his music had washed his soul clean. But at the presidential palace, he felt absolutely nothing. He had just one desire, to take off his clothes in front of the guests and jump into the swimming pool.

In a letter he sent to Farida, he told her that he was the person who'd advised Saddam Hussein to invite the architect Venturi to take part in the competition to build a mosque in Baghdad. Venturi was the indisputable master of architectural kitsch.

What made him give Saddam this advice?

The only reason was that Kamal Medhat realized, both intuitively and rationally, that Saddam Hussein, whose tastes were so populist in nature, would admire the work of the most brilliant

architect in the world. Venturi was an artist who endowed vulgarity, populism and earthiness with a high aesthetic value. Kamal
Medhat might have realized, too, that the grand design that Venturi
created for San Francisco's cafés was not the model likely to attract
the president's attention. But the popular touch that he might add
to the mosque would undoubtedly make the design attractive to
Saddam Hussein, whose taste by that time was very cheap. The
mosque would be a place of worship in the first place, but it
would also be a Western work that appealed to popular taste. It
would become a place combining modern, Western and popular
cultures, a place where more than thirty thousand worshippers
would pray. It would represent an architectural leap forward along
the lines of the president's desires and dreams.

Venturi entered the hall of the presidential palace.

The president stood at the centre, a huge bookcase behind
him. A large chandelier hung from the high ceiling. There were
luxurious sets of upholstered and high-backed chairs. Special
guards without berets stood around. Thick, black moustaches
covered the mouths of the guests. Venturi stood in the middle of
a large circle of architects that included the Spaniard Ricardo
Bofill and Jean Pondo, and behind him was a group of Iraqi
architects and painters as well as Kamal Medhat in his black suit
and bow tie. The model for Venturi's mosque was on display in
front of the president.

It had a high, decorative dome that was borrowed from classical
Islamic architecture and a pastiche of Orientalist images taken from
Hollywood movies and novels about Baghdad. The dome looked
like a huge tree standing in a courtyard. It was bright and airy,
providing shade to the prayer area and the worshippers beneath.
The new mosque was a colossal structure that looked like a casino.

It paid tribute to popular taste while downplaying the stark solemnity of the traditional mosque. Entry into the mosque was meant to be as joyous as stepping into a restaurant or a nightclub.

After the end of the Iraq–Iran war, Kamal Medhat wrote many letters to Farida. Life in Baghdad, he told her, was not only quiet but almost dead. He believed that tranquillity in the Middle East was a most dangerous sign. As soon as the country enjoyed a degree of prosperity, the situation would explode once again. He also told her of other family news: in summary, Nadia's illness, Widad's emigration, Janet's murder and Amjad Mustafa's alcoholism and addiction. Kamal never stopped giving concerts or accepting invitations. But he felt that the post-war years were a time of uncertainty and apprehension. The lifeline of the regime in Baghdad was action and initiative. It couldn't wait behind the scenes for long. Kamal Medhat felt certain that the regime would have to resort to violence sooner or later as the ultimate way out, for it couldn't tolerate stagnation. It feared and dreaded inaction. He was sure that the country was suffering from a psychological disorder after all the revolutions, wars, cruelty and violence. A deadly despair had taken hold of people. The people had become a single mass and the class system had collapsed completely. No real distinctions existed, for all were in the same boat. People were united by fear, poverty and humiliation. Kamal Medhat no longer had faith in the existence of rational judgement. The Middle East was a simmering pot of anger, cruelty and hate. Its politics were based on chauvinism and prejudice. Society was dominated by degenerate values that didn't differentiate between political and gangster ethics. The citizens of the country had finally become the mob.

Everyone was leaving the country or trying to escape. Nadia stood on crutches in front of him, wearing her blue dressing gown. Her face looked withered and sick and her lips trembled. 'Omar can't stay here,' she told him, 'I don't want him to see the atrocities of war. I'll send him to my sister in Egypt.'

Just one day after this conversation between Kamal and Nadia, he bade goodbye to his son, and went back home. He sat in a chair near the window, enjoying once again the sight of trees and flowers. He thought of the fates of his three sons: Meir in the States, Omar in Cairo and Hussein in Tehran.

He trembled to think of their destinies. He shivered to think of a country that held so many closely guarded secrets. A new obsession loomed in the air, a new romanticized notion to blow away minds and thoughts. A deep sense of defeat and malice predominated. Political confrontations abounded, guided only by the unquestioning glorification of nihilism, rebellion and irrationality. The regime exalted the mysterious powers of instincts and blood. Saddam Hussein himself was part of the legacy of nihilism. He was moved by the spirit of the rabble and by malicious, vengeful calculations. His madness came into its own only through the creation of permanent, eternal enemies: first the communists, then the Iranians and then the West. Iraq's existence was defined by the existence of the enemies around it. The country therefore became a marching army that kept moving forward, but heading nowhere in particular, a force avalanching blindly and inevitably towards destruction. Pushed by the West, it rolled with insane speed. It went from one battle to another and from one invasion to the next, to establish the empire of malice and the republic of the mob. The country was in a state of disorder, insanity, limitless violence and unstoppable actions.

The dominant romantic idea was that Iraq acquired its identity from its tragic fate as a country located at the extreme edge of the map, on the one hand, and as a country deprived of access to the sea, on the other. According to nationalist notions, Iraq the saviour was itself Iraq the victim. Iraq was, in fact, being punished for its heroic, prophetic role, for it was a nation with a prophetic mission existing outside human calculations and values. Saddam would come out in his khaki suit, screaming out loud that poor Iraq was surrounded by enemies. Iraq was like Joseph among his brothers. But poor Joseph, who submitted and eventually won the hearts of his father, mother and brothers, was very different from Iraq, which lashed out with all its might.

Kamal woke up in the morning panting with fear, his heart beating like a drum. The radio announced that the Iraqi army had marched into Kuwait and annexed it. He looked at Nadia sleeping in bed, her pulse growing weaker. Medicine bottles, pills, sedatives and a glass of water were placed on the table beside her and her young maid, Fawzeya, sat nearby. International forces had blocked all the routes to Iraq. In a matter of hours, the shops were emptied of goods and closed. The cats began to eat grass when they couldn't find the remains of food in rubbish dumps or homes. The carcasses of starved animals filled the streets.

What was happening to the country?

It was as unbelievable as it was unbearable. Kamal felt a kind of lethal despair and apathy, for he could do nothing except read the papers and listen to the radio carrying political statements.

Years later, he wrote to Farida: 'Those were the worst days of my life. The street was at a boiling point and everybody looked thoroughly miserable. The horizon foretold nothing but an enormous explosion. Everything happened extremely fast. Saddam held on to Kuwait and the Allied fighter planes came to bomb Baghdad and destroy it completely. They didn't leave a bridge, a street, a factory or a palace standing intact. Even the viaducts leading from one village to another were all bombed. In a matter of days, Baghdad became just a village. People transported water by donkey as they did in the past. Primitive instincts bared their teeth and life lost its taste. My sole ambition was to die in peace.'

The little he knew about life outside came from the badly narrated reports of Fawzeya. She often told him things that made him laugh out loud at her inability to fully understand what was going on. Fawzeya had appeared in his life two years earlier, when she was brought to the house by one of Nadia's relatives. She was a beautiful girl with a clear, dark complexion, beautiful large eyes and a fringe of hair neatly styled on her forehead. The day she arrived, she stood holding a bundle of clothes and looking wary and anxious. She wore a green shirt with black buttons whose sleeves were rolled up, revealing her lovely wrists, a tatty pair of trousers and a pair of blue socks. Her shoes were badly polished.

Kamal found Fawzeya stunning. He was astounded by her soft, clear skin and the sparkle of her eyes. He loved the vitality of the bright face, the timid curl of the lips, the high eyebrows and the clear, surprised look at the sight of the house and its master standing before her.

It was love at first sight. He fell in love with her primitive, rural soul. She was made up of pure instincts and innocent emotions as direct as an arrow. Though illiterate and oppressed,

288

she enjoyed the pleasures of life to the full. It was with complete sensual abandon that she ate her meals. Her sensuality swept him off his feet. She had a soul that was in harmony with nature in all its severity, rawness and wonder. Even her peasant dialect sounded deliciously exciting to his ears. Her instinctive behaviour pulsed with the richness of her spirit. Her sexual urge was also strong.

He wrote to Farida: 'I loved this girl with all my heart. No other woman impressed and astounded me as much as she did. I didn't know how ignorant I was of life until I met her. She had an instinctive kind of knowledge, even in sex, that hadn't been spoiled by civilized existence. This illiterate woman taught me the meaning of life afresh.'

Everybody knew that they were having an affair in 'secret', including Nadia, who was on her deathbed.

At that time, Nadia stopped consulting doctors, for the pain-killers were no longer effective. There was nothing she could do to relieve the pain that was concentrated in the middle of her head. No drug could alleviate the pain that gnawed between her temples, bored through her eyes and thumped in her brain to the point of nausea. She lay in bed and the sweat trickled slowly down the sides of her face. She longed for death to relieve her of the excruciating pain. During the bombing of Baghdad, Nadia died. Suddenly, on her bed, she was lifeless. Kamal Medhat let out a scream of pain and hurled himself on her body. Only Fawzeya was with him and together they carried her to her grave. After the burial, he stood at her open grave and cried bitterly.

* * *

Kamal Medhat spent the days of the bombing sitting in complete darkness in front of a thick book and a transistor radio. The bare, plastered room had the pungent smell of bleach. He listened with great interest to the news and learned that the army had been defeated by Allied Forces and had signed the terms of surrender. The masses rose up in the north and south and all news was cut off. The masses began to loot, burn and destroy everything that lay in their path. In response to this rebellion, the state began to strike cities with rockets and artillery.

Kamal's body hurt throughout those days and he couldn't think clearly. As Fawzeya sat in the rocking chair in front of him, he made a silent comparison between two images that haunted his mind in those days: the idyllic and the brutal images of the masses. He loved Fawzeya's illiteracy and her primitive and instinctive nature. He was enamoured of her transparent, pastoral attitude. He realized that governments damaged the masses' natural, poetic instincts by crushing and humiliating them. But Kamal Medhat also had immense fear, contempt and loathing for mob culture. More than anything, he feared the anger of the unruly masses and their instinctive capacity for violence and destruction. The mob swarmed like a horde of locusts devouring everything in front of them. Their basic instinct was to kill, loot and terrorize.

He also believed that the political tendency to uphold mob culture completely destroyed the elite class. The regime, with its vulgarity, cruelty and barbarity, did not only create and nurture the culture of the mob, but it, too, harboured populist and demagogic tendencies. The populace and the government thus stood in headlong confrontation and competed to see which of them could kill and destroy the most. The government elevated belief in murder to a spiritual ecstasy that spread among people like a contagious disease. The people let out their screams against each other in a form of self-destruction that gave them renewed ecstasy. They felt a kind of morbidity, the love of bruised, severed bodies. They were in love with spilt blood, which infused life into their feelings.

The ghostly presence who sat in the chair looking at the garden out of the window was drunk that day with the sight of Fawzeya. He wanted to share the laughter of this helpless peasant woman who'd walked miles that day to bring him some milk. She sat in front of him, telling him of the soldiers returning from the front.

Dark blue circles had appeared under his eyes, from exhaustion, and his eyes were black with pain. He felt that the country was in the grip of mass hysteria that needed to find an outlet. He wanted to express his release from its grip through music, for it alone was capable of making the walls, barriers and darkness disappear. Music alone was able to bring light and a kaleidoscopic sparkle, and to relax his nerves. He stopped for a moment, placed his bow and violin on the stand and began to watch Fawzeya.

Her eyes were full of secrets, radiating light as though from the depths of a cave.

Music and women relieved his sorrows and made him tremble in harmony with the music of the whole universe.

The following day, he went out onto the street. There were soldiers hurrying everywhere and men dressed in traditional gowns as though they belonged to a past era. Faces were tired and angry.

He went straight home. He sat in front of his musical score, thinking with astonishment of the vulgarity that dominated both the regime and the people. People had an instinctive veneration for excrement and blood and an adoration of chaos and confusion. It was the horrifying feeling of living in an anti-world, a world of ferocious claws.

A passage from another letter stated: 'All my friends are gone. Nadia's dead, Amjad's ill, Widad has left, Janet's been murdered and my son Omar is in Egypt with his aunt. I have pain in my joints and the hospitals have no medicine. The streets are dusty, the shops have run out of goods; poverty and crime are everywhere. The people have turned into the masses. The class system and social strata are all gone. There's nothing but a political class that rules with unlimited violence. Only vulgar music and martial songs praising the victories of the regime can be heard. The nationalist movement is gradually becoming Islamist. Saddam prays. He believes that what happened was the will of God. People live in abject poverty and deadly despair, which they try to ease by going back to the fold of religion.'

Kamal Medhat's most tender moments were spent with Fawzeya. He found in her a simple, spontaneous heroism, a kind of self-defence mechanism in the face of a hard, incompatible marriage. Kamal Medhat found in his love for Fawzeya some compensation for his hatred of the masses. He venerated in her the primitive, illiterate human being who remained unspoilt by the regime. Although Fawzeya expressed herself simply and spoke in straightforward, spontaneous statements, she wasn't without complexity. Despite being illiterate and simple, she fought valiantly for her freedom. She'd been married to a cattle farmer in Al-Fadhilia. He was a vain, careless man who'd forced her to marry him. But she'd resisted him ferociously, stood up to him and asked for a divorce.

A few months before the divorce came through, he was killed in the war. In front of the judge, she gave up everything to his family because she'd never loved him.

Kamal Medhat often sat in a chair by the window, listening to a record or playing short pieces on his violin. He sometimes placed his scores in front of him to compose his dream symphony. Fawzeya would walk barefoot on the cold tiles, her tight, black trousers revealing the outline of her buttocks and her tight shirt showing her protruding breasts. She used tassels to tie her hair in a pony tail, and chewed gum energetically while she walked. She would suddenly stop in front of him and look straight at him with her lascivious eyes. She would wink at him, turn quickly around and roll her behind.

Her movements aroused him and made him feel the spirit and power of life. Love alone could explain the latent energy that he wished to express through music. It was a tidal wave of inexplicable passion. Kamal Medhat didn't hate the deprived classes that felt the abject need for bread and faced the arrogance of urban bureaucracy. He loved folk stories in all their details and his music beautifully and poetically expressed the lives of broken, exiled people, drunken farmers, the hungry, illiterate women, lumpen workers and agricultural labourers. But what terrified him was the vulgarity of the regime that crushed those classes and turning them into a rough, ferocious beast, running amok and destroying everything.

What happened during the years that led to Kamal Medhat's murder? Information is, in fact, quite scarce. During the years following the Kuwait war, Kamal Medhat was forgotten. When he walked in the streets, he would meet a wave of people running towards a free meal offered by the government in some square or park. He would stop and look at a crowd of men and women in tatters, starving and barefoot, women's headscarves billowing. They would rush through a side door opened for them by the guards, to eat a free meal of rice offered by the state to the poor. Everything else was hazy and vague. He wrote to Farida: 'Life is cold and empty. Baghdad is a world enveloped by mystery. The streets are filthy, the shops are empty, and the faces are pale, sickly and desperate. Classical music halls have turned into popular haunts for vulgar songs.'

The only surviving image of that elderly musician in the residents' minds was his slow daily walk on the streets of Al-Mansour. They retained the image of a widower having an affair with his maid, a man with grey hair and a light grey beard who was dressed in the same old, shabby clothes that he'd been wearing for years. He often carried a Russian book as he walked on the same street almost every day from his house in Al-Mansour to the end of Al-Haretheya Street and back. He was sometimes accompanied by his maid Fawzeya and he frequently stood in line for his ration of eggs or a piece of chicken distributed to retired state officials, from time to time, by the government.

This was all the information that we managed to get concerning his life between the two wars. We discovered that during the last war, of 2003, he heard the doorbell ring while he was watching the news on television. He got up, pulled the curtain and looked out of the window. Amjad Mustafa was at the door.

It was a huge surprise for Kamal Medhat. Amjad Mustafa was a completely changed man. His eyes were lifeless and his paunch jutted forward. He was short of breath and the effects of addiction were clear on his face. He looked worn out. His body was flabby and his clothes were old and threadbare. He wore an old, navy blue jacket, a tatty shirt and a pair of jeans that were completely faded.

Kamal took him into the lounge and asked Fawzeya to make them some coffee. Amjad Mustafa rushed towards the bar to pour himself a glass of red wine.

'What's happened to you, Amjad? You look so different,' said Kamal Medhat.

'We're all different,' he answered smiling.

Patriotic talk had vanished completely from his conversation. He no longer believed in the divine mission of the Arab nation, which he'd espoused during the past years of victory, glory and historical revisionism. Now it was all the manifest destiny of the American nation, the new drive towards the Tocquevillean dream of democracy and human rights. It was a dream that Kamal Medhat also believed in, despite his fears of uncontrollable populist movements. He wanted change to happen, no doubt. But at what price? Nobody knew. It was still untested, unknown and therefore unfathomable. They could neither push it forward nor stand in its way.

'Who can drive out the US forces?' Amjad asked Kamal Medhat.

'Nobody,' he replied.

'Then let it be. Let's achieve democracy, development and civic rights. Then the nation can decide its destiny.'

Kamal drank his coffee and looked straight out of the window at the thick, wooded garden outside.

'Do you trust America?' he asked Kamal.

Kamal Medhat had absolutely no faith in imperialism, for he

rejected all forms of domination, power and violence. He totally abhorred the spirit of smug victory, whether embodied in Iraqi nationalism or American patriotism.

To refute his argument, Amjad said, 'Haven't you read Saadi Youssef's latest poem, *An Invitation to Tony Blair*? He was urging the British Prime Minister to occupy Iraq.'

Kamal Medhat was astonished to hear that. Could it be true? Then he smiled a little. The dream of change dominated the thinking of all intellectuals. Amjad Mustafa was the victim of his own feelings of extreme oppression. He was an addict suffering the pain of failure and desperate for his lost dream of glory. Like a novice sailor overpowered by the wind, he didn't know how to set his sail. Feeling totally oppressed, he made brief remarks, waved his arms, smoked, cursed and drank red wine in frantic haste.

A few days later, Kamal Medhat was sitting in an armchair by the window in the lounge, watching the movements of the tree branches outside. It was difficult for him to formulate ideas or adopt a stand. Everything was as churned and confused as the movement of the tide. Looking up, he was appalled to see the images of aircraft carriers advancing, fighter planes of all types, Marines with their helmets and military gear marching in formation, and long-range missiles being installed in the desert. Colossal forces were advancing in the desert, led by tanks and armoured vehicles. Other forces were at their bases in the Gulf countries, from which they would march to invade Iraq. The dogs of war were barking and the masses were watching the armed forces taking positions and digging trenches in the streets. Food was becoming scarce and there were numerous checkpoints in public squares and parks. Military and security patrols roamed every alley and street.

Kamal Medhat woke up from his sleep to the sound of huge explosions near the house. For a few moments, he was drenched in sweat. He was worried and afraid. He looked at the damp, rusty room swimming in darkness. With his tall, slightly stooping gait, he went towards Fawzeya, who was sitting close by. Then the sound of another violent explosion made Fawzeya jump and rush to the window. There was a burning car standing parallel to the pavement and a house was on fire. A flower shop had been completely demolished.

He returned to his place near the window and looked at the moon. It was a warm night as the weather forecast had predicted. Everything had been fine until now. He exchanged a few words with Fawzeya. They prepared a meal together, sat down and ate. He cracked a joke and she smiled. She didn't mention anything about his excessive drinking these days. He didn't mention the war or his dread of what the coming days might bring. He raised his glass and drank to her health. When he looked again through the window, the garden had become a block of light.

Ten days had passed since the war had begun. Looking out of the window, Kamal Medhat watched the city being consumed by fire. He saw the fighter planes like black insects bombing everything: bridges, homes, buildings and factories. He watched Baghdad as it turned into a mass of smoke. A dust storm was blowing, uprooting everything in its path while the armed forces escaped with their equipment. Soldiers launched rockets from among the houses. Ambulances carried soldiers swimming in their blood. Soldiers deserted the front while others took shelter in houses and hospitals.

He decided to go out. The moment he opened the door, a

slap of cold air struck him. He buried his neck in the collar of his coat and shrank inside it. He dragged his feet with great difficulty and walked along the pavement. He looked through the window of a semi-burnt-out villa and saw a burnt wooden table and bookcase. Firemen were carrying the wounded and the dead on stretchers.

He continued to walk. Smoke was billowing out of a rose-coloured brick house that was encircled by a wall. On the wall there was a poster inviting people to donate blood and the words 'Death to Americans' were scrawled in black paint. The windows of a house level with the street; a woman speaking to a man holding a nylon bag.

On the final day of the war, he sat in the living room, looking into the corner. The house was completely dark because the power had been cut off. He drew the curtains to bring some light into the room. Fawzeya entered. She seemed disturbed and the words came rushing from her lips. She told him how the army had disappeared entirely from the streets and how people were looting government offices. He was appalled. He knew that the mob would rise once again and realized that they would overtake the whole country. His heart thudded so violently that he felt out of breath.

He went back to his scores and started to arrange them. He tried to write something but couldn't. He suddenly realized that Fawzeya had gone out; she wouldn't be able to resist the attractions outside. He ran after her, panting with exhaustion and in agitation. Trucks carrying looted property passed by him. It was strange to see people stealing their own belongings. Every institution was being looted. The looters even took away the bricks.

Kamal moved among them and nearly bumped into someone carrying a chair, another holding a sack of flour, and a woman running with a refrigerator on her back. Among the crowd he found Fawzeya. She was carrying two bamboo chairs and running away. He gripped her hand and commanded her to get rid of the chairs and follow him. She did so, scowling in annoyance. At home, she protested vehemently, saying it was a free bonanza. Everybody took what they wanted, so why should he stop her? Where was the harm in it?

It was difficult for him to convince her. So he said nothing and returned to his violin.

During the subsequent days all the secrets were revealed. He glimpsed a white man and the flash of a black weapon shining before it fell. He saw another statue incline to the right and topple after being pulled from its base. He saw a woman soldier on top of an armoured car aim her rifle and shoot. Men continued running towards a sleepy-looking black American soldier who stood knee-deep in the brown mud and talked, with a cigarette in one hand and a rifle in the other. The sounds reached him through the window before they became inaudible. The soldier's lips moved continuously while, above the hard collar of his coat, his head appeared slightly larger than a fist. All along the wall, civilians stood near the military gear thrown on the ground. He pointed to the alley and they all dispersed, as fires blazed ferociously in the city. Near the pavement a Marines officer stopped and leaned against the fence. He looked solid in his military uniform. His hair was dusty and a rifle was slung from his neck. Near him lay an Iraqi soldier with a black hole in his temple.

The woman soldier screamed at the people standing on the pavement to go inside. The voice was amplified through a loudspeaker. The sound of bullets rang from afar and the bombs fell on the buildings. Khaki military vehicles roamed the streets of Baghdad with their monstrous noise. Something inside him crumbled and he shuddered.

He sat in his usual place, as he did every day, watching the transformations of the trees and the flowers. The lotus tree stood with its rough, moss-covered bark, its curved trunk and its branches extending beyond the garden fence. The ends of the longer branches sagged low under their weight. He turned up the music on the record player. He heard the distant and enthusiastic voice of a newscaster. The man was not discouraged by the scenes of death everywhere or by the prevailing fear, confusion or screams. He wasn't worried by the horrific explosions, the raging trench warfare, the kidnappings or the medieval-style slaughter. Human beings were being butchered while others had their limbs and guts scattered all over the place. And after the tens of thousands had been killed, silence descended, complete and disturbing. Nothing remained except the cold stare at the sight of violence on the screen, ambulances carrying corpses covered with congealed blood and the gathering up of limbs in tattered, dirty blankets to be dumped in pickup trucks.

Clothing was neglected; conversation was snatched; talk was small and brief. Words came out badly and failed: the repetition of wretched, superficial thoughts. Statements of generalities that had no meaning, intended to convey nothing.

The return of the sons

The most important chapter of Kamal's life in those days was the return of his three sons at the same time after the US invasion. Meir came back with the US forces, bearing ideas of democracy and change; Hussein returned from Tehran with the Islamic Shia movement, feeling happy to be back after a forced exile; Omar came from Egypt, bearing measureless anger and spite at the Sunni's loss of power.

Hussein arrived at his father's house with the help of the address given to him by Kakeh Hameh. He went into the hall and stood in front of his father, who was taken by complete surprise. His son's black hair was parted on the side and a lock of hair fell onto his forehead. He had a thick, black beard and wore black-rimmed glasses, a wide jacket, loose trousers and a white shirt without a tie, which he buttoned at the collar: the typical look of one from the metropolis of contemporary Shia culture.

Quiet and reserved, he sat on the chair, his voice faint and his smile tepid. He was an alternative image of the seventies' communist, who'd vanished completely from Iraqi culture. He spoke quietly about his life, marriage and arrival in Iraq. He wasn't just narrating his personal story, he was trying to create an identity out of his own tragedy, an identity that found its true significance in tragedy.

Kamal Medhat encountered the same attitude in Omar. Coming from Egypt, Omar wanted to embody the old, nationalist intellectual, with his thick moustache that drooped to hide his mouth, his back-combed black hair, his plump cheeks and his harsh gaze. He represented the Arab image of tyrannical, patriotic masculinity. Now, however, it was mixed with the image of the Sunni man who wished to write the history of his identity by recalling the tragedy of the Sunni's ousting from power.

Hussein sat quietly talking history to his father. He believed that Shiite philosophy was a philosophy of history: historical determinism. This was because prophetic revelation had come to an end with the Seal of the Prophets. But history had yet to be sealed. He told his father that the Prophet's role was to communicate God's revealed Word and to establish the *ummah,* community of Muslim believers. But the task came to an end with the end of prophecy.

The devout language, the beard and the black glasses concealed the son from the father. The son talked of a religion that ruled and a religion for the ruled. He was convinced that Western civilization was like sunstroke for Muslims. Western culture meant forgetting existence altogether, while the return to Islam was a return to consciousness and existence. Islam was the amalgam of past and present, which would help establish a just society in future. The awaited, promised Imam was the saviour and the reformer. He was both the aim and the result. We had to achieve the revolution, he argued, in order to overturn the society of Cain.

As Hussein spoke, he evoked in his father's mind Amjad Mustafa's old patriotic convictions, now reclothed in religious garb. The country was always faced with a dialectic that led it to the precipice, for the contradictions of reality were very different from the acrobatics of ideology. The son expressed the ideas of Mohammad al-Sadr and Ali Shariati, while the father sat gaping, too stunned to say anything. He felt the same about his son Omar, who wished to construct a new identity from the contradictions of his brother's. Meir also came to talk to his father of the democratic project that would connect the country with the West. The future would see Iraq turn into a Middle Eastern paradise, like Japan in Asia or Germany in Europe. It was a dream image, designed and fabricated at the best Western think-tanks.

But the father, the tobacco keeper, Kamal Medhat, alone was the true representative of the outsider, the marginalized and the exile, opposing all forms of power and rejecting all ideologies. He was the true image of the tobacco keeper.

Kamal Medhat remembered Pessoa's poem. His three sons were also the three characters of the poem. Meir was born of the character of Yousef Sami Saleh, the keeper of flocks in *Tobacco Shop*; Hussein was the offspring of Haidar Salman, the protected man; Omar came from Kamal Medhat, the tobacco keeper. They were his three names and his three cases of impersonation. Each of their faces corresponded to one of his assumed identities. He realized that each one of them was a faithful reflection of his own ego. Through their characters he discovered the essential answer to the problem of identity. Each one of them was a facet of his personality, a single entity that was split and multiple at the same time. They were a three-dimensional Cubist painting of a single face.

Meir was Alberto Caeiro, the first character of Pessoa's *Tobacco Shop*; Hussein was Ricardo Reis; Omar was Álvaro de Campos. Meir's role was the keeper of flocks, who made himself master of Ricardo Reis (Hussein), the weak and sickly creature. As for Álvaro de Campos, he was Omar, who left for the east (Egypt in this case) and returned laden with great hope, but torn between his sense of greatness and his utter emptiness. Hence his absurdity and lack of balance.

★   ★   ★

303

On the same day, Kamal Medhat walked along the street with Pessoa's *Tobacco Shop* in his hand. He entered a grocery shop near his house to buy cigarettes, or tobacco. The courtyard was almost completely dark because of the power cut. The calm was oppressive. He stood leaning on his ebony walking stick with the ivory handle, his mouth twitching and his gaze contemplative and profound. He saw his neighbour, an old engineer who'd once been a paragon of elegance. The man had always worn white, silk shirts with roomy collars, black velvet trousers with braces and English-style shoes with laces. That day, Kamal saw him wearing the traditional gown and his beard was long. He stopped at the entrance to the shop, smoking nervously and talking with great agitation about the Sunni and Shia question with another neighbour.

The social rift was crystal clear. Kamal Medhat found the split reflected in the whole society, not excluding artists. Although people in general tried to downplay the significance of the division, they tacitly reinforced it. Kamal, who thought that the country had a single story, a single narrative and as a result a single identity, was now shocked to find three conflicting and contradictory narratives. Each faction wrote its own history and narrated its own existence in isolation from the others. He suddenly found that the Shia had a narrative, the Sunnis had a narrative and the Kurds had a narrative. These were not complementary, but were contradictory narratives that confronted each other.

The final letter

Kamal Medhat sent his final letter to Farida via his son Meir when Meir came to visit him at his house in Al-Mansour: 'Death will be here soon. I'm not long for this life. It's true that I'll resist at the beginning, but I'll surrender to it with love in the end. I burn for the final moment. My ecstasy will be indescribable, a moment of orgasmic pleasure.

'I talked to you last time about the tobacco keeper, didn't I? Today I'm thinking, why can't death be the tobacco keeper? I don't regard death as awful, but see him as an elegant gentleman. I will embrace him and call him brother ...'

Part Three

IX

Murder revealed, a life on the periphery and strange lands

'I don't know how many souls I have possessed, for I change at
every moment.'

Fernando Pessoa

A dual existence

In the Green Zone, I led a dual existence. Saddam's small palace
had been renovated by an American contractor and turned into
the US Agency for International Development. The American
army had destroyed it with several smart missiles. When I saw it
immediately following the war, the ceilings had collapsed, the
doors of the lifts had come off their hinges and the pillars had
fallen. The marble staircase was covered with a thick layer of dust.
There was twisted metal and crushed brick. But everything in
it had been restored. The large palace, however, had become
the US Embassy in Baghdad. All the statues of Saddam that had
surrounded the palace had been torn down. Nermine invited me
for a swim in the lake in front of the palace, which had become a
public swimming pool. As we were taking off our clothes, two

female soldiers also came for a swim. They took off their clothes and walked beside the pool in their bikinis, still carrying their machine guns. The pretty soldier with the tattoo, who we'd seen on the plane, was also having a swim. She had another tattoo on her left buttock.

The British pub in the shape of a ship was not far from the pool and sold beer at three dollars a bottle. The only official US post office in the Green Zone, a somewhat small branch, was nearby. A US soldier stood at the entrance to the post office, inspecting the parcels going in. I wondered what he would do if there was anything dangerous in them, but it became clear to me later that the soldier was looking for fake DVDs. After inspecting the parcel, he stamped it. Postage was free.

In the palace gardens there was the Country Club, an excellent pub inside the Green Zone. It stood a few steps from the final checkpoint. The pub was hot and crowded most of the time. Tasteless pop music was playing. Pool tables stood on the left of the circular bar. On the other side was an open area where customers could dance, and in the middle of the pub were a few tables and chairs.

The Bunker, another pub, was always pumping out loud music. Its inner walls were made of concrete. The weird thing was that they were decorated with weapons: the walls were plastered with ornamental mortar bombs.

There was also the bazaar where you could buy souvenirs, carpets and photographs. On the other side stood a number of small buildings: a barber's shop, a car agency, a warehouse and a clothes store. There were also shops selling tape recorders, books, magazines, shoes and bikes, and there was a Burger King. Al-Rashid hotel, where Katrina Hassoun stayed wasn't very far away. Every day, Nermine and I would visit her and spend an hour or two in her company, for there were quality shops selling foreign papers and magazines as well as a shop selling Rolex watches and another selling photographs, Persian rugs and DVDs. From outside, we watched the swimming pool, the casino and the gym. We sometimes spent the time in the corner of the lounge of a small pub. The barman was an emaciated man with sagging skin. He was always dressed in a high collar and red bow tie. He poured wine from a decanter into small glasses. Strangely, this bar had a permanent clientele; every time we went there we found the same crowd. They were four American strategy officers who sat at a round table near the window, playing cards. The winner always ordered beer for the four of them. A hulk of a man with a pink complexion and grey hair sat near them. He ordered full-strength rum and, as he stuffed tobacco into his pipe, watched the card players with eyes full of cunning.

This was how we spent our time in the Green Zone. The Red Zone, however, was a very different matter.

We went under cover of darkness, for armed gangs were everywhere. The map of the city that we had drawn rested on our knees. It was like a chessboard, with black squares for the Shia and yellow for the Sunni; one mistake would definitely mean a fatal checkmate. The car moved forward in the dark while the night cold enveloped the earth and the humidity increased the hardness of objects. The tree trunks were dry and the wind blew over Baghdad, carrying danger. People shut themselves indoors, seeking the protection of roofs and walls. They expected death at any moment. They stayed awake as though watching the night from above, listening to the murmurs of the dead and the kidnapped carried by the wind from afar. A chill, as if from deep underground, haunted the streets and bats hovered in the air, making savage sounds in the dark.

Who killed Kamal Medhat?

Who killed Kamal Medhat? Why? And how? These were the questions that I kept asking myself. They gave me a splitting headache and made me feel like a robot engaged in a long conversation with itself. At times the conversation was superficial and at others inspiring. When it was neither, it made me sick to my heart. When I was unable to explain anything, I started talking like a parrot whose repetitiveness prompts disgust. Nevertheless, I had to move on, even though it was only moving towards a mysterious void. Speaking about Kamal Medhat was like coloured smears on a white wall or a bell ringing to remind us that we had fallen into a bottomless pit. It was like going on a long journey on a war train full of skulls and screaming black masks. It was like arriving in our country for the first time and finding it overrun by black dread and boundless anarchy.

Kidnapping

It was clear that Kamal had been kidnapped from near the post office in Al-Mansour.

He had gone to the engineers' office near the post office. The office manager there said that Kamal had stayed for five minutes, and left without drinking his coffee.

The worker standing near the door said that he'd seen hooded men get out of a black minivan holding revolvers with silencers. Another person standing nearby had additional firepower.

Kamal Medhat went inside the post office and straight to the restroom. He left in a hurry and then went through the door next to the service office. From there he moved to a neglected part of the post office, walking through the back corridors and then to a hall at the back.

Did he sense that he was being pursued? Did he get the feeling that nobody would be able to help him?

Did he anticipate who those men were?

What is clear is that the armed gang wreaked havoc in their pursuit of him. A number of explosions destroyed the back area of the post office.

But Kamal Medhat continued walking through the wreckage and climbed to the telephone centre on the second floor. He opened a side door in order to go down the outside staircase. But he turned back as soon as he saw one of the masked men standing by the stairs. So he climbed down an internal staircase and from a back door he ran, with his feet aching, jumping over a garden fence, hoping to escape through an adjacent house. Three shots were fired at him, holding him up.

He reached a four-storey building, went in and headed to the lift. He decided to climb the stairs on foot because the lift was taking too long and he heard cars on the street. The moment he reached the second floor, the masked gang arrived with their guns and raced into the building.

He was on the move through a doctor's clinic and noticed that the men pursuing him had entered the corridor. But then they vanished, probably having gone upstairs. While he was looking out of the window of the clinic, he saw the black cars on the street and the masked men carrying weapons.

He opened the door to the next room. He was worried they might attack him from the other end of the corridor. How could he shake them off and escape? He continued through the offices, but instead of going right and facing the masked men, he turned left towards the solitary office at the far end of the room. He wanted a car to help him get away.

He saw them behind him, so he entered another building. The lift was open, so he got in and went up. The lift door opened on the fourth floor. He looked right and found a flight of stairs. He went up. After the hot pursuit, he found himself on an open, flat roof. Looking down, he saw dozens of people had gathered near a rundown restaurant to watch the chase.

Perhaps he thought of jumping off the roof.

He was eighty. Feeling short of breath, he placed his hand on his heart. He tripped over a wire and almost fell. He was still panting and sat down. They led him down and took him to a freshly watered field that was full of wild bushes, leafy plants and some mature trees. They led him across the vast green area and put him in the back of a car, which sped away.

Information

All the information on this period was obtained from Mustafa Shaker. We met him in a faded building near Al-Saadoun Street about a week after our arrival in Baghdad. What was this meeting like?

I went to Al-Saadoun Street, where Faris was waiting for me in a grey, decaying building. This was a real Babel of languages and dialects, where journalists of all types and from all places co-existed and which they never left. The neighbourhood was completely sealed by concrete walls and guarded at certain points. Inside were laundries, shops and barbers, and bars filled with Americans and Africans. At the entrances of the buildings and on the street corners were soldiers and Filipino workers. Women sat on balconies and clothes were hung on lines that stretched from windowsills and balconies. Faris Hassan's apartment was smaller than ours in the Green Zone, or so it seemed to me because the tiny living room was filled with clutter, chairs and tables. There was also a bedroom, a kitchen and a bathroom. Though small, the apartment was full of books and CDs. But it wasn't really claustrophobic because its windows had a view of the street and allowed Baghdad's vibrant light to enter. There was also a balcony where journalists could place a table and enjoy supper under Baghdad's stars.

We shook hands with Mustafa Shaker.

He was considered to be the most important journalist in the Middle East. In his long career, he'd written great reports, managed several newspapers and travelled to more than thirty countries. His language was unbelievably eloquent and he was a gifted conversationalist, although he was often forgetful, sometimes even forgetting the names of his friends.

Mustafa Shaker was a short, stout man who was far from elegant. His feet were tiny and his shoes looked like a child's, being ridiculously small. He had fuzzy grey hair and in the middle of his bald head were a few spiky tufts. Because he slept little, his eyes always looked tired. He worked like a machine and his movements were rapid. His hair was dishevelled and he shaved only once or twice a week, which gave his face the white stubble of an old man. Whenever he went to clubs, cafés, theatres, cinemas or galleries, as he frequently did, he was either taken for someone who worked there or as a nonentity. It's impossible to convey how easy writing was for him or his legendary skill in generating ideas and elegant phrases. He was the best journalist I came across in my 'hoopoe' job, a description he would often use in reference to journalism and which he borrowed from the story of Prophet Solomon and his hoopoe. Everybody was aware of his talent, but most people ignored him out of jealousy and envy. None of his generation could stand him. As for our generation, we loved him in spite of his many failings, which included his excessive shyness and courtesy, his greed in monopolizing conversations, and his infantile attitude and competitiveness, which often made him coarse or foolish. But all his flaws were forgiven because of his ability to use language so beautifully and elegantly. He had a winning tone and it was great fun to listen to his anecdotes, political memories or journalistic adventures from various places of the world. I was fascinated by this genius with a mischievous personality and spent hours in discussions with him. I realized that he loved devious, evasive talk, a skill I had mastered, so he grew fond of me and whenever we had a business meeting, we'd stay together and chat for a long time.

Mustafa Shaker spent most of his life managing a magazine almost singlehandedly. After the downfall of Saddam's regime, several newspapers and magazines as well as media institutions had competed for his services, but he wouldn't accept a permanent position. He moved from one place to another until I saw him at the offices of a new newspaper near Faris's apartment on Al-Saadoun Street. I was really happy to see him. We embraced and went into his office.

'How's the hoopoe work going?' he asked in reference to my reporting assignments.

Mustafa Shaker talked to me about the general situation in Baghdad. His unusual expressions always amazed me. It was he who provided me with a letter to the forensic physician at the morgue, indicating that the dead man was my father and allowing me to bury him. He also provided us with the name of a person who possessed a complete set of security and intelligence files and who could provide information in return for a fee.

Finding the documents

Mustafa Shaker gave us a letter for the person with the files from the security and intelligence services. His name was Jabbar Hussein and he lived in an apartment in a poor part of Al-Rusafa neighbourhood in Baghdad. The building was very old and stood near a mosque that had been almost completely demolished by an artillery shell. The minaret had fallen to the ground in one piece. We stopped to buy some cigarettes, and the shop-keeper told us that some months earlier, the mosque had been under the control of a group of armed men. There had been a ferocious firefight with the Marines that had destroyed many of the adjacent buildings, houses and shops. Jabbar's building was dark and tilted to the side. Its façade was destroyed and its staircase had no banisters. Nearby was a spot full of rubbish and dead cats, where rats scurried from one place to another in the darkness.

We arrived at noon. When we entered Jabbar's room, we were

absolutely dumbfounded. It was a complete archive, catalogued and systematically arranged. Once you gave the name you were looking for, he would search and bring you the papers, all for a price, of course.

We sat in wicker chairs. An old rug covered the yellow-tiled floor. Jabbar was a handsome young man of medium height who spoke with a hint of sarcasm. He sat at a wooden desk stolen from some government office, on top of which was a small Iraqi flag. On the wall behind, instead of the president's picture, hung a photograph of his father. The caption beneath it read: 'Photograph of my father. May God preserve and protect him'. Funnily enough, this was the same dedication as the one on Saddam's photographs. This was just a small office in Baghdad that sold documents. Because of frequent power cuts, the windows and curtains were kept open. On the right he'd placed a lantern on a piece of black vinyl, and on a small low table he'd placed his hookah, filled with aromatic tobacco and from which he inhaled and then slowly blew out the smoke.

We asked him about the file of Kamal Medhat.

He was well organized, and had a list of all the names for which he possessed files. He looked at the index, then got up and went to the files stacked behind him. He picked up a file, flipped through it and returned it to its place. Then he took hold of another one, nodded and handed it to me.

I took the file and flipped through its pages. I read his name. I scanned the official notes and the security-service observations about his character. I could have jumped for joy. Faris Hassan began to haggle over the price. I had no wish to listen to Faris bargaining about a price that was no more than the cost of a pair of trousers or a shirt. I asked him to pay the man so that I could get on with my work.

We went down two or three steps and walked through the street's rubbish dump. We stepped on dead cats, an appalling stench filling our nostrils.

We got into the minivan and went straight to Kamal Medhat's house in Al-Mansour.

Most of the material in the file consisted of reports or summaries of reports, some of which were general in nature while others were personal. Only one report really shocked me. Iraqi intelligence had known that he was one of those Iraqis who'd been expelled as an Iranian subject and that he'd gone to Damascus and married Nadia al-Amiry. It was on the record that he'd then arrived in Baghdad and worked with the National Symphony Orchestra. The most important aspect of the report was the security responses given in support of his arrest or interrogation. Some of the documents recommended keeping him under constant surveillance. One important report discussed his relationship with Widad and other private matters. There was also a report on his affair with Janet, for the reports weren't limited to his political attitudes, which categorized him as a free liberal. The word 'free' meant that he had no political affiliations nor any connections with religious movements. Among all the reports was one written by Widad, which had been submitted to a security investigation. She'd recommended him highly and defended him staunchly.

The question is: Did Kamal Medhat know that the state was aware of his previous incarnation? I doubt it.

The artist's house in Al-Mansour

His house in Al-Mansour stood a mere two hundred meters from the statue of Abu Jaafar al-Mansour, the second Abbasid Caliph. The house had a beautiful brick façade and high windows in the style of the seventies. When Faris and I entered, we went through a corridor that led us straight to the library that was packed with books. In front of the dining table was a teak cupboard, which was used for household utensils. On some of the shelves, however, he'd also placed more books, while there was a stack of novels on the floor. There was also a table near the chair in which he used to sit looking out of the window. I found two books on the table. The first was the memoirs of the French violinist Stéphane Grappelli and the second was a selection of poems by the Portuguese poet Fernando Pessoa, translated into English under the title *Tobacco Shop*. The book was open at the poem called *Tobacco Shop* and was filled with explanatory notes written in pencil by Kamal Medhat. It's clear that he'd depended on more than one book in his commentary on the poem. I didn't pay much attention to this at the time, but I took the book and the pencil with me when I left.

There were many newspapers in the bedroom. It was clear that he'd spent most of his time in the dining room. But the door leading to the sitting room at the back remained shut throughout the days of the war.

There was a photograph of a fifty-year-old Nadia al-Amiry, looking beautiful with her blonde hair in two plaits that she curved around her ears. She wore a dark blue blouse and had put a ball of wool on the table. She was half-hidden behind the teapot. Kamal was standing close by with his plastic-rimmed glasses, his light beard and his sad eyes behind semi-dark lenses, smiling at her. Nadia al-Amiry herself looked straight ahead. Kamal Medhat was slightly stooped over the book he was absorbed in reading. With his grey hair and huge hands, he looked more like a worker than a musician.

My mobile phone rang. It was Faris. He said that he'd managed to locate Fawzeya, who was living in Al-Wishash City, the poor district right behind Al-Mansour City.

'How do we get to her?' I asked him.

'Easy. I arranged a meeting with her at ten in the morning.'

The taxi came on Thursday morning. He said we had to wait for an hour or two, until we heard the explosion, before setting off. But I ran out of patience as we sat in the living room waiting for something to happen. Since nothing occurred, we started on our way. Near the bridge we heard the sound of the explosion and our legs shook.

We had to cross the bridge towards Al-Karkh. This was no easy matter, for nobody could predict what would happen. We didn't know what our fate would be this time. After crossing Al-Jumhuriya Bridge in the direction of Al-Karkh, I was overwhelmed by a strange feeling, a mixture of depression and regret. I wondered what had brought me there and why I'd accepted this assignment in the first place. At that moment, it wasn't the fear of death that was uppermost in my mind, but the terror of the torture I might be submitted to.

We reached a poor neighbourhood located right next to a classy district. There were some low buildings standing close to some small farms, in the middle of which ran a canal. It wasn't easy to enter the city. There were potholes and barricades, as well as a group of armed men with rifles. Faris got out of the car and talked to them. He gave them a piece of paper he'd obtained the day before. It was a letter from a militia leader describing the importance of our mission and requesting them to allow us in.

I don't know if he actually offered the militia leader money to facilitate the mission, but Faris had included a sum of money in the budget. We then walked along the street. Stagnant water filled the potholes that had taken over the street. The houses standing behind the wealthy district of Al-Mansour graphically illustrated the gulf separating the classes. The militias of the poor Sunni and Shia areas were fighting over Al-Mansour, which was inhabited by the middle and upper classes.

We stopped in front of a very poor house whose façade had been practically destroyed, and knocked on the door. Fawzeya came out to greet us, wearing a wide pair of trousers and a black shirt. She'd covered her hair with a scarf. She lived with three of her sisters and her mother on the salary provided by Kamal Medhat. She was grieving, but was one of our most important sources of information.

She invited us to sit down, and we sat on plastic chairs opposite her. In front of us was a broken wooden table. She told us that he'd had a strange feeling two days before the event, when he'd received a death threat.

This was new information for us. She described his behaviour in detail.

He'd been sitting in the large chair with his eyes open. She thought it was one of his many ways of meditating. But his state of bewilderment seemed like a person who didn't belong to this world. She came up to him and asked him what was wrong. He told her that he'd received a threat. His voice was hoarse as he said it. Then he sat by the window until night fell and the whole house was dark. In the darkness, she saw his large eyes, grey hair and peaceful face, as he held a coffee cup.

His frizzy hair seemed ashen and his bones were fragile with premature ageing. He still felt unsteady because of the insomnia. 'I know they're going to kill me,' he added gravely.

I asked her why she thought they wanted to kill him. 'Perhaps because of the American who visited the house,' she said.

Faris and I blanched. 'An American visited him? What American?' we asked.

'I don't know. An American visited him at night and left.'

'Did you see him?'

'It was night time and dark.'

'How do you know?'

'I was in the house and saw him.'

'Did the threat say that they saw him with the American?'

'It didn't say anything about his . . .' she said.

(We learned later that it was his son Meir.) Then she told us how he'd emerged from the bedroom the next day in his pyjamas. He'd placed the dish of shaving soap on the marble sink beside the washbag containing his shaving kit. There was also a candle in case of power cuts, which happened frequently. He'd put on his square-lensed glasses with the black plastic frames, which he always kept in the pocket of his pyjamas, and trimmed his beard, which he never shaved completely.

After shaving, he'd paced to and fro in the room, trying hard not to look at himself in the mirror. He'd brushed his teeth using English toothpaste, clipped his fingernails and toenails, wrapped himself in a blanket and gone to sleep.

The visit by the stranger and his guards the night before was the last visit he'd ever received. For quite some time, he'd been mistrustful of everybody. He'd placed important papers, photographs and newspapers in two boxes. She was the only one who'd believed him when he'd said that he was really going this time.

'Did you love each other?'

'Yes,' she said.

She had trampled on the traditions of an ultra-conservative society. They were not lovers in secret, but in the open. It was a public scandal. She had shown him increasing love and affection as his sight dimmed and his flesh became loooser. He smoked heavily. She sat beside him and talked to him while he listened to her in his pyjamas, always with a book in his hand. By day, the only sounds to be heard in the silent house were her voice and his laughter.

We left Fawzeya to her grief and loneliness and decided to go to the department of forensic medicine to arrange for the burial of Kamal Medhat's body. We had an appointment with the doctor in the morning.

When we went in, the doctor was expecting us: Mustafa Shaker had already been in touch with him. I handed him the letter.

He gave me a piece of medical gauze to cover my nose. We followed him. He stopped and pulled hard on a handle. Kamal Medhat's body lay before us. Faris and I saw his open mouth and his crushed forehead, which was loosely covered with sticking plaster. One eye was open and looked reddish and cloudy.

We filled out the hospital forms and took him from the morgue. He was registered as my father. We had to take him straight to the cemetery. But which one? The Jewish cemetery in

Al-Habibeyya, the Shia cemetery in Al-Najaf, or the Sunni cemetery in Al-Karkh?

'Where should we bury him?' asked Faris.

'The nearest one,' I said.

It was Al-Karkh. So we got out of the taxi and headed to the administrative office of the cemetery.

Faris knew the undertaker and said that he also dealt with militants. He treated us as if we were Sunni. We sat in the office, a simple room with Quranic verses mounted on the walls and a wooden cupboard with some files. The man in charge wanted to know what kind of grave and shroud we required. There was a tomb of alabaster and another just in the ground with a tombstone. There was also a tomb and headstone of brick. We said alabaster.

The undertakers placed him in the coffin and lifted it up. A sheikh sat at the head of the grave, reciting verses from the Quran. They removed the blood-stained wrappings. I saw him as he looked in the photograph sent by Farida Reuben. They removed the plaster from his head, revealing a hole in the forehead. His nose was delicate and straight. A young man brought a sponge and a bar of soap. They poured buckets of water over him as they sprayed white camphor.

They buried him and threw earth over him. It was only then that I felt the tobacco keeper was actually dead.

The following day, we went to a US prison near the airport to meet a leader of one of the militias that controlled the Al-Mansour area. I wanted to meet one of the men who'd murdered or slaughtered more than a hundred people in that vicinity. Kamal Medhat was reputed to be one of them.

We got out of the car. I shook hands with the head of the

guards and others who were lower in rank. They were clean-shaven young men armed with machine guns. We told them about our mission, but they didn't allow us to enter. Instead, they threatened to kill us if we didn't leave within a few seconds.

We got in the car and headed back. We passed by a concrete block next to which was a small café. I asked the driver to stop so that we could have a cup of tea. I felt bitterly thirsty and thoroughly exhausted. In fact, I felt paralyzed, disgusted and suspicious of almost everyone.

It was time to realize that I wouldn't arrive at any conclusion regarding the militias and armed factions that were attacking and destroying the country. I'd wanted to reach some conclusion, or understand those who'd kidnapped and killed him. I filled the saucer with cigarette butts while I tried to analyse some of the forces in control of the area. I went over in my head all I had heard or seen. There were accusations of American, Iranian and Arab involvement in violence in Iraq. One heard of all kinds of attacks by militias, armed groups or the US Army: rape, kidnapping, torture and fatal beatings.

Where was the truth? The stories of the Sunni and the Shia didn't make any sense at all. I told Faris Hassan that the future would demonstrate that all our assumptions were baseless.

'But the rift still exists,' he said.

'True, but only because of the violence, nothing else,' I replied.

But who directed the violence?

Society was collapsing. Women were fetching water from stagnant pools to wash their clothes and dishes. There were many ways to die, cholera not the least of them, but what euphemisms could be used for those who formed gangs to kidnap and murder? Utter anarchy reigned, for there were powers with licence to kill:

the US Marine Corps, private security firms, Shia militias, Sunni militias, organized crime and an enfeebled state that had no presence in many districts. So how could we discover the fault lines of the conflict? How could we define the identity of the enemy? Sectarianism? Imperialism? Foreign Intervention? Was it the desperate defence of private wealth, the class system, international law, or the conflicts of governments? How could one label what was happening?

All the reports that Nancy Awdeh and I had read were vague, flimsy and based on non-existent evidence, most of which was contradictory or incomprehensible. The available evidence disproved all the claims that had been made by the US State Department. The Iraqi army's weaponry, estimated in tons, had been left out in the open to be plundered. There was an intricate network of militias and armed groups, similar to the right-wing Latin American death-squads that had been supported by the US against the left. Although there was nothing to prove that the US was backing particular militias in Iraq, there was no real desire to eliminate them entirely. There was only the desire to create a balance of forces. And what was the cost of creating such a balance? There was talk of wars of interest among several countries being fought out on the streets of Baghdad. But who could tell which faction was fighting which? Were the Shia killing Shia or the Sunnis killing Sunnis? The killings only succeeded in eroding our feeble national memory.

After another day of research, Faris Hassan came along and announced that our work had entered the danger zone. He'd received a signal indicating that a decision had been taken to kidnap and liquidate me.

I told him that I'd always felt it would come to this. Immediately, I jumped up and called a friend of mine who worked at Iraqi Airways to book seats for Faris and myself on the next flight out of Baghdad. I changed my trousers and shirt, and ran to pack the essentials into my small black leather bag that I would carry over my shoulder. I tied everything else up with string, leaving behind a great many things that I no longer needed. I was very selective of what I put in my bag, for I was extremely agitated and tense.

Faris said that he would go and negotiate with the militias.

'Don't. Don't go to them! I've already booked a flight for you,' I screamed at him.

But as usual, he insisted on meeting them because he knew them and had had dealings with them in the past.

After midnight, I received word from the friend working at Iraqi Airways that the flight had been booked. At dawn, I came downstairs to the lobby. I asked the security guard of the building to keep all the stuff I didn't need in the left luggage office. The guard had worked before at one of the American bases, and I liked talking to him, for he was one of a kind. With his worn, pallid face, bulbous nose, large fat lips and thick glasses he looked like a Bollywood actor. As I was speaking with him, I noticed for the first time the presence of foreign women workers in the Green Zone. They looked like overdressed Pigalle café whores. They walked with great pride and gazed around them from beneath the edges of their urinal-shaped hats.

I left the guesthouse, got on the minibus and sat at the back. I hid my camera in my bag. The driver was a dark young man called Marwan, a resident of Al-Karkh. He was brave and experienced. Nermine had told me I could depend on him.

Baghdad's image fluctuated before my eyes: war, expulsion, kidnapping, terrorism, failure and occupation. The picture moved like a chain swinging to the right and left. I uttered a few incomprehensible words. I thought of a myriad of things during the hour it took the minibus to reach the final checkpoint of the Green Zone, near the Arch of Triumph. The vehicle took a little turn into a dusty road. At a checkpoint, a man in civilian clothes stood examining car documents. His face was expressionless and his eyes were rigid, inattentive and careless. On the road, we saw a lot of tanks and armoured vehicles that had been damaged by missiles, a sign that the area had witnessed numerous battles.

As soon as we'd turned onto the airport road, I felt that we were being followed. A car was pursuing us along the narrow street. Marwan had already spotted it in the wing mirror and quickly decided to take evasive action. When we left the narrow street, we were overtaken by another car with three men in it. Their machine guns were directed at our car. This prompted Marwan to take another narrow street to avoid our tyres being targeted. At the end of the street, we saw a corpse thrown onto the pavement, its intestines hanging out, its head severed and placed beside it. As we turned onto another road, we saw more corpses stretched out in the middle of the street. Marwan drove over them as though going over a small ramp. When I looked back, I saw that the corpses had burst open. Fluids and blood were spurting out, as if from a hosepipe.

'It's nothing. Just a body!'

After an hour, I arrived at the airport feeling utterly drained. I completed the procedures quickly. When the plane was high in the air, I cast a quick look at Baghdad. It was covered with a pall of dust and its river had the colour of mud. I began to repeat the last words of 'Tobacco Shop': Eat your chocolate, little girl. Eat your chocolate! Believe me, there are no metaphysics in the world beyond chocolate. Believe me, all the religions in the world do not teach more than a sweetshop. Eat, dirty girl, eat!

My whole body was shaking.

2006-08

Baghdad – Tehran – Damascus

Amira Nowaira is a professor of English Literature at Alexandria University. She has previously translated Susan Bassnett's book *Comparative Literature: A Critical Introduction* (with Azza El-Kholy - Blackwell Publishers, 1993), Iqbal Qazwini's *Zubaida's Window* (Feminist Press, 2008) and Randa Abdel-Fattah's *Where the Streets Had a Name* (Bloomsbury Qatar Foundation Publishing, 2010). She lives in Alexandria.